GARDEN OF EDEN

They lay down on the billowing grass in the center of the gardenia-scented enclosure. In the trees beyond, a mockingbird sang, and below them the creek that fed the bayou splashed and bubbled. Pale sunlight warmed and dappled Jessamine's ivory skin, while the slight breeze teased a shiver of anticipation out of her lovely body.

"You're perfect," Ransome said huskily.

"I was just thinking the same thing about you," Jessamine responded.

"You're not afraid of me? Of what we're about to do?"

"I love you. I want to give you pleasure."

He bent over her. "You'll have pleasure, too."

"I've heard some women do," Jessamine said. "Do you think I may be one?"

In answer he kissed her, his fingers tracing lazy circles on her sun-kissed breasts. . . .

YESTERDAY'S
ROSES

Yesterday's Roses

LYNDA TRENT

AN ONYX BOOK

NEW AMERICAN LIBRARY

NAL BOOKS ARE AVAILABLE AT QUANTITY DISCOUNTS WHEN USED TO
PROMOTE PRODUCTS OR SERVICES. FOR INFORMATION PLEASE WRITE
TO PREMIUM MARKETING DIVISION, NEW AMERICAN LIBRARY. 1633
BROADWAY, NEW YORK, NEW YORK 10019.

PUBLISHER'S NOTE

This book is a work of fiction. Names, characters, places, and
incidents either are the product of the author's imagination or are
used fictitiously, and any resemblance to actual persons, living or
dead, events, or locales is entirely coincidental.

 Onyx is a trademark of New American Library.

SIGNET, SIGNET CLASSIC, MENTOR, ONYX, PLUME,
MERIDIAN and NAL BOOKS are published by NAL PENGUIN
INC., 1633 Broadway, New York, New York 10019

First Printing, October, 1988

1 2 3 4 5 6 7 8 9

PRINTED IN THE UNITED STATES OF AMERICA

To our other family:

Linda Ballard, Dottie Littlefield, Dorys Ward,
and Patricia Harriman

With special thanks to Eleanor McElyea for answering our questions on Creole Louisiana, to the Rusk County Memorial Library for once more finding just the right books for us, and to Sheila Clay for the inspiration for the title.

The fairest things have fleetest end,
Their scent survives their close:
But the rose's scent is bitterness
To him that loved the rose.

—James Kenneth Stephen

I

Roseland: 1865

The sun that brief December day
Rose cheerless over hills of gray,
And, darkly circled, gave at
  noon
A sadder light than waning
  moon.

> —John Greenleaf Whittier

1

"TWENTY-FIVE HUNDRED DOLLARS!" REUBEN ROARED at the sheriff. "My Roseland was auctioned for only twenty-five hundred dollars?"

The sheriff, who had only months before returned with Reuben from the war, looked about the porch in embarrassment. "I know it's a damned shame, Reuben, but Magnolias went for less than that last week. It's happening to everybody. I hate that Yankee bastard I have to work for, but being sheriff is the only thing I know how to do."

Reuben drew a deep breath to calm himself as he stared at the friend with whom he had shared so much. "William, what's going to become of us all? I have Delia to think of. Our children."

"I don't know. I just don't know. Before the war I knew everybody in Iberville parish. Now half the people are strangers, and I can't understand most of what they say." He paused, then asked, "Have you or Delia got any family you could go to? Maybe it's not so bad other places."

"You know as well as I do how bad it is everywhere. I was just remembering how scared I was when we saw those plantations that has been gutted by fire just up the river from here, and how relieved I was to see that Roseland had been spared." Reuben ran long fingers through his dark brown hair. His brow was furrowed in concern.

William Macy scowled. "It's a dirty shame, Reuben, and I could choke on this, but I've got to tell you to move."

For a long time Reuben silently stared out across Roseland's barren fields, once lush with cotton plants and the assurance of prosperity; then he turned back to his friend and asked, "What if I refuse?"

"I'd have to arrest you and put your family out. I wouldn't have any choice. You know how it is around here now. Don't make me do that to you."

Reuben ran his hand up and down the enormous white

13

column beside him that supported the veranda overhead. "Roseland is my home, William. It's been in the Delacroix family for generations."

"I know. But now it belongs to—" he consulted the legal papers he held—"Ian and Eliza MacKinley."

A harsh sound rumbled in Reuben's throat as if he couldn't bear even to hear their names.

"I can give you a month, but that's all. The Mac-Kinleys are moving down from New York then."

"New York!" Reuben ground out. "Yankees in Roseland!" He put his forearm against the column and clenched his fist. "I know it's not your fault. It's just so damned wrong! MacKinley," he spat. "Even their name leaves a bitter taste in my mouth."

"I know it. You're not the only one to feel this way."

"Is everyone around here being bought out?"

"Not all, but too many. Arnaud Leslie managed to hang on to his place 'cause he had enough money to pay the taxes. Early in the war he put a good bit of what they had in a bank in England while most of the rest of us converted ours to Confederate scrip."

As though he hadn't been listening to the sheriff, Reuben asked, "And you'd arrest me?"

"I'd have to, Reuben, if it came to it." He tipped his hat and called out a farewell as he left.

Reuben didn't trust himself to speak. The sale of his plantation had been inevitable, but now that it had come to pass, it was too much for him to bear. As he stared impassively into the distance, Delia came out onto the porch. After a pause she put her hand on his arm. "Was that William Macy I saw leaving? Why didn't he come inside?"

In a lifeless tone he said, "He was here on business. Roseland has been sold." He heard his wife catch her breath.

"I had hoped no one would bid on it."

"Not bid on Roseland? Who could pass up a plantation like this?" Reuben struggled to maintain his composure, then added, "It only brought twenty-five hundred dollars."

"That's all?"

"Not even enough to pay the outrageous taxes they tried to collect," he said with scorn.

"Where will we go? You've always lived here."

He put his arm around her and cradled her blond head on his shoulder. "We'll think of something. We still have that ten acres down in the bottom. The taxes on it were very little. They said the property was almost worthless, and they may be right, but at least it's still ours."

"You mean move there? Into that old shack?" Delia was appalled by the thought, and her mouth dropped open. Her ancestors, like his, were Creole, and proud of their French heritage and culture.

"Would you rather sleep in a ditch?" he snapped, before seeing the hurt in her gray eyes. "I'm sorry, *chérie*. The idea galls me no end, but I don't know what else we can do. I don't like the thought of having to live there any better than you do." As difficult as this all was for him, Reuben knew it would be worse for Delia. The dogtrot log cabin had been built by his *grand-père* as a temporary shelter while the Rose-land mansion was being constructed. No frills had gone into the rough cabin. When Reuben's father was master, he had hired a doctor and provided him with the cabin as living quarters. The doctor had kept the house in good repair, but that was about it. The dogtrot cabin was little better than the cabins in the slave quarters behind the big house.

Delia stepped closer and put her arm around him. "When do we have to move?"

"We have a month. Maybe something will come up and we can stay here." But he knew there was no chance of that at all, and so did she.

Three weeks later, as Reuben paced in the library, he heard voices from the foyer. When he investigated, he found a strange couple and a teenage boy milling about at the foot of the stairs. "I didn't hear anyone knock," Reuben said. "Who are you?"

The startled woman jumped, and the whiskered man wheeled to face Reuben. With a crisp accent, colored by a faint Scottish burr, the man said, "What are *you* doing here, may I ask?"

"My name is Reuben Delacroix and I live here!"

"I'm Ian MacKinley."

Reuben Delacroix and Ian MacKinley glared at one another in silence as tension filled the room. At length the plump woman stepped forward. "I'm Eliza MacKinley and this is our son, Ransome." She looked around the hall. "Your home is lovely."

"Don't fawn, Mother. It is ours now," her husband said, his side whiskers puffing. To Reuben he said, "We expected you to be gone by now."

"Sheriff Macy said we had a month from the date of sale. That's not until next Monday." He was aware that Delia had come down the stairs and was standing behind him, but he kept his eyes fixed on his enemy.

"I'm Eliza MacKinley," the woman repeated to Delia, "and this is—"

"Not now, Mother!" Ian interrupted. He turned back to Reuben. "We were able to dispose of our home in Albany sooner than we expected and we're ready to move in here now."

"That's too bad, because we haven't moved out yet. You agreed not to take possession for another four days."

"Be that as it may, my family and I are here now and ready to take possession."

"Yes. Do you suppose we might look upstairs?" Eliza asked.

Reuben tensed at the audacity of these people as he glared from one to the other. When his face began to turn red with his mounting anger, Delia put her hand on his arm. "You and your family can go to—" Reuben began, but stopped abruptly when Delia tightened her grip on his arm. Restraining himself, and in deference to his wife, Reuben finished his sentence more genteelly, saying, "—to the boardinghouse in town."

"I'm not moving to a boardinghouse when I have a plantation!"

"Mr. MacKinley, please!" Eliza importuned. "All our furniture hasn't arrived yet. We'd be more comfortable in a boardinghouse." She moved closer to their son, who remained silent.

"Have you other children, Mrs. MacKinley?" Delia asked in an effort to ease the mounting tension.

"We had an older son," Eliza answered automatically, then cut her eyes to catch her husband's admonishing scowl. "But Dennis died at Gettysburg."

"Our eldest died at Vicksburg."

"Next you'll be swapping recipes and forming a sewing circle," Ian growled.

"No, they won't," Reuben said tightly.

"Just see that you're out by the first of next week!"

Reuben drew himself up proudly. "Mr. MacKinley, I'd be obliged if you were to get off my land." Reuben refused to be stared down.

After an uncomfortable moment MacKinley said, "Get in the buggy, Mother, Ransome." With one last menacing glare at Reuben, he followed them out, slamming the door behind him.

Delia glanced across the foyer to her black butler, who had just stepped into the doorway and was standing there wide-eyed. "We must start packing, Sam."

"Where we goin'?"

After a glance at Reuben, Delia said, "We still own the back ten acres. We'll be moving into the house there." She wondered if this setback in status would make Sam and Tabitha want to leave. All the other former slaves were already gone.

Reuben's shoulders dropped; his face was haggard as he sighed in defeat. "I guess we have no choice. We'll dismantle two of the slave cabins, one for you and your family, Sam, the other for a barn." He looked again at Delia. "When I asked you to marry me, I never dreamed I would ever move you into a shack a stone's throw from the swamp."

She put her hand into his. "It's not your fault, Reuben. And you know I'd go with you anywhere. That house won't be so bad." She didn't meet his eyes, however, for she wasn't an accomplished liar, and they both knew what it would be like there.

"Which cabin do you want, Sam?" Reuben asked as he looked up and down the double row of almost identical cabins that had once housed his numerous slaves. For a moment Reuben's thoughts turned to those days before the war when this area was buzzing with the daily activity that had made Roseland thrive. He had hoped that even though his slaves had been freed, they would stay to work the plantation for wages. He felt he had always been good to them and fair in his dealings with them. But when he finally returned from the fighting, every cabin but one was vacant. Only Sam and Tabitha had loyally remained, and for that he was grateful. Pulling himself from his reverie, he said, "I'd like for you to take your pick."

"I believe I'd just as soon have the one we been living in." He nodded toward one that was slightly larger than the other cabins. Because of his status as butler and Tabitha's as house servant, they had been given one of the better ones. It had two small rooms and a shed attached to the back, where their daughter, Doll, slept.

"Jerome, number those logs on Sam's cabin from bottom to top so we can get it back together again," Reuben said to his sixteen-year-old son. As Jerome obediently began the task, Reuben said, "We'll take the long house for the barn. I'll mark it. Sam, you swing the mules around so the sled is close to the cabin. We don't want to carry those logs any farther than we have to."

"Yes, sir."

Reuben purposefully strode to the end cabin, a long building that had housed the single men, and began marking the logs. As he thought of all the work ahead of them and how damned unfair this all was, his strokes became angry slashes. He could hear his daughters, Jessamine and young Adele, calling to the dog they planned to take. Delia, Tabitha, and Doll were inside the house packing.

He wiped his face on his sleeve and told himself it was sweat, not tears. Roseland had been the Delacroix empire for almost a hundred years. Her cotton had been in demand as far away as England; her thoroughbreds had been known all over America as being fine and sound animals. What kind of legacy would he leave his own son? A dogtrot cabin on the edge of the encroaching swamp? Reuben jabbed the pencil at the log so hard it snapped in half, and he had to take out his pocketknife to resharpen it.

Delia hadn't uttered a word of complaint, though her face was drawn and her eyes were the dusky shade they always became when she was repressing her emotions. He could almost have borne this adversity better if she had railed at him, because then he could fight back and work out some of his anger. But Delia was an aristocrat, and true ladies never raised their voices.

Jessamine, at fourteen, had not reacted to the news with her mother's reserve. Headstrong and rebellious, Jessamine was determined not to leave her home among the roses to go live by a swamp. Doll, who had been her companion since birth, had taken Jessamine aside and talked with her. No one knew what Doll had said, but whatever it was had calmed her friend. Now Jessamine was being reasonable, packing without an argument. Adele had cried off and on, but she was only ten and couldn't be expected to understand why she had to leave her playhouse behind. In time, Reuben hoped she would come to accept it, but he questioned whether he could ever accept it himself.

Although the cabins were very sturdy, they were fairly easy to disassemble. The wooden pegs that joined the logs at the corners snapped in half under a blow from a hammer and chisel, and the shingle roofs came apart by sections. Working as quickly as they could, the three of them stacked the pieces of Sam's cabin onto the large sled. Under Sam's direction, the mules pulled the load down the road to the bottomland, and by dusk the walls of Sam's home had been stacked across the side yard from the dogtrot cabin.

Straightening his tired back, Reuben surveyed the house that was to be his new home. "I can't quite picture Miss Delia in there, Sam."

The black man wiped his sweaty brow with a big bandanna from his hip pocket and followed his former master's gaze. "No, sir. I can't neither. Ya'll going to be crowded in there for sure."

"When we get a food crop planted, we can take time and add rooms onto it. Do you know anything about planting?"

"No, sir. Not a thing in this world."

"Well," Reuben sighed, "neither of us knew anything about moving cabins either, but we did it. Sam, you're not thinking about leaving me, are you?"

Sam drew himself up tall. "No, sir. I been living on Roseland long as you have. I ain't fixing to take off."

Reuben looked over at the man. According to family gossip, they shared a grandfather, though Sam was the deep brown of mahogany. Whether it was true or not, Sam was as proud as any Delacroix. Reuben slapped him companionably on the shoulder. "We'll get through this somehow. Maybe those damned MacKinleys will go bankrupt in a couple of years and I can buy Roseland back."

"Yes, sir." Sam looked at the stack of grayed logs. It didn't matter much to him whether his house sat by a swamp or behind the plantation house. Now that necessity had made him a field hand, the work was the same.

Reuben called to Jerome, who was standing on the hill looking down at the moss-draped swamp. The boy turned and ran back with the easy gait of youth, and joined his father and Sam on the sled. Reuben slapped the reins on the mules' rumps as a signal to take them home.

For the next three days the men worked at moving and reconstructing the cabin and barn, while the women and girls sorted through generations of belongings, faced with the very difficult decisions of what could go and what must be left behind.

Delia tried not to think at all about what was going on

as she made her way through the trunks of winter and summer clothes and the seemingly endless shelves, drawers, and pantries, pretending that this was no more than a thorough spring cleaning.

Doll had been sent out to dig up the silverware that had been hidden when Yankee soldiers were raiding the area several years before. Some of it had been traded, a piece at a time, for food and supplies when times were getting really bad, but most of the pieces Delia's mother had given her as a wedding gift still remained. Methodically Delia placed each piece of her silver, still in its wrappings, into a drawer to be moved.

Now that her initial upset was over, Jessamine was being as obedient as Jessamine ever was, and Delia was glad for that. The girl was old enough to see the necessity of the move and to know they couldn't take everything with them. She even seemed to be viewing this as an adventure of sorts, not unlike having been shipwrecked on a desert island. Delia had heard her tell Doll that story only the day before. Adele was still being difficult. She wanted to take everything she owned, and Jessamine had been scolded for boxing her younger sister's ears in vexation. Delia found herself giving in on several of Adele's tearful requests when she should have held firm. She rationalized that it was because Adele was her youngest, but in truth she was partial to Adele, for she was the only one of her children who was Nordic blond like her own family. Both Jessamine and Jerome were vivaciously dark like their father, though Jessamine did have the distinctive gray eyes of the Spartan family.

For a forbidden moment Delia let herself recall her eldest son, Spartan, named for her family and as blond as a young Viking. And now gone. There was a marker for him in the family cemetery, but his body was in a grave in faraway Vicksburg. Delia's busy hands stilled. "Tabitha, we'll be leaving our family graves behind as well! I never thought of that."

Tabitha's light brown hands continued sorting the linens. "Yes, ma'am," she agreed as she glanced at her former mistress. "Ya'll can come back and put out flowers, I imagine. Even Yankees wouldn't stop you from doing that."

"It wouldn't be the same—having to ask permission to visit my own son's grave."

For a minute Tabitha was quiet, then said, "Yes, ma'am. I got graves of my own what needs tending." Of her numerous brood, only Doll had survived infancy, and she wasn't even Sam's real flesh and blood, Tabitha having been pregnant with her when the Delacroixs bought her.

"I know, Tabitha. For a minute I forgot. That was selfish of me," Delia spread her wide full skirts and knelt to help with the table linens. "Mrs. MacKinley said she had lost a child too. She'll surely see that our graves are properly kept up." She held up a tablecloth, delicately embroidered with silk. "Whatever will I do with this? My mother made it and the matching napkins for my hope chest, but it fits the big table with all the leaves in place. I can't leave it behind for those people."

"Pack it in here, Miss Delia. I can cut it down to fit the small table and make two cloths out of it."

Regretfully Delia folded the fine linen. It seemed a sacrilege to cut it in half, but otherwise it would be useless and would just take up space.

Adele followed Jessamine into the room, a large basset hound in tow. "We found Sounder," she announced.

"You get that dog right out of my house," Delia responded automatically.

"I didn't think it would matter anymore," Adele said with a tremble of her lower lip. "I wanted to show him my room."

"All right. But then take him outside. I won't have him making a mess, and Eliza MacKinley thinking I let the house be used as a kennel."

Adele hurried upstairs, the dog hard on her heels. Jessamine knelt by the woman. "I can take the cat and kittens, can't I? They don't eat much, and Velvet is a good mouser."

"One cat and one litter of kittens," Delia conceded. "I imagine the others will find us soon enough on their own."

Jessamine smiled and a dimple appeared in her left cheek. "Thank you, Mama. Where's Doll?"

"In the kitchen. Go see if she is finished. It's almost midafternoon. We have to leave soon."

Jessamine went from the formal dining room with its elegant cherrywood furniture into the wide entry hall and stopped for a moment to collect a few additional memories to take with her. To either side of her curved Roseland's graceful double stairs, rising in a wishbone shape to meet at the landing that spanned the upstairs hallway. For a minute Jessamine gazed up at the crystal prisms of the chandelier. She looked to her left through the open library door to the shelves upon shelves of books. She swallowed hard to keep from crying. Mama might think she had accepted the idea of leaving, but that was far from the truth. Jessamine loved Roseland with an intensity that was less obvious than Jerome's, but every bit as deep. Almost reverently she went into the library and breathed in the scent of leather and pipe smoke that always seemed to be there. She and her father used this room more than anyone else in the family, and she was more attached to it than to the bedroom she shared with Adele. Gently Jessamine touched the bright gold letters on the leather spine of one of her favorite books. How could she leave them behind? Would the MacKinleys take care of them and not let dust or dampness ruin them? Impulsively Jessamine gathered several volumes that she couldn't part with and ran upstairs to pack them into the nooks and crannies left in one of the trunks.

When Jessamine finally got to the kitchen, she was out of breath. Doll looked up as she hurried in, and when she noticed Jessamine had come alone, Doll beamed her a bright friendly smile, and Jessamine returned the gesture. "How's things coming in the house?" Doll asked.

Jessamine took a deep breath, and her smile faded as she recalled the scene inside. "Mama looks as if she may cry, and your ma looks as if she already has."

"So have I," Doll admitted. "I don't know why, exactly. One place ought to be same as another. Leastways that's what Pa says."

"You mean 'anyway,' not 'leastways.' " One of the girls' newest joint endeavors was to teach Doll to speak correct English and to read. Jessamine said conspiratorially, "I'm taking some of the books from the library."

Doll's face lit up, but only briefly. "You know Miss Delia told you to leave them alone."

"Papa took the ones he wanted. Mama doesn't understand because she only reads the newspapers and magazines. *Godey's Lady's Book* and the *Illustrated London News* aren't the same as *Modeste Mignon* and *Vanity Fair.*"

"Do you think I'll ever learn to read books like that?"

"As fast as you're learning? I'm sure you will."

"I just hope Ma and Miss Delia don't catch you teaching me. They would have a fit."

"Dogs have 'fits.' Our mamas would be angry," Jessamine corrected.

"They sure would be."

Jessamine helped Doll pack the horsehair sieves and the long-handled stirring spoons. "Just think—tonight we'll be in our new place. Ten Acres. That's what I'm going to call it."

"It fits," Doll said. "I'm looking forward to getting back into my own room. We've been using Bertha and Will's cabin, and it has fleas."

"I hope our house doesn't."

"It won't. There hasn't been an animal sleeping inside of it since the doctor died and his dog took up over at the Ramseys' place."

"I had forgotten Dr. Harris died there. Do you suppose his ghost is in the house?"

When Doll laughed, her white teeth flashed in contrast to her *café-au-lait* skin. "Don't you worry about no ghost showing up. Once we get all this stuff moved in, there won't be room for one."

Jessamine smiled. She and Doll had been born the same day and had shared everything, from a wet nurse to their first steps to their newest escapade of teaching Doll to speak like the Delacroixs. "My window faces yours at Ten Acres. We can wave across at each other."

"Better not let our mamas catch us. Ma told me just last week that I shouldn't be so friendly toward you. She said it wasn't being respectful."

"But we're friends, Doll. You're the closest friend I have. I'll bet you're Jerome's best friend too. We've always gone everywhere together, like the Three Musketeers."

"I know it. I'm just telling you what Ma said."

Jessamine frowned. "I'll tell you a secret, Doll. I hate the MacKinleys. I know Father Theriot says that it's wrong to hate, and I know I never saw them before, but I hate them anyway. They're the reason we're having to move down by the swamp and leave Roseland."

"I heard Mr. Reuben say that if it wasn't them it would have been somebody else."

"You've lived here all your life too. How can you be so calm about having to leave!"

Doll smiled. "My people grow up knowing they might be sent away at any time."

"You mean sold? My family would never have sold you!"

"Ma said she thought the same thing about her old master and the plantation where she grew up. Then one day she was told to get in the wagon, the next thing she knew, she was on her way to the auction at New Orleans."

"Slavery was wrong. Mama and Papa have both told

me that all my life. There just wasn't any other way to get things done.''

"I expect now you'll find a way," Doll said in her soft, melodious voice.

Jessamine nodded. "Are we taking the cranes from the fireplace?"

"Ma says there's a wood stove there."

Jessamine wrinkled her nose. "Food tastes funny cooked on a wood stove. The Leslies have one and it's just not as good."

"We'll get used to it."

"I wish you wouldn't be so darn complacent about all this!"

"Jessamine, you're going to find there's not much in life you can't live with if you have to," Doll counseled. "And you better hope to high heaven your mama don't catch you saying 'darn.'"

"'Doesn't,'" Jessamine retorted.

In time the last trunk was loaded onto the sled and the extras were stuffed into the boot of the buggy. Reuben sent Sam and his family on ahead, then went back for Delia. After a last look, Reuben eased his wife out the front door. Delia paused on the wide veranda and gazed out over her rose gardens. "I still can't believe it, Reuben. I just can't believe I'll never live here again."

"Somehow we'll get it back," her husband said in a tight voice. "The MacKinleys are going to find that it's not all that easy to run a cotton plantation. Especially not without slaves. Maybe they won't be able to make it here and will sell out. In a few years we may be back on our feet again and can buy it back."

Delia knew the odds were against that, but she didn't voice her feelings. "I can't stand the idea of that awful man in our house. Do you suppose they'll change the draperies or the paper on the walls?"

"Why would they change a thing? Roseland is perfect just as it is."

She looked again at her roses. "Did Mrs. MacKinley appear to you to be the sort of woman who likes to garden? My roses need care to stay pretty."

"Come on, *chérie*. At this rate we won't get there before dark."

With a sigh, Delia let him lead her to the buggy and help her up onto the spring seat, while the children piled into the back. Quickly Reuben climbed aboard and slapped the reins on the horse's back. Delia and the children looked back at Roseland for as long as they could see even the tips of the tall chimneys. Reuben stared stonily ahead.

In a short while he reined the horse into the clearing around the dogtrot cabin. "We're home," he said with mock cheerfulness.

"I've named this place Ten Acres," Jessamine said as her father helped her mother out of the buggy. Neither of them responded. They both looked sad, even though he was trying to smile.

Delia held on to the mud board for a minute as if she felt faint. She had been to the cabin from time to time over the years, of course, but she had intentionally avoided it since she learned it was to be her home.

The cabin stood on a knoll beneath a chinaberry tree on one side and an enormous oak on the other. From the front it looked like two giant boxes joined by a covered porch or dog run. The windows were few and small. The whitewash that had once brightened the log walls was long since gone, eroded by dampness and harsh sun. At one corner stood a barrel that had served as a cistern, and out back was a clump of cedar trees that discreetly hid the "necessary" house from view.

Slowly Delia crossed the uneven yard and climbed the plank steps. Two doors faced each other across the breezy dog run. She lifted the latch on the door to the right and stepped into the sitting room. Trunks and boxes were everywhere, and two narrow beds stood head to head in one corner.

"Jessamine and Adele will sleep here," Reuben said in a tone of forced good humor. "Jerome will sleep up there in the loft."

Delia's stunned eyes followed the narrow steps up to the loft tucked between the roof and the ceiling of the room below.

"You can hang curtains so they will have more privacy."

Not trusting herself to speak or to meet Reuben's eyes, Delia crossed the open porch and entered the other half of the house. It was a mirror image of what she had just seen, with an identical stone fireplace on the outside wall. Here were more trunks and the heavy bedstead from their bedroom at Roseland, along with the marble-topped washstand and rosewood chest that matched the rest of the furniture. At the end of the bed was Delia's well-loved rocker.

Reuben went to it and pushed it gently before stopping its motion with his fingertips. "I brought it for you as a surprise. The room is crowded, but I know you set great store by this furniture.''

Hot tears welled up in Delia's eyes, then trickled down her pale cheeks as she looked again at the incongruously elegant furniture against the cabin's rough-hewn walls. Sightlessly she reached out to pat Reuben's arm and let her fingers trail down his sleeve as she walked toward the rocker.

Moving like a sleepwalker, Delia eased herself onto the familiar seat and rested her arms on the arms of the chair. Pushing experimentally, she rocked back and forth as she stared straight ahead at the grimy window, seeing neither dust nor cobwebs.

Reuben stood in the doorway, anxiously watching her. Was she never going to speak? He wondered if he had somehow made a mistake in bringing their bedroom furniture. He had thought at the time that she would be pleased, but it looked remarkably out of place in the crude room, and Delia just sat there rocking as tears coursed down her face.

''I want to buy a wagonload of seashells,'' she said at last. ''Just as soon as we can afford it. That should make enough lime to whitewash this place inside and out. By the time I'm through, this house will be as clean as the other one was.'' She stopped rocking. ''Where's Jerome?''

''That's the other surprise. Look out the front window.''

Delia peered through the thick layer of grime. ''What is he doing?''

''He's planting roses. Just before we left, he dug up a few of your favorites. If you don't want them on both sides of the steps, you had better speak up fast.''

Delia turned to Reuben with a wavering smile. ''How could I have been afraid?'' she reproached herself as she hurried into his embrace, tears streaming down her face. ''I have my things about me and even my roses. Above all, I have you. I love you, Reuben.''

He held her tightly and willed himself not to join her sobs. ''Someday, somehow, we'll get Roseland back,'' he promised in a fierce voice.

2

IAN MACKINLEY OPENED THE WIDE FRONT DOOR OF the Roseland mansion with a flourish and stepped back to let his wife and son enter the foyer. "Welcome home, Mother."

Eliza swept by her husband and hurried to the beautifully curving stairway, her small feet rushing in tiny steps to keep up with her plump body. "Oh, Mr. MacKinley, what can I say! It's magnificent! I can hardly wait to see the rest of it!" She clasped her hands under her second chin and the faded red topknot of her hair wobbled precariously.

"Mother, there's a dog out here," her son exclaimed. "Is he ours?" His voice creaked up unexpectedly as it sometimes still did before settling back in the deeper tone brought to his voice by his recent advancement into puberty.

"Sure, son, sure." Ian beamed magnanimously. "Everything here is ours. I bought it lock, stock, and barrel." He laughed as if he were making a joke, and his belly jiggled under his brocaded vest.

"Blue!" Eliza proclaimed in rapture. "I'll paper this foyer in federal blue."

"Whatever you say, Mother. Look in here. It's a library." Ian pushed open the door and stepped inside. "Pull back those curtains and open the windows, son. It's stuffy in here."

Ransome did as he was told and sunlight streamed in, burnishing the boy's auburn hair to dark flame. "Look at all the books! There are more of them here than at Aunt Polly's!" He walked almost reverently around the room, touching first one and then another. "Do you suppose they read them all?"

"I doubt it," said Ian, who was not a reader himself. "And I don't want you spending all your time in here. You have acres and acres to roam. I'll go to town tomorrow and

27

buy you a horse—I let that Rebel family keep what livestock
they had.''

To Eliza he added, ''I'll see about hiring hands as
well. If we're going to grow cotton, we'll need a lot of help
about the place.''

''Cotton growers,'' Eliza sighed. ''Just imagine!''

''Boy, by the time you inherit all this, you'll be a
wealthy man. This is just the break we've been looking for.''
He clapped Ransome on the shoulder. ''No more cities for
us.'' As always when he was excited, Ian rolled his R's in
an unmistakably Scottish manner.

Ransome, who had spent all his fifteen years in cities,
nodded and smiled as he knew he was expected to do. Up
until now he had secretly had doubts about leaving all his
friends and moving to a place he had never seen before,
where all his neighbors would be the former enemy.

''I just wish my mother had lived to see this place,''
Eliza murmured as she touched the velvet draperies.
''Wouldn't she be proud?'' Although her parents had im-
migrated to the United States from Killarney, Ireland, when
Eliza was a toddler, she still retained a hint of an Irish
brogue.

''She would indeed.''

Eliza poked her head through the doorway in the back
wall. ''This would likely be your parlor, dear.'' She proceeded through a side door and across the foyer. ''Here's
the ladies' parlor. My, how nice. I'll buy paper in a bold
print for this room. My, how that woman must have loved
pink! It's everywhere! Blue is much nicer, in my opinion.''
She went toward the front of the house and into the dining
room. ''My!'' she exclaimed. ''Mr. MacKinley, come look
at the size of this table!''

Ian and Ransome joined her, and they all gaped at the
cherrywood table with its twelve leaves. ''It's a big one,''
Ransome confirmed.

''I haven't a cloth to cover it,'' Eliza lamented as she
began to rummage through the drawers of the massive sideboard. ''Thank goodness! There're linens in here.''

''Like I said, I bought it all, just as it stands.''

Ransome studied the length of the table and said,
''They must have children to need a table that size.''

''Yes, they do, but it doesn't matter,'' Ian answered
in his normally brusque manner. ''We won't be associating
with them.''

Eliza's blue eyes looked troubled. "Where did they go when they moved out? You know, I felt a bit sorry for that Mrs. Delacroix. Is that how you say the name?"

"No need to waste time and thought on the likes of them. Don't you remember how that dirty Rebel treated us? He all but threw us out."

"Well, it was his home. Maybe—"

"There's no maybe to it! I bought this place and paid hard cash for it. We've worked for years to get a chance like this. Don't go looking back now." He thrust his hands into his pockets as he surveyed the crystals in the twin chandeliers over the table.

"But where did they go, Father?"

"Delacroix had a few acres on the back side of Roseland that he had under a separate deed. I heard they moved there. It's across the woods. The sheriff said there's a swamp there too."

"A real swamp? With alligators?"

"Ransome, you're not to go near it," his mother warned.

"And you're especially not to go near the Delacroixs. We'll meet more suitable people. People of our own kind. A number of places around here were bought by families from back home."

"From New York?" Ransome asked.

"From the North. We'll meet them, and they will be our friends. And while we're on that subject, I want to tell you another thing, son. Now that we're living here in Louisiana, you won't be able to completely avoid contact with these Rebels, but I don't want you being friends with any of them."

"Yes, sir. But you already told me that before we got here. It's just that—"

"Ransome, there are no buts to it. You can't trust them. They're bad—the whole lot of them."

Ransome looked back at his father, his steady brown eyes doubtful. "Surely not all of them, Father."

"Don't ever let me hear you say that again," Ian thundered. "For all we know, Reuben Delacroix himself might have pulled the trigger that killed our Dennis!" He pointed at Eliza, who was groping blindly through a spontaneous flood of tears for her lace handkerchief. "There! See what you've done? You've made your mother cry!"

"I'm sorry, Mother." He really was. Ransome disliked causing any unpleasantness. If he could have his way, no one would ever raise his voice in anger. Especially not his father. Ransome was almost as tall as his father, but Ian's bellowing still caused him to flinch in fear. Unlike his dead brother, Dennis, Ransome had never learned the knack of pacifying his father with a lie.

Room by room, they explored the house. Whenever Ian discovered a bare spot where furniture had stood, he roared as if he had been robbed. Eliza calmed him with a flutter of her hands and a shushing sound; Ransome stayed out of reach.

Ransome chose the second largest bedroom for himself. From his window he overlooked the curving drive and could see past the spreading branches of a magnolia tree to the woods that flanked a small creek. Beyond the woods, he had been told, were the treacherous swamp and the dreadful Delacroixs.

Ransome sat on the window seat, wondering about the family whose house they now occupied. When he had seen them that first day, he hadn't found Mr. Delacroix any more fearsome than his own father, and certainly not as loud. Why his father had declared the man to be so dangerous wasn't evident.

He examined the wide bed with the tall headboard where he would be sleeping in the nights to come. From the looks of it, he guessed that it must have been used by one of the Delacroixs' sons. He had heard the woman say her eldest was dead. Had this been his bed? Roseland, with its endless rooms and moss-shrouded trees, was a perfect haunting ground for a restless spirit. Ransome let a delicious shiver of fear creep up his spine before he remembered he was too old to believe in ghosts.

The slight smile faded from his lips as reality crowded back in on him. If he were to tell his parents of such notions, his father would ridicule him and his mother would certainly have one of her "spells." No, if he was sharing the room with a ghost, he would simply have to live with it.

As Ransome went out into the hall, his father came barging out of the largest bedroom, his mother pattering fast to keep up with him. "They took the whole blamed roomful!"

"I'm sure they needed their bed for their own use. Ours is due to arrive at any moment."

"That's not the point, Mother. I bought the house and all its belongings!"

"I would have put it in the attic anyway, I'm sure," she said, trying to mollify him. "Goodness, I don't think I could sleep on a Rebel's bed. Surely you couldn't either. Think of the dreams we would have!"

Somewhat calmed, Ian glared down at his wife. "I suppose—but it's the idea of it that irritates me."

"Personally, I see it as one less thing we would have to move. You know how difficult it is to move furniture. We might have had to live with it, and it might have looked simply dreadful. Our bed and dresser will look much nicer in here, I'm sure." She went down the hall as if the matter were all settled and looked into the room Jessamine and Adele had shared. "All this pink! My!"

Ian and Ransome left her making lists for wallpaper and paint as they went out to inspect the grounds. In the barn Ransome took note of the clean stalls, each topped with a brick ledge to prevent the horse from "cribbing." As they quickly moved through, Ransome read the names of the Delacroixs' horses on the wooden plaques over the feed boxes. He was surprised that they had owned so many horses. In the city few people kept more than two or three.

Ian begrudgingly nodded his approval. "Good barn. Won't need much work."

Ransome couldn't see anything at all that needed repair, but he kept quiet. The carriage house was built onto the side of the barn, and beyond that, according to his father, was what must have been the overseer's house. From the looks of it, the place had not been lived in for several years. Ian made a point of telling Ransome that the Delacroixs had at least left this furniture. Ransome saw no reason why they should have taken it. All the pieces were handmade and far less beautiful than the ones in the main house. If it had been him leaving Roseland, Ransome thought, he too would have chosen the better furniture over the crude pine.

"I'll hire an overseer tomorrow," Ian said in Ransome's general direction. "I'll need someone to deal with the hired hands. A gentleman planter can't spend all his time supervising a cotton field, now, can he?" He barked out a laugh as if this were high humor.

"No, sir," Ransom responded obligingly.

"You're much too quiet for a boy who's nearly

grown,'' Ian said as they left the frame house and walked along the path toward the bayou that flowed past Roseland on its way from Cavelier to the Mississippi River. ''You ought to run and yell more—like Dennis used to do.''

Ransome nodded. He had heard all this before.

''He was quite a lad, your brother was. He would have made a fine man.'' Ian set his heavy jaw and blinked several times before pulling out his pocket handkerchief and loudly blowing his nose.

Ransome noticed the hound dog he had seen earlier come out of some bushes, and he snapped his fingers to call to it. As the dog trotted over, wagging his tail in a friendly manner, Ian said, ''Now, boy, you've got to learn to command this dog to come to you. The dog needs to see you as his master, the one to be obeyed. Just snapping your fingers isn't good enough.''

Ransome wanted to point out that the dog had already come, but instead he turned his attention to the dog. As he stroked the silky head, he asked, ''What's your name, boy?''

''Name him anything you please. He's yours.'' Ian didn't give the dog more than a glance.

Ransome patted the dog again before he straightened. ''I expect he already has a name. I wonder what it is.''

Ian ignored him. ''Look there. Those must be the slave quarters.'' He hardened his face as if he expected to find all manner of atrocities as he strode toward the cabins.

There were two rows of neat cabins that faced an open quadrangle. Behind the cabins Ransome could see small gardens and chicken yards. Several hens, herded by a dark red rooster, clucked and scratched under the shade of an enormous oak in the center of the quadrangle. Ransome wasn't sure what he had expected to see, but these houses looked no different from small farmers' houses up North.

Ian drew his bristling eyebrows together in a frown as he paced over to a gap in the row of cabins. ''Look here! One is missing! And there—another one stood there!''

''Maybe they burned down or something.''

''Don't talk rubbish. There are no ashes, no charred wood. Look there! Skid marks! That damned Rebel stole my cabins!''

Following his father's accusing finger, Ransome saw where there were indeed marks such as a sled would make. ''Maybe they were moved to another part of the grounds.''

''They were stolen! And I mean to get them back!''

"But, Father, we don't have any slaves or anyone else to live in them. Why do you want them?"

"Because they're mine! Can't you understand that, boy? When somebody takes something that belongs to you, you're honor-bound to take it back. We just got through fighting a war to prove it. Those damned Rebels seceded from the Union, and we damn well brought them back."

"I thought we were fighting over slavery."

"That too. Go get the buggy."

Eliza stepped out onto the veranda as Ian and Ransome climbed aboard. "Mr. MacKinley? Where are you off to?"

"You want to see something that will set you against these Rebels once and for all?" her husband called out. "Go back there and look at the slave quarters!"

"My God," she gasped as she turned pale. "What's back there!"

"Delacroix stole two of the cabins!"

Eliza put her hand out to steady herself against one of the soaring white columns. "Is that all? Heavens. You frightened me half to death." She pulled out her lace handkerchief and fanned herself in relief.

"All! All!" Ian roared. "Mother, you're as bad as he is." He jabbed his thumb at his son. "We're going to go over there and get back what is rightfully ours." He popped the reins on the horse's rump and the buggy jerked forward.

Ian mumbled in his wrath as he guided the horse down the road that led away from town. Ransome ignored his father. This whole matter was pretty embarrassing as far as he was concerned, but he was very curious about the Delacroix family. What better way to find their house than to let his father take him there?

They hadn't gone a mile before the road ended in a clearing that held a log cabin of an unusual design, as well as two cabins that looked very familiar. Two men, one black and the other white, were on the roof of one building and a boy about Ransome's age was tossing shingles up to them.

Ian was out of the buggy before the wheels came to a rest. The white man on the roof wrinkled his face into a scowl as he shaded his eyes from the glaring sun to see who had ridden up. As the man scrambled off the roof, Ransome recognized him as Reuben Delacroix. The black man stayed where he was, but quit hammering in order to listen.

"What the hell do you mean by stealing my cabins!"

Ian MacKinley yelled as he closed the space between Reuben and himself.

"The terms of sale stated I could take what I deemed necessary for survival," Reuben answered sharply. "Sam and his family needed their house and I needed a barn. Who the hell do you think you are to come over here and accuse me of stealing!"

Ransome caught the boy's eye and they exchanged a long look. He found himself thinking he would be more comfortable sharing his room with a ghost than this boy. Slowly he got out of the buggy.

"Jerome! Get over here!" Reuben commanded. "Tell this damned Yankee that we needed the cabins."

So the boy was named Jerome, Ransome thought. And his father clearly put stock in the boy's words, for he was asking him to testify just as if Jerome were a grown man. Ransome watched in fascination.

"That cabin over there belongs to Sam and his family," Jerome confirmed. "That's Sam up there on the roof. We had to have a barn. Winter will be on us before you know it, and we have to have shelter for the stock." Jerome glanced back at the young Yankee boy as if he too were curious.

"Who cares about the word of a boy?" Ian scoffed. "Besides that, he's your son. Naturally he's going to side with you."

"Jerome may not be grown, but he was the man of the house after Spartan and I went to war. He has a level head and he doesn't lie."

Ransome wondered if there were any chance of making friends with Jerome. The next closest neighbor was three miles away, and they might or might not have anyone his age. Perhaps Jerome wasn't as unfriendly as he looked.

Ian poked his thick finger at Reuben's chest and said, "You move those cabins back or you're liable to find them burned to the ground!"

Jerome shoved forward and knocked Ian's hand back. "You talk to Papa like that and I'll pin your ears back! And your son's to boot!"

Ransome fought the urge to step back, and held his ground, as did his father. No chance of friendship here, he thought. A flash of color from the porch of the larger house caught his eye. Two girls, one white and one dark, had emerged to see what the commotion was all about. Ransome's eyes met those of the white girl. He couldn't look away. Even though they were separated by the yard, he felt as if he were standing next to her.

Jessamine stared back at the handsome boy whose hair was the same shade of red as her bay horse. He had to be the son of the despicable man arguing with her papa and Jerome, but he seemed different. Very, very different. Her black eyelashes widened and her lips parted. Jessamine had never felt anything like the emotion she was feeling now. The boy was tall—even taller than Jerome, though he didn't look any older. His eyes seemed to hypnotize her. They were a chocolate brown and looked very intelligent. Jessamine felt as if she knew him without having exchanged a word. Unconsciously she took a step forward as he did the same.

Doll poked her in the ribs. "Don't you be looking at that Yankee boy like that. Your mama will wring your neck."

Jessamine brushed Doll aside. She like the strong set of his jaw and the way his hands were already square across the palm like a man's. She had heard these were signs of great loyalty and a strength he might not even know he possessed.

Completely ignoring the ruckus, Ransome slowly crossed the yard and stood gazing up at her as if he were having a vision of some sort. "My name is Ransome MacKinley," he said in a voice filled with wonder.

"I'm Jessamine. Jessamine Delacroix." She jumped when Doll jabbed her again.

"I found a hound dog over at Roseland that must have been yours. Do you want him back?"

"This place is so small, we couldn't bring all our pets. Will you please take care of him for us?"

"Sure. What's his name?"

She smiled and a dimple appeared in her cheek. "That's Baron. He's a good watchdog."

"You better quit talking to him," Doll hissed in Jessamine's ear. "I hear our mamas coming."

Ransome gave her a slow smile. Jessamine felt as if the porch were reeling beneath her feet.

"Ransome! Ransome, get over here. You hear me?" Ian bellowed from the buggy.

"I have to go."

Jessamine glanced over her shoulder to see her mother opening the door to come out. "Sometimes I walk down by the swimming hole in the creek early in the mornings. It's nice down there," she whispered to Ransome, then smiled.

"Ransome!"

He gave Jessamine another of his heart-stopping grins and turned to go to the buggy, where his father sat in fuming rage. As Ian sent the buggy wheeling out of the yard, Ransome glanced back at the porch. Jessamine's mother and a black woman had joined the girls on the porch, so he didn't wave, but he wondered if Jessamine had been hinting for him to meet her in the morning. He couldn't think of any other reason for her to have said what she did.

"Those damned pigheaded Rebel bastards are a curse on this earth!" Ian fumed. "He flat-out refused to return my cabins! He as much as threatened my neck if we didn't leave. And that son of his is just as bad. If I ever catch you talking to that boy, I'll have your hide! Do you hear me, Ransome? As far as we're concerned, the Delacroixs don't exist and never did!"

"Yes, sir," Ransome dutifully said as he refrained from smiling. He had all afternoon to walk the creek and figure out where this swimming hole might be.

The following morning was cool with the scent of late summer, and the lowlands were shrouded with fog. Jessamine dressed hurriedly and as silently as possible behind the curtain that hid her bed. When she heard Adele moving restlessly behind the adjoining curtain, she froze until her sister's breathing was even again. She grabbed the yellow sunbonnet that matched her gingham dress and held her wide skirts close so they wouldn't rustle. She glanced up at the loft and was relieved to see Jerome hadn't pushed back his curtain for the day. Everyone was still asleep.

She let herself out and tiptoed across the porch and down the steps. As soon as her feet touched the dewy grass, she lifted her skirts and bolted for the woods.

Birds sang in the treetops in the distance and a slight breeze fluttered the draping gray-green Spanish moss. As she neared the creek, the grass beneath her feet changed to a thick emerald moss. Wispy fog filled the creek bottom, lying soft and silent. And somewhat eerie. She had seldom been down here with it so foggy, and had a bit of trouble maintaining her bearings. Things looked different. References beyond ten or fifteen feet ahead were lost. She shivered as she strained to see the curve of the bank that marked the swimming hole. Would he be here?

In the mist ahead, a slight movement caught her attention, and she stopped, rigidly still. What if it was one of the wild razorback hogs that often frequented the creek? As she strained to see, a breeze thinned the fog, revealing the boy's shape. Although she was relieved that it was he and not a javelina, a different uneasiness came over her. Jessamine had only recently begun to realize boys were more interesting to her than girls, and she wasn't accustomed to the odd sensations she had felt from time to time when she was around one of them.

He stepped forward and stopped.

"I hoped you would be here," she said over the hammering of her heart.

"It wasn't too hard to find. I just followed the creek." His voice sounded different from any she had ever heard before. He talked faster, and apparently his voice hadn't finished the change Jerome's had recently been through, as it shifted to a higher pitch on some words and lower on others. Jessamine was amused, but from her recent experience with Jerome's voice change, she knew better than to say anything about it.

She slowly approached him. "Around here we call it a *coulée*. Do you like it here in Cavelier?"

"I don't know yet. It sure is different from Albany." His clipped accent reminded her of snowy fields and warm fires.

"You know we shouldn't be here. I mean, even if there weren't hard feelings between our families, a girl shouldn't meet a boy alone in the woods."

"Do you want me to leave?"

"No," she said with a shy smile.

He grinned back. "Sit by me here on this log and tell me about yourself."

Jessamine demurely spread her bright skirt over the huge log and sat on its mossy trunk. "There's nothing at all to tell. I was born at Roseland, and I lived there all my life until two days ago."

"Did you mind moving?" he asked awkwardly.

"Of course we did. Wouldn't you? We've worked our fingers to the bone scrubbing that dog-run house. Tabitha said you can't make a silk purse out of a sow's ear—but you can make the sow's ear clean." She looked at him curiously, wondering why she felt as if she already knew him. She had always made friends easily, but this seemed different.

"Is Tabitha the Negro girl I saw you with?"

"No, that's Doll. Tabitha and Sam are her parents." She drew a deep breath and said in a rush, "You mustn't tell a soul, but Doll and I are best friends."

"Why are you telling me a secret?"

"So we can be friends, of course. Now you have to tell me one."

"I can't do that. I don't even know you."

"If you don't, you're taking advantage of my confidences and then we can't be friends," she protested.

Ransome was even less accustomed to flirting than Jessamine, and all this seemed to have scrambled his thoughts. For several moments he struggled to recall something he could share; then he brightened. "Before my brother, Dennis, went off to war, he got drunk. Not just tipsy, but weaving drunk. I slipped him in through the window and sat on him until he fell asleep."

"You sat on him?" she said with a giggle.

"If my mother and father had found out, they would have been really upset. Dennis wasn't allowed to drink." He smiled. "Are all Louisiana girls so outspoken?"

"Probably not. Papa says I've never met a stranger. I'll tell you another secret, just for free. I used to slip off down here and swim with Doll whenever Jerome and Spartan weren't likely to come by."

"You can swim?" He swallowed and tried to disregard the picture in his mind of her bare limbs in the clear water.

She nodded. "So can Doll, but since ladies don't do things like that, I can't tell anyone."

"You shouldn't be telling me this." He couldn't stop thinking about her in the water. "Does your brother know you come here?"

"No."

"Does that mean you aren't close?" Ransome thought of how the boy had dared speak up to his father and wondered if he would ever be able to do that himself. Although he admired Jerome's bravery, he was a bit intimidated by it.

"Well, of course we are. He was always my favorite brother. It's just that Jerome is sort of stuffy about things like that. He thinks I should act like a lady, but I can tell you that's really boring at times. Doll and I can tell him just about everything else." She threw him a sideways glance. "I don't think I'll tell him about you, though."

"Father was sure upset at Jerome for talking up to him like he did."

"When Jerome thinks something is right or wrong, he doesn't mind saying so. He can be very outspoken too."

"I don't know quite how to say this, so don't get mad, but I never knew Southerners made friends with their slaves."

"You mean Doll and me? That's different. We were born under the same star. Tabitha says that's why we're so close. You can't know Doll and not like her—that's what Jerome says."

"Yes." Ransome was thinking how fog would always remind him of the gray of her eyes. Only, her eyes sparkled, more like quicksilver. He decided he was liking Louisiana better every minute.

Jessamine looked around. "The fog is starting to lift. That means the sun is well up and everyone will be wondering where I am." She stood up and shook her skirts to knock off the clinging bits of bark and moss.

"Will you come back again?"

"I'll be here every chance I get. I don't want to make anyone suspicious, or they might follow me and make us stop meeting. I know—if I think I can get out the next morning, I'll wedge a leaf in the railing of the bridge the evening before. All right?"

"All right. And if I can't come, I'll go down and put a pebble on the railing. Are you going to tell Doll?"

"I imagine she already knows. She's like that. Besides, she was standing close enough to hear me tell you to come here. We can trust her, though."

He nodded, feeling suddenly awkward. "I guess I'll see you soon, then."

She smiled and put her bonnet on her head, framing her face in yellow calico.

Bending stiffly, Ransome kissed her cheek, and part of her bonnet as well. Then he blushed at his daring.

Jessamine tiptoed and put a quick kiss on his cheek before she turned and ran back the way she had come.

Ransome stood staring after her as if he had been enchanted and turned to stone. Slowly he raised his fingertips to his cheek. No girl had ever kissed him before. A wide grin spread across his face.

3

THE CHINABERRY TREE BESIDE THE TEN ACRES cabin had changed from an umbrella of gold to a bare skeleton of branches that poked toward the sky. Then its waxy balls dropped to the ground like pellets of yellow hail. Winter had come to the swamp.

"I knew it was going to be a hard one when I seen how fluffy the squirrels' coats was," Tabitha told Delia. "The tree bark is thick too. We might even see snow."

Delia looked out her window to the leaden sky and pulled her shawl more closely about her shoulders. "It's a wonder we're not all down with something." Her usually serene voice was tight with concern. Reuben had had one cold after another, and now Adele was sniffing and sneezing.

"How's Mr. Reuben doin' today?"

"He says he's better, but I fancied he still felt a bit feverish. He won't stay in bed, though."

"No, ma'am."

"Since he came back from the war, he's been too thin. I'm afraid all the privations broke his health for good."

"I been trying to dose him with lady's-slipper tea, but he won't drink it. I even tried some sulfur and molasses, but he wouldn't take it neither. I don't rightly know what to do with him."

"Neither do I. He hates being sickly, but he won't let me doctor him. Maybe if we cooked meat more often." She looked hopefully at Tabitha.

"Where we gonna get it? Sam was out till good dark last night and didn't get a thing but that old possum."

Jerome came into the house in time to hear the last exchange. His young face was marked with studious unconcern as he stacked the evening's firewood in the box.

Delia unconsciously rubbed the worry lines in her forehead with her fingertips. "I don't know how we're going to hold out until we can get another crop planted and harvested. We've got barely enough to get by on.''

"I could go live in town,'' Jerome offered. "I might be able to get work.''

"No. We stay together,'' Delia said firmly. "Besides, your papa needs you here. There's too much work around here as it is.''

"I sure wish we had had time to build us a smoke-house and bring more of that cured meat.''

Jerome dusted his hands on his pants and listened quietly. He could almost taste the ham they had to leave behind.

"We brought all we could manage at the time,'' Delia said. "Hindsight doesn't help anybody.''

"Yes, ma'am. That's the truth.''

Adele, who had been asleep on her parents' bed, came into the common room. Her cheeks were bright red and her eyes were glassy.

"Come here, honey,'' Delia said as she pulled her daughter's cheek to her own. "Tabitha, she's running another fever.''

"Is she for a fact? Come over here, baby, and set yourself down by the fire while I make you some gingerroot tea.''

"I don't like ginger tea,'' Adele complained fretfully. "My head hurts.''

"It's the fever, and the tea will bring it down.'' Delia looked over Adele's head to Tabitha, her eyes full of concern. "Where did Jessamine and Doll go?''

"Last I saw of them, they were heading towards the woods to look for nuts.''

"This late in the year? The squirrels have long since gathered them.'' Delia dampened a cloth and bathed Adele's flushed face. "It seems as if Jessamine is always gone these days.''

"Yes, ma'am.'' Tabitha looked out the window toward the woods. She thought Jessamine's absences were mighty peculiar too.

Meanwhile, well into the woods by the swimming hole, three heads were bent over a book. "Read this part here, Doll,'' Jessamine instructed.

Holding the book with obvious pride, Doll carefully read the passage and smiled from Jessamine to Ransome.

"Perfect!" he pronounced. "I've never seen anybody learn to read so quickly."

Doll lowered her eyes modestly. "Jessamine has been teaching me off and on for quite some time. It's easy to do something if you want to bad enough."

Ransome pulled another book from his canvas bag. "Read this one next. It's by Charles Dickens."

"*Nicholas Nickleby,*" Jessamine read aloud. "I don't remember this one from our library."

"I brought it with me when we moved here."

Jessamine tried to fit it into her pocket, but couldn't. "Don't bring such big ones. I can't slip them into the house."

Doll pulled off her apron. "Here. Roll it up in this, and I'll bring it in like I've been gathering eggs or something."

"We told them nuts this time, remember."

"There aren't any nuts on the ground this late in the year," Ransome said.

"It was all I could think of at the time, and Tabitha had that look on her face as if she were getting suspicious."

"I sure don't like slipping around," Doll said. "I'm scared Ma will find out and tell Miss Delia. You know what would happen then." She rolled her dark eyes expressively. "They wouldn't let us leave their sight from then on."

"Nobody will find out." Jessamine was already poring hungrily over the first few pages. "You're going to enjoy this one, Doll."

"I don't like having secrets from Jerome, either," Doll added. "You know he's never kept anything from us."

"What would you have us do?" Jessamine asked in exasperation. "Invite him along? You know how he feels about Ransome's family."

"I know it. It just don't seem right."

" 'Doesn't,' " Jessamine and Ransome corrected together.

"How do you explain where these books come from once you get them in the house?" Ransome asked. "Hasn't anyone ever noticed how many different ones you're reading?"

"Papa is the only one interested in books other than us," Jessamine told him. "And lately he's been too busy to notice."

Doll stood up and shook her skirts. "We have to be

getting back. If Ma is suspicious, she'll be watching for us.''

Jessamine handed Doll the newest book, concealed in the apron. ''You go on and stall them. I'll be along in a little while.''

Doll looked from Jessamine to Ransome, who was suddenly intent on examining a dead leaf. ''I shouldn't go off and leave you out here. You know that.''

''We've been over that before. Ransome and I just want to talk a bit.''

Doll studied the white girl for a few moments. ''I don't mind waiting.''

''What's that supposed to mean?''

''I just feel edgy. Like something's about to happen to us. I don't like it.''

''Surely you trust me,'' Ransome protested. ''You know I wouldn't do anything to harm Jessamine.''

''I know it.'' Still she hesitated. Doll also knew far more than Jessamine about the relationship of men to women, due to the lack of privacy in the slave quarters. She had seen other ''good'' girls brought down with babies, and she doubted white girls were much different from black ones in this respect. Still, she couldn't very well say so. Nodding, she walked away.

''Doll didn't mean anything by that,'' Jessamine said when they were alone.

''I wasn't offended. I really wouldn't ever do anything to hurt you. You know she's right, though. If we ever got caught out here by ourselves, they would all think the worst.''

''It wouldn't be any worse than if they caught me talking to you at all, or us teaching Doll to read.''

Ransome doubted that, but he rather admired Jessamine's naiveté. It made him feel very protective. He reached out and took her hand and smiled down into her expressive eyes.

Doll wasn't happy about leaving the two of them alone, but she couldn't very well go back. What would she do if their friendship got carried away and Jessamine wound up in trouble? Jessamine had told her that Ransome had held her hand and had even kissed her. Doll decided it was time for her to sit Jessamine down and tell her the facts of life as she had learned them from the kitchen maids at Rose-land.

As she was crossing the yard, Tabitha stepped out of the barn and motioned to her. Doll's steps faltered. The hidden book seemed to be burning a hole in her apron as she went to her mother.

"Where you been? Where's Miss Jessamine?"

"She'll be along directly."

"Uh-huh. What you got there in your apron, girl?"

Reluctantly Doll unwrapped the book. "Jessamine told me to bring it to the house for her."

"*Miss* Jessamine," her mother snapped. "What's she doing off in the woods with a book?"

Doll took it back and rewrapped it, guiltily thankful that her mother couldn't read and didn't know this was a new one. "I don't know. She just was."

"That's fine for her, but not for you. I worry about you, girl. Here lately you got to where you talk just like the white folks. How come you doing that?"

Doll shrugged and refused to meet her mother's eyes.

"Next thing I know, you're liable to start putting on airs and getting uppity. That'll get you in bad trouble, Doll. I knows what I'm talking about!"

"Ma, you just don't understand. Times are changing."

"Not for us they ain't. Not so as I can see it. You think just because Mr. Lincoln said we is free that we gonna stay that way? Girl, you not that dumb. White folks is in charge of it all. If they decides to take up slavery again, they can do it."

"But the war—"

"Ain't nothing sure but death. You know that. I hear they is something new called the Ku Klux Klan. That's a bunch of white folks what meets to put down carpetbaggers and our people that takes to putting on airs. They real mean and strong, this Klan. Folks over to the church was speculating that they might take over the government and bring slavery back."

"You don't reckon they will!"

"Can't nobody know for sure. In the meantime, you'd be real smart to remember who you is and who they is."

Doll was silent, and she tried to be still but couldn't stop her hands from trembling.

"What's eating at you? Don't shake your head at me.

I know you as well as I know myself, and there's been something fretting you for days.''

"Ma, something's going on, and I don't know what to do about it.''

"Maybe you'd better tell me about it. Is you in some kind of trouble?''

"No, ma'am. Not me. The thing is, Jess . . . Miss Jessamine has been meeting the MacKinley boy, and they have become friends.''

"They ain't!''

"Yes, ma'am.''

"If her papa finds out, he'll whip her for sure. What's that child thinking on?''

"Well, he is real nice and friendly.'' Doll watched closely to see if her mother seemed to be worried about the same thing that had occurred to her.

"She better quit slipping off to see him. She's gonna be a young lady right soon, and things will be different then.'' Suspiciously she said, "You didn't go off and leave them out there alone, did you?''

"Miss Jessamine told me to. I was thinking, Ma. Do you think I ought to tell Mr. Jerome? He might be able to talk some sense into her.''

Tabitha weighed the idea for a minute, a frown wrinkling her brow. "You stay out of it, girl. Miss Jessamine and that MacKinley boy are too young to be up to any meanness. Don't tell Mr. Jerome, neither. White folks is too unpredictable. You don't never know what they going to do next. Best thing for us to do is stay out of their way as best we can and don't see nothing and don't know nothing.''

Doll nodded. "Yes, ma'am.''

With her frown deepening, Tabitha studied her daughter. Doll was growing fast, and already her breasts were starting to take shape. With her cream-colored skin and heavy black hair, Doll was on the verge of blossoming into a real beauty. "I seen you and Mr. Jerome walking down by the swamp yesterday.''

"Yes, ma'am. He was showing me a squirrel nest.'' Doll looked surprised at her mother's sudden switch of subject.

"You've seen squirrel nests before. Don't you go off alone with him unless you can't help it.'' When Doll looked confused, Tabitha said, "Mr. Jerome is getting to be a young man. I don't want you getting in trouble.''

"Jerome?"

"*Mr.* Jerome!" Tabitha corrected her, shaking her head in exasperation. "It's things like that what worries me half to death 'bout you."

"You haven't got any reason to worry, Ma. I'm no older than Miss Jessamine."

"It ain't the same, child. It just ain't the same. You go on to the house now. Miss Adele is sick again, and Miss Delia is beside herself."

Doll did as she was told, but her thoughts were confused. She had never considered that Jerome would ever be anything but one of her best friends. She had never thought of him in any other way, and she wondered what her mother had meant. At times her mother's veiled warnings were hard to figure out. Shoving such thoughts aside for another time, Doll climbed the porch steps and entered the house.

Adele was in her bed, and as Doll went to see about her, she surreptitiously hid the book she was carrying under Jessamine's mattress. She placed the back of her hand on Adele's forehead to check for fever, and all at once a shock of images coursed through her mind: images of the family huddled together and crying; of Adele lying still and waxy white; of newly turned earth. Doll jerked her hand away. Immediately the half-seen pictures faded, leaving only the dread they had evoked.

"What's wrong?" Delia asked her.

"Nothing, Miss Delia. Nothing at all." Doll swallowed and glanced with fright at Adele as she unconsciously rubbed her hand over her homespun skirt. She was still trembling and filled with foreboding.

"Start peeling these potatoes for supper," Delia said. "Jerome is digging some cabbage out of the mounds." She went to Adele and held a cup of tea to her lips. Adele drank it, but she grimaced at the bitter taste.

Doll sat down at the table, and as she methodically peeled the potatoes, she puzzled over what had happened when she touched Adele. This wasn't the first unusual and unexplainable experience for her, but it was different from the others. On several occasions before when Doll had touched something that belonged to someone else, she had gotten strange pictures in her mind, as though she could see the person who owned the object using it. But this thing with Adele was not like that at all.

This time she seemed to be seeing the future and Adele had seemed to be dead. Doll felt sick at the idea.

The door opened and Jerome came in with two cabbages. As Doll took them from him, she whispered, "What's wrong with Adele?"

"Not much. She just has another cold."

"She sure has been sick a lot here lately."

"It's this drafty cabin," he complained. "I have wind whistling around my head all night."

Overhearing the last part of their exchange, Delia said to Jerome, "You aren't getting another earache, are you?"

"No, ma'am. I just wish I could find all the cracks in this old house so I could plug them. It seems that as fast as I fix one place, the wind comes through another." He looked at Doll. "Is your cabin this drafty?"

Doll met his eyes and was aware of an intensity there that she had never noticed before. Looking back down to her work, she answered, "No, our cabin has fresh chinking up to the roof, so it stays pretty warm." She resumed peeling the potatoes, but her thoughts had turned from Adele to Jerome. He had the Delacroixs' dark hair, as did Jessamine, but his eyes were brown, as were his father's. Already his jaw was taking on the firm line of adulthood, and he looked and acted older than his sixteen years. The burden of responsibility he had had during those years when he was the man of the house had matured him early. Doll looked up to find Jerome watching her. He smiled at her, and she felt a warm glow begin to spread inside her. Bashfully she looked away. He was going to be a heartbreaker. Doll was sure of it. She put aside the unsettling images she had seen in connection with Adele.

4

Dinner at the MacKinley house had always been a solemn affair, but now that they lived at Roseland and took all their meals on the enormous dining table, the emphasis on proper manners and refinements was more stringent than ever. Ransome supposed it was because his parents were so new to this level of luxury, but whatever the reason, he wished it would stop. He spent most meals worrying whether he was using the right fork and concerned that he might spill gravy on the tablecloth.

He looked up to find his father frowning at him from the head of the table. "I saw you coming in from the woods today. It seems as if you're always coming or going in that direction."

The food in Ransome's mouth went to sawdust, and he swallowed convulsively before saying, "I like to walk down by the creek."

"And that's another thing," his father said. "You've started saying 'creek' instead of 'crick.' "

"I guess I picked it up from school," he offered lamely.

"I told you we should have hired a private tutor," Ian said to his wife. "He's starting to pick up that detestable Southern manner of speech!"

"No," she said doubtfully. "Surely not."

"The Delacroixs live close to that part of the woods," Ian continued. "You aren't meeting that boy of theirs, are you?"

"No, sir," he said firmly. "I promise I've never met Jerome Delacroix in the woods or anywhere else."

"There, Mr. MacKinley. You see?" To Ransome Eliza said, "Your father has been worrying that you were making friends with him."

"No, ma'am. I'm not." Ransome tried to eat faster to escape the table without further interrogation.

48

"I saw Delacroix in town the other day," Ian said. "We didn't speak, naturally, but he gave me a look that would unnerve the dead," he said with a roll of his R's.

"Imagine," Eliza said vaguely, as if she were trying to picture what sort of look would do that.

"I'm telling you, boy, don't you ever have anything to do with those people. They're all rotten to the core."

Ransome carefully laid down his fork. Unaccustomed anger was building in him. He remembered how Jerome had faced up to his father that day, and he wondered if he would ever be able to do the same. He wasn't fearful, as a general rule, and had had his share of fistfights and won most of them, but he couldn't recall a time he hadn't been terrified of his father. "May I be excused?"

"Don't you want any cake?" Eliza asked. "Cissy cooked it today."

"No, thank you." Ransome knew the cook would give him a slice later despite his father's orders to the contrary. All their new servants liked Ransome and seemed to go out of their way for him.

"I do hope he isn't coming down with something," Eliza clucked. "Mrs. Johnson says half the town is sick."

"I feel fine, Mother."

"Leave the table, then," Ian conceded. He motioned to the butler, who stood by the door. "Bring us some more coffee."

Ransome escaped the room and used the opportunity to replace the book Jessamine had borrowed. He went upstairs, but instead of going to his own room, he went to the unused pink one—the one Jessamine had said she and Adele had occupied. His mother had not yet repapered in here, and Ransome could almost feel Jessamine's presence in the soft colors and frilly curtains. He sat on the windowsill and drew the curtains back in place so no one entering the room would know he was there.

Ransome sat quietly enjoying the solitude and serenity as the twilight of evening faded to darkness. Before long he heard his parents coming upstairs for the night. His mother was talking animatedly about a bolt of brocade she had bought that day, and as they passed the doorway he could distinguish his mother's two steps for each one of his father's. Ransome was glad he was finally past the age when his mother checked on him at bedtime. Tonight he wasn't sleepy, and his mind was too full of Jessamine for him to read.

The house grew quiet, and even the faint sounds of the servants in their attic rooms ceased. The full moon topped a bank of clouds on the horizon, casting silver beams over the fields and expansive lawn. From his vantage point Ransome could see the row of outbuildings that bordered the backyard. As he watched, engrossed in his memory of how Jessamine had kissed him on the cheek again that afternoon, he saw a figure move out of the deep shadows. At first he thought it was Jessamine herself; then, as the person moved into the moonlight, Ransome saw it was a man who seemed to be heading for the smokehouse.

Ransome hurried out into the hall and paused to consider whether he should wake his father, but decided he was old enough to handle this alone. Silently he made his way down the stairs, two at a time, and rushed out the back door. In his haste, he almost stumbled over Baron as the dog excitedly greeted him in the yard, wagging his tail as if he were determined to disjoint his body. Ransome paused for a moment, curious that his watchdog had paid no heed to the intruder; then it occurred to him that he had been foolish not go get his squirrel gun before rushing out here like this. As he looked around for some object that he might use to defend himself, he heard the smokehouse door open and saw the man emerging with a bundle under his arm.

Grabbing a nearby board and running toward the thief, Ransome called out, "You! Stop right there!" When he recognized the intruder as Jerome Delacroix, he stopped short.

Jerome froze as though he thought he might fade into the shadows if he remained motionless, but Baron leapt over to him and began trying to lick his face.

"Jerome? Is that you?" Ransome lowered the board in his hand and stepped closer.

Not taking his eyes from Ransome, Jerome silently patted the dog that had been his longtime hunting companion.

"What are you doing in our smokehouse?" Ransome asked.

Jerome's eyes flickered to the ham he held and back to his accuser. "Adele is sick and we need food. I butchered and smoked this hog myself, and I figured you'd never miss it."

"You need food? You're hungry? Why didn't you ask me? I'd have given you the meat."

"Listen, Yankee, we don't want charity. If Papa knew I was here, he would skin me alive."

"Do you want some sausage too?"

Jerome stared incredulously at the MacKinley boy. He hadn't expected him to be so generous. That made Jerome feel even worse about stealing the meat—and no matter how he tried to justify it, he was stealing. Anger welled up in him. No Delacroix had ever stolen anything before. Jerome shoved the ham at Ransome. "Take it back! I don't want it anymore!"

"But if you're hungry, you should—"

"We don't take charity!" Jerome dropped the ham and turned and ran back into the woods. He felt completely miserable. Why had he even considered this? He was lucky Ransome hadn't collared him and hauled him off to the sheriff.

He ran blindly through the trees and down the hollow to the little moss-covered bridge. He bent over the rail, gripping the cedar bark as he choked on his own disgust. Not only was he thoroughly embarrassed at having been caught stealing, but now he was obliged to that damned Yankee for letting him go. Jerome struck the railing hard with the palm of his hand and tried to gulp back the hot tears that were welling in his eyes.

Lifting his head, he let the stinging tears run down his cheeks. Life was so hard these days! Adele sick, and his papa with a chronic cough that shook him from head to foot. Jerome suspected he was often running a low fever as well.

Jerome felt responsible not only for his own family but also for Doll's. He didn't know how they would all live until the next harvest. At times like this he felt so young and helpless. With each passing day it got harder to remember what it had felt like to be a child and a pampered younger son.

Shoving the tears off his cheeks, Jerome squared his shoulders and started for home. All this wouldn't have happened if they had been able to stay at Roseland, where there was a garden to supply enough food for them all and where there were no drafts whistling through the walls. "It's those damned MacKinleys' fault!" Jerome muttered to himself as he found his way through the woods. He would never forget this night, he swore, and the depths to which those MacKinleys had forced him to sink. He would hate them all his life, and he would never forgive them or forget.

5

REUBEN AND SAM PLANTED THE SPRING CROP ON the hill that gently sloped down toward the swamp. Sam shook his head dolefully when they rested the mule. "Good thing that mule played out when he did. I'm plumb wore out."

"We'll get used to it." Reuben was as tired as Sam, but he automatically rejected speaking about it to his former slave; he had to be an example of fortitude. Slowly he eased himself down on the unplowed grass beneath a lone tree and leaned back on its trunk. When he drew a deep breath, his persistent, ragged cough shook his thin frame.

Sam glanced at him from the corner of his eye. "Next winter we'll have plenty of corn to fatten you up, Mr. Reuben. That'll put you back on your feet."

"I'm fine. It's just a cough." Reuben narrowed his eyes and looked down toward the swamp. "It's purely a shame we can't drain that damned thing."

"Drain the swamp?" Sam chuckled softly at the absurdity of the idea. "Might be a sight easier to sop up the Red River with a dishrag."

Maintaining his serious tone, Reuben continued thinking aloud. "There should be some use for it. Something that would bring in some money, before the crops ripen."

Sam looked at the still black water that encircled the numerous cypress trees. A green film of duckweed covered most of the surface. The inky depth might be one foot or twenty feet, no one knew. The tufts of needlelike grass along the bank might be supported by firm ground or be masking treacherous quicksand. "That old swamp's not to be trusted, Mr. Reuben. Folks goes in there and some don't never come out. I seen a mule swallowed by quicksand once. Poor old thing didn't stand a chance."

"I know it's dangerous," Reuben said as he was looking at the trees and not the water. "You know, there's probably not a better wood in the world than cypress. It won't rot, and it finishes out as nice as oak.'' An idea was starting to form in Reuben's mind. Nobody owned the swamp—nobody wanted it. It covered hundreds, maybe thousands of acres and was full of cypress. ''All a person would have to do to own that swamp is to go to the surveyor's office and claim it. They couldn't charge much taxes on a swamp. Everybody knows it isn't worth anything.''

''Why would you want to go and do that?''

A light was growing in Reuben's eyes as he said, ''If we could get those cypress trees out of there, they could be worth a lot of money. I'll bet if a man worked from a floating platform, he could get in there to cut them. What do you think, Sam?''

''Yes, sir. I guess you could. But it sure would be hard work, and I don't know who you could get, what wouldn't be afraid to do it. That swamp's a mighty scary place.''

Reuben leaned forward and clasped his hands around his knees as his thoughts raced. ''And if we built a sawmill to cut the trees into lumber, it would be worth even more and would be easier to haul.''

''Mr. Reuben, that seems like a good idea, but does you know how to do all that?''

Reuben wasn't listening to Sam. He was too busy planning. ''We could put the sawmill over there on that knoll.'' Reuben again gauged the distance from the swamp to the hill to be sure it would be close enough to the source of trees, and double-checked the elevation of the hill to be sure it wouldn't flood. ''A lot of people are going to have to rebuild now that the war is over, and they're going to need a lot of lumber to do that.''

''But, Mr. Reuben, I don't know nothing about being no mill hand. I just now got used to being a farmer. That's the free name me and Tabitha decided to take for ourselves—Farmer. I been meaning to tell you that.''

''I assumed you would take the name Delacroix, but Farmer is fine. I'm just a bit surprised.''

''We thought on it and decided it wouldn't be fittin', with us living on the same farm.''

''Farmer is a good name, Sam.''

''I can't be named Farmer if I'm working a sawmill.''

''Sure you can. We'll be farming as well. How about if I put you in charge of the land once I get some men working under me in the mill?''

"Mr. Reuben, how you gonna buy saws and things like that? You can't build a mill without saws, and you can't afford saws without a mill."

"I thought of that. We still have that silver we dug up before we left Roseland."

"But, Mr. Reuben, Miss Delia, she—"

"I know, Sam," Reuben interrupted. "That's the silver her mama gave us as a wedding gift, and it's very special to her. But I'll handle it. We won't need to buy much to begin with, and as we start making a profit, we can expand."

"But, Mr. Reuben—"

"Don't worry, Sam. I can convince her." Reuben smiled as he stood up and looked again at the swamp. For the first time in a year he felt like himself. "Let's finish this plowing, Sam Farmer. I've got a future to plan."

Late that night after everyone was in bed, Reuben put his arm around Delia and pulled her close to him. He nuzzled in the warm hollow of her neck, and she put her arms around him.

"Aren't you tired? Sam said you two plowed that whole hillside."

"I'm not that tired."

"You're still so thin. I worry about you."

"I needed to lose some weight. I'm just lean." He raised up on his elbow and looked down at her in the dark. "You're still the prettiest belle in the whole parish."

"Reuben, the very idea." She laughed quietly with pleasure at his compliment. "We have grown children and gray is starting to show in my hair."

"Not gray, but silver. Silver among the gold." He bent and kissed her.

"You certainly are full of compliments tonight. Why is that?"

"I haven't been paying enough attention to you lately, *mon amoureuse.*"

"The last time you called me that, Adele soon came along. You aren't planning to have more children, are you, because I have more than enough to do as it is."

"No, no. Calm down. I just meant what I said. You're a beautiful woman, and I've been taking you for granted these last few weeks. Well, not for granted, exactly. I mean, I appreciate all the work you do, and goodness knows I couldn't manage without you." He grinned at her and glided his hand over her nightgown to feel the curves of her body. "You're still as slender as a girl."

"Reuben, what are you up to?"

"Nothing." He kissed her again and felt her lips open beneath his. Confidently he moved his hand up to cup her breast.

"I know you better than that," Delia said as she pulled back.

He silenced her with a lingering kiss and felt her begin to respond. "One of these days, I'm going to put you back in a fine house," he promised between kisses. "You'll have your roses again, and plenty of servants to do your bidding. Maybe we'll even have Roseland again."

"Oh?" Her voice was husky with the pleasure his touch was giving her. It had been a long time.

He stroked her breast through the thin cotton of the nightgown and her nipple hardened beneath his palm. "If the MacKinleys can't make it as planters, they will have to sell out. If we have the money, we can buy it back."

"Where do you plan to get this money?"

Before answering, he kissed her deeply and unbuttoned the front of her nightgown. "I was thinking of starting a new business. One that would put us back on our feet. Like a sawmill."

"A sawmill?"

"That swamp is free land and full of cypress. I couldn't find a better wood anywhere."

"A sawmill," she repeated. "Where are we going to get the money to build a sawmill?"

"All we need are saws and tools. Sam and I can build it ourselves."

"You aren't thinking of selling Ten Acres to get the money! Where would we go?"

"No, no. Don't get so excited. Nobody said anything about selling Ten Acres."

"Who could you borrow money from these days? The bank is managed by Yankees—all of them are. They won't lend us money."

"No, I imagine we'll have to sell something." He held his breath and kissed the tender spot on her neck just below her ear. "Like your silver, for instance."

"My *mother's* silver?" She pushed him away and sat up, pulling her nightgown back over her breasts.

"I know you had to part with some of it while I was

gone, but surely there's enough left to trade for some saws and things."

"Not the silver! That's all I have left except some linens. Reuben, how can you suggest such a thing?"

He pulled her back into his arms. "I know your mother gave it to you so you could have pretty things around you, but I can't stand the idea of you having to spend the rest of your life living in a dogtrot cabin. I want more for you than that, and the only way I can get money is to earn it. You know we can't grow a big enough crop here to do more than make do until the next crop. After a few years in this drafty cabin our health will break, and then I won't be able to run a mill. No, Delia, now is the time if we're every going to get back on top. We aren't getting any younger."

Delia was silent as she laid her cheek on her husband's chest. She knew he was right. Her poor Reuben had been through so much. Even though his heart beat with a reassuring thump, his chest was thin and he hadn't regained much strength, if any, since he'd returned from the war. "Somehow I never thought we would get old," she said softly. "I guess I thought time would make an exception of us, and somehow we would be young and strong forever."

"We don't exactly have one foot in the grave. I plowed several acres today, and still have the strength to make love to you."

She patted his rib cage absently. "Yes, I know. This sawmill—will it really make money?"

"I don't see how it could fail. Not only is there building going on in town, but I can ship it down the bayou to New Orleans. I plan to ride to town tomorrow and file a claim on the swamp so the trees will belong to us."

Delia nodded reluctantly. "I guess what's left of Mother's silver would be well-spent in starting a sawmill, if there's enough. She told me once that my grandmother sold all her jewels to buy my grandfather a sailing ship. That's where the Spartans got their family wealth. I would be following a family tradition."

Reuben let out a sigh of relief. "You won't be sorry, *ma petite*. In time I'll buy you more silver."

"I trust you, Reuben, but what you don't know is that I had to trade some of the silver this last winter for food. I didn't tell you then, because I didn't want to burden you. But if this mill doesn't bring in some money by next fall, and if our garden doesn't do well, we won't have anything left.''

''Trust me. I know this will work.'' He tilted her head up and kissed her with all the love in his heart. ''I won't let you down, Delia.''

She nodded as she thought that the silver looked miserably out of place here anyway. With a sigh she gave herself over to his lovemaking.

The next morning, before Reuben began bundling up the silver, Delia headed out for her garden. She had agreed to sell the silver, but as it was her last vestige of true security, she couldn't bear to watch it leave. While she was busy planting the beans, peas, and cabbages, Reuben left for Cavelier.

Tabitha worked beside Delia, covering the seeds as Delia sowed them. ''When I went to church last Sunday I noticed they was gettin' ready to pitch cotton over to the Ramseys'.''

''I'm surprised the Ramseys are able to plant this year. But they have several grown sons to help. I guess that makes a difference. This does seem a bit early, though.'' She ignored Tabitha's reference to church. Although she and Sam had both been Catholic, as were the Delacroix, Baptist missionaries had recently converted them. The blacks had built a church of their own down the road toward town, and Delia had heard the congregation was still growing. Delia disapproved of the switch in religion, but she no longer had a say in the matter, so she avoided the subject.

''I sure hope we don't get another freeze,'' Tabitha said as she patted the rich brown dirt over the seeds.

''March will be here in a week. We aren't likely to see any more bad weather. Where are the girls?''

''Miss Jessamine and Doll went to look for poke greens and mushrooms. Miss Adele went with them.''

''I do hope they don't gather poison ones.''

''Doll knows what to look for.'' Tabitha hoped that mushrooms and greens were all the girls would find in the woods. She hadn't asked Doll since that day in the barn, but she was pretty sure Jessamine was still slipping out to meet the MacKinley boy. If Jerome happened upon them, there was no telling what he might do. ''I haven't see Mr. Jerome lately.''

"He was going crawfishing. I hope he brings in enough for jambalaya."

"Yes, ma'am. That sure would be good." Tabitha glanced toward the woods and hoped Jerome was working the swamp and not the creek.

"Have you noticed Jerome's attitude lately? All winter he seemed mad at the world. I hoped his disposition would improve with warmer weather, but it hasn't."

"He took it real hard, having to leave Roseland. I reckon it was because the plantation would have been his someday now that Mr. Spartan is gone."

"Perhaps that's it. Somehow he seems to blame the MacKinleys for all our misfortunes. So does Reuben."

"Yes, ma'am," Tabitha replied as noncommittally as possible. She was too smart to take either side with white folks.

"Maybe men need a target for their anger. Does Sam do that?"

"No, ma'am. Sam ain't mad at nobody."

"No. No, of course not. I was only thinking out loud. Where is Sam?"

"He be pacing off the spot for the sawmill. He said they was going to start building it right away."

"This will be good for us all," Delia said firmly. "Next winter they won't have to work out in the rain and weather as they did this last one."

"Yes, ma'am."

"Adele is much better lately, don't you think?"

"Yes, ma'am. She's picking right up. I believe she's putting on some weight."

"We're going to make it, Tabitha. It was a terrible winter, but now I can tell we're going to make it."

"I've never been more glad to see spring in my whole life," Tabitha said fervently. "At times I thought it would never get here."

"So did I," Delia murmured. "So did I."

By the time they finished planting the rows of vegetables, both women had discarded their shawls. The weak February warmth seemed to be a promise of an early spring, and the fallow ground looked much more fertile than the crop-worn dirt around Roseland. Tabitha even hummed to herself as she worked, and Delia wished she could forget social propriety and join in.

"Mama! Mama!" Jessamine called as she ran out of the woods. "Adele fell into the *coulée!*"

Delia froze for an instant, then lifted her skirts and ran toward her daughter. "In the creek? Where is she!"

"They're bringing her. Luckily Ransome MacKinley happened by and he pulled her out."

"You weren't on their land!"

"We were walking along and talking, and I guess we were on it a little bit." As she spoke, she pointed to the woods. "Here they come."

Delia saw the tall MacKinley boy and Doll, but her eyes were glued to the limp figure that the boy carried. "Adele!" Delia screamed as she ran to them and took her child. She staggered under the sodden weight of her little girl until she gained her balance.

Tabitha gasped. "Is she . . . ? She ain't drowned, is she?"

"No, ma'am," Doll said. "Rans . . . Mr. Ransome jumped in and saved her. She's cold to the bone, though."

Delia glanced back at the boy and saw he was as wet as Adele. "Come into the house and get some dry clothes on. I'm sure Jerome's clothes will fit you."

"I think I'd better not," the boy said as he was backing away. "I've already got a lot of explaining to do by going home wet. I could never explain having on Jerome's clothes."

"It's a good thing you . . . happened by," Jessamine said. "Otherwise I would have jumped in after her, and we might have both drowned."

Delia looked from Jessamine to Ransome, and a doubt crept into her mind about the coincidence. Then Adele trembled with a chill and whimpered, and the thought flew out of Delia's mind.

She turned and ran with Tabitha at her heels toward the house.

The cook fire had died down to coals, but Tabitha soon had the fire roaring as Delia stripped Adele to the skin. Doll got the girl's warmest nightgown and helped Delia pull it onto Adele's shivering body. Delia sat on the hearth and held Adele in her lap like an overgrown baby with quilts piled on top of her.

Adele kept her eyes screwed shut as tremor after tremor shook her thin body. Delia's eyes met Tabitha's and they exchanged a look of deep concern.

By afternoon of the following day, they both knew

Adele was in trouble. "We got to get help for her," Tabitha whispered as she felt the girl's hot forehead. "I never seen fever go so high so fast and not go back down."

"There hasn't been a doctor in town since Dr. Harris died."

"There's old Asiza."

Delia looked up reprovingly. "She's only a legend. There is no such person."

"Yes, ma'am, there is. She live back in the swamp. I reckon Sam could find her if he took the pirogue."

"Sam isn't going off in a boat on some wild-goose chase. Reuben needs his help. We were up most of the night with Adele. Reuben is asleep on his feet."

"I could find her," Doll spoke up.

"You've never been in the swamp in your life. No. I won't hear of it. Adele has been sick before. She will be all right."

"Yes, ma'am," Tabitha said reluctantly. "But Asiza—"

"She isn't real! That's a legend told around here. No woman could live alone back in the swamp, even if she *were* a witch. Adele needs medicine, not voodoo. Mix some more sulfur and molasses, Tabitha. Doll, you brew another pot of ginger tea." Delia sat on the side of Adele's bed and repeatedly bathed the girl's face in cool water.

When Reuben came in that night, his face was drawn as if ten years had been added in the day's time. "Is she any better?"

Delia silently shook her head.

"It's those damned MacKinleys' fault!" he exploded. "If we were still living at Roseland, she wouldn't have been ailing all winter and run-down to the point where falling in the *coulée* would make her sick."

"If the MacKinleys hadn't bought Roseland, someone else would have," Delia said in a tired voice. "Your dinner is there on the table. Go eat."

"You're not hungry?"

"I ate earlier," she lied. She couldn't bear the thought of food when Adele was so sick.

"You're right, Papa," Jerome angrily agreed. "It's all their fault."

"That's enough, Jerome!" his mother snapped. "Sit down and eat your dinner. You too, Jessamine. You'll have to help me watch Adele tonight."

"Doll said she would sit up with me so you can sleep, Mama."

"I can't leave her." Delia looked down at her youngest. Adele's every breath was audible, and dark circles had formed under her eyes.

"You can sleep on my bed," Jessamine suggested. "If she gets worse, you'll be right here."

"Perhaps."

"You have to get some rest or you'll get sick too," Reuben said. He came to her and put his arm around her. "Come and eat a bite or two."

"I said I had eaten."

"I don't believe it."

She let Reuben lead her to the table and dutifully ate a small plate of peas, greens, and cornbread.

After dinner Jessamine washed dishes and went out on the tunnellike porch to join Jerome. "It's getting cold. You ought to come inside."

"I just can't stand it," he said through his clenched teeth. "Those MacKinleys sit over there in our house eating food from our garden at our table, and here we are in this predicament. I hate those MacKinleys. I do for a fact."

"Well, you shouldn't hate them all," she retorted sharply. "If Ransome MacKinley hadn't come along when he did, Adele would have drowned. She fell in at the swimming hole where the water is deep. He jumped in and pulled her out."

"He did? I don't believe it!"

"I was there, Jerome. I saw him do it." She frowned up at her brother. "You may not like them, but it's because of Ransome that Adele is still alive."

He looked at his sister closely. "Roseland is a big place. How did it happen that he came along at just the right time?"

"How should I know?"

"I'll tell you one thing, Jessamine, you better not be making friends with that boy or I'll beat him within an inch of his life."

"You can't! He's bigger than you are!"

"He's not used to hard work, and I'm stronger. You had better not be meeting him. Do you hear me?"

"I hear you." She glared at her brother and strode back into the house.

Jerome scowled out at the night. Ransome had saved Adele! He would never have guessed any MacKinley would do anything for a Delàcroix. Unbidden the memory arose of that night he had tried to steal the ham from the Mac-Kinley's smokehouse. Ransome had let him go and had never told anyone of the incident. Jerome struck the side of the house in his anger. Of all the people in the world to be indebted to, Ransome MacKinley was the worst. Just as Reuben blamed the family for their misfortune, Jerome's hatred for Ransome MacKinley bordered on obsession.

By the following afternoon, Adele was worse. She moved restlessly in bed and picked at her bedclothes as if in spasm. Delia's face was drawn and pale as she announced, "It's pneumonia."

"I thought so last night," Tabitha confirmed as she watched the labored shallow breaths that barely stirred the covers. "What we gonna do?"

"There's nothing to do but what we already are doing." Delia's voice was impassive, and her eyes held a haunting fear.

"I could try to find Asiza."

"No! I told you, there is no such person. Don't you dare mention her again! That's all just superstition, and I won't have any of it talked about in my house."

Tabitha nodded and sullenly mumbled, "Yes, ma'am." When white folks decided something was so or not so, there was no point in trying to tell them anything.

By the following day Delia could hear the saws and faint hammering from where the men were building the floating platform. Reuben knew Adele was sinking, and he worked himself at a furious pace to block his thoughts of what might happen to her.

Doll and Jessamine were in the woods looking for dock and the onionlike ramps that grew wild in the hollows. Neither was speaking much because they were afraid to talk about Adele and nothing else filled their minds.

"She didn't look so good today, did she?" Doll asked at last.

"I thought she seemed to be breathing easier," Jessamine replied, stubbornly refusing to face reality. "I heard Mama say the next day or so will be the turning point."

"I should have been watching her closer. It was all my fault she got so near the bank."

"Adele is ten years old, Doll. She's not a baby that needs constant watching. Quit blaming yourself. If anything, it's my fault for taking her with us to meet Ransome."

"It's nobody's fault. Adele just fell in. It could have happened to any of us. Thank goodness Ransome jumped in. I couldn't move!"

"Neither could I. She went under so fast. If he hadn't kept diving for her, she wouldn't have come up at all."

"It was her skirts. They were so heavy when they got wet." Doll ran her hand over the shapeless ducking she wore. Unlike Jessamine and Adele, she wouldn't wear a fitted bodice and full skirt for several more years. Some of the girls in the quarters had worn ducking until they were married.

Jessamine paused in pulling the pale green shoots of the ramps. "Wasn't it brave of him? I've never met anyone like him. On one hand he's so gentle that you'd think he has no gumption. Then something like this comes up, and he risks his life without even a second thought. I'll bet there was trouble when he got home. He has left a pebble on the bridge rail every day to show he can't meet me."

Doll was listening, but more and more she became aware of a hard knot of dread deep in her middle. Sitting back on her heels, she let the dread come to her, and she looked at it with that part of her mind that understood such things. Hazy pictures formed along with half-audible echoes. Instinctively Doll let her thoughts relax and the pictures and voices became clearer.

Her eyes flew open wide, and she jumped to her feet. "We have to go home. Hurry!"

"What? What are you talking about? We don't have enough dock to make a mess of greens."

Doll grabbed her arm and hauled her to her feet. "Come on! We have to go now!" She turned and ran back toward the house.

Jessamine called after her, but when Doll didn't even look back, she picked up both baskets and ran after her.

They arrived at the house just as Reuben was stumbling from Adele's silent bed to drop like an old man into the hide-bottomed chair at the table. Delia and Tabitha were both sobbing quietly, and Sam looked miserably awkward as he fingered the brim of his hat. Not fully comprehending what was going on, Jessamine stepped up beside Doll and looked down at Adele. Except for the women's sobs, the room seemed oddly quiet. Then Jessamine realized that the sound she missed was Adele's ragged breathing. Doll looked too shocked to speak, so Jessamine turned to her mother,

her face stricken with understanding. Delia drew her into her embrace, and Jessamine felt the tears sting her own eyes.

"I'll go find Jerome," Doll volunteered. She left the house and started down the barn as if she knew instinctively where to look for him. Shadows were lengthening across the yard, and the hens were fluttering up to the low limbs of an apple tree to perch for the night. Doll pushed open the door of the barn and saw Jerome. For a minute she stared at him through the gloaming as he brushed his horse. When he became aware that she was watching him, he cocked his head to one side with curiosity.

"I believe you had better get up to the house," she said at last.

Jerome stopped brushing the horse, and hung the brush on a nail as he closed the stall door. Doll seemed to be acting very strangely. "What's happened?"

"It's bad, Jerome. Real bad."

He crossed over to her and gazed down at the familiar planes of her face. She reached out and touched his bare arm, and in the dim light their skin was the same shade of bronze. "It's not Adele, is it?" he whispered, hoping he was wrong.

She nodded as tears filled her eyes. Jessamine didn't know it, but Adele was Jerome's favorite sister. He was going to take this especially hard, and there wasn't a thing she could do to ease him.

A groaning sound came from deep in his throat as he ran past her toward the house. At the cabin door, his father pushed past him on his way out, not speaking a word, his face grimly set. The room was in a turmoil when Jerome burst through the door. Everyone seemed to be talking and crying at once. Adele lay unmoving on her narrow bed. Jerome took a step toward her.

Tabitha was suddenly by his side, and she said in a low, harsh voice, "You get on the mule and go after your papa! He's on his way to Roseland to kill Ian MacKinley!"

"What?"

"He says Miss Adele would be alive if it wasn't for Mr. MacKinley." Tabitha turned him around and pushed him toward the door. "You're the only one that can stop your papa from murder!"

As Tabitha's words sank in, a muscle clenched in Jerome's jaw. The MacKinleys were at fault, but he couldn't let his father commit murder. As he ran from the house,

Reuben rode past him as if he didn't see him. As quickly as he could, Jerome tied a rope on the mule's halter and rode after his father.

The families waited at Ten Acres in painful apprehension. An hour passed, then two. Because Delia was in no condition to do anything but cling to Jessamine and cry, Tabitha washed Adele, and she and Doll put her in her Sunday dress. Sam stood on the hearth and nervously poked at the fire, because there was nothing else for him to do. Then a noise outside drew everyone's attention. Riddled with anxiety, they all strained to listen. They heard only one set of footsteps on the porch. It was Jerome who came through the door, moving with slow deliberation. "It's all right," he said in an exhausted voice. "We never got as far as Roseland. Papa's putting the animals in the barn. He's pretty badly shaken, but he's all right."

Delia collapsed like a rag doll against Jessamine and sobbed her relief. Jessamine drew what felt like her first deep breath since she and Doll had run home from the woods. She was thankful that Jerome had stopped her father, especially so because that meant that Ransome must be safe as well. Shortly, Reuben walked in, moving as if his body were numb. Delia rushed to him, and he fiercely embraced her.

Much later, Doll followed her parents across the yard to their cabin. Tabitha shut the heavy door as Sam knelt to build a fire against the chill of the night. "I thought sure Mr. Reuben was gonna kill that man."

"So did I," Sam agreed. "I never seen a man so mad. He charged out of that house like a rabid bull."

"I'm wore out. That poor little child! Ever' time I think about Miss Adele, I want to cry some more."

Sam went to her and enfolded her in his strong arms as Doll watched from the doorway to her room. "I know. I know. She was like a ray of sunshine, was Miss Adele. It won't seem right without her."

"You know what I kept thinking as me and Doll laid her out? I kept thinking how the first thing you and Mr. Reuben gonna make in that sawmill is Miss Adele's coffin."

"Hush. Don't you say that. It's bad luck." He held Tabitha closer and rocked her gently from side to side. "It's real hard on everybody, but these things happens to folks."

"At least Mr. Jerome kept Mr. Reuben from killing

that Yankee. They would have hung him for sure. Then where would Miss Delia be?"

"Mr. Jerome is gonna be a fine man someday. I know he hates those MacKinleys as much as his papa does, but Mr. Jerome is levelheaded. He don't go off in a tailspin like most boys his age. He's gonna make a fine man."

Doll went into her room and closed the door. Dawn was already showing beneath the thin gingham curtain at her window. She lay down fully dressed on her bed and gazed up at the sloping roof. Yes, she agreed, Jerome was going to be a fine man someday.

Ian MacKinley glared at his dripping-wet son. "So you jumped in to save her, did you! And then carried her all the way home? You could have caught your death, you young fool!"

"I couldn't let her drown, Father," Ransome protested. "She couldn't swim in all those skirts and petticoats. It was too deep for her to wade out."

"She had no business there in the first place. I'll bet that trash trespasses on my land all the time. You should have let her drown!"

Eliza sharply drew in her breath.

"I would never have let Adele drown!" Ransome cried out. "I think you're awful to say such a thing."

Instantly Ian's beefy hand clouted Ransome on the ear, sending him sprawling onto the floor. As the boy struggled back to his feet, he shook his head, trying to get the ringing to stop. Eliza gripped her crumpled handkerchief, and her wide blue eyes darted in terror from her husband to her son, but she dared not go to his defense.

"Well?" Ian thundered when the boy stood unsteadily before him.

"I'm . . . I'm sorry, Father," Ransome managed to say. He hoped his father would let him off with no further punishment, but he knew better. His eyes crept toward his father's black cane, and his skin went clammy.

"There's only one way to deal with this," Ian said harshly.

Ransome tightened his lips and waited.

"You're leaving!"

The boy looked up in amazement. He hadn't expected this.

Ian glared at Eliza. "Mother, pack the boy's bags. He's going back to his aunt and uncle."

"Mr. MacKinley, don't you think—"

"Do as I say, woman!" he bellowed. As Eliza scurried out, he said in a tone of heavy disgust, "Let's see what my sister can do with you. Albany schools will be better for you than anything Cavelier has to offer. At least you won't be sneaking around here anymore." He grabbed up the heavy cane and advanced on his son. "You're going to learn to obey me, boy. One way or another, you'll learn to obey."

Ransome gritted his teeth as the first blow fell across his back. Tears rushed to his eyes, and he gripped the back of the settee to keep from falling. Years of beatings had trained him to silence, but before his father finished, Ransome's breathing was ragged with stifled sobs.

Abruptly Ian stopped, and as if nothing more than a scolding had transpired, he strode from the room.

Ransome wasn't sure what to do. He was in pain and wanted to go to his room, but his clothes were still wet and he was hesitant to use the stairs. Tears stung his eyes. *Go all the way to Albany alone? What if I get lost?* he worried. A dull hate for his father left him cold and empty inside.

When a sound behind him startled him, Ransome painfully turned to find Jenkins, the butler, motioning for him to come. Silently the tall man handed the boy a towel and shepherded him back toward the warm kitchen.

Although Jenkins had seldom paid him any particular attention, Ransome was grateful for this act of unexpected kindness. He glanced out the window in the direction of Ten Acres. He didn't want to leave his new friends, but his father's word was law. At least he would be far away from the man he hated and feared. He would be glad to see Aunt Polly and Uncle Edward again. To bolster his courage, he tried to think of the terrifying trip ahead of him as an adventure.

"Someday I'll be back," he said, more to himself than to the butler.

Jenkins patted his shoulder and gave him one of his rare smiles.

II

Ten Acres: Spring 1870

A youth to whom was given
So much of earth—so much of
    heaven,
And such impetuous blood.

> —William Wordsworth

6

TABITHA BUSTLED ABOUT THE NEW KITCHEN AT THE main house, putting the finishing touches on the men's dinner as Doll packed the food into a large basket. As she worked, Tabitha cast quick glances at her daughter. Doll had grown into a remarkably beautiful young woman seemingly overnight, and Tabitha still couldn't accustom herself to the change. Doll's face had lost its childish roundness and her large almond-shaped eyes were like dark jewels in her light tan skin. Her hair was heavy and black, but not coarse like Tabitha's, and she wore it in a neatly braided bun on the nape of her neck. Aside from Doll's seductively soft eyes, Tabitha was most worried over her daughter's voluptuous figure. Always tall and slender, Doll had developed ample, firm breasts and rounded hips, and an elegance of bearing that kept her mother awake nights.

"You take this basket to Mr. Reuben down to the swamp. And you come straight home, and don't you talk to none of the workers," Tabitha enjoined.

"Yes, ma'am."

Tabitha frowned. Even Doll's voice was sultry and sensuous. "Don't talk to nobody."

"Ma, what's wrong with you these days? You act as if I can't be trusted out of your sight."

"It's not you I don't trust," Tabitha said as she shoved the heavy skillet to the back of the wood stove and used a metal hook to replace the burner cover. "It's like I woke up one morning and took a good look at you, and I ain't got over it yet."

"What's wrong with the way I look?"

"Nothing. That's what scares me. There's been many a girl plainer than you what has come to harm."

Doll laughed and her even white teeth flashed. "Ma, Mr. Reuben wouldn't lay a hand on me and neither would

71

Jerome. And they watch the other men whenever Jessamine or I are around.''

"There you go again! It's *Mr.* Jerome and *Miss* Jessamine. For years I been telling you not to call them by they proper names like that! And listen to how you talk. You sound as white as they do!''

"Mr. Reuben and Miss Delia can't hear us out here, and there's nothing wrong with speaking properly.''

"Yes, they is! I worry about you day and night. You ought to find you a beau and be thinking about getting married.''

"I'm only nineteen, Ma.''

"By the time I was your age, I had me a baby.''

Doll looked across the table at her mother, her expression changing from argumentative stubbornness to one of sincere curiosity. She knew she had been the result of her mother's first pregnancy. "Who was my father, Ma?''

Tabitha stared at her daughter, momentarily stunned by her frankness, then slowly sat down on the straight-backed chair.

"I know it's not Pa,'' Doll said gently. "I've known that for a long time.''

"What difference does it make? Sam has been your pa since the night you was born.''

"I know, and I love him, but I wonder.''

"I guess you got a right to know. Maybe then you'll listen closer to my cautions. I growed up on a plantation near New Orleans. When the old master died, I was just turned about eighteen, I guess. The new master, his son, had a bride, and they took over the big house, where I was a maid. Well, I wasn't bad-looking when I was young, and my looks caught the master's eye. Before long, his wife was expecting and sick all the time, so he come after me. I didn't want him to, but he did, and before I knew it, I was his woman.''

"What was his name?''

"His name don't matter,'' Tabitha snapped. "You ain't never gonna need to know that.'' Her voice softened as she said, "He was the prettiest man I ever seen. His hair was black like his eyes, but his skin was white—as white as this here tablecloth. I never seen anybody so white. He seemed to nearly shine. Well, before long my ma said I was gonna have a baby, and she was right. The missus, she have a baby boy and the master he think that baby hung the moon. Wasn't nothing he couldn't do for his wife right then. She knowed about me and all, so she point to me and say, 'Get rid of her.' Next thing I knows, I'm on the slave block in New Orleans.'' Tabitha's voice trailed off as she struggled to contain her emotions.

''That was the worst time of my life,'' she continued softly. ''No matter what happens, won't nothing be worse than that. I was hauled off from my parents and my brothers and sisters and throwed in a pen with a lot of strangers. Next day we had to bathe in cold water and rub grease all over us so we would shine like we was real healthy. Then they herded us like cows behind a platform and took us up one at a time. Folks was crying and carrying on, families being split up, children, even babies, being torn out of their mamas' arms. It was like being in hell.

''Then it was my turn. I had to strip down to the waist and trot back and forth on that platform so the white folks could see I was big with child and still quick. Some of them come up on the platform and pinched my skin to see if I was as young as the auctioneer said. You know older skin don't go back in place as quick as young skin do. Then I was sold. A man bought me for a thousand dollars on account of my age and because I was getting a baby soon. Afterward I was put on a wagon with a few others, and we was brought to Roseland. That's when I met Sam. We took a liking to each other right off, and Mr. Reuben said we could get married. He married us hisself, under that old oak grove by the side of the big house. Sam has been your pa ever since then.''

Doll was quiet for a time; then she reached out and covered her mother's work-roughened hands with her own.

''That's why I worry about you, girl. You're a whole lot prettier than I was, and there's white men all over this place and no young black ones, except what Mr. Reuben hires to cut trees or work in the mill. You need to meet more of your own kind. Settle down.''

Doll saw the worry in her mother's eyes, and she nodded. ''I understand, Ma. But times have changed. There is no more slavery, and if they were going to bring it back, I think it would have happened by now. As I said before, Mr. Reuben keeps a close eye on his men, and I'm in no danger here.''

Tabitha shook her head slowly. ''I just can't make you understand, can I? Go on with you, and take them their food.'' She stood, resignation slowing the movements of her thin body. Worry lines etched her face.

Doll longed to reassure her mother, but she knew it was useless. She was like a hen with one chick, and the older she got, the more she fretted about everything. Doll knew she would never be able to explain the friendship she had for Jessamine and Jerome. To Tabitha slavery would always exist, and now that Doll knew about her own beginnings, she could better understand why. She also realized for the first time that her life with the Delacroixs had been remarkably sheltered.

Black willows and cottonwoods bordered the swamp, and bald cypresses grew in profusion amid the swamp itself, their knees protruding above the water's murky surface. Spring flowers grew all the way down to the water's edge, and butterflies competed with bees for the blossoms. Jerome was working alone from the floating platform that had been moored at the base of a cypress that soared some seventy to eighty feet into the air. He had already sent the five other men on his crew to begin to work on another tree a safe distance away while he made the final, crucial cuts. In the past five years Jerome had felled many a tree and had become an expert at dropping them within inches of the target.

A breeze blew through the cypress's feathery leaves and lifted the curtains of Spanish moss draped all around, as he smoothly swung his ax into the remaining few inches of tree. In the still water below, a bug as small and black as a jet bead created an arrow-shaped wake as it swam by. A turtle swimming beneath the surface caused the emerald duckweed to bob up and down. Jerome was accustomed to the wild beauty of the swamp and paid it no attention. All his concentration was set on felling the giant tree in precisely the right spot to ease the job of getting it out of the swamp.

Without warning, the breeze picked up, and as he looked skyward, the top of the tree wavered and began its downward plunge—straight toward Jerome. He shouted and dived toward the brackish water, his cry smothered by the crashing of the cypress tearing through smaller branches and vines and saplings. With a sharp crack, the trunk gave way, and Jerome swam as fast as he could to avoid being crushed. The tree struck the water with a splash and the wave pushed Jerome past the knees of an adjacent cypress and onto a strip of seemingly innocent sand. He clawed at the surface, trying to right himself, but his hands and arms passed through the soupy mixture, finding nothing solid to push back against. "Quicksand!" he shouted. "Help!"

Doll was too far away to hear the tree fall or to hear Jerome's shouts, but suddenly she got the same sick feeling in the pit of her stomach that she had the day Adele died. Since that day in the woods she had hoped she would never have that particular "knowing" again. But here it was, overwhelming her. Jerome was in bad trouble. She lifted her skirts as she ran into the swamp.

When the tall trees closed around her, she looked about frantically. No one was in sight, but she knew she should run along the ridge of cottonwoods and willows. As she searched frantically, she called, "Jerome? Jerome!"

"Here!" she heard him say. "Over here!"

She ran down to the water's edge and saw Jerome floundering a short distance away in the shifting sand. He was already waist-deep and sinking fast. She dropped the basket and grabbed a nearby limb. With no thought for her own safety, Doll splashed into the water up to her knees and thrust the limb out to him. He missed on the first attempt, then caught it in one hand. Only his arm and head were visible by that time.

Doll pulled on the limb, praying that the end wouldn't break off in Jerome's hand.

As she pulled and the sucking sand began to release him, Jerome kept completely immobile until his other arm was free. Then, very carefully, he worked his way up the limb to a thicker part of the branch. Soon he floated free into the water.

Doll dropped back onto the bank as Jerome swam over and pulled himself out. He shook the water off his hands and ran his fingers through his dark hair. "It's a good thing you heard me shouting," he said at last.

Doll was still shaking too hard to reply, but she nodded. Gently she reached out to pick a strand of green moss off his shoulder.

"You're trembling," Jerome said as he knelt next to her.

"You scared me half to death."

He glanced in the direction from which she had come. "I don't see how you heard me when the men didn't."

She shrugged her shoulders as if she didn't understand. And she didn't, at least not exactly. She had never tried to explain her unusual ability to sense things that she had no way of knowing, because she was afraid people might think she was crazy or cursed. She reached out and touched his face. "Are you sure you're all right? You aren't hurt?"

Jerome gazed deep into her eyes and found it difficult to speak. Lately he had felt extraordinarily close to Doll, as if no distance could separate them. "I'm all right." He covered her hand on his cheek with his own and was surprised to feel how delicate her fingers were and how right it seemed for her to touch him.

Suddenly there was a loud rustling as the other men came hurrying through the brush. Doll jerked her hand away and lowered her eyes as she got hastily to her feet.

"What happened to you?" Reuben asked. "You're all wet."

Jerome scrambled up and pointed at the fallen tree. "It nearly came down on me. When I jumped from the platform, I somehow landed in that quicksand. Luckily Doll came running up and pulled me out with a tree limb."

All the men looked toward Doll, and a wave of embarrassment washed over her. Shyly she bent down and picked up the basket of food. "I brought out the dinner, Mr. Reuben."

"It's a good thing you did. I would never have been able to get out of there alone," Jerome said, his eyes lingering on Doll a bit longer than was prudent.

Apparently uncomfortable with the degree of gratitude his son was expressing, Reuben rather quickly said to her, "We're much obliged to you. We had no idea that Jerome was in trouble."

Sam stepped forward and took the basket. "You go on back to the house now, I'll bring the basket home with me when we come in tonight."

As Doll started to leave, she noticed two young black men there that she had never met. One of them was staring at her as if he had never seen a woman before. She looked away quickly. Her mother might be zealous in guarding her against the white men, but Sam hadn't limited his concern only to them, and he had not missed the exchange of glances. "Now, you run on along, Doll. We got work to do."

She smiled up at his stern face and said, "Yes, Pa."

Jerome watched her leave from the corner of his eyes as he half-listened to one of the men teasing that this proved he was still wet behind the ears. When she was gone, he turned his full attention to the men on his crew and grinned at them good-naturedly. Even though he was their supervisor and the boss's son, he was the youngest and he encouraged the camaraderie of their ribbing. As they did every day, Reuben handed out the food and Sam and the other blacks sat in their own circle while Jerome, Reuben, and the other whites gathered into theirs to eat. Up until that day, Jerome had never given the division at mealtime a thought. Now his mind was full of Doll, how her hand had caressed his cheek and how her skin felt exactly like his own.

After supper the Delacroixs went out to sit on the porch to enjoy the cool of the evening. The breezeway originally between the two halves of the dogtrot cabin had been enclosed to serve as a parlor, and the men had extended the roof overhang to cover the new veranda that encircled the front of the house from the dining-room addition on the left rear to Jessamine's new bedroom on the right. The entire exterior of the house had been covered with white clapboard siding, and all the floors redone in polished cypress from the busy mill.

Delia sat in the porch swing next to Reuben, smiling at him contentedly. Although her hair now had nearly as many silver strands as gold, his was as dark as it had always been. "How did your work go today?"

"Fine. Jerome took a swim about noon."

She looked at her son, who sat on the steps under the bower of sweetly scented roses. "It's awfully early for a swim, Jerome. You'll catch a cold."

"Papa is teasing you. I fell in. Or rather I jumped in to keep a tree from falling on me."

"Jerome! Reuben, you're supposed to be keeping an eye on him!"

"Honey, he's a grown man now. Doll pulled him out with a tree limb."

Jessamine had come out to join them, and she poked her brother in the ribs. "Since when can't you swim?"

"No one can swim in quicksand," he murmured under his breath.

"Quicksand!" she gasped. "Mama, Jerome fell in quicksand!"

Delia frowned at both her men. "I knew that swamp was too dangerous. Jerome, I don't want you going back in it."

"Oh, Mama," he sighed with exasperation. "It didn't amount to anything."

With a puzzled expression Jessamine said, "It seems strange that Doll didn't mention it to me." She frowned. "I was talking to her all afternoon while we were sewing on my new dress."

"You know Doll isn't the sort to go around bragging," Jerome said gruffly.

Reuben was filling his pipe with deliberate movements as he studied Jerome. "Why are you in such a bad mood, son? Maybe next time I should tell Doll to leave you in the swamp." He lit a match and held it over his pipe bowl. To Delia he said, "He's been snapping at everybody all afternoon." As he drew gently on his pipe, a cough shook his shoulders, but it had become so much a part of him, no one paid it any heed.

"I don't know why everybody is so concerned with me all of a sudden."

Turning back to Jerome, Reuben continued, "That new boy, Tom Smith, said something about Doll, and you nearly took his head off. Personally, I think she could do a lot worse than the likes of him. He's a hard worker, and it looked to me like he had his eye on her."

As Jerome recalled, with a scowl, the muscular young man his father was speaking of, Doll and Tabitha came out of the kitchen and crossed the yard to their own house. Jerome's eyes followed Doll until she was inside. "I don't like Tom Smith. I don't think he would be good for her."

"Well, for goodness' sake," Delia laughed. "It's not as if we had a say anymore. She's free to choose among her kind just like you are."

Jerome silently acknowledged the truth in his mother's statement. He wasn't at all sure why he had been so defensive of Doll, except that they had been friends for so long a time.

"If you ask me," Reuben said to Jerome, "You should ride into town tomorrow and see that Leslie girl."

"Susanna? Why should I do that?"

"Since we're not working then, you would have all afternoon to court her. She's a pretty girl. Before long someone will be asking for her hand."

Jerome rested his forearm on his bent knee and leaned back against the porch rail. "I guess she is pretty, at that."

"She's a sweet girl," Delia agreed. "Don't you like her, Jessamine?"

"I suppose."

Jerome glanced back at the Farmers' house. "Mama, you sound as if you have her all picked out for me."

"Nonsense, Jerome. What at idea," Delia said complacently.

Reuben was puffing hard on his pipe and had shrouded himself in a cloud of smoke. "I wouldn't mind seeing us connected to the Leslies. They have become one of the most prominent families in town. That cotton gin of his must make a lot more than our sawmill. People may stop building houses or we may run out of trees, but nothing will ever replace the need for cotton. His and Thayer's gins are the only ones within two days' drive."

"They aren't hurting for money," Jerome agreed.

"And Susanna is a pretty girl," Delia put in almost offhandedly.

"I guess I'll ride in tomorrow."

"Take the buggy, son. It's nicer for courting."

Delia shaded her eyes and looked out toward the road. "Now, who can that be? Are you expecting anyone, Reuben?"

"That's just Louis Broussard," Jessamine replied. "He said he might drop by to see me."

"Why on earth didn't you tell us?" Delia said as she patted her hair smooth and straightened her skirt. "I'll bet there isn't even a slice of pie to offer him."

Jerome gave his sister a teasing grin. "By that sappy look on his face, I don't expect he came for pie, Mama."

"You know it's rude not to offer something to company." To Jessamine she said, "Don't worry, I'll find something."

Jessamine kicked her brother's shin as she stood to meet the young man. "Hello, Louis. Are those flowers for me?"

Louis Broussard smiled self-consciously and handed Jessamine the bouquet of jonquils as he shyly acknowledged her parents and Jerome.

"Goodness," Delia said, "I have a dozen things to do in the house. Reuben, you'll help me, won't you?"

Reuben looked at her in surprise, then tapped the tobacco from his pipe as he stood to shake Louis' hand. "It was nice seeing you."

Louis almost tripped over Jerome in his eagerness to reach Mr. Delacroix's hand. "Thank you, sir."

"Jerome, if you have something else to do, I don't want to keep you," Jessamine said when her parents had left, but he continued to sit on the steps.

"I don't have anything I—"

"Jerome?" Delia called through the window. "I need you in here."

With a grin, Jerome went in the house, and Jessamine sighed in relief. "Have a seat, Louis. The flowers are beautiful." She sat where her mother had been in the swing.

"No prettier than you are, Miss Jessamine."

She smiled and the deep dimple appeared in her cheek. "How are your sisters?"

"They're quite well. Belle is getting married next week, you know. I suppose Hattie will be next. Unless I am, that is." He blushed to the roots of his pomaded hair.

"Oh? Are you thinking of getting married?" she asked with interest. "I hadn't heard."

"Not just yet. I mean, I just thought of it today. Miss Jessamine, would you—"

"Look, there are the Ramsey brothers. Why, they're stopping here." She waved her hand at the two young men who had dismounted at the front gate.

Louis frowned. "I didn't know you had other company coming."

"Nonsense, we're all friends." She cast him a sideways glance through her long black eyelashes. Her gray eyes sparkled at the prospect of three beaux all on one porch. "Hello, Robert, William. What brings you to Ten Acres?"

"We just thought we would ride over and pass the evening," Robert said. "Hello, Louis."

When Louis stood to shake Robert's hand, William took his place in the swing beside Jessamine.

"It's going to be a beautiful night," she sighed. "I wager by tomorrow there will be a full moon. Look at the flowers Louis brought me. Aren't they pretty?"

Robert and William both gave Louis a disparaging look. "I was going to pick some flowers for you, but Robert was in a hurry to leave."

"Well, you must bring some next time," Jessamine said flirtatiously. "You know how I love flowers."

"I saw in the newspaper that one of your neighbors will be coming back to town this week," Robert said as he pulled a chair close to Jessamine's end of the swing.

"Which neighbor is that?" she asked lightly as she breathed in the jonquils' springtime aroma.

"Ransome MacKinley."

Jessamine's eyes flew open and her lips parted in surprise.

"Don't you remember him? Surely you must. His parents bought Roseland."

"Yes. Yes, of course I remember him. He's been away a very long time. He's coming home, you say?"

"That's what the paper said. We don't have much to do with the MacKinleys," William said. "Papa says they're too brash."

"My father says we should let bygones be bygones," Louis stated rather pompously. "Only last Sunday Father Theriot's lesson was on forgiveness."

"When did you say Ransome will arrive?"

"One day this week. The paper didn't mention which one."

Jessamine dimly heard her suitors arguing good-naturedly about whether or not the priest had intended for Yankees to be included in such forgiveness, but her mind was on Ransome MacKinley. She hadn't seen him since that day five years before when he had rescued Adele from drowning in the creek. She had heard that he was sent North to live with an aunt and go to school. In all that time he had not once been back to Roseland, nor had he written to her. For a while she had missed him and was angry with his family for sending him away, but in time she had set aside all thoughts of him, and until this moment she had thought she had dismissed him from her mind. But with the reminder of him, her mouth felt dry and her palms were damp with nervousness. Why was this happening? she wondered. True, he was the first boy she had ever kissed, but she had been only a child then. As she allowed the memory of Ransome MacKinley and their clandestine meetings to return, a smile lit her lips, only to be erased by the thought of his overbearing father, who had sent him away for saving the life of her sister. She was anxious to see him again, but what if he had changed? She certainly had. What if she couldn't even recognize him? Or worse, what if he had become like his dreadful father—after all, he had been living with his father's sister for years.

Her reverie was broken as she heard William commenting that Jerome was watching them through the window. As she turned and frowned at her nosy brother, he let the curtain fall back into place. "Would you look at that?" Jerome said to his mother. "Now there's three of them out there!"

"Come away from the window," Delia said. "Your sister is a beautiful girl. Naturally she has beaux. I had better put more food on this tray." She carried it back toward the kitchen.

"She draws them in like a pot of honey draws flies."

"It's to be expected," Reuben said calmly. "Before long, she'll be getting married. She needs to look them all over to be sure she picks the right one." He winked at Delia, who had paused in the doorway. "You should have seen the crowds on your mama's front porch."

Delia smiled in appreciation of Reuben's compliment, but took on a more serious bearing as she said, "I do hope she doesn't choose that Broussard boy. He's so dull."

"He seems to worship the ground she walks on," Reuben said as he wistfully fingered his smokeless pipe. Delia didn't allow smoking or chewing in her parlor, and he respected her wishes, but at times he wished she would make an exception. "Maybe she will accept one of the Ramsey boys. I think Robert is warming up to a proposal. On the other hand, Vincent Macy may be in the running too."

"He isn't French Creole. His people are Acadians."

"True, but his father is still the sheriff, and the family is well-thought-of. You know his father and I became friends on our way back from the war."

"Not Vincent Macy," Delia said firmly. "She has plenty of boys to pick from whose families came from France."

"Vincent Macy would be better than that MacKinley boy. I read in the paper that he will be home for the summer."

Jerome frowned. "He had better stay away from my sister."

Delia looked at the demitasses and pralines on the tray. "He did save Adele that day."

"That doesn't matter," Reuben said with unusual sharpness. Then more gently he added, "On that issue I stand firm. There must never be any connection between our family and theirs."

"There will never be, as far as I'm concerned," Jerome declared. "Those people are nothing but . . . carpetbaggers." That word was the strongest one he dared to use in front of his mother, and for the time it would suffice, as it carried almost as much disgust as some of the more descriptive expletives he knew.

Delia nodded. "I agree. The less we see of them, the better. In a town as small as Cavelier, we can't help running into them now and then, but we have no reason to speak to them."

Reuben folded the newspaper and laid it on the fire dogs in the hearth before lighting it. "Now she won't be able to read the news of his arrival, and with luck, she won't even know he is in town."

Delia nodded her approval and went out to add more coffee and pralines to the tray.

Out on the porch, Jessamine was smiling and flirting and wishing with all her heart that the young men would leave. She wanted to be alone with her thoughts about Ransome. He had been handsome as a boy. What would he be like as a young man? The memory of his gentle voice and quiet determination made her pulse race. He had been so different from Jerome, whose fiery Creole temper so often burst in quick anger, then dissipated as rapidly. Ransome had had deep emotions, and she suspected that they were much more permanent than Jerome's.

When the Ramseys had had several cups of the strong coffee and had finished off the pralines, they realized they could no longer politely outwait Louis' departure, so they left. Jessamine's face felt stiff from smiling, but she couldn't very well tell Louis to leave as well, so she did the next best thing and remained standing so Louis couldn't sit back down.

He shuffled from one foot to the other and finally said, "I guess I should be going as well."

"Must you?" she said, but when she saw his eyes light with hope, she quickly added, "But how selfish of me. Of course you must. You have to ride back to town, and I'm sure it's quite late."

"May I come again?"

"Of course, Louis. You may come at any time. We are friends, after all. Are you coming to our Calico Ball this Saturday night?"

Louis' wide mouth split into a grin. "I wouldn't miss it for anything, Miss Jessamine. Will you save me a dance?"

"I'd be pleased to dance with you. I'll see you Saturday." She waved as he went down the walk to the gate where his horse was tied. At last she could be alone to think about Ransome.

7

"I FEEL WEAK AROUND MY HEART EVERY TIME I think of you nearly drowning in that awful swamp," Susanna Leslie said as she gazed up at Jerome. The sunlight touched her hair beneath her pink bonnet and brightened its usual mousy brown to near-blond. Her blue eyes were large and guileless, and although they lacked Jessamine's quick intelligence, they were certainly adoring. The pink dress she wore set off her tiny waist and small but firm breasts to the best advantage, and she looked as sweet as a sugarplum as she walked by his side down the main street of Cavelier.

"Luckily for me, Doll Farmer was nearby, and she pulled me out." Jerome slowed his pace to Susanna's more leisurely one, and paused while she looked in the milliner's window. Cavelier was bustling that day, and he was careful to stay between Susanna and the dusty street.

"Doll? Isn't she that cuffy girl that worked for your family?"

"We don't call them that at Ten Acres. And Doll is grown now," he said stiffly.

Susanna waved her fingers in a shooting motion. "You know what I mean. My goodness, you Delacroixs spoil that family rotten."

"If it hadn't been for the Farmers we would have had a hard time of it. And Doll saved my life."

Susanna gave a silvery laugh as she strolled to the next shop window. "Jerome Delacroix, how do you run on. It was her *duty* to save you. To hear you talk, a person would think you're beholden to her."

Jerome frowned slightly. He wanted to tell Susanna in no uncertain terms that not only did he feel indebted to her, but Doll was one of his closest friends, but he knew that to do so would be to spread the word all over town. Susanna loved to gossip. Feeling as guilty as a thief, he held his

84

tongue. His friendship with Doll was special, and he didn't want to be teased about it or to have to defend it.

"I'll bet these gowns come all the way from Paris," Susanna said as she studied the beautiful creations. "Those that are made here just don't compare." Like many Creoles, Susanna's allegiance still lay closer to France than the United States.

"That yellow one would look nice on you," Jerome said gallantly.

"Yellow? With my skin? My, my, Jerome, you'd say just anything, wouldn't you?"

He had no answer for that, so he smiled at her rakishly. When they came to the end of the boardwalk at a cross street, Susanna put her dainty gloved hand in the crook of his arm, and Jerome led her across the street and onto the safety of the boardwalk on the other side. When he was with Susanna, he was ten feet tall, and every inch a man. She had a way of making him feel heroic with just a glance. He pretended to be looking at another display of dresses while he perused her figure in the reflection of the glass. Susanna's lines were rounded and petite, and her flirtatious ways taunted him to wonder what she would look like wearing just her chemise—or better yet, nothing at all. Because he stayed so busy at the sawmill, Jerome had had little contact with Cavelier's female population, and he wasn't nearly as experienced as he led his friends to believe. In fact, he had never once gone to bed with a woman. He thought about this as he watched Susanna's hips swaying saucily. He guided her around the corner and away from the more unseemly dock area.

Several blocks away, a side-wheel paddler had docked and was disembarking passengers and noisily unloading cargo and livestock. Many of the young boys in town had come to share the excitement, and as they scampered over the docks with their dogs yapping at their heels, it seemed as if everyone was either trying to get from boat to land or land to boat. Amid the confusion, a tall, good-looking man stepped off the gangplank and counted out some money to a black porter. "Take these trunks to Roseland," he said. "There will be someone there to receive them."

The porter grinned at the size of the tip and nodded. "Yes, sir!"

Ransome MacKinley pulled his gold watch from his vest pocket and consulted its intricately filigreed face. Not only had the trip from New York taken a day less than he had anticipated, but the boat had arrived earlier in the day than he had thought it would. Because his parents weren't expecting him until the following afternoon, no one had come to meet him.

As he looked about, he noticed that the town seemed even smaller than he remembered, but five years in Albany, New York, no doubt changed his outlook. At his Aunt Polly's house, dirty patches of snow still dotted the lawns, but here spring was in full bloom. The air was scented with narcissus and hyacinth and wisteria.

The intervening years had brought changes to Ransome. He was tall, well over six feet, and muscularly lean. His extreme shyness was gone after the years of schooling and daily association with his Uncle Edward and Aunt Polly, both of whom had been very outgoing and loving toward him. They had encouraged his self-confidence and praised his successes. Ransome was now possessed of a quiet strength and a calm determination. His hair had darkened to a deeper shade of auburn and his face was more ruggedly handsome than pretty. No one could suspect Ransome MacKinley of having weak purposes or shallow emotions.

He walked up the dock toward the town proper, his stride one of a man who seemed to own whatever ground he touched. The only thing to do, he decided, was to hire a horse and ride out to Roseland. He smiled when he thought how surprised his mother would be at his early arrival. However, Ransome spared no thought for his father, as he was determined to enjoy his homecoming.

Once he was in town, Ransome was struck by how little everything had changed. There were more people, a few new stores, but in general Cavelier was the same. He might have been gone five weeks instead of five years. He heard snatches of musical Creole French mixed with the cajun patois and black dialect. Cries of women selling crawfish and strawberries and flowers rang from the narrow streets, accompanied by the creak of carriage wheels and the jingle of harnesses. He felt divided in his loyalties, half of him longing to return to Aunt Polly's cheerful household and the other half yearning for the mysterious bayous and mosses and the fiery eyes of the French people who lived here.

Jessamine Delacroix. The name had returned to his thoughts on his journey home, along with the memory of the fascination he had had with just being around her. When it occurred to him that she might be married by now, he felt a twinge of loss.

Preoccupied with his thoughts, Ransome rounded a corner and ran headlong into a young couple. Stepping back and tipping his hat in apology, he recognized the man as Jerome Delacroix. The young lady was a stranger to him. For a moment the two men were eye to eye, both too startled to react. Then each took another step back, and Ransome smiled. "Hello, Jerome. It's been a long time. Is Jessamine in town with you?" He held out his hand in an offer of friendship.

Jerome's dark brows gathered in a frown, and he ignored Ransome's hand. "So you're back."

"Yes, I just arrived." Ransome glanced at the woman and waited to be introduced as common courtesy demanded.

Instead of introducing the woman, Jerome put his arm about her waist and swept her away, as she looked up at him in bewilderment. Over his shoulder Jerome called back, "I can't stop you from being here in Cavelier, but you stay away from my sister!"

Ransome watched in amazement as Jerome led the baffled woman away. Slowly he shook his head. Things hadn't changed at all. He turned toward the livery stable and recognized a young man who was driving out in a smart buggy. "Louis! Louis Broussard! How are you?"

Louis reined to a stop and grinned down at him in recognition. "Ransome MacKinley! I had heard you were coming back for a visit."

"It may not be for just a visit. Father wants me to learn how to run Roseland now that I'm out of college. I may be here to stay."

"Welcome back. Do you have a horse?"

"No, I just arrived and was on my way to the livery stable to hire one."

"Get in. No need to do that. I'll be happy to give you a ride to Roseland."

Ransome stepped up onto the seat beside Louis and said, "I'd appreciate it."

"No trouble at all!" Louis barked a command in French to his horse as he popped the reins, and they rolled smoothly out of town.

Ransome listened to Louis' flow of conversation and inquired after everyone except the one foremost in his mind. He was almost afraid to ask about Jessamine and learn she was married or promised to someone. When they reached Roseland's gates, Ransome swung down to save Louis a trip up the drive. "Thanks for the ride."

"No bother. As I said, I was coming this way."

"Oh? I didn't know this road went anywhere but to Ten Acres."

"That's where I'm going. I've been walking out with Jessamine Delacroix lately, and I was on my way to see her."

"Oh." Ransome looked up at Louis' fleshy face and his plump hands.

Louis smiled and tipped his hat. "I'll be seeing you."

Ransome stared after him. Louis Broussard and Jessamine? Surely not!

As he walked up the curving drive, he tried to reconcile the idea of Jessamine walking out with Louis. He was all right as a friend, but surely Jessamine wasn't serious about him! At this distance, Roseland was hidden from view by the impressive avenue of live oaks that made a green tunnel over the drive. To either side were lush lawns, shaded by enormous trees, and banks of azaleas and camellias. At the end of the avenue, Roseland suddenly came into view with a spectacular soaring of columns and winged galleries and clusters of chimneys.

Beyond the budding gardens and fountains, Ransome could see the cotton field where the overseer, Oliver Gibbons, was directing the field hands as they chopped the cotton to remove the weeds. A mockingbird sang in the magnolia above Ransome's head, and he looked up to see waxy flowers as large as dinner plates. He might not want to be a planter, but Ransome could think of no place prettier if he had to be one.

He went up the wide steps and across the deep shade of the veranda. Before he could put his hand on the doorknob, the door was swung wide by a well-dressed butler. "Welcome home, Mr. Ransome," he said in a cultured British accent.

"Thank you, Jenkins." Ransome went into the foyer and looked about at the blue-and-silver walls and soaring twin stairs. "Nothing has changed."

"So, sir. May I take your hat?"

Ransome gave it to him and turned to see his mother come out of the parlor. "Ransome!" she exclaimed as she trotted over to him.

He caught her to him in an affectionate hug and noted

with surprise that her head only reached to his chin. "Mother! How good you look."

"You've grown so tall! Mr. MacKinley, come and see! Our Ransome is home."

Ransome tried not to stiffen as his father appeared in the doorway. The memory of the caning his father had given him when he learned Ransome not only had been meeting Jessamine in the woods but also had even risked his life to pull her younger sister out of the creek on the MacKinley land was still raw. Ransome's back had still been bruised when he was put on the boat to Albany and his exile with his Aunt Polly. "Father," Ransome said with cool reserve.

"Good to see you, boy. Come into the parlor and let's have a good look at you."

"He's not a boy any longer," Eliza observed proudly as she dabbed at the corners of her eyes with her scented handkerchief. "My, how you've grown! I believe you take after my papa's side of the family, doesn't he, Mr. Mac-Kinley? Looks so much like a Fitzpatrick."

Ian gestured toward a settee that had recently been reupholstered in horsehair in the latest fashion. "Sit down. Have a cigar."

"No, thank you."

"You don't smoke? Don't tell me you don't drink either! What's that sister of mine done to you?"

"I'll have a brandy, Jenkins," Ransome said to the butler, who waited by the door. "Roseland is as beautiful as ever."

"Yes, it is, but only due to constant hard work. That's why I sent for you. I'm getting on in years, boy, and you need to learn how to run this plantation."

"I'm not sure I want to learn."

"Nonsense! I haven't worked my fingers to the bone for nothing. Schooling is all right in its place, but you've had more than enough. Too much is as bad as too little. This is your legacy. You have to learn to manage it."

Eliza nodded. "Someday we'll be old and dependent on you. We expect you to move in here with your family and keep things going."

"Family?" He took the glass of brandy from the butler's tray and cupped it in his palm to warm it.

"Well, you will marry. Someday," Eliza said. "Everyone does."

Ransome took a sip of the fiery liquor. "I don't have anyone in mind. Do you?"

"Actually, we are having a party tomorrow," Eliza said happily. "A homecoming party. I've invited all the eligible girls in Cavelier."

"All of them?" Ransome's dark brown eyes gazed steadily at his mother.

"All the *proper* ones. I especially want you to meet Priscilla Danbridge. Her mother is my closest friend."

"You'll like her," his father said, stroking his salt-and-pepper side whiskers.

"Is that an order?" Ransome's voice was soft, but his eyes never wavered from his father.

"What an idea!" Eliza laughed. "As if we would arrange your marriage for you! I had no idea you had become such a josher, Ransome."

Ian didn't smile as his small eyes took in his son's measure. Ransome had thought he'd conquered his fear of his father, but he found his stomach was churning in the same way it had when he was a boy. As soon as his father dropped his stare, Ransome breathed with relief and reached out to touch the long silk fringe on the lamp that stood on the marble-topped end table. "You've added some things, Mother."

"It's so hard to keep up with styles, because Cavelier hasn't a thing that interests me. Everything has to be ordered."

Ransome looked at the clutter of family photographs that littered the table and picked up the one of Dennis in his Union uniform.

"I put flowers on Dennis' grave before I left Albany, just as you asked."

Eliza took the picture from him and looked at it sadly. "He was so young, so very young. He never lived to be as old as you are now. It gives me a funny feeling to think of it, but it's true."

"Aunt Polly sends you both her love."

"I'll write and tell her you arrived safely. She has done a good job in bringing you up." Eliza put the photograph back in its place among the others.

An awkward silence tightened in the room. Ransome sipped his brandy and waited it out. If he had learned anything as a boy, it was not to speak too freely. His father at last heaved his bulk up from the chair and reached down for his cane. "Come on, boy. I'll show you around."

Ransome stared briefly at the silver-tipped black cane. Was it the same one that had made his childhood so miserable? Putting his brandy aside, he followed his father out of the parlor. He had, indeed, come back home.

8

IT WAS SATURDAY, AND REUBEN AND JEROME HAD
moved the furniture from the parlor into the back room and
rolled up the rug to make room for dancing. Tabitha and
Doll had hand-polished the cypress flooring until it looked
as glossy as syrup candy. The musicians had been en-
sconced at one end of the room, and at the other end was
the table of refreshments. For the men there were brandy
and whiskey, and for the ladies the much sweeter anisette.
For both there was strong black coffee to be served in
demitasses. As the guests began to arrive, the music struck
up in a lively air.

Jessamine was the undisputed belle of the Calico Ball,
and the young men vied for each dance even though she had
filled up her dance card days in advance. Her lyrical laughter rang out as she turned in a swirl of bright calico and
lace in Robert Ramsey's arms. Louis Broussard and William
Ramsey waited out the dance, glaring at each other jeal-
ously. At the end of the tune, Jessamine playfully selected
William with a tap of her folded fan, and as the next one
began, he swept her back to the dance floor.

"Your sister is having quite a time," Susanna said
with scarcely concealed envy. "I declare, she's going to
dance a hole in both her shoes."

"It wouldn't be the first time, and likely not the last,"
Jerome said over the music.

"I'm glad I let you write your name on every line in
my dance card." Susanna tossed a glare at the queue of
young men gawking at Jessamine. She was reading a note
that had just been handed her, and Susanna was dying to
know the contents. But rather than let anyone learn of her
curiosity, she disdainfully said, "I'd just die if Louis Broussard asked me to dance."

"He had better not," Jerome warned her with mock
anger, then smiled down at her, noticing how willowy her

91

waist was and recalling how her small breasts grazed his chest from time to time. He had been thinking a lot about Susanna these past few days. She had an untouchable quality about her that he found irresistible. "Would you like to walk in the flower garden? There's a full moon."

"Now, Jerome, you stop that!" Susanna swatted him coquettishly on the shoulder as if he had made an indecent suggestion.

Jerome grinned at the petite woman's flirtatious gesture. He had heard that the girls who pretended to be so shy were often tigers in bed. "I like your dress. It's the same blue as your eyes."

Susanna smiled sweetly and pursed her lips to make a hint of a dimple appear at the corner. "You don't think it's *too* blue, do you?" She opened her eyes wide because she knew very well they were the same shade as the fabric. That's why her father had paid so much for it.

"I wouldn't change it at all. Nor you either."

She fluttered her eyelashes and looked prettily confused. "Why, Jerome!" She took his hand and urged him onto the floor.

Moments later, the music ended and they finished in a breathless swirl. Jerome leaned over to whisper in her ear, "Mama has a new rose the same color as your cheeks. I'll bet you've never seen one like it."

"She does?" Susanna looked down coyly. "I'd love to see it, Jerome." When he smiled and took her arm, she added, "But don't you get the wrong idea, now. We're going to look at the rose and nothing else!"

As they left the house, Jessamine's delighted laughter trailed out after them.

Across the hollow and beyond the woods, Ransome was also in the midst of a party. His collar felt too stiff and the room was uncomfortably stuffy, but his mother had refused to open the windows and chance having her guests attacked by mosquitoes and june bugs. A polite murmur of conversation rose and fell like waves in the room, accentuated occasionally by the click of a teacup against a saucer or the jingle of a bracelet.

Ransome smiled at the pale young woman next to him and tried to recall her name. Priscilla, that was it. Priscilla Danbridge. That horse-faced woman across the room was her mother. Fortunately, Priscilla bore little resemblance to her mother, and Ransome hoped, for the girl's sake, that she never would. He tried to concentrate on what she was saying, but she spoke in such a soft monotone that he had no idea what she was talking about.

He saw his mother trip up to Amelia Danbridge, and they put their heads close together in a whispered confidence before turning as one to smile in his direction. Ransome wished Priscilla would speak up and that the heat would soften the starch in his collar before it abraded his throat.

Ian McKinley strode proudly through the crowd as if he were a king surveying his subjects. When he saw Ransome talking to Priscilla, he came to them. "Having a good time, Miss Danbridge?"

She mumbled something that might have been affirmative, and Ian clapped Ransome on the shoulder. "Good, good! Show her the garden, son. Women put a lot of stock in flowers by moonlight." Guffawing at his own wit, Ian went to join the other men.

Ransome concealed his annoyance and said, "Would you like to see the flowers, Miss Danbridge?"

She nodded and took his arm as if she couldn't be quite expected to find her own way across the room.

The night air was particularly cool by comparison with the stuffiness inside, and Ransome breathed deeply in relief. At least out here away from the noise, he might be able to understand her.

They strolled down the steps and across the curving path to the rose garden. In the center, a fountain splashed silver droplets onto the head of a cherub and a swan. The night air was perfumed, and a slight breeze rippled the curtains of moss that dripped from the live oaks. "Have you lived in Cavelier long, Miss Danbridge?"

She mumbled a response, and this time Ransome asked her to repeat what she had said a bit more loudly.

"Heavens, no," she repeated in a raspy nasal twang that sounded like a gate hinge in need of oil. "We've only been here a couple of years. Personally I detest the South."

A surprised grin spread over Ransome's face, and despite his attempt at restraint, he began to chuckle at the disparity between her appearance and her voice. It was no wonder that she had been speaking so softly.

Although she had no idea what she had said that he

found so humorous, she began to chuckle with him, and soon they were both laughing aloud.

Eliza let the curtain fall back into place and squeezed Amelia's hand. "They're getting along perfectly. I haven't seen Ransome laugh like that since he came home!"

Amelia twittered and nodded as if this were a delicious secret. "I think I hear wedding bells in the offing, Eliza."

The two friends giggled together like co-conspirators. Eliza saw Ian's disapproving frown and tried to assume a more decorous expression.

Jessamine could scarcely stand still while Doll fastened the row of tiny pearl buttons up the back of her sprigged-muslin dress. "I just can't wait, Doll. Can't you fasten me up any quicker?"

"With you moving all over the room? Stand still. It's not even good daylight yet."

"Are you still cross with me? Don't be, because I'm happy enough to burst."

"Yes, and I know why. But I'm telling you, Jessamine, you're just asking for trouble!"

"No, I'm not. Doll, you don't understand how I feel. I haven't seen Ransome McKinley in years, and I'm so looking forward to it. You know we were in love before his papa sent him away. Of course, we were just children then, but I still think of him fondly. I just couldn't believe it last night when I received that private note from him asking me to meet him at the swimming hole early this morning. The rest of the evening, I couldn't think of anyone but him." She sat on the edge of the bench in front of her mirror as Doll brushed her long black hair that hung well below her waist.

"Do you think I don't know how you feel? You think it's romantic and forbidden and full of excitement. I can tell you, though, that forbidden love isn't really like that. It's purely dangerous. A person could get her heart broken by caring too much for the wrong person."

"How do you know?" Jessamine asked in surprise. "Are you in love with someone and didn't tell me? I know! I'll bet it's Tom Smith. He works for Papa!"

For a minute alarm sparked in Doll's dark eyes; then she carefully said, "I'm not in love with anybody. Especially not Tom Smith."

"Then you must have read too many books. I should never have given you that copy of *Jane Eyre.*"

A faint smile lifted Doll's lips as she coiled Jessamine's glossy hair into a thick bun. "That must be it."

"Well, *this* romance may end happily ever after." Jessamine pinched her cheeks to make them rosier. "I wish I had some rouge."

"Jessamine!"

"Don't look so shocked, Doll. I wouldn't use much. Well, it can't be helped. I'll pinch my cheeks again just before I get there."

'Isn't there anything I can say to keep you from doing this? If your papa or Jerome finds out, there'll be a mess of trouble, for sure."

"Then they had better not find out, had they? Don't look so upset or you'll give me away." She squeezed Doll's hand. "Someday I'll do a big favor for you." She took up her leghorn hat and sailed out, leaving Doll staring after her.

The party the night before had gone on until very late, and everyone else was still asleep, so Jessamine had no trouble slipping away unseen. The woods were cool and green with drifts of creamy mallows in the sunlit areas and deep purple spiderwort in the shade. Clusters of redbuds were blooming among the trees, and butterflies fluttered like free-floating flowers above the tender grass.

Jessamine soon heard the whisper of the creek as it splashed below the swimming hole, and she held her skirts carefully so she wouldn't trip. At first she didn't see him and was afraid he hadn't come; then he saw her and stood up to greet her. Her breath seemed stuck in her throat.

Ransome was more handsome than she had remembered, and he was very tall. His body was lithe, and moved in a way that reminded her of the panthers that roamed the swamp.

Slowly Ransome removed his hat and stared across the glade at the woman. He had known Jessamine would be pretty, but he hadn't expected her to become a vivacious beauty. She was slim, but her breasts were full and well-rounded. Her arms beneath her gossamer shawl were graceful and her neck was slender. Her features were a startling combination of innocence and natural seductiveness. No princess could have had a more regal bearing.

As she moved slowly to him, he compared her with

his memory of her. She wasn't much taller than she had been when he left for New York, but she was all woman. Her large gray eyes were shaded by the longest eyelashes he had ever seen. She stopped a few feet in front of him and gazed directly into his eyes. Her dewy pink lips parted slightly to reveal her white teeth as she quietly said, "Hello."

"Hello," he responded. Her voice was soft and as clear as spring water.

Ransome wasn't sure what to do. He wanted to sweep her up in his arms and kiss her until the world dissolved around them, and on the other hand he wanted to worship her as he would a goddess of purity.

Jessamine felt her pulse race as she searched his dark, velvety eyes. She was too much a coquette not to recognize what she saw there. "Have you been waiting here long?"

"No, not long." His deep voice seemed to touch her very soul and bring to life an emotion much deeper than infatuation.

With careful movements, not taking her eyes from his, Jessamine slowly untied the ribbons of her bonnet and removed it so that she stood before him with the intimacy usually reserved for a parlor.

Ransome was never sure who made the first move, but as he bent his head to kiss her, she tiptoed up into his embrace. Her lips were soft beneath his and her breath sweet in his mouth. Love, tempered with an instinct to protect her and guard her from harm, flooded through him as he gathered her to him in a hungry embrace that wiped away five years of separation.

Jessamine held him as she had never held anyone before, and kissed him as she had dreamed of kissing a man all the long nights since she had become a woman with a woman's desires. She realized now that her reticence to become seriously involved with any one particular suitor had been because of her deep feelings for Ransome that she had closeted away to protect herself from the pain of their separation. She was made for Ransome as surely as he was made for her, and she would have no other. Drawing back, she gazed deeply into his eyes and felt their souls touch. Ransome lifted her and whirled her around before he kissed her again. Jessamine's lips parted beneath his, and she let him teach her to kiss in the ways of love.

9

TABITHA SAT ON THE LOW STOOL BY THE HEARTH and stirred the simmering pot of filé gumbo. Sam sat in the cane-bottomed chair and leaned back against the log wall as he lit his corncob pipe. The soft crackling of the fire and the pale glow of the lamp on the table made the scene so cozy that Tabitha was almost uneasy. Everyone knew that too much contentment bred trouble. Across the room Doll lounged against the doorjamb, gazing out into the night.

"The crickets are singing for rain," Doll said. "I can hear the bullfrogs down in the swamp too."

"They singing because they happy to be frogs," Sam said as he puffed life into his pipe. "The little ones are saying 'knee-deep, knee-deep,' and the big old bullfrogs is calling for 'a jug o' rum, a jug o' rum.' "

Doll smiled. "That's what you used to tell me when I was a little girl." She heard a cricket tune up beneath the small porch as the cool breeze brushed against her face.

"Mr. Reuben, he thinking about making some chairs and such as that along with the lumber," Sam said to no one in particular.

Tabitha tasted the gumbo and sprinkled in a little more salt. "You don't know how to make furniture." She pulled the skillet of johnnycake toward a warmer spot in the fire.

"I don't, but Tom Smith does. He was trained as a skilled joiner before the war."

"I sure do like that boy. He come over to the kitchen the other night to offer us a bucket of shrimp. I think he mainly come to see Doll." She sneaked a sideways glance at her daughter. "He seems real nice."

"I'm not ready to settle down, Ma."

"You're nineteen years old. How long you think you have to hem-haw around? Men like this Tom Smith don't come down the road every day."

"Now, Tabitha, maybe Doll has her eye on somebody

over to the church. That young man that led the singing last Sunday was grinning at her the whole time.''

Doll turned her face away toward the darkness.

"You see that? She ain't interested in nobody." Tabitha wrapped a cup towel around the handle of the skillet and pulled it out of the fire. With a practiced flip of her wrist she popped the johnnycake onto a plate. "You need a man of your own, girl. As pretty as you be, you can still have a choice, but when they're gone, they're gone."

"Don't worry about me, Ma." Doll ambled back into the room and finished setting the table with the dishes that had been cast off from the main house.

"Your ma is right, baby. A woman needs a husband to see to her. We was meant to pull in pairs, not to go off on our own. The preacher said so."

"I know, Pa. There simply isn't anyone I want to marry, or to even have court me."

"Listen to how she talks," Tabitha fretted. "If you eyes was shut, you'd swear that was Miss Jessamine talking." She looked through the assortment of condiments on her table and selected the one with the picture of cayenne peppers on it.

"Ma, it hasn't hurt for me to learn to speak properly and to improve myself. Why, if that pepper company changes its label, you wouldn't know how to buy it."

"Are you saying you can read too?" Tabitha demanded.

Doll faltered. "I can read enough to make out labels and follow written recipes." She wasn't about to admit that she had read every book in Mr. Reuben's growing library, as well as many from Roseland.

"There's nothing wrong in that," Sam mollified as he reached out the window and tapped his pipe out on the side of the house. "She can get a better job someday if she can read some."

"In some places it's still against the law for a colored girl to read," Tabitha objected as she ladled up the gumbo.

"Then I reckon she ought to stay away from those places." Sam winked at Doll, and she tried to smile back.

"Sam, are you too thickheaded to see why I'm worried? Look at her! White men likes to set up octoroons like Doll as fancy women down in places like New Orleans!"

Sam looked at his daughter in surprise. "Has some man come to you with a idea like that?"

"No, Pa."

"Well, then, I don't reckon we ought to worry about it." He sat at the table and said, "Ain't we got no butter for the cornbread?"

Tabitha shoved the pat of butter toward him and frowned as she cut the johnnycake into wedges. "Some folks can't see nothing 'less it's under they noses." She reached for the stoppered bottle of vinegar and oil. "Look here, Doll. What do you see?"

"I see oil floating on top of vinegar." She poured them each a cup of black chicory coffee.

"Look what happens when I shakes it." Tabitha vigorously agitated the bottle, then held it in front of Doll's eyes. Slowly the beads of oil rose to the top again, leaving the vinegar below. "We is like the vinegar down there on the bottom. White folks is like the oil on top. They gonna stay on top no matter what, and they ain't gonna mess with us."

Tabitha shoved the bottle back onto the cabinet. "I sees a pretty black girl that talks white and thinks white, and I sees trouble just waiting to happen. What's wrong with our people that you have to always try and be different?"

"Ma, nothing is wrong with them. I'm proud to be who I am. But why should I settle for less than I can be?"

"Less! You think I'm less than you are?"

"No, no, Ma. I didn't mean that." Doll shook her head. "I can't explain it. I like to hear words spoken properly and to dress in pretty clothes and think about more than what to cook for supper or how to clean a stain out of one of Miss Delia's napkins. Can't you see that, Ma?" She gazed beseechingly at her mother.

"All I see is trouble coming."

Tabitha thumped the bowls of gumbo down on the table and flopped into a chair. Her protruding lower lip warned Doll to silence.

Without a word among them, the Farmers ate their evening meal to the chorus of crickets and frogs. Doll knew that both her parents would be up in arms if they knew the path her thoughts were taking lately.

Jessamine strolled hand in hand with Ransome through the woods beside the meandering creek. "I guess you have a girlfriend up North," she said.

"No, as a matter of fact, I don't." He reached out to pull aside a branch for Jessamine to pass. "I understand you have a beau."

"For goodness' sake, Ransome," she said with a laugh. "Of course I do." When he frowned, she added, "None of them are serious beaux, however."

"That's not what I heard. I understand Louis Broussard and Robert and William Ramsey practically live on your front porch."

"Jealous?" she teased as her silvery eyes sparkled.

"Yes, as a matter of fact, I am. What if your father decides you should marry one of them?"

"Papa wouldn't order me to marry a man I didn't love."

They came to a bower where thick gardenia bushes hid a circular patch of grass. When she was a child, this had been Jessamine's playhouse. "I used to think this place was enchanted," she said as she led him into the secluded spot. "One day I found it purely by accident. I was half-grown before I learned Papa and Sam had planted it for me." She spread her skirts and sat on the lush grass. "I'll bet they wouldn't be too happy if they knew my old playhouse is now my trysting place."

"I know they wouldn't be." Ransome sat beside her. "Then you really aren't in love with anyone?"

Jessamine smiled secretively. "I didn't say that."

"Which one?" he demanded indignantly.

She cast him a furtive glance and said, "Can't you guess?"

"No, I can't." He ran his long fingers through his auburn hair and shook his head. "All I can think about is you. After each time we've been together, I go over all you said and all you did, and how that dimple appears when you laugh. While I'm waiting to see you again, I'm in an agony over whether you'll be here or whether someone will see us together."

"No one knows about this place. It even took me a while to rediscover it. The woods are thicker, since your father doesn't keep goats in here as we did."

He pulled her to face him. "Don't you see what I'm saying, Jessamine? I can't get you out of my mind."

"I know," she said softly.

"If you're in love with someone, I have a right to know."

She looked away and said, "Tell me about New York. Is there snow there most of the time?"

"No, only during the winter. I was in Albany, not the arctic circle."

"There—you're upset with me!"

"Don't play the coquette with me."

Jessamine's smile faded. "It's the only way I know to be."

"You could just be yourself. Before I was sent away from here, you were smarter than any of my other friends and not afraid to say what you liked or didn't like. Now I get the feeling you weigh each word for the effect it will have before you say it. Are you just playing with me, Jessamine? If so, you had better come right out and tell me, because I'm serious about the way I feel." He looked at her and made her meet his eyes.

"You don't know what you're asking. A lady doesn't just blurt out anything she thinks or feels. That's not fair."

"Is this fair to me? I can't come sit on your front porch so I can compete with every man in Iberville parish. Your father would shoot me on sight."

"No, Papa wouldn't. But I'm sure he'd ask you to leave." Her thought sprang to the day Jerome had to rush after her father and talk him out of trying to kill Ransome's father. That had been very frightening, but it had also been a long time ago.

"If I can't court you, how can I hope to convince you that I'm better for you than any of the others? We need to follow our own rules here."

"Do you mean that?"

"Yes. We took an oath once that no matter what happened, we would never lie to each other."

"I haven't lied to you."

"You haven't been completely honest either. Do you or don't you love someone?"

"I do," she replied softly.

Tension hung heavily in the leafy enclosure. Ransome had thought he could bear honesty better than deception, but now he wasn't so sure. Changing the subject abruptly, he said, "I didn't want to come back, you know. At least not yet."

"You didn't?"

"I have no desire to be a planter, but Father insisted I come home."

"What did you want to do instead?"

"I wanted to be a lawyer. I had even been accepted for law school when he wrote and demanded I come home." Ransome smiled mirthlessly. "Lawyers make a lot of money. If I had become one and made my fortune, I could have come down here and thrown all my riches at your feet." He knelt in front of her in the pretense of spreading gold and jewels at her feet. " 'I'm the most famous lawyer on all the East Coast,' I would have said. 'Come away with me and be my bride.' " He dropped back to her side.

"Is that a proposal?" she asked in a small voice.

"Sure. Why not?" he answered with a scoffing laugh.

"Then I accept."

Ransome was shocked by her response. She had said she was in love with someone else. In disbelief he turned to her. "What did you say?"

She put her hand on his cheek and looked deep into his eyes. "I love you, Ransome. If that was indeed a proposal of marriage, I accept it."

Ransome's mouth parted in amazement, and he said, "You love *me?*"

"How can you be so surprised? Haven't I kissed you in a way no lady should ever kiss anyone but her intended? Haven't I waited for you all these years?"

"You waited . . . for me?"

"I didn't marry anyone else, did I? I don't know how it is in Albany, but in Cavelier the girls marry young. I'll be twenty next month and that's older than most of my unmarried friends." She hesitated and said almost shyly, "Do you love me?"

"Love you?" he whispered. "How can I describe what I feel for you in such a small word? I fell in love with you that day on your front porch when we scarcely exchanged a word. When I came home and found you grown into a lady, I was half-afraid because I loved you so much. Are you sure you want to marry me? You know what our families will say."

"I think we should each tell our own separately. I want Papa and Jerome to get used to the idea before they see you."

"I don't like the idea of you facing them alone." Ransome was thinking of the scene that was certain to transpire with his own father. "He won't hurt you, will he?"

"Papa? Of course not. He has never laid a hand on

me in my life. Jerome won't be happy about it, but he's only my brother.''

"Perhaps we should elope."

"No. Then Papa really might shoot you. And Mama would never forgive you for depriving her of my wedding. "Oh, dear, you aren't Catholic, are you?''

"I could learn to be."

"Good. That's good. That will put Father Theriot on our side. He loves to make converts.''

Ransome pulled her closer and cupped her cheek in his hand. "I love you, Jessamine. God, how I've longed to say those words!''

"I love you, Ransome. I thought you would never come back.''

"I'll never leave you again. Part of me belongs to you." He kissed her gently at first, then more deeply as he felt her eager response. Gently he laid her back on the billowing grass and matched his body to hers.

Jessamine held him close and let her hands explore the breadth of his shoulders and the straight line of his spine beneath his coat. His hair was thick beneath her fingers, and crisper than her own. "Don't they sell pomade in Albany?'' she teased.

"I don't like grease in my hair. If I did use that stuff, you couldn't be doing that.''

She ran all her fingers through his hair and smiled. "Never use pomade. I think I'm going to be doing this often.''

Ransome rested his hand on her waist and noticed that she was laced so tightly that he could almost span her waist with his hands. Her breasts swelled enticingly against her bodice in a most provocative way. "Do you want a long engagement?''

"No. My hope chest has been full for ages.'' She smiled and added, "I'm not supposed to tell you that.''

He chuckled. "Now you're sounding like the Jessamine I remember. Do you recall all those books we passed back and forth?''

She nodded, her hair dark against the green of the grass. "Papa has started a library at Ten Acres. When we are married we'll have a lot of books to choose from.''

"When we are married," he repeated. "I like the sound of that.''

"Will we live at Roseland?''

"I don't know. It never occurred to me that you would say yes. At first I suppose we will live in Albany so I can finish law school."

Her eyes sparkled in anticipation. "Will I see snow?"

"Every winter. I guarantee it. More than you'll wish for." He rubbed the back of his finger along the curve of her jaw. "After I get my degree, we'll come back here. By then our parents will be ready to welcome us. Maybe there will even be a grandchild for them to fight over."

"Ransome, you make it sound so perfect." Her face glowed with her happiness. "I feel as if I could float up there in the treetops."

"So do I."

"There isn't a chance that your father won't let you marry me, is there?" she said with a slight frown. "He doesn't ever speak to us, or we to him."

"He won't be happy about it, but what can he do?"

"He could disown you, for one thing. Ransome, I don't want to come between you and your family. It would break your mother's heart. I know it would mine."

"What do you suggest?"

"We should hint to them that we are seeing each other first. Let them get used to that idea, then say we aren't seeing anyone except each other. That way Papa can get to know you, and your father can meet me. Then we'll tell them we want to get married."

"That seems a bit devious."

"It is. Do you think it will work?"

"Perhaps. I know another war will break out if we just tell them point-blank that we've decided to marry."

She nodded. "We'll try it this way first. Tabitha used to say you can catch more flies with honey than you can with vinegar."

He kissed her again. "It's going to be hard to wait until we're married, as much as I love you."

"I know, Ransome. I know. I guess we'll just have to do our best and hope they come around soon."

Ransome automatically straightened his coat and adjusted his cuffs before going into the parlor. Through the door he could hear his mother's ceaseless prattle and his father's occasional gruff reply. Despite his age, Ransome felt as if he were a boy again who was about to confess to a heinous crime. The old fear of his father's rages made his mouth go dry. He had expressed great confidence when he was with Jessamine, but he had no guarantee that he wouldn't be thrown out of the house for even mentioning her name. He still hated conflict, and he wondered if he shouldn't have pressed her to elope.

Taking a deep breath, Ransome entered the room and silently closed the parlor doors behind him. On the mantel, the clock ticked in accompaniment to Eliza's knitting needles, and as he crossed the room, its reedy voice proclaimed the hour to be ten o'clock.

"My, we're up late tonight," Eliza said as she glanced at the clock and folded away her knitting.

"Father, Mother, could I talk to you for a minute?"

Ian looked up suspiciously and set his heavy jaw like a bulldog. Eliza smiled and nodded, causing her jet earrings to bounce. "What is it, son?"

Ransome crossed over to the mantel and rested his elbow upon it as he considered how to begin. "Since I came back to Roseland, I've been seeing someone. She's become very important to me. I thought you should know."

"It's Priscilla Danbridge!" his mother exclaimed in a rapture of happiness. "I knew it! Amelia will be so pleased! But of course she must know about it already if you've been calling. How sly of her not to mention it to me!"

"She's a good choice. Her father is rich. It never hurts to love a rich one."

"It's not Miss Danbridge."

The room grew quiet and Eliza's smile faded. "Then who is it, dear?"

"Jessamine Delacroix."

"Those Cajuns!" Ian exploded.

"She's not Acadian, she's Creole."

"Oh, my!" Eliza's plump face crumbled into despair. "Not the Delacroix girl!"

"Out of all the parish, you had to see her? Knowing how I feel about that family?" Ian's face was becoming alarmingly red, and he fingered his cane as he drew in hissing breaths.

"I know there were hard feelings after the war, but that was a long time ago," Ransome said, forcing himself to remain calm.

"Not down here it wasn't! They talk about the war as if it's still going on!"

"It's true, Ransome," Eliza said. "I saw Mrs. Dela-

croix in a store not long after her little girl died and tried
to give her my condolences, but she cut me dead with a
look such as I never hope to see again. It seems they actually blame *us* somehow for the girl dying—even though you
pulled her out of that creek.''

''And was beaten half to death for doing it,'' Ransome
added spontaneously as his anger rose.

''You'd think that would have taught you a lesson,''
Ian bellowed. ''Now I hear you're taking up with them
again. Leave it to you to pick the one family I absolutely
hate!''

Eliza cast a fearful glance at her husband. ''Ransome
only said he had seen her, Mr. MacKinley. Surely—''

''Shut up, woman! I heard what he said!''

Ransome looked from his furious father to his quailing
mother. Had the violence Ian had shown him as a child
found another target during his absence? Bile rose in Ransome's throat at the idea.

''If you see that girl again, I'll disown you!'' Ian
yelled as he strode toward Ransome, brandishing his cane.

Ransome stood his ground and met his father glare for
glare. Eliza jumped to her feet, her words tumbling over
each other as she headed for the door. ''My goodness, look
how late. No wonder we're snapping at each other. I think
we should all get a good night's sleep and just forget about
this unpleasantness.''

Ransome waited until his mother had had time to be
well on her way to the bedroom she no longer shared with
his father. ''I told Jessamine that you wouldn't be reasonable about it.''

''You mark my words, boy. If you think I caned you
for fishing one of their scum from the creek, wait until you
see what I do if you try to court one of them.''

''Don't do anything foolish, Father.'' Ransome's voice
was still calm, but steel laced his words. After another long
look, Ransome turned and unhurriedly left the room. As he
mounted the stairs, however, his hands shook. Would his
father try to take out his anger on his mother? When he
reached his bedroom, he left his door slightly ajar so no
sound would escape his notice. If he heard one alarming
sound, anything at all, he would run to his mother's rescue.
Since returning to Roseland, he had seen Eliza's weaknesses
as he never had before. Now that he was home, he could
protect her. He wondered almost absently whether other

families were as his was, but that didn't matter. He vowed that when he had a wife and children of his own, he would be nothing at all like his father. For a moment he let himself imagine Jessamine as his wife, with a laughing, tumbling brood of happy children. Yes, he affirmed to himself, he would be a very different husband and father from the man downstairs.

"Papa, I would never have thought you could be so mean!" Jessamine sobbed on Delia's shoulder as Reuben paced back and forth in the parlor.

"Have you lost your senses, girl? Did you think I would welcome having you walk out with one of the damned Yankees that took our very home?" He pointed a trembling finger toward the east window. "Poor little Adele is lying in her grave out there on the hill because of those Mac-Kinleys! Now you say you want to have one come calling?"

"Reuben, she never said she thought of marrying him," Delia said soothingly.

"Marry! I'd see her dead first! Or better yet, him!"

Jerome scowled at his sister as if he had never seen her before. Behind him, Doll stood half-hidden in the doorway.

"No, Papa!"

"Now, Reuben, we'll have none of that talk," Delia said firmly. "He's not going to call him out, honey. Quit crying."

"Then I will!" Jerome stated.

"You'll do no such thing!" his mother snapped.

Jessamine sobbed brokenly. "I thought you would want me to be happy, Papa."

"I do. And I know he would make your life miserable. You have nothing in common with those people. Why, they aren't even Catholic!"

"Ransome said he will convert."

"Ha!" Reuben jabbed his finger in the air in her direction. "So you only met him by chance, did you? And he offered to change his religion so he could go for walks with you? Ha!"

"Jessamine, we only want what is best for you," Delia said.

"Ransome *is* best for me!"

Reuben stopped pacing and faced his daughter. "This very afternoon Louis Broussard came out to see me. He said he has been hired by Arnaud Leslie, and has every expectation of becoming a partner in the gin. He asked me for your hand, and by God, I have a mind to give it to him!''

Jessamine pulled away from her mother and glared at her father. "You wouldn't!''

"Why wouldn't I? The best marriages are the ones arranged by the parents. Look at your mother and me!''

"You already knew each other and were in love!''

"That has nothing to do with it. You know Louis and find him acceptable as a gentleman caller. He's both Creole *and* Catholic. No one in his family ever lived farther north than Shreveport.''

"I'll never marry Louis Broussard," Jessamine hissed. "Never! You may haul me to the altar in chains, but I'll never make the responses!''

"Now, now. Both of you calm down," Delia said, stepping between her husband and daughter. "No one is forcing you to marry Louis.'' She motioned for Doll to come forward. "Doll, take Miss Jessamine to her room and help her get ready for bed.''

Jessamine let Doll lead her away, but her steps were jerky with anger. Once they were in her room, Jessamine sat on her bed and fell back in the pillows. "Put that nightgown down, Doll, and come here.'' She patted the other side of the bed.

Doll sat down and regarded her friend's pale face. "I haven't seen Mr. Reuben so mad since Adele died.''

"Neither have I. Jerome was just as bad. If Jerome makes one move to duel with Ransome, I'll . . . I'll . . .''

"Your mama isn't going to allow any dueling.''

Jessamine rolled to her side and curled up. "He says he loves me," she whispered confidentially.

"What? Ransome said that?''

Jessamine nodded through her tears. "He asked me to marry him.''

"You're not going to! Your papa would skin you alive!''

"He's awfully mad, isn't he?''

Doll leaned nearer. "I'm telling you, Jessamine. You're playing with fire. Loving a man you can never have will only bring you misery.''

"How do you know? When you say that, you look as if you're speaking from experience.''

Doll looked away and got off the bed. "How could I? You know I never walk out with anybody."

She picked up the nightgown and laid it on the foot of the bed. Tabitha was right about one thing—you couldn't tell a white person everything that popped into your mind. Not even when it was Jessamine. Or Jerome. Doll's troubled eyes went back to Jessamine. She knew all too well what her friend was feeling, but her own love was even less possible than Jessamine's. "Put on your nightgown before your mama comes in to check on you."

Jessamine reluctantly obeyed. "I love him, Doll. When I'm with him, it's as if I'm more than I was before. Does that make sense? He wants to be a lawyer. Can you imagine? You have to be awfully smart to do that." She smiled waveringly. "Ransome can be anything he sets his mind to be. There's a strength in him that he doesn't even know he has."

Doll said softly, "If I were you and all that stood in my way was my family and his, I would go see old Asiza."

"What? Asiza?"

"She could give you a charm or something to turn your luck."

"Doll, I'm surprised at you! Asiza isn't real. If she ever existed at all, she must be dead by now. I don't think she was ever anything but a legend. Didn't you tell me once that 'Asiza' is a Dahomey word for 'spirit'?"

"Asiza isn't her real name—it's what she is."

"Have you ever seen her?"

"No, she lives way back in the swamp and never comes out."

"There. You see? How could she manage that?" Jessamine pulled the pins from her long hair and let it fall down her back. "I don't need a charm anyway. Ransome loves me, and someday I will be his wife—whether Papa and Jerome approve or not."

Doll said nothing, but wasn't as confident about the outcome as Jessamine seemed to be.

10

SAM DROVE THE DELACROIX FAMILY INTO TOWN and came around to help the ladies down the buggy steps and through the gate of the black wrought-iron fence that enclosed the front yard of the Leslies' house.

Reuben nodded and said, "Go around back, Sam. I'll send for you when we're ready to leave."

Delia looked up at the square two-story house that sat on a narrow lot. "There was a time when the Leslies aspired to reach our station in life," she mused in a low voice. "How times have changed."

"I wish I had had Arnaud Leslie's forethought to put my money in an English bank. Today they are probably the wealthiest family in Cavelier. Perhaps in this part of Iberville parish."

"I don't see how they can bear to live squashed up against their neighbors like this," Delia said.

"I think it's quite convenient," Jerome said in defense of Susanna's home. "Everything is within walking distance."

"What difference does that make when they have to feed their horses whether they use them or not?" Jessamine asked. "I would hate to live in town."

"Well, you had better get used to the idea. You may end up marrying Louis," Jerome retorted.

"Don't pester your sister," Delia said under her breath as the Leslies' butler swung open the door.

Marie Leslie's front parlor was resplendent in the fashionable hues of crimson and royal blue made possible by the new aniline dyes. The draperies, lamps, mantel drapery, and bell pulls were all adorned with gold fringe. Every tabletop or other flat surface in the room was covered with small framed photographs and various bric-a-brac. On the walls were numerous pen-and-ink sketches and watercolors

110

of tempestuous seashores and mountain vistas, all suspended by gold silk cords with tassels.

Marie and Susanna Leslie sat in adjoining chairs, awaiting their guests, their heads almost touching over a music box that was playing strains of "Ave Maria" to complete the tableau. When their company entered, they both looked up as if in pleasant surprise, though both must have heard the Delacroixs' entrance.

"Delia, how good of you to come for dinner." Marie kissed the air to either side of Delia's cheeks. "And Jessamine! How pretty you look."

Jerome smiled down at Susanna, who managed to blush a delicate shade of pink. Her dishwater-blond hair had been tortured into curls such as a debutante might wear, though her debut had been several years before. Her pale blue dress was stylishly cut, with most of the fullness at the back and a flat *tablier* front like an apron. The square neckline was more fashionable than Jessamine's rounded one, showing an expanse of her snowy bosom. She allowed Jerome to kiss her small hand, and smiled so that a slight dimple appeared at the corner of her mouth.

Arnaud Leslie entered the room and greeted their female guests before he shook hands with Jerome and Reuben. "Sorry I wasn't here when you arrived, but I had business to see to. I'm organizing a White League for Cavelier and had to attend a meeting. You know there is an election coming up. Can't afford to let the cuffies take over this one like they did the governor's election." Arnaud was brusque and hearty and walked with quick movements. Even when he was angry, he usually had a smile pasted on his face.

"Now, you aren't going to talk politics," his wife admonished. To Delia and Jessamine she confided, "That's all we hear around this house, politics, politics, politics."

Arnaud continued, "You ought to join us, Reuben. I've almost convinced most of the men in Cavelier. We're a nonmilitary army and our aim is to keep the voters white."

Reuben made a noncommittal answer. Politics had never been his strong suit. He was much more interested in seeing Jerome betrothed to Susanna, and eventually in line for the Leslie fortune.

"We carry guns, but that's mainly for show." Leslie laughed. "Once we show them, we seldom have to use them!"

Jerome lifted the lid of the music box and the tune began again. "Is this new? You don't have a beau that I don't know about, do you?"

"How you talk! No, Papa brought me the music box as a gift when he was in Baton Rouge last week."

Jerome touched one of her silken curls and watched with fascination as it bounced. Susanna struck his hand playfully with her fingertips and tossed her head so that all the curls jiggled riotously.

Jessamine watched the coquettish exchange, and wondered if she had ever appeared to be that foolish herself. Since the ugly scene with Papa over her seeing Ransome, she had been closely watched, and as a result, she had become quieter. Rebellion seethed beneath the surface, however. She thought Susanna was as brainless a bit of fluff as anyone she had ever seen, yet both Reuben and Delia were practically panting for Jerome to marry her.

"I understand from Jerome that you and Louis Broussard are an item," Mrs. Leslie said to Jessamine.

"Did he say that? Whatever for, I wonder," Jessamine answered, ignoring her mother's warning glance. "Louis and I are friends, but nothing more."

"You should set your cap for him, my dear. My Arnaud says that young man will be very important in Cavelier someday. He has quite a head for business."

Jessamine started to point out that Louis was as dreary as any man she'd ever met, but refrained when she recalled there was a family connection of some sort between the Leslies and the Broussards.

The butler announced dinner and each of the men offered an arm to a lady. Jessamine, of course, had no escort and felt oddly out of place as she took her father's other arm. If she didn't marry, this would always be her lot in life, and over the past few days she had become more and more resolved to have the man she loved or no one.

After the potage St. Germain, the crawfish *étouffé* and *choux glorieux* were served with dishes of minted carrots and fried okra. Jerome scarcely tasted his food for the fascination he found in Susanna's dainty bites and birdlike appetite. To watch her, a person would think she scarcely ate at all. No wonder her waist was so tiny, he mused. After only a few morsels, she laid her fork on her plate, touched the corner of her lips with the linen napkin, and folded her hands demurely in her lap. Jerome was enthralled. He knew

Jessamine had a healthy appetite, and that her slimness was a marvel to the family. Here, however, was a porcelain doll of a woman who was delicate beyond his every dream.

Susanna, as if unaware of his covert gaze, sighed and made her breasts mound fuller beneath the dress's tight bodice. Jerome almost dropped his fork at the unexpected sight of the straining fabric.

Dessert was orange soufflé, a specialty of the Leslies' cook. Jerome barely tasted it. And as with the main course, Susanna made a delicate foray toward it, but had no more than tasted it before she motioned for the butler to take it away. She looked across at Jerome and widened her blue eyes when they encountered his.

Jessamine ate her soufflé down to the last morsel, despite her mother's reproving glance. If they thought they could turn her into a simpering fool like Susanna Leslie, they had another think coming! Jessamine had always been able to eat as she pleased and not gain weight, so she thought it ridiculous to pretend otherwise. Since that terrible fight with her parents over Ransome, a change had come over her—one her family didn't like nearly as well as she did.

"Governor Warmouth will ruin us for sure," Arnaud Leslie was saying to Reuben. "He's nothing but a Yankee dictator! Half our House of Representatives are as black as Silas over there." He jerked his thumb at the passive-featured butler. "Even the lieutenant governor is a cuffy! We should have shot them before we gave them the vote."

Jessamine frowned her disapproval. She knew the problems as well as anyone else, but she also knew that Silas had feelings just as Doll did. Unable to restrain herself further, she said, "It's only right for the state leaders to be elected by the vote of all the people."

"Hush!" Delia exclaimed.

"Begging your pardon, Miss Jessamine," Arnaud Leslie said with his infuriating smile and a mock bow, "but you can't understand the intricacies of politics. It's better to leave such worries to your menfolk."

Jessamine forced a smile to her face and retorted, "Personally I think women should be allowed to vote, and then the state's leaders would finally represent *all* the people."

"Jessamine!" Delia gasped. "Please excuse her, Mr. Leslie. She had an upset recently, and I believe she is still in shock. A private matter of family importance only, but she has been remarkably outspoken of late."

Jessamine blushed to the roots of her hair, and she felt as reproached as Delia had intended for her to be. Even Jerome was looking at her in amazement. The Leslies were frankly shocked.

Mrs. Leslie quickly covered the awkward moment by rising to lead the women back into the drawing room. "Let's leave the men to their cigars, shall we? I have a recipe for lemon glacé that I know you'll love, Delia. I'll lend you my ether machine to make the ice when you decide to try it."

"Miss Susanna, will you show me the gazebo?" Jerome asked. He bowed toward her father. "With your permission?"

"Certainly. You do that." Her proud father beamed. "I was young once myself."

Susanna preceded Jerome out of the house and down the front steps to the lawn. "Jessamine certainly is shocking, isn't she? Imagine a lady even wanting to vote!" She batted her eyelashes at Jerome. "I think all true ladies want to be ruled by their husbands. At least I will—someday."

Jerome felt as if he would burst with pride for simply being so privileged as to walk beside her. "Jessamine isn't like that. She tends to speak her mind, but she isn't brash."

"You're so loyal, Jerome."

"She's my sister. Of course I'm protective of her."

They strolled across the shade-dappled grass, and Susanna paused to pluck a daisy from the profusion of them in the flowerbed. "I love daisies, don't you? They're so shy and humble." She paused, hoping Jerome would see the correlation between the flower and herself.

"Jessamine prefers gardenias."

"They're so robust!" she protested. "I declare, their scent is fairly cloying." She drew the white petals beneath her chin. "A gardenia is so . . . passionate." She glanced covertly at Jerome.

He was in a daze as she led him through the flowers, humming with bees, into the privacy of the vine-shrouded gazebo. He looked back toward the house, but the view was totally obscured by a curtain of honeysuckle. The gazebo was even more secluded than he had guessed.

"I hear the Ramseys are giving a Starvation Party next week," he said as he stepped nearer. "May I drive you over?"

"My goodness." She pouted in a tempting way. "I'll be so glad when things go back to normal. Starvation Parties and Calico Balls, and everybody having to bring a covered dish of food. It's a disgrace. Whoever could have imagined such things when we were children." She looked over at the carriage house, where Sam was talking with the Leslies' groom, and with acrimony said, "I think it's as much their fault as it is the Yankees', and I hate them for it."

"It's not Sam's fault any more than any of his people's. The Yankees are the ones to blame."

"Oh, Jerome, everybody knows you Delacroixs spoil your people. You'll be sorry one of these days. Papa says there are still bands of Negroes roaming through the state robbing and murdering and goodness knows what else."

"The Farmers aren't like that. Neither are the other Negroes that work for us."

"Have it your way, Jerome. Personally, I always feel uneasy around them these days. A person can't tell what may be going through their minds."

Ignoring her bias, Jerome put his arm around her waist and bent his dark head closer to hers. "Can you tell what's going on in my mind?"

"Now, Jerome, you just stop that!" She stepped nearer him and batted her eyelashes again. "The next thing I know, you'll be demanding a kiss, and I told you in your mother's rose garden that there would be no more of that!"

"Surely you wouldn't miss just one kiss," he bargained. "No one can see us in here."

Susanna looked about carefully. "Well, perhaps just one." She lifted her face up toward his and pursed her lips as she shut her eyes.

Jerome covered her lips with his own, but he was far more conscious of the way her slender body swayed against his and how her breasts brushed his chest. He pulled her closer, his kiss becoming more passionate. She kept her lips firmly closed, but let him kiss her for as long as he pleased.

He rubbed his palms over her small waist and back, and noticed how much easier it was to kiss a woman now that the dress styles had changed from those cumbersome crinoline hoop skirts to ones that were closer-fitting in the front and fuller in the back. His hands grew bolder and he reached up to touch the curve of her breast.

"Jerome!" Susanna exclaimed as she pushed him away. "What sort of person do you think I am?"

"I didn't mean anything," he protested. "Susanna, you aren't crying, are you? Don't cry."

Tears hadn't occurred to Susanna until he mentioned them. She looked away, willing her eyes to brim with moisture. Gazing back at him, she let Jerome see the full extent of her effort.

"You *are* crying!"

"I just . . . I just hate what you must think of me to try to . . . to touch me like that." She pressed her lace handkerchief to the corners of her nose, but let the tears slide down her cheeks.

Jerome took the wisp of lace from her and dabbed her cheeks dry as he looked at her in misery. "Susanna, I don't think ill of you. Why, I respect you more than any woman I know."

"You have an odd way of showing it, Jerome Delacroix. No one but my husband will ever touch me . . . there."

Jerome looked at her with thoughtful consideration. Susanna was pretty, in addition to being his family's choice for his wife. She wasn't passionate, but he would have been amazed if she had been, because Susanna was a lady to the very core. In that brief touch, he hadn't satisfied his yearning or even his curiosity as to how she felt beneath the ruffles and laces of her dress. Only her husband would be allowed to touch her in that way, she had said. Didn't that imply she was willing to let her husband awaken her passion?

"We should be going back," he said.

She took her handkerchief and nodded. "We don't want out parents to become alarmed at our absence. A reputation is a precarious thing."

"Your reputation is safe with me. I would protect it just as I would you."

"Would you, Jerome?" She gave him an angelic smile, and he seemed to melt inside.

As they walked back to the house, Sam turned to Andre and chuckled. "Those two got courting written all over them."

Andre stopped polishing the harness to watch the couple pass through the garden. "I sure don't envy the man what gets her. She can sure throw a temper fit."

"Miss Susanna can? Come on, now."

"It's a fact."

Sam shook his head. "Looks like Mr. Jerome is gonna set his head for her anyways. Young folks in love is blind in one eye and can't see out of the other."

"How is Tabitha and Doll these days?"

"They fine. You wouldn't have to ask, if you'd been coming to Sunday meeting. You haven't been there a single time this month. Andre, you hide from church worse than anybody I knows."

"I ain't lost nothing down there. Ain't no reason to go look for it."

"What you need is a good woman to straighten you out."

Andre laughed. Sam was always trying to convert him to religion or marriage. "Is Doll seeing anybody? They's some new families moved down the road a piece. Some of them have sons what is ripe for marrying."

"That girl won't give none of them the time of day. Tom Smith watches her like she was an angel or something, and she just looks straight through him."

"That's purely a shame. He's a good man." Andre glanced toward the house. "Better put the horse back in the traces. Here comes Silas to get you."

Sam nodded to the dignified butler, but he felt ill-at-ease around him. Until Roseland was lost to the Mac-Kinleys, Sam had enjoyed the status that Silas still retained, and he was a bit envious. " 'Afternoon, Silas."

"Afternoon, Sam. Mr. Reuben said to come fetch you around. You going to the 'protracted' meeting? I hear it'll be going on at the church every night for a week."

"Tabitha wouldn't let me miss a night if I wanted to. Are you?"

"I sure am."

Sam fastened the horse's harness to the buggy and led him out into the coach yard. "See you then, Silas. Wouldn't hurt you to come too, Andre." He climbed onto the seat and clucked to the horse.

Later, as they drove toward Ten Acres, Reuben turned to Jerome. "How did it go in the gazebo, son?"

Jerome was startled by his father's probing question. "What do you mean?"

"Your papa means that we approve of Susanna," Delia said. "Marie couldn't very well say anything directly about it, but I think she is hoping for the match too."

"Arnaud is willing, I believe. He quit talking politics

long enough to tell me he is opening another gin and buying a couple of riverboats to take the cotton to New Orleans. Off season, he plans to ship other goods back and forth.'' Reuben turned toward Jessamine. ''Louis Broussard will manage the new gin. It would be good for us to tie in with the ginning and shipping out of Cavelier.''

Jessamine frowned. ''I don't have any intention of marrying Louis. He's as dull as whey.''

''He asked me again for your hand.''

''He didn't! Why didn't you tell me, Papa?''

''I was giving you time to think more favorably of him.''

''You didn't tell him yes!''

''I told him your mother and I are in favor of the match, but that the decision will be yours.''

Jessamine relaxed somewhat. ''Good. If he ever gets around to asking me, I'll tell him no.''

''You had better be cautious,'' Delia said. ''You're almost twenty, and there aren't many men to choose from since the war. The Ramseys are a fine family, but they've lost their fortune and may still lose their land if taxes continue to go up.''

''Mama, I'm not interested in marrying a man for his money.''

''That's all well and good now, Jessamine, but you'll find as you get older that security is as necessary as a wedding band. As for love, I've told you it will grow when two people are kind and respect each other.''

Jessamine lifted her chin. ''I have my sights aimed higher, Mama. I'll marry for love or I'll never marry at all.''

''You don't know what you're saying, child.''

''I'm not a child any longer. I grew up the night I learned you care more for a stupid feud than you do for me.''

''Don't you talk to your mother that way!'' Reuben snapped.

''Papa, you may as well listen to what I'm saying, because I'm as stubborn as you are. I'll marry Ransome MacKinley or I'll marry no one at all!''

The rest of the drive was finished in stony silence. Jerome was frankly shocked that his sister had spoken so strongly to their parents, and he was puzzled by the degree of emotion she must be feeling that would lead her to affirm that she would have Ransome or no one. He loved Susanna, he was pretty sure, but that was different. If Jessamine didn't marry, she would be an old maid. Before the war had decimated such a large portion of the male population, any girl her age would have already been considered well past her prime for marriage. With fewer men now, the urgency was even greater. If she didn't choose a husband soon, she would likely have to settle for a widower, if one became available someday. Everyone knew that wives almost always outlived their husbands unless they died in childbed. Jerome wondered if Susanna loved him so strongly that she would save herself for him or no one.

When they reached Ten Acres, Jerome walked for a while, trying to sort out his thoughts. When he saw Doll go into the henhouse, he glanced around to be sure their parents weren't watching, and he followed her in. The building was long and narrow, and pungent with the smell of chickens and corn.

Doll looked up and smiled, her white dress a splash of light in the dim room. "Did you have a good time?"

"The Leslies' cook can't compare with your ma," Jerome commented as he reached in a square wooden box and lifted a brown egg out of the hay. "Jessamine still says she won't marry anybody but Ransome."

"She loves him." Doll shrugged gracefully. "That's the way love is. You can't marry one man if you really love someone else."

"That's what I don't understand. Jessamine couldn't have seen him more than a couple of times in her life, but she's willing to throw away her whole future for him."

Doll avoided Jerome's eyes. "She loves him."

Jerome handed her the egg, and when his fingers brushed hers, the mere touch brought a stirring within him. "Are you like that? I mean, if you were in love, would you refuse to marry anyone else, even if it meant you might never marry at all?"

"Yes." She turned away abruptly and reached for another nest. "Old Prissy outdid herself. Two!" She held up the eggs before placing them in the basket.

"Why don't you ever walk out with anybody? I've never once seen you look at anyone twice. Not even Tom Smith."

"Tom Smith again! I wish I had never heard of him. Why is everybody determined to marry me off?"

Jerome handed her another egg and this time when their fingers touched he wasn't as quick to draw back. "I'm not eager for you to marry Tom, or anybody else in town."

Reluctantly Doll raised her almond eyes to meet his. A late ray of sun, slanting through the side window, turned the air to gold dust around them. The hens' contented murmurs and clucking seemed part of the magic as time paused for them and differences vanished.

Jerome felt an almost irresistible urge to reach out and touch her smooth cheek as he had so often when they were children. But they were children no longer, and he dared not raise his hand. "They want me to marry Susanna Leslie," he said at last.

Doll's eyes widened as she considered what to say. "What do you want?"

"I guess I want to marry her too."

"You just guess you do?" Doll gave a wry laugh. "You don't sound to me like a man in love."

After a long pause he said, "I guess it's different with a man. I don't love her the way Jessamine seems to think she loves Ransome, but I'm more logical than Jessamine will ever be."

"Are you, Jerome? Or is what you feel not love at all? I know you, and I know that if you were in love you'd go through heaven and hell to get her. You're that kind. Just like Jessamine is."

"What are you saying?"

"I'm saying that you may want her body more than you want her." A rare spark of anger flashed in Doll's dark eyes.

"I'm going to forget you said that! Imagine talking about Susanna like that!"

"You sound just like her when you talk like that! Go on out of here and let me finish my chores, before I have to do them by lantern light." She turned her back on Jerome and heard him stride out of the henhouse. He never saw Doll's tears. Tears that were more real than any Susanna had ever cried.

11

FOR THE NEXT TWO MONTHS JEROME SPENT EVERY available evening in the Leslies' parlor. Marie and Arnaud became as accustomed to seeing Jerome leafing through picture albums or exclaiming over the wonders of Niagra Falls as depicted on the stereoscope as they were to seeing Susanna. When anyone gave a party, it was assumed that Susanna and Jerome would attend together, and Marie's women friends hinted at the possibility of an approaching engagement.

The more Jerome saw of Susanna, the more infatuated he became. Soon he was measuring every woman to Susanna's scale. Susanna, in her turn, was sensing his growing ardor and moving in for the matrimonial kill.

"Jerome, which do think will be prettier here?" she asked as she turned the box she was decorating first one way and then the other. "The little pink shells or the round white ones?"

He studied the box as if the decision were of grave importance. "The white ones, I think."

"But I put pink ones on the front, and I believe I should be consistent with the design, don't you?" She smiled at him over the lid of the box. "Will you pick out the prettiest ones for me?"

Jerome obediently poked around in the tray of tiny assorted seashells to find the pinkest ones. Boxes decorated with designs made from seashells had become the fashion in Cavelier of late, and he suspected someone was making a small fortune collecting shells from the beaches and selling them inland. He selected several and held them out in the palm of his hand.

Susanna coated a small area on the box with thick mucilage and picked the shells out of his palm, one by one, her fingers stroking his skin in the process. "I like this new fad," he said with a grin.

"Now, Jerome, I know that look, and you just stop it. I could hardly pick up the tiny shells without touching you, now could I?"

"That's what I like about it." He leaned closer until he could smell the faint lavender scent of her gown. "I'm liable to steal a kiss if you aren't careful."

"Don't you dare! Mama could walk in at any minute!" She pushed him away in mock shyness.

Jerome smiled as he searched in the tray for more pink shells. As he did, his thoughts were on Susanna and what it would be like to come home to her every day. Working at the logging business and sawmill had been exciting the first few years, but the work was sometimes tedious, and Jerome's head had been turned by Mr. Leslie's broad hints that he might be made the manager of the man's new shipping line. Although Leslie hadn't exactly said so, Jerome knew the position was one that would go to Susanna's husband as part of her dowry. Jerome had been brought up from the cradle to live an almost princely life, and he hadn't been able to adjust to their greatly diminished standard of living any more than his parents. To Jerome, domestic happiness and money were synonymous. He still couldn't believe his luck in being favored by a girl who was not only pretty but also from a rich family.

Susanna used a hatpin to push the shells into the glue. The rosy lamplight that filtered through the red satin lampshade made her skin glow as if she were constantly blushing. Her face was intent upon her deliberate movements as she pushed a shell first one way and then another. As the June nights were warm, she wore a low-cut dress that exposed the shallow cleavage of her small breasts. Her bare arms were round and her hands small, with pale fingernails as delicate as the shells themselves.

Seemingly unaware of Jerome's scrutiny, Susanna pursed her pink lips in the semblance of a pouting kiss and lowered her long eyelashes to make a lacy shadow on her cheek. As he watched, she moistened her lips with the tip of her small pink tongue. The room suddenly seemed too hot, and Jerome tugged at his scratchy collar.

When Susanna's fingers again grazed his palm, Jerome caught her hand. She looked up at him as if in surprise. "Susanna, there's something on my mind. Something I must speak to you about."

"Yes, Jerome?" She let her small hand lie within his, and swayed slightly toward him.

"I've become very close to you of late," he said as he had practiced on the ride to town. "As you know, our cypress lumber business is becoming quite profitable, and I have reason to believe I have a secure future to offer a woman. I believe our parents are in favor of what I'm about to say, as well. Susanna, will you become my wife?" The words sounded stilted to him when he said them aloud, but Susanna clearly didn't think so.

She gasped as if she had been holding her breath and pressed her free hand to her mouth. "Become your wife? Jerome, I'm so surprised!"

"I guess I should have led up to it more eloquently, but you looked so pretty, the words just slipped out."

"I would be honored to be your wife!"

Jerome leaned forward to kiss her, but Susanna leapt to her feet and hurried to the door. "Mama! Papa! Come here!"

Awkwardly he hurried to his feet as her parents rushed into the room. By the look on her mother's face, he wondered if she might have been listening to their entire exchange, but she let Susanna speak as if she had no idea what her daughter was going to say.

"Mama, Papa, Jerome has asked me to be his wife!"

"Forgive me for not speaking to you first, Mr. Leslie, but I had intended to do so if Susanna gave me the encouragement."

"I told him yes, Papa."

"Well, it seems settled then!" Arnaud beamed with obvious pride at Jerome, and crossed the room to shake his hand and slap him warmly on the shoulders. Marie tiptoed up to kiss both his cheeks. Jerome grinned in embarrassment. He was still somewhat surprised by his own words.

"When have you set the date?" Marie asked as she embraced her daughter.

"We haven't talked about it yet."

Susanna clasped her mother's hands. "Perhaps in October, Mama? That will give us plenty of time to find just the right dress. And I want to bring in my cousins from Shreveport. I would like Cousin Célina and Cousin Virginie to stand with me and little Joséphine would be lovely as a flower girl."

Jerome was amazed at how fast the plans were being

made. He had somehow thought such things required more contemplation. "I don't want to rush you, Susanna. If you want the customary year's engagement, I'm quite prepared to wait."

"Nonsense, my boy," Mr. Leslie said heartily. "October is months away. How long can it take to pick out a dress and bring three cousins from Shreveport?"

Jerome smiled, but he felt a bit weak. Everything was going so fast! "I just didn't want to seem to be rushing her."

"Four months is no rush. Besides, girls look forward to this day all their lives. By October I'll be needing a manager for my riverboat trade, as well. A position like that should go to a son and, well, you're the son we never had, my boy." He companionably slapped Jerome on the back again.

"Thank you, sir."

"We must write to the Louvieres in Paris and tell them," Marie was saying to Susanna. "I'll have Cousin Zélia contact a dressmaker and have samples of silk sent to us so we can choose just the right one. We'll order one of those lovely veils that the Carmelite nuns embroider. You can't get needlework like that in the United States. And I'll write to your Tante Julie and Nonc Christophe first thing in the morning."

Jerome was amazed at how eager Susanna's parents seemed to be to make the wedding plans. It was almost as if they had been made long in advance and were now being voiced for his benefit. The first niggling doubts began to creep in, but Jerome knew he couldn't possibly back out now.

"Let's leave the details to the women," Arnaud suggested amiably. "I'll walk you to your horse."

"I suppose it is late." He looked wistfully at Susanna, who tossed him one of her sweetest smiles before conferring again with her mother. Somehow Jerome had always expected a proposal to be less public and more romantic.

Before he knew it, he was on his horse and headed for home, trying to determine how he had so thoroughly lost control of the evening. By the time he reached Ten Acres, he had convinced himself that he was lucky to have been accepted so quickly by Susanna and so wholeheartedly by her parents.

The lights were on in the parlor, but Jerome hesitated. He had to tell his parents, but he wanted to put it off as long as possible. For some reason he wasn't nearly as excited about the turn of events as the Leslies were, and he wasn't sure he could convince his family that he was. He went to the barn and unsaddled his horse and gave him a measure of feed as he thought about his future.

"I thought I saw you come home," Doll said as she stepped into the doorway. "You're home early." She hung her lantern on a nail.

He patted his horse's rump on his way out of the stall, closing the gate behind him. "I didn't see you outside."

"I was sitting on my porch, enjoying the cool breeze." She stepped closer. "What's wrong? You look as if there's trouble."

"No. No trouble." He made an effort to smile. Leaning on the stall gate as if he were watching his horse eat the grain, he said, "Have you ever done something impulsively, and then wondered if you did the right thing?"

"Sure. Lots of times."

He frowned and studied the palms of his hands before looking back at the horse.

"Jerome? What is it?"

"I asked Susanna to marry me tonight." He didn't look at Doll or notice how silent she was. "As soon as I asked her, she said yes and ran to get her parents. Next thing I know, the wedding is set for October and I'm the manager of the Leslies' riverboats." He shook his head. "I don't know, Doll, but it seems as if it should have been . . . well, different." When he looked back at her, she had moved into the shadows by the empty stalls, and he couldn't see her face.

"I know I'm a lucky man. I'm getting a pretty bride and will be well on my way to making a fortune. Like Papa is always saying, if we don't have money, we'll never be able to buy Roseland back."

"Roseland! Are you wanting to marry that girl to get money to buy a place that's not even for sale?"

"No! Of course not. Susanna will make a perfect wife. She's sweet and dainty, and our families are all for it. Especially hers. Dammit, Doll, I felt like a hog that's been trussed up for the slaughter. Now, why would I feel that way?"

"Maybe you don't love her."

"Nonsense. Of course I love her. Didn't I tell you how perfect she is?" He frowned at the horse and pulled a wisp of straw from the manger and twirled it between his thumb and forefinger. "It just seems like something is missing." He turned to Doll and tried to discern her features in the shadows. "I'm glad you came out. I needed to say these things to somebody, and I can't even tell Jessamine how I'm feeling."

"But you can tell me?" Doll's voice was too serene, as though she was refusing to say exactly what she felt.

"Are you all right? You sound odd. Come into the light here so I can see you."

After a pause, Doll stepped forward. Her dark eyes were unusually bright, and she held her head high. Jerome studied her familiar features. He had known Doll all her life, and she had always been his friend and confidante. He could tell by the set of her shoulders and the tilt of her chin that she was upset. "Was Mama harsh with you about something?"

"No."

He stepped nearer and touched her cool cheek. She moved away as if his touch startled her, but he wasn't quick to draw away. The light tan of her skin seemed rich after Susanna's paleness and her eyes were dark and liquid, as if they held a deep secret. Whatever it was, Jerome knew she would never tell. Doll's secrets were always kept hidden even from Jessamine and himself. "You aren't feeling bad, are you? Your skin is cool." He ran his thumb along the curve of her chin, then remembered himself and dropped his arm.

"I feel fine."

Jerome knew he should step sway, smile, and tell Doll he was only experiencing a bachelor's natural reticence. Instead he stood there gazing at her as if he hadn't known her all his life. Doll was tall—almost as tall as he was—and gracefully curved. How had he seen her every day for almost twenty years and never realized until this moment how sensuously beautiful she was? His thoughts startled him, and he stepped back.

"I'm going in to tell Mama and Papa and Jessamine," he said to break the spell. "Do you want me to light you to your cabin?"

"No. No, I can find my way." She, too, stepped away as if she had felt the same thrumming tension that he had.

He watched her turn and glide through the dim light and out into the darkness. A frown creased his brows as he blew out the barn's lantern and made his way to the main house.

Jessamine tapped her fingers impatiently on her forearm as she strained to hear Ransome's approach. For two months her parents and Tabitha had been watching her very closely, and it had become increasingly difficult to get away to meet Ransome. More than a week had passed since she last saw him, but she wasn't sure how much longer she could risk waiting for him. She had sent Doll to the bridge to set out the signal for Ransome, but she didn't know whether he looked for the wedged leaf every day.

She heard the faint sound of footsteps in the grass, and with great care she peered through the opening in the circle of gardenias. Ransome saw her, and quickened his pace. As soon as he stepped inside the bower, Jessamine threw her arms about his neck, and he lifted her from the ground in an exuberant hug. "I was so afraid you wouldn't come," she said as she buried her face against his neck.

Ransome let her slide down his lean body to the ground. "I've waited every day for your signal. I wasn't sure what had happened this last week, but I didn't think it was wise to come to your house or try to send another message. I didn't want to get you into bigger trouble."

"It's been a bad week. Papa and Jerome still get furious every time I bring up your name. Thank goodness they don't know we plan to get married! Papa's been watching me like a hawk lately. I wouldn't be here now except the house is upside down over Jerome proposing to that silly Susanna Leslie. The way Mama and Papa are carrying on, you'd think he was marrying some princess. What's been happening at your house?"

"Nothing is any different. They're still against me seeing you. Father keeps saying I'm the last heir in his branch of the family, and I must make what he calls a proper marriage. Jessamine, I love you. Elope with me and we'll tell them all to go to hell."

"I can't, Ransome. How can I turn my back on my family and my home? You don't seem to understand what it means to me. Here in the South our family ties are sacred. This land is part of me. It's who I am. Don't you see?"

"No, I don't. Go to Albany with me. We can be married at my Aunt Polly's, and when I become established in my law practice, I'll buy you as much land as you want.''

"It wouldn't be Roseland. It wouldn't be Ten Acres. I can't turn away from my entire heritage. How can you? Neither of our families would ever speak to us again.''

"I would rather have you than my family or this land.''

"Ransome, please understand. I love you so much. I just think we can get them to understand if we wait awhile longer. I've told my parents that I won't marry anyone but you. Once they see that I mean it, they will reconsider.'' She touched his cheek and let her eyes linger on his lips. "I love you, Ransome. Please be patient.''

He pulled her to him and held her close. "Even if your parents agree, mine never will. Father never changes his mind and Mother does exactly what he tells her.''

"Perhaps she will surprise you. Mama seems to always agree with Papa, but I know she really has as much say in family matters as he does.''

Ransome shook his head. "It's not like that with my parents. If Dennis were still alive to carry on the name, they might give in, but not as it is.''

She laid her cheek on his chest and closed her eyes. "I wish we were like Jerome and Susanna, and our parents were practically in a froth to see us married. Jerome doesn't realize how lucky he is.''

He lifted her chin and gazed into her eyes. "If you want to wait, we'll wait. Father is determined to turn me into a planter, so I'm not going anywhere. In time maybe a miracle will happen.''

"I'll wait for you forever, if need be.''

Slowly he lowered his head and tasted the honey of her lips. She molded her body against his, and returned his kisses with a passion that rose to meet his own. Her lips parted eagerly, and her tongue met his, teasing and exciting him even more.

"God, Jessamine! How can you ask me to wait and kiss me like that?''

Her eyes were as dark as a stormy sky with her intense longing for him. "You make me feel like a woman,'' she said softly. "When you kiss me, I want to give myself to you and I don't care at all that I mustn't.''

A muscle tightened in his jaw, and he cupped her earnest face between his palms. "We have to be strong, love. Otherwise you know what could happen.''

Slowly she nodded.

"I want you so much, I feel as if I'm on fire whenever I think about you. At night I dream that I hold you close and that no one can part us."

"I want you too."

"But it's not just that I want to make love with you, though God knows I do. It's that I want to wake up with you, and see you over our own dinner table, and tell you all the things that have happened to me during the day. I want to hear you tell me what the neighbors are doing, and see you grow large with our child."

Jessamine's eyes misted with the love she felt as she said, "Ransome, will you ever realize how strong I have to make myself not to elope with you and turn my back on all I have ever known? If I didn't feel my family would see reason in time, I would have left with you the day you proposed. I've loved you since the first day I saw you, and the Mississippi River will quit flowing long before I stop loving you."

Once more he bent to kiss her, and Jessamine felt her senses reel as his strong arms held her close. She knew all too well what an afternoon of indiscretion could bring, but more and more frequently, she didn't care.

12

EVERYONE WAS THRILLED OVER THE NEWS OF SU-
sanna Leslie's engagement to Jerome Delacroix, but when
the subject was brought up in mixed company, Susanna
blushed and demurely refused to discuss it. Jerome, however, accepted his friends' congratulations with a boyish
grin. Parties were planned in their honor, and Jerome began
making arrangements for their honeymoon.

On a Sunday afternoon in mid-June, Susanna and Jerome went into the country with several of their friends for
a picnic. Susanna spread a bright-colored quilt on the ground
and put out the luncheon she had packed. "I hope you like
deviled eggs," she said. "It's Mama's recipe."

"I'm sure I will. Did you cook this yourself?" he said
as he eyed the spread with anticipation.

"Well, of course I did. You don't think I can't cook,
do you? The very idea. Of course, we'll have a maid, but
all the Leslie ladies are taught to cook." With a furtive
glance at Jerome, Susanna said, "I know a secret."

"Oh?"

"Papa has bought us a house as a wedding gift!"

"He has! A house? What house?" Jerome was a great
deal more curious than excited.

"It's the big white one with all the azalea bushes on
Natchez Street. The one with the dark green shutters and
tall front steps."

"Oh." Jerome knew the house. It was relatively new
and had been patterned after a French style that was popular
in New Orleans, with the living quarters on the second floor.
The exterior of the house was adorned with black wrought-
iron railings reminiscent of French lace.

She pouted. "You don't sound very pleased."

"I had expected to have a say in where we were to
live."

130

"Well, how could you, and it still be a surprise? Really, Jerome. I think you're just awful not to be pleased."

"I am pleased. Just surprised, that's all."

"I knew you would be! And it's only a block away from my parents' house, so Mama can come over every day."

Jerome felt it was prudent that he not mention that he found that bit of news to be no enticement. Susanna's mother already seemed to be dictating their lives.

Their friends spread quilts nearby, and everyone talked and laughed as midge flies floated in the sunlight and ants attempted forays onto the quilts after the crumbs. As the afternoon wore on, two by two, the others left to return to town. At last only Jerome and Susanna were left at the picnic grounds.

She briskly packed the remains of their meal into the basket and started to get to her feet.

"Wait. Let's not go yet."

"Why not? Everyone else has gone."

Jerome looked at her and smiled. "I'd just like to be alone with you for a while. We almost never are."

"Here? Without a chaperon? What will Mama think?"

"She won't know the others left early. Besides, we're getting married in just a few months."

"That's true." She sat back down on the quilt and folded her hands demurely in her lap.

Jerome leaned over and gave her a quick kiss. "I've been wanting to do that all afternoon."

"We ought to go back, you know."

"I know." He kissed her again, moving his lips over hers. Susanna put her arms around his neck and pulled him down onto the quilt. Jerome raised his head and looked at her in amazement.

"Well, we *are* getting married, Jerome," she said primly. Then she smiled and pulled him down for another kiss.

Jerome needed no urging. He had burned to possess her for months. He put his hand under her hips and drew her beneath him. He had removed his coat earlier, and her hands felt hot on his back as she stroked him through the material of his shirt. She felt so yielding beneath him that he moved his hand up to cup her breast. To his astonishment and great pleasure, she didn't push him away this time.

He ran his finger along the neckline of her dress and

over the small mounds of her breasts. Susanna made no move to encourage or to dissuade him, so he slipped beneath the fabric and the band of cloth that made her breasts swell so femininely.

A hot pulse raced in his temples as he realized he was, at last, touching her breasts. The fingers of his free hand moved over the row of buttons down the front of her bodice.

"Jerome! We mustn't," she protested breathlessly.

He drew back, his eyes almost black with his desire. "If you tell me to stop, I will, but I don't want to."

"All right," she said shyly.

He unbuttoned her dress and pushed it away. A few moments later he had removed the linen band from around her chest and was staring at her small breasts, gleaming white in the filtered sunlight. He had expected her breasts would be larger, but surmised that they had only appeared that way because of the ruffles and padding of the bodices of her dresses. Nevertheless, the nipples pouted invitingly, and when Jerome lowered his head to draw one into his mouth, she protested only feebly. He couldn't determine how to remove the lacings that cinched her waist without removing her dress and petticoats as well, so he left the lacings in place. Somehow her breasts seemed even more bare above the tight garment.

He ran his hand up under her skirt as he kissed her again, and managed to loosen the drawstring that fastened her bloomers. When he eased them down, she protested demurely, but he could tell her resistance was no more than a token gesture.

Jerome touched the nest of curls between her thighs, letting his instincts guide him as he tried to awaken Susanna's passion. She was obedient, even willing, but he didn't feel the togetherness he had expected at such a moment. She had not tried to stop him, but she also kept her lips firmly closed.

He loosened his trousers, and Susanna refused to look at him as he bared himself to her. Instead, she screwed her eyes shut tight. He tried to guide her hand to touch him, but she jerked it back; and when his hard maleness touched her thigh, she flinched. "Susanna? do you want me to stop?"

She shook her head from side to side, but made no verbal reply.

Pulling her farther beneath him, Jerome nudged her legs apart, knelt between them and slowly entered her. Susanna bit her finger and gave a choked scream, then was silent. He had never felt anything so wonderful in his entire life. She was amazingly hot and wet, almost uncomfortably tight at first. Then Jerome began to move slowly, unaware of anything but this incredible new sensation.

Deep down he wanted to give her the pleasure he had heard some women could experience. He kissed her and teased her breasts, struggling to hold back until she showed greater passion.

"Hurry!" she muttered through clenched teeth. "Please!"

Thinking this meant she was enjoying what he was doing and would have even more pleasure if he moved faster, Jerome began thrusting deeper and more rapidly. Suddenly he seemed to explode from within, and he held Susanna tight as satisfaction thundered through him.

After a while he raised himself and pulled away from her. She lay motionless and quiet for a minute, then sat up and began rearranging her clothing.

The expression on her face was anything but pleasant. "Didn't you enjoy it at all?" he asked finally.

"Enjoy it? Certainly not! I'm not supposed to enjoy it!"

Jerome was flabbergasted. The boys he had talked with about such things had never mentioned anything of the sort. In fact, they had all bragged that they were so good at it, the girls always had a good time. "I hear some women do."

"No *lady* would." Her fingers faltered on the row of buttons and her voice trembled. "I'll become accustomed to it. In time."

Silently Jerome dressed and helped her fold the quilt.

13

AUGUST HUNG HOT AND HEAVY OVER THE SMALL town of Cavelier, and the sweltering swamp was hazed with mosquitoes and midge flies. Jerome's working hours were split between learning to operate the shipping business under Arnaud Leslie's tutelage and helping his father wrestle cypress timber from the swamp.

Jerome sat on a felled tree and wiped the sweat from his brow. "Papa, how are you going to manage without me?"

"I'll hire another man, maybe two. With that new order from the coffin company over in Lafayette, we'll have even more business than before, but we'll manage. I'm even buying another team of mules from the Ramsays." He looked questioningly at his son. "Don't you like shipping?"

"It's all right, I suppose. But sometimes I can see a better way to do something, and Mr. Leslie won't even listen to my idea. That's pretty frustrating. If he would let me have my own say, I think I could increase profits by half again what we're making now."

"You always have had good business sense. Lord knows where you got it, though. Except for my daddy, none of the Delacroixs—or the Spartans either—were known for being good businessmen."

"That's not true, Papa. Look at how well Roseland was doing before the war."

"But I managed to lose it, didn't I?"

"Papa, that wasn't your fault. That just couldn't be helped. Besides, you haven't done so bad since then." Jerome nodded in the direction of the mill. "Look at all the improvements you've made. People all over Louisiana are writing to you about timber."

"Well, if nothing else, we Delacroixs know how to survive, son. We've always done what we needed to do."

Jerome was silent a minute. "Papa, can I talk to you? About Susanna, I mean."

"Why, Jerome, don't tell me you need to hear about the birds and the bees," Reuben said with a grin.

"No, no. Nothing like that. Here lately I haven't been seeing much of Susanna, and when I do, she seems out of sorts, but won't tell me why."

"Marriage is a big step, son. Most women get nervous before their weddings."

"But it's almost as if I'm not as important as the ceremony. Do you know what I mean?"

"It's just the excitement, son. Susanna is getting ready for the biggest day of her life. I imagine her mother is working day and night to be sure Susanna's trousseau and hope chest are finished before the wedding. A girl is bound to be edgy at such a time. It's nothing. By the time you're married in October, she will be her sweet self again."

"I suppose you're right." Jerome stood up and reached for his ax. Methodically he lopped off the cypress limbs from the felled tree and stacked the ones big enough for fenceposts in one pile and the smaller ones in a heap to be burned after the next rain.

Something else was bothering him even more than Susanna's preoccupied brusqueness. He was beginning to have serious doubts about whether he loved her. He knew it was his own fault, but he wasn't eager to go visit with her, and he was beginning to find her conversation shallow and dull. He had spent long hours at night trying to convince himself that no lady would be interested in discussing either the sawmill or the riverboats, but he couldn't seem to find any other subject of interest either.

Once the priest married them, Jerome knew he would be married for the rest of his life, and in light of his reservations, that seemed like a very long time indeed. He wanted to tell his father about his doubts, but he couldn't seem to say the words. Not only would his parents be disappointed if he broke his engagement, but there would be a scandal, since everyone in town was expecting the marriage to take place.

Jerome fastened the chain around the stripped log and whistled to the mule. Preoccupied with his concerns, he followed the mule up the bare ridge toward the mill, the animal needing no guidance for it had made that journey more times than Jerome had.

Perhaps, he thought as he maneuvered the log into place with the others, Susanna was also feeling some doubts. That would explain her occasional sharp retorts. She might be wishing for a reprieve herself. The more Jerome thought about it, the more certain he was. As he headed back for another log, he was whistling merrily.

That night Jerome took extra care in dressing, and was scarcely tired at all as he rode into town. He had convinced himself that Susanna was as unhappy with the arrangement as he was, and that she would welcome his suggestion that they postpone the wedding or even cancel it altogether.

He tied his horse and loosened the saddle cinch so that the animal would be more comfortable, and went up the porch steps. On his second knock Marie Leslie opened the door herself and frankly stared at him for a minute before stepping aside and motioning for him to enter.

Although puzzled by her somber expression, Jerome cheerfully said, "Evening, Mrs. Leslie."

"Good evening, Jerome. Susanna is in the parlor." Her voice sounded strained, as if she were suppressing a strong emotion, but she offered no explanation or clue as to what the cause might be.

Jerome looked at her curiously, but was too well-mannered to ask what was wrong. He assumed she and her husband had had an argument. When he went into the parlor, however, he noticed that Susanna's face was puffy from crying. She barely glanced at him before turning her face away. "Susanna? Is something wrong?" When Mrs. Leslie slammed the parlor door closed behind him, he jumped.

He went to Susanna and sat beside her on the settee. "Did you and your mother have words? Where is your father?"

"He's at the gin, thank goodness. Jerome, I have to talk to you about something terribly important." Her voice quavered and her lower lip trembled.

"Is it about the wedding?" Jerome asked, and when she nodded, he put his arms around her and pulled her close. "I've been thinking about that too. Maybe we should postpone it until spring or—"

"Postpone it!" she gasped. "We have to move it up! Jerome, I'm going to have a baby!"

He stared at her in disbelief, his mouth dropping open. "What?" he managed at last.

"A baby!" Susanna spat out. "My life is ruined!"

Jerome released her and sat back in stunned disbelief. "You're going to . . . ? Are you sure?"

"Certainly I'm sure! Would I say such a thing if I wasn't?"

In a loud whisper Jerome pleaded, "But we only did it once! I didn't think that you . . . I mean . . ."

"Well, you were wrong. Now I'm . . . I'm *enceinte,* and we have to get married right away."

He swallowed nervously. "I understand a person can't always be sure so soon. That was only two months ago. Maybe . . ."

"I'm positive! Mama says we can have the priest post the banns right away and be married by the end of the week."

Jerome stood up and paced to the far side of the room and back, before he again looked at her. "Your parents know?"

"Only Mama. If Papa knew, I think he would kill you."

Jerome drew a deep breath, the first breath of any sort he could remember having taken for several minutes. "So that's why you've been so edgy."

"What did you expect? Of course I'm upset. My whole life is ruined."

"No, it isn't. We'll get married right away, and no one has to know why. When the baby comes, we'll say it was born early."

Susanna let out a sigh of relief. "I was so afraid, Jerome. I thought you might leave me like this."

He went back to her and once more put his arms around her, though he felt numb inside. "I would never do such a thing, Susanna. You must have known I would stand beside you."

"After all, it is your baby," she murmured against his shirt front. "It is your fault, after all."

Jerome didn't reply, but he felt as if nothing would ever be right with him again.

14

JESSAMINE GLANCED OVER HER SHOULDER AS SHE hurried to meet Ransome. At the last minute, her mother had decided she must try on the dress they were making for her to wear to Jerome's wedding. Jessamine had been hard pressed not to fidget while Delia and Tabitha first lowered the hem, then raised it again, and finally put it back the way it had been and painstakingly pinned the yards of pale blue silk. She only hoped Ransome would still be there in the secret bower.

The afternoon sun was slanting low in the sky and promising some measure of comparative coolness. To the south, massive clouds were building, and Jessamine knew there would be rain before morning. Summer rain on the bayou, however, only added to the oppressive humidity and did nothing to relieve the heat.

She lifted her full skirts and ran the last few yards, then slipped through the break in the glossy green bushes. The gardenias were in bloom and their heady scent enveloped her along with the cool shade. "Ransome!" she murmured happily as he turned to her and held out his arms. "I'm so glad you waited."

"When I saw the leaf wedged into the bridge railing, I told Father I was going into town and wouldn't be back before dark."

Jessamine laid her cheek on the cotton ruffles of his shirt. His dove-gray coat fit his lean build perfectly, as did his buff-colored trousers. She stroked the fine material of his coat, savoring the expensive texture. Ransome always dressed and conducted himself as a gentleman, in sharp contrast to his obstentatious father.

He held her firmly, his cheek resting on the top of her head; and as he stroked her back with his sensitive hands, Jessamine felt the comforting protection of his strength flow through. "If only Mama and Papa would just get to know you. I'm sure they would see they have the wrong impression of you.''

"Maybe. If I were your parents, I wouldn't like anyone who wanted to take you away.''

"Take me away?''

"I'm no planter, Jessamine. Father treats his workers worse than when they were slaves. He barely pays them enough to live on, and when they can't make it, he lends them money to keep them indebted to him. That way they can't quit their jobs. He even has families living in the old slave quarters, and the conditions back there are becoming unbearable. He won't listen to any of my suggestions, and gets angry if I try to make the workers more content with a bonus or extra measure of grain. Why did we fight the war if we were going to keep the Negroes enslaved under the name of sharecropper? No, I want to go back to New York and get my law degree.''

"Can't you get a law degree somewhere closer?''

"I received a notice that I've been accepted into the Albany Law School. I even think I would be able to work for a firm there after graduation.''

"Albany is so far away.''

"It is a long way from here, but it may as well be in China for all the good it will do me. Mother says Father's health isn't as robust as it seems, and that he needs me to carry some of the load. I don't like living under his roof, but I can't walk out on Mother. Besides, if I'm here, I can watch over her.''

His voice was calm, but there was a grim determination just under the surface.

"Watch over her? What do you mean?''

"Never mind,'' he said as he lifted her chin and smiled down at her. "We have so little time together, let's not waste it with talk of unpleasant things.''

Jessamine smiled, and he bent to kiss the dimple in her cheek. "You look radiant,'' he said as he studied her face.

"I'm in love. I hope that someday you learn to love living here in Louisiana as much as I do.''

"I love you. That's enough for me.'' He kissed her and felt her petal-soft lips part beneath his. As their kiss deepened, his nerves seemed to hum like the honeybees in the camellia blossoms. He clasped Jessamine to his chest and held her tightly.

"How can we bear to wait for something that may never come? Marry me, Jessamine. Marry me now. Today."

Her anguish shone plainly in the silver of her eyes. She drew his face down for her kiss. "I love you, Ransome. I love you. Just give me a little longer to convince my parents."

He groaned in his frustration and pulled her tight against him, as his fingers tangled in the heavy coil of hair on the nape of her neck. Once the hairpins were loose, her sable tresses tumbled down her back to below her waist. Ransome had not seen Jessamine's hair down since she had become an adult, and the sensuousness of the dark waves triggered a hunger in him that only Jessamine could quench.

For a moment she studied his eyes, her thick hair lifting in the breeze like a cape; then she began to slowly unbutton the front of her curry-hued dress.

"What are you doing?" Ransome whispered, knowing all the while the answer to that question by the expression on her face.

"What would you guess I'm doing?" she teased as her slender fingers released one small jet button after another, first exposing a wedge of creamy skin, then the round curve of her breasts.

"Jessamine, don't tempt me like this. I'm only human."

"I'm not tempting you. I'm giving myself to you." Her white lace camisole was now visible.

Ransome was spellbound. This was something he had dreamed about and ached to experience with her for a long time. Now that it was actually happening, he could only stare.

Jessamine opened the princess-style gown to her waist, then stopped. She wanted him, but she wasn't going to force herself on him. Only a moment passed before Ransome took his cue. Slowly he lifted his hand and ran his finger down the open bodice, grazing her warm skin with the most gentle of caresses. His dark eyes followed his finger, savoring the beauty of her exposed cleavage. Gently he caught her wrist and drew her closer. For another moment he studied the gray depths of her eyes. He had no doubt from what he saw there that she was willing and unashamed.

When he lowered his head, Jessamine tilted her face to receive his kiss. Again his hand traveled the line of her open dress, this time letting the backs of his fingers glide over her smooth skin. When he reached the remaining buttons, he released them. Moving almost reverently, he brushed the dress from her shoulders, and it pooled about her feet like dark gold. With slow deliberation, he untied the satin ribbon that held her petticoat, and it joined the gown on the ground.

He drew back to look at her as his pulses hammered. She was more beautiful than he had even dreamed. Her breasts were full and her nipples pouted against her lacy camisole, the tail of which was neatly tucked into the waistband of her drawers. A pale blue ribbon that matched the trimming around the legs of her drawers had been used to tie the garment at her waist. Her thin cotton stockings were rolled and tied just below her knees. Jessamine let him gaze at her, with only minimal modesty.

Not taking his eyes from her, he removed his coat and tossed it aside, and without hesitation unbuttoned his shirt and cast it aside as well.

Ransome's muscles weren't as heavy as her brother's, but as she rubbed her face over the smooth, hard expanse of his chest, she noted that they were whipcord taut. She passed her hand over the swell of his chest, where his flat nipples were as hard as her own, and down the satin ridges of his stomach.

"Are you certain, Jessamine?"

"Yes," she whispered. "Yes."

He knelt and removed her shoes and rolled away her stockings before removing his own shoes. Moving gently so he wouldn't frighten her, he stood and pulled her camisole over her head. "You aren't wearing lacings," he said as he stroked the firm skin of her waist and drank in the charming sight of her breasts.

"I've lost weight lately, and besides, I hate lacings. They pinch."

"Then never wear them again." He raised his hand to cup the rounded fullness of her breast, and she caught her breath at the sensation of his hand being where no one had ever touched her before. Her nipple grew achingly hard against his palm, and she swayed toward him.

Ransome kissed her as he untied the ribbon at her waist and pushed her lower garment down over the swell of her hips. He cupped her buttocks in his palms and drew her to him as his kisses grew hungrier and more demanding.

Jessamine moaned as if she were trying to hold back her passion.

"Love me," he whispered, a mere breath away from her lips. "Show me your love, darling."

Awkwardly at first, Jessamine fumbled with the buttons that held his trousers, and as she did so, her breasts brushed twin fires across his chest and lean belly. Finally she conquered the buttons and impatiently pushed away his trousers and undergarment.

Ransome stepped out of his clothes, and held his breath as Jessamine surveyed him as intently as he had studied her moments earlier. Then a small, seductive smile lifted her lips, and she came back into his embrace.

They lay down on the billowing grass in the center of the gardenia-scented enclosure. In the trees beyond, a mockingbird sang, and beyond the leafy walls the creek that fed the bayou splashed and bubbled. Pale sunlight dappled Jessamine's ivory skin, and the slight breeze teased her nipples to tautness.

"I've never seen anyone so beautiful in all my life," Ransome said huskily. "You're perfect." He spread her hair like a cloud over the grass.

"I was just thinking the same thing about you."

"You're not afraid of me? Of what we're about to do?"

"I love you, Ransome. I want to give myself to you and to give you pleasure with me."

He bent over her. "You'll have pleasure too."

"I've heard some women do. Do you think I may be one?"

He grinned. "I guarantee it."

As he kissed her, his fingers traced lazy circles on her sun-kissed breasts; then he gently rolled one nipple between his thumb and forefinger. Jessamine murmured and arched toward him as she caressed his bare back and narrow hips.

Ransome left pearls of kisses down her graceful neck, and lower, until he reached her breast. Taking his time, he licked her nipple, circling it with his tongue and flicking it to dewy hardness before taking it into his mouth and sucking sensuously as Jessamine moaned with pleasure.

She had never felt or even expected such a delight. Passion was quickening her pulse as his lips and tongue taught her delights she had never suspected. His large hands spanned the swell of her hips, lifting her to him and cradling her with restrained power.

Slowly, as if every inch of her pleased him, Ransome stroked his hand lower but when he began to caress the sensitive skin of her inner thighs, she stiffened. Fear gripped her as she recalled from overheard conversations among the kitchen maids at Roseland that it hurt a woman to be taken by a man, especially the first time.

Ransome immediately stopped, sensing her discomfort. For several moments he spoke to her, murmuring words of love and reassuring her that he would be careful not to hurt her. When she relaxed again, he covered her lips with his own and resumed stroking her satiny thighs, moving ever so slowly upward until his hand reached the dark nest of curls. Gently he urged her to part her legs, and she willingly complied. His fingers explored her femininity, and from her responses to his touch he learned what pleased her most. She felt a slick wetness and a tight centering of pleasures as he continued his unhurried exploration.

Jessamine felt she should at least pretend embarrassment, but her desires overwhelmed her. She wanted more but wasn't sure exactly what it was that she desired. But Ransome seemed to know perfectly as his fingers stroked the small bud that was the most sensitive part of her entire body. A rapturous feeling began to spread through her with amazing quickness.

Jessamine murmured his name as he brought her to greater and greater heights. All at once her world seemed to explode into brilliant prisms of sheer pleasure, and she held him tightly.

With her eyes filled with wonder, Jessamine looked up at Ransome, wanting to ask what had happened to her and not knowing the words to describe it. He grinned down at her and again started to stroke her.

When the breathtaking ecstasy again started to build, Ransome knelt between her thighs. She cried out as he began to enter her, but he stopped and soothed her fears before continuing. Slowly, gently, he worked his way into her, filling her, helping her become a woman. His woman. For a moment he lay still, letting her become accustomed to him. Then his fingers again found the seat of her desire as he started to move rhythmically within her.

At first Jessamine was uncomfortable; then his body and his knowing fingers reawakened her desires. She moved with him, guided by love's instinct, and when she again felt the explosion of pure love, he clasped her tightly and thrust himself to his own completion.

For a long while they lay in each other's arms, not speaking, for words were unnecessary. Jessamine stroked his firm jaw and ran her fingers through his auburn hair.

"We belong to each other now," he said softly. "I'm your man and you're my woman."

"I love you," she murmured. "I never knew how wonderful this could be."

"I didn't hurt you?"

She shook her head, the mild discomfort forgotten. "Is it always like this between a man and woman?"

"No. Not always. Our love makes the difference."

"Someday we'll be married," she whispered as she nuzzled his ear. "We'll sleep like this every night and wake up in each other's arms every morning."

"We can get married now, if you'll just say the word."

"Where could we live? With your parents? With mine?"

"We could go to my Aunt Polly, and in no time we would have a place of our own."

"It would break my parents' hearts to see me move North. Especially so very far away. And with a MacKinley. Will you wait for me just a bit longer?"

"I'll wait for you forever if I need to. I won't give you up for either of our families' sakes."

She smiled. "Would you give me up for any reason at all?"

"Only if I knew you didn't love me and that you no longer wanted me."

"Then you'll never give me up at all, because I'll love you forever."

They kissed and held each other in a gentle embrace that was born of love and satisfied passion. "Look, it's getting late."

Jessamine rolled over to look up at the sky. The thunderheads were nearer and glowed pink against the deeper gold to the west. Overhead the sky was deepening to indigo and the half-moon was already above the trees. "I have to go," she said reluctantly.

"I know," he said with a sigh before he kissed her again. "I wish you never had to leave me."

"Someday I won't."

They dressed in silence, each dreading the moment of departure. Despite Jessamine's protests, Ransome walked her back through the darkening woods.

"Don't come any farther," she warned as they neared the edge of the trees. "Someone might see you."

He drew her to him for another kiss and smiled down at her. "I love you."

"I love you." She tiptoed up to kiss his cheek, then turned and walked briskly away before she lost her resolve. She felt different, inside and out. Her breasts were tender from his caresses, and she still felt the impression of his loving deep within her. She hoped her cheeks weren't as pink as they felt, and that the sparkle in her eyes wouldn't betray her.

When she entered the house, no one except Doll seemed to even be curious about her long absence. Doll was setting the table and Jessamine pretended to inspect what she was doing in order to be near her friend.

"What have you been up to?" she whispered.

"Oh, doll, I love him so! He wants me to elope with him."

"You can't do that! It would break your Mama's heart."

"What about my heart? You don't know what it's like to love a man you can't have."

Doll made no comment and continued to lay out the flatware beside the plates.

"He wants to go back to Albany, New York, and become a lawyer."

"What about Roseland? I saw Mr. MacKinley in town the other day, and if you ask me, he's not healthy. He can't run a place the size of Roseland without Ransome."

"Of course he can. Their overseer is Oliver Gibbons, and he knows more about cotton farming than any other man around here."

"Just the same, the old man didn't look right. He had a funny color around him."

"A what? I don't know what you're talking about."

Doll closed her mouth firmly. She rarely made a slip like that. Her strange ability to "know" was as confusing to her as it was to her friends and family.

"I don't want to move North, so I told Ransome I want to wait until we can make peace between our parents. Then we can stay here in Louisiana."

Doll gave her a pitying look. Couldn't Jessamine see how unlikely that was? Doll needed no special knowing to realize the feud went too deep to be resolved with words, or even a marriage.

The front door opened and Jerome came in. His face looked pale and drawn, and Doll instinctively took a step toward him.

"You're home awfully early for a courting man," Reuben said in surprise.

"You and Susanna haven't had words, have you?" Delia asked as she looked up from her sewing.

"No." Jerome looked at his parents, then through the doorway to Doll. Looking back at his mother, he said in a tight voice, "We've moved the wedding date up."

Doll carefully laid the last of the silverware in place.

"We're going to get married right away. Next Friday, in fact."

Delia rose and put her hand on Jerome's arm. "Why so soon?"

He shrugged and managed a smile. "It was her mother's idea. It seems she and Mr. Leslie were married on that day, and since Susanna's trousseau is finished, there's no reason to wait."

Reuben's face broke into a smile, and he clapped his son on the back. "That's good news, son! See? I told you Susanna wasn't about to change her mind. You were worried for no reason at all."

Jerome looked back at the doorway and his eyes again met Doll's. She turned away and glided silently out of the room and into the night.

15

DOLL FARMER STOOD ALONE IN THE COVER OF THE woods across the road from the Church of St. Mary of Lourdes. The rose-red brick building that housed the Catholic church was larger and much prettier than the whitewashed Baptist church down the swamp road where the blacks attended services. Until they were freed, Doll and her parents had sat in the balcony of this church every Sunday morning along with the other slaves whose masters allowed them a religion. Today Doll wouldn't have entered that church on pain of death because even at that very moment Father Theriot was uniting Jerome Delacroix and Susanna Leslie in unbreakable bonds of matrimony.

Doll had known the moment was coming, but she had hoped that by October she would have gained the strength to accept it. The sudden move of the ceremony to August had left her unprepared. For days she had felt hot tears rising and had either choked them back or fled to the root cellar or barn to shed them. She had avoided Jerome to the point that Jessamine had even come out of her own daze of love to ask what was wrong between them. Luckily for Doll, all their parents were much too busy to notice. But Jerome had looked hurt whenever he saw her leaving a room as he entered.

She put her hand on the rough bark of a sweet-gum tree as peals of music rang forth from the church. It was done now. Instead of the knifing pain she had felt all week, Doll was mercifully numb. A great stillness had grown inside her, and she felt almost resigned. She wasn't sure why she had come. Perhaps to see Jerome one last time before he was married, or perhaps to prove to herself that the wedding had indeed occurred.

As the first of the people began to come out of the church, Doll eased back into the woods. She didn't want to

147

be seen, and she certainly didn't want to see the new couple.

She made her way through the tangle of sweet gums and pin oaks and walked down the dusty road toward home. At least, she thought, she would be spared the daily sight of the newlyweds, for Jerome had already moved his belongings to the big white house in town that had been provided for them by Susanna's parents as a wedding present.

By the time Doll reached home, twilight was gathering. She had never been alone on Ten Acres, and it felt odd not to see or hear other people. Her parents were at the Leslies' home, and probably wouldn't be home before noon the next day, as the Leslies had hired them to help serve food and clean up after the wedding party. A small army of servants had been required to roast the pig and put together the wedding feast and to serve it. A wedding—especially one between a Leslie and a Delacroix—was not to be taken lightly.

Doll took the lantern from its peg just inside the barn door and sloshed it to be sure it was full of coal oil. She took some matches from the tin box beside the door and set out for the swamp.

At the small pier below the sawmill, Doll set the lantern down and carefully stepped into Reuben Delacroix's pirogue that he kept moored there. Gingerly she eased herself onto the low board seat, and when the tiny boat stopped rocking precariously from side to side, she placed the lantern in front of her and pulled the paddle from beneath the seat. She cast off the mooring rope and used the paddle to push away from the pier. For the first time since deciding to do this, Doll had a twinge of foreboding. She wasn't at all familiar with the swamp, and she didn't know if old Asiza was still alive, or whether she even existed at all. However, with grim determination she paddled down the bayou and into the swamp.

The tall cypresses laced their fernlike leaves above her head and black willows dotted the bank along with tupelo gums. The sunlight was weak here, even on the brightest of days, and the low sun scarcely penetrated the tangle of Spanish moss above and the bushes below. A bright green film of duckweed covered the water's surface and silenced the sound of the pirogue.

The current in the sluggish bayou was barely discernible, but Doll knew better than to try to use it as a direction marker, for the bayou's movements, such as they were, depended on the ebb and flow of the not-too-distant Gulf of Mexico. In the morning it might be drifting one way, and by the evening it would have reversed. She would have to depend on her intuition to guide her.

A red-winged blackbird clung to a slender reed by the bank and a snowy egret craned his neck to watch her approach. When she drew too near for his comfort, the graceful white bird flew away with a muffled flapping of wings. In one of the numerous inlets, a bull alligator slipped silently beneath the black water, and Doll warily followed his progress by the slow-moving ripple in the surface until he swam too deep to stir the water. She swallowed nervously. The alligator had been almost as long as the pirogue, and they had been known to overturn much larger boats than hers.

As she ducked under a veil of gray-green Spanish moss hanging from a low limb, she remembered stories her father had told her of cottonmouth moccasins dropping from such limbs out over the water into passing boats, and she hoped that wouldn't happen to her. Algae-and-slime-encrusted logs that poked out of the water were crowded with as many turtles as their surface could hold. Resurrection fern blanketed the enormous sloping tree trunks and branches.

Doll considered going back before it became too dark to see, but she knew that only one person in all the world could help her now. Asiza's charms were known to be very potent. Lighting the lantern against the pending darkness, Doll forced herself to continue her journey.

In spots the pirogue seemed to be sliding over mud rather than water, but in others, she had a sense of very deep water beneath the thin bottom of the boat. As darkness fell, the frogs tuned up in an almost deafening chorus. Clouds of lightning bugs flashed along the bank like stars lost from the heavens.

Often Doll paused and let the boat drift as she held the lantern high, trying to determine the path of the main bayou, but the light was little help, as it pierced only a few feet into the darkness. Sometimes one way looked all too much like another. A cold sweat broke out on Doll's brow as she heard the scream of a bobcat not too far away. Panic rose, and she closed her eyes and drew several deep breaths.

All at once the knowing was upon her. Calm settled over her like a mantle, and she turned the pirogue away from the main arm of the bayou. As if she were following a well-known path, Doll guided the small boat through the heavy darkness. Moss brushed her face, but she no longer had any fear. She knew she was safe. She knew where she was going.

After half an hour she saw a light far off in the swamp. Doll smiled and paddled with long, sure strokes. Several minutes later, she slid silently up to a pier that barely cleared the water. She looped the mooring rope over a piling and stepped out.

A few yards away, on a *chenier* covered with massive live oaks, was a cabin. Although Doll had made no sound that could be heard over the orchestra of frogs, the door opened and a woman stepped out onto the small porch and said, ''So. You are here at last.''

As Doll went closer, she held her lantern out ahead of her for a better look at the woman, and couldn't help staring at her. Asiza was big. Not just tall, but massive and heavy-boned. Her skin was not merely black, but was blue-black, and her features were patrician and haughty. She was clad in white from her tightly wrapped turban to the hem of her loose caftan. Large bangles of gold hung from her ears and neck, and she wore several gold bracelets on each arm.

She looked Doll over from head to foot, and silently stepped aside to let her enter. ''Welcome to my home,'' she said in her oddly accented voice.

The house contained only one room. Two chairs were drawn up to a crude table, a low cot was on one wall, and a hammock had been suspended from one wall to the other. Pots and baskets of all sizes and descriptions were scattered about the room.

Bunches of fragrant herbs hung from the rafters, and a low fire was burning on the hearth.

''You sound as if you expected me,'' Doll said after she had looked around for a moment.

''I did. I heard you deciding to come here days ago. Then I heard you get in the pirogue and come into the swamp. I led you here.''

''How could you hear me?'' Doll protested as she warily watched the woman. ''Nobody led me here. I found it on my own.''

A wide smile spread across Asiza's face, showing her strong white teeth. ''Nobody does nothing on their own. Didn't you feel me pulling you this way?''

Slowly Doll nodded.

"Well, then. There you are," Asiza dipped a gourd into a pot, simmering on the hearth, and poured the contents into a wooden bowl. She held it out to Doll.

Doll's eyes widened, and when she started to shake her head, Asiza chuckled. "It's just crawdad gumbo, child."

Feeling foolish, Doll took the bowl, and Asiza filled one for herself. They sat on opposite sides of the table, staring at each other. Now that she was here, Doll couldn't seem to form a thought, let alone a word.

"What am I to call you, child?"

"Doll. I'm Doll Farmer."

"Doll." Asiza beamed at her as if she had discovered a treasure.

"You're Asiza," Doll said in an awed voice. "You really exist."

"Yes, I really do. Tell me, Doll, why have you come way back here in the swamp in the dark of the night?"

"I need a charm."

"I see. A love spell to bind a young man to you."

"No. No, I want to break a love. One that can never be."

Asiza looked at her with greater interest. "Someone who loves you, maybe?"

"No, it's for someone I love."

"I don't get much call for charms to break love. Most folks would want one to override the young man's will and bring him to heel. But you want to set him free."

"He's already free. I want to free myself."

Asiza put aside her bowl of gumbo. "Love is too rare a gift to break."

"Then you can't help me?"

"I didn't say that. Most folks want charms or amulets. Not freedom."

"You mean other people find their way here?"

Asiza chuckled softly. "You'd be surprised, child. You would be for a fact. But I don't get many that have the knowing that you have inside."

Doll's eyes widened in astonishment at the woman's use of the word she had always used to describe her strangeness.

"Yes, child, there are others like us. When I was younger than you, I found my Asiza. She taught me all she knew. I been waiting for you for years. Calm yourself. I can hear your thoughts flapping like a cage full of birds. Old Asiza's not fixing to turn you into a toad or something.''

Doll swallowed nervously. ''I don't want to have anything to do with voodoo magic. I just want a charm.''

''I don't do no voodoo. That's devil meanness. I don't need it. I got the power without it.''

Asiza went to a shelf and got a black bowl. Carefully she wiped it out with a clean towel and ceremoniously poured some water into it from a cracked porcelain pitcher. She carefully placed the bowl of water in the center of the table between the two of them.

Asiza's bracelets clinked musically as she swept her hands, palms down, over the bowl. She closed her eyes and let her body sway as she concentrated all her energy into the water. Opening her eyes, Asiza gazed into the bowl and said softly, ''I see. No wonder you have to break your love of him.''

''What? What do you see in there?'' Doll asked with some alarm.

''Calm, calm. I can't help you if I don't see what needs to be done.'' She nodded. ''Jerome, he is called. Jerome Delacroix. And he is white.''

''Yes,'' Doll whispered, her voice barely audible through her dry throat.

''He got married today. That's how come you're here.''

Doll nodded, her face entranced. ''How do you know that?''

''I see it. There. In the water.''

''I don't see anything.''

''That's because you're looking with your eyes.'' As Asiza tapped her forehead, she said, ''You got to see truth here. But there's something that you don't know about this Jerome.''

''I know everything about him. I've known him all my life. He loves Susanna Leslie, and he married her today just like you said. I want him to be happy, but I can't for the life of me see why he loves her.''

''She's *enceinte*. He had to marry her.''

''No! You're wrong. This wedding has been planned for months.'' Doll looked away from Asiza for a while, then turned to meet her eyes again. ''She is?''

''She is for a fact.''

The dull pain of loss that Doll had felt since the day

she learned Jerome was engaged returned, and she stood to go. "If you can't help me, I should leave."

"Sit, sit. Have I waited all these years for someone with the knowing, only to have her leave with nothing? I can't break your love, child, because whatever we do always comes home. I could teach you to love another young man or to warm a man to love you, but real love is too precious to put aside."

"Then what will I do?"

"Your ability to love is a gift from God. In time you will know what to do, but first I must teach you many things and help you develop your special talents. Perhaps your purpose is to learn to heal the sick, or to be a wise woman, or to be like those prophets the white church talks about." Asiza took Doll's wrist and pulled her gently back into the chair. "You come to me often, and I'll teach you all I know. You'll find your true talent."

"How can I come back? I almost couldn't slip out this time."

"You'll find a way. You'll find it because you already know what you are."

Doll stared at the woman.

"Now, look into the water. Not at the surface or at the bowl beneath it, but into the middle of the water." Asiza's smooth voice was mesmerizing. "Look into the water. Be the water."

And Doll found that she could.

16

THE OCTOBER DAY THAT HAD ORIGINALLY BEEN SET for Jerome and Susanna's wedding brought a fresh coolness to Cavelier. The sweet gums turned shades from gold to red to russet and the willows became showers of pale yellow as the limbs gave up their leaves in preparation for winter. Jerome looked at the calendar beside his desk and the red circle he had put around the fourth, wishing he had somehow been able to avoid this marriage. In the past six weeks more had changed about Susanna than her expanding girth.

The office was quiet as he was the only one who hadn't gone home from work. Outside his window he could see the silvery water of the bayou and the dark silhouette of their company's small riverboat that would be loaded the next morning. He went to the cabinet and took out a brown bottle of whiskey, almost ceremoniously pouring himself a small glassful. He had tried to convince himself that this nightly ritual was necessary to warm his body for the ride home, but he knew the nights weren't that cold, and he lived only a few blocks away. Tossing the amber liquid down his throat, he poured another and returned to his desk.

Slumping into his leather desk chair, he shuffled through the neat stack of papers on his desk. The words "Roseland" and "MacKinley" appeared on many of them. As much as it galled Jerome to ship Ian MacKinley's baled cotton, he had to admit the man supplied his father-in-law's companies with a great deal of business. Fortunately his own dealings were always with the overseer, Oliver Gibbons, and not with the old man.

Jerome looked at the gold watch he carried in his vest pocket and drained the rest of the whiskey. He was later than usual and Susanna would be waiting. With the ebony cane in hand that he used for protection when he walked home late, he locked the offices for the night and stepped out into the cool, damp air. The adjoining wharf was stacked with burlap-wrapped bales of cotton that had been ware-housed while waiting for the level of the bayou to rise with the fall rains so the boat could make its journey toward the Mississippi more safely. Each bale bore the stamp of the Leslie gins, Roseland's mark, and the symbol that meant New Orleans. Words were not used because none of the dockhands could read. If only, he thought, words would not be necessary when he reached home.

He crossed the street and headed toward the residential part of town. Although the streets were all but deserted, he avoided the deep shadows, because even though he carried no payroll or other valuables, a thief wouldn't know that. He walked this way so often he could have done so blindfolded, taking his cues from the baying of the Macys' coon hounds and the yapping of the Broussards' terrier. He missed the animals on Ten Acres. Aside from the necessary horses, Susanna was insistent that they have no animals about. Not even a cat to catch rats in the barn or a yard dog to protect the place.

Jerome turned into his yard and pulled the wrought-iron gate shut behind him. The house was large and square, and seemed to be hulking among the shadows of azaleas, camellias, and magnolias. The only light on the porch was that from the wide front windows. Even though he had asked her several times, Susanna had not put out a lamp for him. Jerome climbed the steep front steps and put his hand on the cold door handle.

Inside there was no smell of dinner cooking. Susanna had forgotten to give orders to the cook again. He hung up his coat and hat on the hall tree and put his cane in the umbrella rack. Only when he went into the parlor did he announce that he was home.

Susanna looked up from the tray she was painting and frowned. ''You're late again.'' She tossed the brush down on the canvas-covered table with the others that had dried hard with paint.

''I had a lot of work to do. The Roseland cotton goes out tomorrow.''

''And yesterday it was barrels of cane syrup from the Broussards, and before that a load of mules from the Ramseys. Papa never works this late, so why do you?''

''He does during ginning season.''

Susanna's lower lip protruded, and she rose with a flounce. ''I wish we had never gotten married. There's a

party tonight at the Duprees', but I can't dance like this."
She gestured at her rounding stomach.

"The baby will be born in time, and then you'll feel
like dancing again."

"No, I won't. I'll be an old wife, tied down with
household duties."

Jermome gave her a long look before he said, "What
are we having for dinner?"

"Cold ham left over from last night. I was so busy
with this tray that I forgot to tell Dulcie to cook dinner.
Honestly, Jerome, you'd think that girl could remember
some things for herself."

"Telling her what to cook is your job. You know that.
Dulcie can't be expected to know what you want to eat. The
few times she tried to work on her own, you got angry with
her. We're lucky she hasn't quit."

"Pooh! I've been thinking of firing her anyway. Those
cuffies have gotten so uppity."

Jerome knew he was being baited, so he ignored her.
He looked down at the gaudy tin tray on which Susanna had
painted a bouquet of flowers, but they were so poorly done,
he couldn't recognize a single variety. "Nice," he said
dryly.

"It should be. It took me all day." She ran her hands
over the heavy nankeen fabric of her dress. "Before long
I will have to have this gown resewn. It's getting tight
again."

Jerome felt guilty as he went to her. She was so young,
after all, and he doubted their explanations for marrying
early had fooled anyone. No doubt she still felt bad, and
now was becoming bulky as well. He put his hands on her
waist and she moved away, but not before he felt the ridges
beneath the dress. "Susanna! You're using lacings!"

"Well, I had to go out with Mama earlier, and I
couldn't very well leave the house without my lacings."

"The doctor told you to leave them off until after the
baby is born."

"What does he know? It won't hurt anything for me
to look nice."

"It may hurt the baby!"

"Nonsense. Mama says that's simply ridiculous."

Jerome pulled her around to face him. "You'll do as
the doctor says. We aren't going to chance harming our baby
just so your dress will fit!"

"Mama also says I shouldn't have to do . . . that . . . anymore. Not now that I'm beginning to get larger."

"We've discussed this before, Susanna. The doctor says you're perfectly healthy and we can make love for several months yet."

"Hush! What if Dulcie heard you?" Susanna glared at him. "If you were any kind of a gentleman, you'd respect my wishes and move into another room."

"Is that what you want? Not only for me not to touch you, but to not even sleep in the same bed?"

Susanna looked down at her clasped fingers, then back at him petulantly. "Yes. Do you think I want you to see me dressing and undressing every day? My parents have always had separate rooms."

"Mine haven't."

She tossed her head. "My family doesn't live in an old cabin by the swamp, either."

Jerome clamped his mouth shut. In the past few weeks Susanna had frequently made cutting remarks about his family and their reduced means. "Before the war you'd have considered yourself lucky to land a Delacroix!"

"Would I?" she asked sarcastically. "I don't consider myself very lucky now."

Jerome turned on his heel and stalked out of the room. How had he ever thought she was sweet and delicate? She was a shrew if there ever was one!

He took the entire drawer that held his shirts and carried it into the room across the hall. Yanking out an empty drawer, he dumped the contents in and slammed it before going back after another. As he was carrying the last of his belongings out of Susanna's room, he paused, then went to the drawer where she kept her undergarments. Her other lacings were jumbled there along with her camisoles and drawers. Jerome grabbed up all the lacings, then angrily stared at the bed for a moment before striding out.

When he was in his new room, he thrust the lacings well up under his mattress where Susanna wasn't likely to find them. After the baby was born she could have them back, but not before.

As he gazed out at the night, he wished he had another glass of whiskey. Only his stubbornness kept him from going downstairs to get one. Susanna might drive him from her room, but she would never drive him to become a drunk. He had far too much pride for that.

17

DOLL WENT OFTEN TO SEE ASIZA. ONCE SHE KNEW what trees to look for and the small signs of the swamp, she lost her fear of it, though not her respect. The swamp was still dangerous and could trap the unwary without warning.

Asiza always knew when Doll would arrive and would be waiting for her at the dock or on the high porch. Doll never discovered how Asiza knew to expect her, but it happened without fail. Although Asiza's tiny house was now familiar to her, and although Asiza had taught her as much each visit as Doll's head could hold, Doll was still in awe of the mysterious woman.

Doll guided the pirogue beside the dock and got out with a familiar step. Suddenly she stopped, frozen by what she was seeing. Asiza was sitting on the steps to her house, and not three yards away was the biggest bobcat Doll had ever seen. The old woman was calmly smoking her pipe as she spoke in a low voice to the cat. Then the cat looked in Doll's direction, gave a low growl, and padded silently into the swamp.

"I never saw a tame bobcat!" Doll said as she cautiously approached the woman. "How did you train him like that?"

"He's not tame, him. He just happened into the yard."

Doll's eyes grew round. "Then why didn't he run away when he saw you or attack you?"

"He didn't feel no fear in me, child. You know how I taught you to put your mind into the bowl of water? Well, you can do the same thing with an animal or anything else, if you don't hold nothing but love in your heart."

Doubtfully Doll looked in the direction the bobcat had taken. "I'll never be as wise as you, Asiza. Not if I live to be a hundred."

Asiza emitted a characteristic chuckle. "Is that how old they say I am? Well, they're wrong."

Doll studied her mentor closely. Asiza could be either a young woman who looked old or an old woman who looked young. She was truly ageless. "My pa said his parents told him about you. How old are you?"

She shook her head. "I don't rightly know. I came here as a child from Haiti and was set free before I was as old as you are. I don't keep track of the years. Don't see no reason to. The seasons come and they go like they always have. Some days I feel like I'm as ancient as this swamp, sometimes I'm as new as a robin's egg."

"Why were you set free?"

"I saved my mistress's life. We was out in the woods and come upon a pack of wolves. You don't see many 'round here these days, but back then they was a real problem. I did what you just saw me do with that bobcat and sent them away." She thought back a minute. "The day I was set free, I took the name Asiza. That's a Dahomey word for a spirit that lives way back in the forests. I came here and built my house with the help of an old hermit that used to live near here. I been here ever since."

Asiza reached into the pocket of her flowing white robe and brought out an amulet made of bright beads and feathers. "I made this for you. There's not a French or English word that says it right, but it means bring-love."

Doll tried to hand it back. "I told you I don't want a love spell put on Jerome."

Asiza refused to take it. "Then don't use it. But you need to know how. Once you have a power, it's yours, and you can use it or not, but it's still your power. Don't turn down knowledge just because you don't think you need it right now."

Reluctantly Doll nodded. She knew Asiza was right. But she was afraid that she might not be so self-sacrificing if she had a charm to make Jerome love her.

"Yes," Asiza said with a smile, as if Doll had spoken aloud. "We all got to wrestle with our demons, don't we?"

Doll nodded and closed her fingers around the charm.

18

"YOU DON'T NEED NO PLACE OF YOUR OWN," SAM said firmly.

"Yes, I do, Pa. I'm a grown woman now. I need to have my own place."

Tabitha shook her head in bewilderment. "Where you get such ideas, girl? A place of your own? Whoever heard of such?"

"Look, Ma." Doll pulled a folded square of paper from her pocket. "I bought four acres of land out behind the back of Ten Acres. This is the deed. I own it."

Slowly Tabitha took the paper and looked at it uncomprehendingly, then handed it to Sam. "What do you mean you bought land, Doll?"

"I've been putting money back for a long time now. This land is on the swamp and only cost ten dollars an acre. I bought it free and clear. All I need is for Pa to help me build a house."

"You want to live on the swamp?" Sam exclaimed. "Are you simple-headed? Don't nobody want to live on the swamp."

"It was all I could afford. It has enough dry ground for a garden and a pasture for a mule and a cow. It has a high spot on it with some big live oaks where I plan to build a house." One reason she had chosen this spot was that it reminded her of Asiza's place. "It's just down the bayou a little way. We'll still see each other when I come in to work."

"Is somebody fixing to set you up as his fancy woman?" Sam demanded suspiciously.

"No! Pa, you know better than that."

"I ain't never heard of no woman wanting to live off by herself unless she had a good reason."

Doll lifted her head defiantly. "I want to, and I'm nobody's fancy woman." She met his eyes to show him her determination.

160

Tabitha handed the deed back to her. "Why didn't you come to us and talk about this before you spent all that money? I just can't understand what's gotten into you."

"I knew you and Pa would try to talk me out of it, and I knew I was going to do it anyway." She knelt beside her mother's chair and looked up at her, imploring her to understand. "Ma, can't you see that I can't be content to live in the back room all my life? It's time for me to grow up."

"It's time for you to get married," Tabitha retorted. "Who wants to marry a woman that would go off and live by herself in the swamp? When you get married, you'll go live with your husband, and the money you spent on this swampland will be wasted."

"I'm not going to get married, Ma."

Tabitha looked at Sam, then back at Doll. Again she shook her head slowly. "I can't figure you out. When you get old and sick, who's gonna take care of you? A woman needs a man."

"I'll take care of myself, Ma." She stood and looked at her father. "Will you help me build it, Pa, or should I ask the men down at the church to help me out?"

"And have everybody think we don't take care of our own? I'll build you the house, but I'm telling you I don't want to."

Doll smiled. "Thank you, Pa. I know just what I want. I want one big room in front like this one, and two little rooms in the back. Nothing fancy. And maybe a barn with room for a mule and a cow."

"And I guess you want a feed lot and a smokehouse too?"

"I don't need a smokehouse. Not right away." She went to Sam and hugged him. "I love you, Pa."

Sam grimaced and shifted his weight as he always did when he felt he had given in too easily on an issue. "I'll talk to Mr. Reuben and see about getting the lumber to build it strong so you won't blow away in the first storm." He looked at Tabitha with a drawn expression that asked her where they had gone wrong in raising their daughter.

"Not get married," Tabitha grumbled. "Who ever heard of such a thing!" She scowled at her daughter. "You better get up to the main house. Miss Jessamine was asking for you a while ago."

"She's my age, Ma, and she isn't married."

Tabitha snorted. "She's also white. The same rules don't go for them."

Doll left before Tabitha could say more. Recently her mother had begun to voice her dislikes of the whites all too often for Doll's comfort. She had not lived the life her mother had, and had a great deal of difficulty understanding her bias. The older Doll had become, the more she realized that her attitude toward the whites was perhaps unique, possibly because she was so nearly white herself. To her, they were no better or worse than anyone else. They were just people, most of whom had more money, but people nevertheless.

She found Jessamine in the springhouse, one of the few places where they could talk with little likelihood of being overheard. "I was beginning to think you weren't coming," Jessamine said. "Mama will be looking for me soon." She pulled her shawl more closely about her against the coolness of the springhouse.

"I had to talk to Ma and Pa. Look." She pulled out the deed and handed it to Jessamine.

"You bought the land? You really did it?"

Doll nodded with barely suppressed excitement. "It's the four acres I showed you back beyond the ridge. And I finally talked Pa into building me a house, too."

"Did you! I'm so happy for you. A place of your own! I have to admit I'm a bit jealous. Sometimes it seems as if I'll live here with my parents forever."

"Half the beaux in town would love to change that," Doll teased.

"You know how I feel about that. I'll have Ransome or I won't marry at all. But it won't come to that. I can see Mama starting to get nervous already. I've refused to walk out with any young man for months, and she's afraid her stubbornness will cause me to be an old maid. Any day now she will start convincing Papa to let me marry whomever I want."

"You seem so sure of yourself."

"I am. There hasn't been an old maid in the family in four generations, and Mama doesn't want me to be the first. You just watch and see. By this time next year I'll be Mrs. Ransome MacKinley."

"I hope you're right." Doll turned to rearrange the pats of butter wrapped in cheesecloth on the shelf over the stream that ran through the building. "Have you seen Jerome lately? He looked thin when he was here last."

"We went in to see them last Sunday after church. Doll, you wouldn't believe what a poor housekeeper Susanna is. There was a film of dust on everything, and I'll bet the floor hadn't been swept in days. She asked us to stay for supper, but by the way she said it, we could tell she didn't mean it."

"I had hoped they would be happy." When the words were out of her mouth, she hoped that she didn't sound as wistful as she felt.

"How could he be, with a simpering little fool like Susanna? Only she doesn't put on those helpless airs anymore. Several times she even spoke sharply to Jerome with us sitting right there in the room with them!"

"She did that?" Doll looked back at Jessamine in surprise. No lady ever made such a breach in etiquette as to speak derisively to her husband in front of company. "Is he really not happy, then?"

"He never said so, but I can tell he isn't. Jerome has changed. He doesn't laugh as much as he did, and he seems more withdrawn—like he is when he's hurt or feeling bad about something."

Doll withdrew to the privacy of her thoughts for a moment as she sniffed the crock of milk to determine whether it was still fresh. "I guess they're glad about having a baby on the way."

"I wouldn't count on it." Jessamine lowered her voice conspiratorially. "I overheard Mama telling Papa that Susanna looks and acts as if she's farther along than she says. My guess is that it will be born sooner than we have been told."

Doll managed to look surprised. So Asiza had been right once more! Maybe the old witch woman had been right when she told her that she would know what to do with the spells she had been learning during those journeys into the swamp. The thought that one could be used to bring Jerome to her wasn't as fleeting a thought this time as it had been, and Doll had to force the notion firmly aside.

"I'm going to miss seeing you in the evenings." Jessamine said, breaking Doll's reverie. "When you get your own place, you won't be so close."

"I'll be here every day but Sunday. I wish you could come to see me."

"I do too. I don't see why it isn't all right. I think that's so ridiculous. Why should it make a difference if we visit here or at your house?"

"I know Miss Delia wouldn't want you to come to my house to visit. She's always said that a white person can't go to a black person's house. You know she scolds me about that every time she knows we've been talking about anything but running the house."

"Thank goodness Mama doesn't know we're still friends. I'm trying to be above reproach until she convinces Papa to let me marry Ransome." She smiled and added, "But I'll get out to see you whenever I can slip away. Between slipping out to see you and Ransome, I'll seldom be here at all!"

Doll laughed. Of all the unusual friendships she had ever heard of, this one was the most unlikely—and one of the best anyone could hope to have.

A few weeks later the work on Doll's cabin was completed, and she immediately moved in. At first the silence was difficult to get used to, with no one moving about or talking. The early years of Doll's life had been spent in the noisy community of the slave quarters. Even after they moved to Ten Acres, Doll had lived across the yard from the Delacroixs and in the same house as her parents. She had rarely been alone.

Sam had built the house in the midst of the protecting oaks and high on pilings so that she would be safe in case of flooding. As he had told her, any flood that could wash away that house would drown everybody in town. Sam still wasn't happy about her move.

Jessamine had given her a table that once stood in a corner of her room, and Delia had sent over two chairs from the kitchen. Doll stroked the smooth oak wood and smiled at the vision it triggered of Jessamine using the table and enjoying it.

Dusk was falling, so Doll lit the coal-oil lamp her mother had brought as a gift the only time she had come to see the house. The lamp's base and chimney were made of pale green glass, the nicest one her mother had owned. Doll had been touched by the gesture, for she knew her mother was still as much against her living away from home on her own as her father was.

For the first time Doll had some doubts. As night fell,

the frogs and crickets began their reedy songs, and back in the swamp she heard the roar of a bull alligator. Doll soon realized that she greatly missed the familiar sounds of other people in the house.

She took one of her chairs out onto the porch and sat with her arm resting on the railing. The house was nestled in the stand of massive oaks that hugged it closely as if standing guard against a storm. It was almost like being in the playhouse Jerome had built up in a tree as a boy. With that comforting idea, she began to relax. Beyond the live oaks' leaves, she saw the rose and purple hues of the arching sunset sky. The orange ball was turning red and was swelling as it began to settle behind the treetops of the nearby forest. Across its vivid face was a finger-shaped wedge of golden cloud. At the far edge of the stand of live oaks, a white-tailed deer cautiously emerged to graze.

As she watched the idyllic scene, Doll's thoughts returned to Jerome and to what Jessamine had said about him being unhappy with Susanna. The idea was painful to her, because she knew it was true. Would it be so wrong to cast a love spell on him, when he wasn't happy where he was?

She took two pebbles from her pocket, one dark and one light. Held in her left hand, they warmed quickly. Doll made circular passes over them with her right hand, her fingers outstretched. Soon she felt the tug of power tingling in her palm, just as Asiza had taught her. Doll began to hum softly, a tune as old as the nearby swamp itself, and every bit as mysterious and secretive. The pebbles grew warmer, and she felt a surge of energy passing through her.

Suddenly Doll broke off the chant and clenched the pebbles tightly in her fist. No! She wouldn't use Asiza's magic on Jerome! If he didn't come to her of his own free will, she didn't want him to come at all.

Doll threw the pebbles away from her as far as she could. The deer bolted and ran back to the safety of the woods, and Doll closed her eyes with relief. She had almost given in to the temptation, but she knew she wouldn't again. In her mind she could almost hear Asiza's soft chuckle and see the nod of her head.

Ransome finished going over Roseland's account books and closed the ledger. The plantation was making a profit, but he saw several places where his father had cut corners that had cost them money in the long run. There were other entries so vague as to be suspicious, about money paid to unlikely people. Eliza had hinted to Ransome that Ian had started to gamble with some regularity, and Ransome had little doubt that these odd entries were evidence of payment of his gambling debts.

He stood and matched the time on his pocket watch to that of the mantel clock. He was to meet Jessamine in ten minutes. He automatically straightened the blotter on his father's desk and put the pen back in the inkwell and the ledger into the desk drawer. His father insisted that the library to be kept neat. Ransome looked around at the books and remembered how years before he had slipped them out one at a time to Jessamine, and how they had taught Doll to read and write. Someday, Ransome vowed silently, he would see to it that Jessamine had all the books she could ever want to read.

He went out onto the porch, looked around, and finding no one in sight, hurried down the steps and across the lawn to the bordering woods. Usually on his way to see Jessamine, he nonchalantly started off down the road as if he were headed for town, but then cut back into the woods once he was out of sight of the house. But it was late, and he was impatient to be with her. Already he could imagine the softness of her lips and the way she sighed with pleasure when they made love.

From the end bedroom on the second floor, Ian MacKinley was casually surveying the fields outside his window when he noticed his son striding purposefully toward the woods. Ian's lips protruded as he puzzled over why Ransome would be going to the woods with such haste. His bushy eyebrows knit together and his loose jowls trembled as he put two and two together and came up with Jessamine Delacroix. Ransome had often been absent at odd times during the day, but this was the first time Ian had actually caught him coming or going. He grabbed up his silver-tipped cane and started for the stairs.

Ransome hurried through the woods that were now as familiar to him as his own bedroom. Soon the weather would be too cold for them to meet in comfort. The only consolation was the shortness of the Southern winters.

Jessamine was waiting for him by the bend in the creek. When she saw him, she ran to his arms. "I was afraid you had forgotten!"

"Could I ever forget you?" He kissed her hungrily.

"Why are you out here? It will be warmer in the bower with the bushes to shut out the wind."

"I couldn't wait those extra seconds for you," she said with a laugh. "Every minute I'm away from you seems like a week."

"Only a week? Surely you're not getting tired of me already," he teased.

"That's not very likely. Ransome, I saw Susanna and Jerome yesterday, and I think it's true that he had to marry her quickly. That made me think that perhaps the same thing might happen to us!"

Ransome stared down at her. "You aren't . . ."

"No, not yet, but surely I will be, if we keep meeting in the bower. Don't you see how that could work in our favor? If I was going to have a baby, even Papa would insist we get married."

"But, Jessamine, I don't think that's a very good idea. What about your reputation and good name?"

"If we got married right away, no one would know for sure. Susanna's reputation isn't ruined. Everyone is saying she must be carrying twins because she has grown so large so fast. They all believe that she was pure as the driven snow on her wedding day."

"Maybe some think that, but not everyone. There's talk going on behind her back, and it isn't pretty. Some say she just did it to trap him and that she doesn't love him now and never did."

"Nonsense. I can't imagine anyone believing such as that. Besides, my point was that if it did happen to me, it would be easier for us to convince our parents that we should marry. I wasn't suggesting that we do it intentionally. But accidents do happen."

"I know. I should have thought of that sooner. When we get married, I want you to be able to walk down that aisle with your head held high and not have to worry about any ugly rumors. We haven't been careful enough. Aren't there herbs or something you can take to prevent it from happening?"

"I guess there may be something I can do, but I don't have any idea whom I could ask. But I suppose you're right and I should ask someone. Let me tell you my other idea about how we can convince them to let us get married. Mama is practically beside herself with worry over my being an old maid. Robert and William Ramsey have both given up on me and proposed to two other girls. They're to be married in a double ceremony. If Louis Broussard stops dropping by, Mama and Papa will think I've lost my last chance for a match they approve of. That leaves them a choice of accepting you for my husband or being responsible for my spinsterhood.''

"If I thought Louis was a real rival, I'd break his neck."

"Are you jealous?" she asked with her coquettish smile. "How flattering."

"Don't play the belle with me," he said with a pretended growl as he swept her up and whirled her around. As her feet touched the ground he threaded his fingers in her hair to shake loose her bun, and kissed her with a lover's possessiveness and ardent passion.

Neither of them heard Ian MacKinley's approach until he was upon them. Red-eyed and red-faced, he roared, "Turn her loose!" He struck Ransome across the back with his heavy cane as he shouted, "Get away from that hussy!"

Ransome thrust her out of his father's reach so that he bore the blows alone. The silver tip of the cane caught his cheek, and blood spurted from the cut. Ransome was almost too stunned by the blow to hear Jessamine's screams. A surge of protectiveness cleared his head, and he lunged at his father. The impact of his fist against his father's jaw carried the weight of all the years of repressed pain and fear suffered by himself and his mother, as well as the need to protect Jessamine from him.

Ian reeled back but caught himself against a tree. With a bellow he charged at Ransome, his cane raised in both his beefy hands. Suddenly he staggered to one side as a puzzled look crossed his face. He opened his mouth as if he wanted to speak, but no words came out. The cane dropped from his loose fingers, and he fell heavily to one side, crumpling upon the ground and lying deathly still.

Jessamine pressed her hands against her mouth to stifle her screams and stared in horror at the inert man, then back at Ransome. "Is he dead?" she gasped as he knelt by his father's side.

"I don't know," he managed to say as he leaned his ear against his father's chest. For a long moment he said nothing, then announced, "No. No, he's alive!"

She rushed to bend down beside him. "Are you hurt

badly? Oh, God, Ransome! I thought he was going to kill you!''

"So did I!" He felt for his father's pulse and patted his face to try to bring him back to consciousness. "He didn't hurt you, did he, Jessamine?"

"No. No, not at all." She touched Ransome's cheek where the blood still flowed and a blue-purple bruise was already showing. "Ransome," she half-sobbed. "Dear Ransome!"

He stood and pulled his father to a sitting position until he could get his arms about him and lift him. Staggering under the man's ponderous weight, Ransome said, "I have to get him home fast. He may be dying." As he stumbled away, he said, "I'll get word to you as soon as I can."

"I love you, Ransome," he heard her call to him. "I love you!"

By the time he reached the house, his steps were faltering. Several times he had thought he couldn't possibly make it, but had kept going. Oliver Gibbons, who was just leaving the house, saw him and came running to help.

"Ride to town," Gibbons shouted at the nearest hired hand. "Get the doctor!"

Together he and Ransome managed to get Ian upstairs and into bed. The man was a deadweight and showed no signs of consciousness at all.

"What the hell happened?" Oliver asked as he noticed the blood on Ransome's face as Ransome removed his father's collar and loosened his shirt.

"He came at me with that damned cane. This time I couldn't take it."

"You're bleeding." The man offered his handerchief.

Ransome touched his cheek as if surprised to find it was cut. His back hurt so badly, he hadn't noticed his cheek. He pressed Oliver's handkerchief against the cut.

Eliza came rushing into the room and gave a choked shriek. "Ian!"

Ransome glanced at her. It was the first time he had ever heard her call his father by his first name. "I think he had a stroke."

She pressed her lace handkerchief to her mouth and her blue eyes opened wide. She looked from her husband to her injured son and asked no questions.

The doctor arrived within the hour, and Ransome and Oliver Gibbons were relieved to be able to stop their futile efforts to rouse Ian with cold cloths and smelling salts. Dr. Griggs was new to Cavelier, but not to the earmarks of a fight. He curiously eyed the bruise on Ian's jaw and the worse wound on Ransome's cheek and shook his head. "When did this happen?"

Ransome told him about everything but Jessamine, and the doctor nodded. "Has he shown any signs of knowing anyone?"

"No. He's been like this since he fell."

Dr. Griggs put his ear to Ian's chest and listened carefully. "He seems stable. It's hard to tell. You're right about this being a stroke. He's not showing signs of a heart attack." He examined Ian's fingernails for any indication of cyanosis. When Ransome turned, the doctor saw the bloodstains that had soaked through the back of his shirt. Ian had evidently beaten his son most brutally. Dr. Griggs frowned down at the inert man on the bed.

"Will he be all right?" Eliza asked fearfully.

"I don't know. He may regain consciousness or he may not. You may as well know the worst. If he does come to, he may be partially, or even totally, paralyzed. We'll have to wait and see."

Ransome stared at his father's ashen face. He had actually struck his own father! The awesomeness of his act went over him like cold water. Ransome had no doubt at all that this blow to his father's face had caused his stroke. Guilt such as he had never known before threatened to overwhelm him. He wanted to run to Jessamine and ease his pain by holding her, but he dared not leave. His father seemed to be holding on to life by a slender thread, and if his father died, his mother would need him more than ever. Besides, he knew Jessamine would be at her house now, and Ransome's experiences with his own father colored his judgment of fathers in general. What if he went to Jessamine, and as a result, her father beat her?

He tried not to wince as the doctor treated the cut on his cheek and carefully peeled the shirt from his aching and bleeding back. No matter how badly he wanted to see Jessamine, he knew he would never expose her to such danger. He clenched his teeth as the doctor applied a medicinal salve to his back.

19

FOR DAYS RANSOME SAT BY HIS FATHER'S BEDSIDE as the man hovered between life and death. Eliza, who wasn't up to the strain, spent most of her time clutching her smelling salts and dabbing at her eyes with her handkerchief as she wandered about the house. She was an expert at always appearing to be busy when actually accomplishing nothing at all, and now this habit kept her occupied. Ransome envied her the industriousness that filled her time, for he had nothing to take his mind from the invalid in the huge bed. Even with his father's orders silenced, Roseland didn't need Ransome, because the plantation continued to run smoothly under Oliver Gibbons' expert guidance.

However, Gibbons was openminded, and as Ransome passed more and more of each day with him, trying to keep his mind off his father, he discovered that Gibbons would listen to his suggestions for improvement of Roseland's operations. Working together, Ransome and Gibbons put into action several ideas to produce more cotton and to clean up the field workers' cabins. But when that was done, Gibbons suggested that Ransome might be of more use on the inside, then left Ransome standing there alone while he went off to attend to the plantation's duties.

Ransome knew his mother needed no help with the house, since it had been so ably run for years by Jenkins, the butler, and the housekeeper, Mrs. Bailey. They had taken care of everything for Eliza, and Ransome suspected his mother had no idea that she wasn't the sole force behind the smooth dinners and elegant entertaining.

Nowhere in the scheme of Roseland was he needed, even though the doctor had told them all from the day his father was stricken that there was a chance Ian might never become himself again. Although Ransome had seen him move his left arm and leg, his right side remained puffy and still and his face was drawn down in a permanent scowl on that side.

Ransome shifted in the leather chair at his father's bedside and studied the man's profile. All his life he had feared and even hated this man. Now he was terribly afraid his father was dying and that it was all his fault. The momentary satisfaction of seeing his tormentor's head snap back from his blow wasn't enough to compensate for the overwhelming guilt he felt, though Ransome knew that he would do the same thing again to save Jessamine.

He wondered what she must be thinking and feeling. Since that day, he hadn't left his father's side long enough to meet her in their trysting place. As remorseful as he felt from causing his father's stroke, he knew he would feel even worse if his father died while he was meeting with Jessamine. So he sat and he waited.

Ian MacKinley's thick fingers moved on the bedcovers, and several moments passed before Ransome realized his eyes were open and that this time he was conscious of his surroundings. In a lithe movement Ransome stood and leaned over the bed. His eyes met his father's.

"You!" his father said hoarsely and with a pronounced slur. "Where am I?"

"You're in your room. Lie still and I'll call Mother." Ransome hurried to call Eliza and rushed back to the bed. "Do you hurt anywhere? Can I get you anything?"

Ian moved cautiously. "Am I tied down? Why can't I sit up?" His words were barely understandable. He reached up and felt his face as if it belonged to a stranger. "My God," he whispered. "I can't feel my hand on the side of my face. And it feels . . . What's happened to me!"

"Stay calm, Father."

"How did I get here? What happened to me!"

"You've had a stroke. Don't try to move. The doctor said you must remain calm."

Ian was silent for a moment as he felt along the useless arm. "What caused it? Why would I have had a stroke? Why don't I remember it?" His voice was rising in alarm.

"The doctor says you may recover in time. You're not to give up hope," Ransome said.

Ian let his left arm drop back as if he were exhausted. After a moment he said, "That cut on your cheek. How did it get there?"

Ransome touched the wound. Despite the doctor's attention, it would leave a noticeable scar. "You hit me with your cane."

Slowly Ian nodded. "The woods. You were in the woods. It's coming back now. You were there with the Delacroix slut. Yes, I'm starting to remember."

A veil seemed to drop behind Ransome's eyes, and he didn't answer. When Eliza bustled into the room, Ransome moved away to look out the window.

"Mr. MacKinley! You had us so worried. We were afraid you would never wake up."

Ian ignored his wife's pats and touches and frowned at his son's ramrod-straight back.

"I'll have the cook make you some beef broth," Eliza said. "You haven't eaten in days. Not really, that is. How do you feel?"

"Like hell. Has that doctor been here?"

"Dr. Griggs? To be sure he has. He comes out every day about dinnertime."

"What did he say about me?"

Eliza glanced at Ransome and back at her husband. "He says you may recover just fine."

"May? Tell me exactly what he said."

"What does he know? He's a young man. Scarcely older than Ransome. I'll send to Baton Rouge for a more experienced man."

"What did he say!" Ian's voice sounded alien and harsher than ever before. Eliza jumped and drew back her hand.

Without turning, Ransome said quietly, "He said you'll be paralyzed, at least to some extent, on your right side."

Ian struggled to sit up, but it was as if half his body belonged to someone else. A strangled roar of fear and rage burst out of him and brought Jenkins on a run.

With Eliza ineffectually patting his numb side and Ransome and Jenkins keeping him from flailing himself off the bed on the other side, Ian finally calmed somewhat.

"Rest easy, Father, or you may have another stroke," Ransome said as he pinned his father's left arm.

Ian's mouth drooped and a fine foam of spittle dotted the right corner. "You! You've done this to me! I remember it all now!"

"No, no, Mr. MacKinley. No one has done anything

to you. We must all remain calm,'' Eliza pleaded as she dabbed her husband's lips dry.

"I wish it had been you that died in the war instead of Dennis!'' Ian's mumbling words were intelligible enough to be plainly understood as he glared at Ransome, and Eliza gasped.

Ransome leaned nearer. "Do you really think Dennis would have carried you out of the woods? Think about it!''

Ian's face mottled dark red with anger. "Get out of my house! Do you hear me? Get out! And don't come back!''

Ransome straightened, his face stiff to hide his hurt and anger. Eliza put her hand on his arm to keep him from leaving the room. "Don't go. He doesn't realize what he's saying!''

"Yes, I do!'' Ian bellowed, spraying spittle across the sheets.

Ransome looked from his mother to his father and Jenkins and back again. "I'm afraid he does know, Mother.'' He took her hand and stroked it in what was a rare show of affection in their family. "For a long time now I've wanted to return to Albany and enter law school. I think I would be a good lawyer.''

"Leave Roseland?''

"Do you really think I can stay here after this?'' he asked gently.

Ian was making garbled sounds and trying to rise despite Jenkins' restraining hand. "Oliver Gibbons can run the plantation as well as or better than I can. Jenkins and Mrs. Bailey will look after you. If you ever need me, I'll return by the first boat.''

Eliza's wide eyes filled with tears as she nodded. She seldom faced reality, preferring to live in her safer world of pretense, but now she put her hand on her son's arm and said, "I know you're right, Ransome. I just don't want it to be like this.''

Again Ian lunged and yelled, "Get that bastard out of my house! I won't rest until he's gone!''

"I think you had better leave,'' Eliza said reluctantly. "All this excitement may be the death of him.''

Ransome turned back to Ian. "I'm sorry, Father. I never meant for this to happen. Say you at least forgive me that.''

"Never," Ian shouted in that curious monotone slur. "Never!"

Ransome turned silently and left as Eliza sobbed softly. This turn of events wasn't entirely unexpected, and Ransome had wondered if it would come to this. He went to his room and pulled out the bag he had carried with him on his return to Roseland. He had almost finished packing when his mother entered the room.

"Perhaps you could stay here, but just not go in his room," she suggested. "He would never know you're here."

"No, Mother. He would hear me in the hall or see me from the window. Besides, I wouldn't put you in the position of having to lie to him."

"But, Ransome! All the way to Albany?"

"Aunt Polly will be glad to have me back. Since Uncle Edward died she has been lonely."

"I know, but it's so far! Perhaps I could have Polly move down here."

"That wouldn't solve the problem, Mother."

"No, no, I guess it wouldn't."

Ransome buckled the bag shut. "Have Jenkins pack everything else in my two trunks and send them to the docks, please." He paused and looked across at his mother. "I have to tell you something. I'm going to ask Jessamine Delacroix to go with me."

Eliza's eyes opened wider and her mouth dropped. "After all that's happened?"

"I love her. We've been in love for a long time."

As if she were a puppet and someone was pulling her strings, Eliza MacKinley drew herself up. "I can't accept one of those Delacroixs in my family!"

"Not even for me?"

"No! You know how Delia Delacroix has cut me down for years, and how Reuben Delacroix even stole two of our slave cabins. How can you suggest marrying their daughter?"

"You too?" he asked sadly. "Somehow I thought . . . But never mind. It doesn't change anything."

Eliza followed him to the top of the stairs, but when he bent toward her, she was cool as she offered him her cheek, and made no effort to kiss him good-bye. Ransome smiled wryly and went downstairs. When he looked back, his mother was going to his father's room.

Ransome hitched the bay gelding to the buggy and tossed his bag in the back. Whoever brought the trunks to the dock could take back the horse and buggy.

The horse wanted to turn toward town, but Ransome reined him down the swamp road that led to the Delacroixs'. He drove to the front gate and tied his animal at the hitching ring. The yard dog barked as Ransome strode up the steps and onto the porch. He knocked, and as he waited for an answer, he looked about him. Jessamine had said they had made improvements in the place, but he hadn't expected it to look so nice. The old dogtrot cabin was completely hidden by the new clapboard siding, and it was easily twice as large as he remembered.

Doll answered the knock on the door, looking as surprised as if one of the cypress trees from the swamp had suddenly turned up on the porch. "Is Jessamine here?" he asked.

"Yes. Should you . . . ? I mean, come in." She held open the door and stared at him as he entered, then hurried away to get Jessamine.

Delia, who had been in the kitchen, came in to see who was in the parlor. When she saw Ransome, she stopped stone-still, the welcoming smile frozen in place.

"Hello, Mrs. Delacroix. I've come to see Jessamine."

Delia, unable to form a response, continued to stare at him in shock as Jessamine ran into the room.

"Ransome! What are you . . . ? Your father! He didn't die, did he?" she gasped.

Delia turned accusingly toward her daughter.

"No," Ransome said. "He's paralyzed on one side, but he's going to live." Looking back to Jessamine's mother, he said, "Mrs. Delacroix, I know this seems terribly sudden, but I want to marry your daughter."

Jessamine pressed her fingers to her lips and forced her eyes from Ransome to her mother.

"Marry!" Delia exclaimed.

"We love each other and I'll give her a good home and security. I'm on my way to Albany, where I intend to become a lawyer." He paused and said, "I know I'm not saying this correctly, but I've never asked for a woman's hand before."

"Albany," Jessamine whispered. "Now?"

"My bag is in the buggy."

"Get Reuben!" Delia commanded Doll, who was hovering in the doorway. "Hurry!" To Ransome she said, "You expect to walk in here and have me give you, a MacKinley, my only daughter, just for the asking? I never!"

"Mama, please hear him out. It's true—we are in love."

Delia ignored her daughter. "I don't know what has been going on here, but I can tell you that you've made a big mistake. Take my daughter to Albany? We don't even know you! And what I know of your family I don't like!" Her usually soft voice was clipped and unsteady with emotion.

"I know there has been bad blood between us, but—"

"Bad blood! My Adele lies in her grave because your family took our house. We almost starved that first year while you ate the food we planted! You even begrudged us the house for Sam's family and our barn!"

"That was my father, not me."

Reuben hurried into the room, his coat off and his shirt sleeves rolled up just as they had been when he was splitting wood. When he saw Ransome he stopped as short as Delia had. "What are you doing here?" he demanded.

"I've come to ask permission to marry Jessamine," Ransome answered, his dark eyes studying Reuben for signs of possible danger.

Jessamine ran to her father and caught his hand. "Please, Papa, say yes. I love him!"

Reuben shook her hand away and looked at Delia. "What the hell is going on here! Do you know anything about this!"

"He says he wants to marry her!"

Ransome said, "I know this should have happened in a different way, but I'm leaving for Albany and I want Jessamine to come with me. We'll be married at my Aunt Polly's house."

Jessamine hurried across the room to him. "Yes, Ransome. I'll go with you!"

"No!" Reuben roared. "You'll do no such thing!" He crossed in angry strides and faced Ransome almost nose to nose. "You get the hell out of my house, MacKinley. If I ever see you here again, I'll shoot you!" He caught Jessamine's arm and pulled her away from Ransome.

"Don't you dare hurt her," Ransome said in a menacing tone. "The last man that tried to lay a hand on her in anger will never walk again!"

Delia pushed Jessamine toward Doll and thrust her body between the men. "No one is going to hurt Jessamine and no one is going to take her away. Mr. MacKinley, I'll thank you to get out of my parlor."

Ransome paused, but while he would have almost welcomed the chance to fight Reuben Delacroix, he couldn't hit a woman. To Jessamine he said, "The boat sails at five o'clock."

"Get out!" Reuben growled, edging closer.

Ransome met his glare evenly for a long minute, then looked back at Jessamine. For a moment his eyes softened and love for her shone in their depths.

"Do as he says, Ransome," Jessamine said unsteadily. "I can't bear it if the two of you fight."

After a pause, Ransome turned and left. Jessamine grabbed Doll's arm and whispered, "Run! Go through the woods and catch up with him. Tell him I'll meet him there before five!"

Doll's face was anguished, but she nodded and slipped away, while Delia struggled with Reuben to prevent him from going after Ransome.

"I love him, Papa!" Jessamine cried out over his angry protests. "Can't you see that he's right for me?"

Delia put her hand firmly on Reuben's chest and said, "That's enough, Jessamine! Go to your room."

Jessamine gave both her parents a withering glare, but left. As soon as she reached her room, Jessamine began grabbing her things together. Ransome had been wrong to come here! She had been wrong to insist that they wait! Her heart still ached at the memory of that terrible day in the woods and at the new scar on Ransome's cheekbone. Ian MacKinley paralyzed! She packed all the belongings that would fit in her one bag.

A click at the door made her jump and wheel. When no one came in, she ran to it and tried to open it. It was locked. "Open this door!" she shouted. "Papa! Mama! You can't do this to me!"

Only silence answered her. With her face set in anger, Jessamine yanked up her bag and threw open the window. Although the window was too far above the ground for her to jump out, she sat on the windowsill, stuffed her full skirts through the opening, dropped her bag to the dirt below, and reached for the limb of the nearby chinaberry tree. As a child she had escaped this way more than once.

The bark on the limb was smooth, almost slippery, under her fingers, and it swayed much more than she remembered. Thankfully the bark on the trunk was rougher, affording her a surer grip, as she shinnied down. When her feet touched ground, Jessamine brushed the bark from her dress, picked up her bag, and turned—to run headlong into her father. "Papa!" she gasped.

Without a word, he wrenched the bag from her and led her into the house. She balked and protested, but she was no match for her father's strength. Once more he deposited her in her room and locked her in.

Jessamine ran back to the window and again threw her bag out. Once more she maneuvered herself through the window and reached for the limb. As she did, she felt a tremor run through it. Looking down, she saw her father chop again at the tree trunk, his anger driving the ax blade deep into the soft wood.

Slowly Jessamine climbed back into her room and sat on the floor, her forearms resting on the windowsill. The chinaberry tree shuddered, cracked, and fell to the ground with a leafy thud. Reuben glared up at her, drove his ax into the raw tree stump, and strode away.

"Starving yourself won't change anything," Delia said with thinning patience. "You've hardly eaten a bite all week."

Jessamine shrugged. She knew Doll would smuggle her some food as she had every night since Ransome had left for Albany.

"Reuben, can't you do something with her?" Delia asked.

Reuben studied his daughter. "She's as stubborn as your side of the family. When she gets hungry enough, she'll eat."

Delia gave him an exasperated look. "I don't suppose any of the Delacroixs are stubborn?"

"We're firm in our decisions," Reuben said with a wink at Delia. "Jessamine, you're being unreasonable. Someday you'll thank us for this."

"Never!"

"I heard in town that Ian MacKinley had a stroke and really is paralyzed," Delia said. "Jessamine, what did Ransome mean about some man trying to hurt you? Surely he wasn't talking about his father!''

Jessamine saw her father's body tense as he fixed his stare on her. As always when she was questioned about that day, she said, ''I don't want to talk about it.''

''If I ever find out that Ian MacKinley even thought about harming you, I'll—''

''Now, Reuben. That surely can't be it. Not even a MacKinley would stoop to such.'' Delia passed him the bowl of black-eyed peas and more cornbread. ''Hurry up and finish eating.''

''Why?'' Jessamine asked suspiciously.

''Well, you never know. We might have company.''

''Is that why you have on your new dress? Who's coming?''

Delia smiled with relief to see Jessamine come out of her apathy enough to say two sentences in a row. ''I didn't say we are, I said we might have company.''

As if that were a cue, Jessamine heard the front gate squeak and then a few moments later she heard footsteps on the porch. ''Tabitha, will you go to the door?'' Delia said as she stood up and skillfully intercepted Jessamine, who was heading for her bedroom. ''Let's go see who it is.''

''I have a feeling you already know,'' Jessamine said stiffly.

As Delia drew Jessamine into the parlor, Tabitha was taking their visitor's hat. ''Louis Broussard! How good to see you. Look, Jessamine. We haven't seen Louis in weeks.''

Jessamine looked accusingly at her parents, but she knew as well as Delia did that escape wasn't possible.

''Hello, Mr. and Mrs. Delacroix. Hello, Miss Jessamine. Nice weather we're having.''

Etiquette dictated that he could not sit down until both women were seated, so Jessamine perversely continued to stand. When Delia noticed what her daughter was doing, she caught her hand and drew her down onto a chair. ''It is indeed nice weather, isn't it, Reuben?''

''It was a dry summer, but we got through it.''

Louis sat on the edge of the settee, looking very uncomfortable. ''That's a nice dress, Mrs. Delacroix.''

''Thank you, Louis.''

Jessamine made no effort to put Louis at ease or to ask him to sit on the porch with her as she had on numerous occasions before Ransome had come back into her life. Delia gave her a reproving glance when Louis looked away, but Jessamine pretended not to see it.

After a long and awkward pause, Louis said, "I saw William Ramsey in town today. He and his bride are back from their honeymoon, and he said Robert and his new wife will also be home soon." He glanced hopefully at Jessamine, who was pretending to be interested in the stitching on one of the cushions.

"I hear Vincent Macy is getting married before long," Reuben said.

"Before we know it, all of you will be grown and have homes of your own," Delia added. "How time flies."

Jessamine sighed. Neither of her parents was being very subtle about the subject of marriage. She wondered whether this visit was Louis' idea or her parents'.

Louis cleared his throat and cast his eyes sideways at Jessamine. "Will you step out on the porch with me?"

"No, thank you," she replied. This time both her parents reproachfully eyed her.

Turning to Jessamine's parents, Louis said, "Well, I guess there's no reason to beat around the bush." He had to clear his throat again before continuing. "As you know, I haven't exactly been a stranger around here." He chuckled as if his statement were a sally from a keen wit. "What I want to say is, well, will you do me the honor of allowing me to have Miss Jessamine for my wife?"

"What!" Jessamine shouted as she leapt to her feet, her mouth agape.

"Why, Louis, I suppose—" Reuben began.

"Papa, don't you dare answer for me!" With blazing eyes she advanced on her luckless suitor, who had had to stand when she did. "Louis Broussard, this is the lowest thing I've ever seen you do! Proposing to me like this! Whom are you asking? Me or them?"

"I . . . I'm sorry, Miss Jessamine. Will you marry me?"

"No!" She backed him into the side table, causing her mother's bric-a-brac to jiggle alarmingly. Louis edged toward the door. "I don't want to marry you. I don't love you. Even if I did, you owe me more than to spring it on me like this! Leave my house at once!"

Louis was stammering as he felt behind his back for the doorknob.

"Jessamine!" both her parents gasped in unison. Delia jumped to her feet and stepped forward. "Please forgive her, she hasn't been well lately."

"Mama, I'm perfectly all right and you know it. Louis, did they put you up to this?"

"Your father suggested that perhaps you wouldn't be completely averse—"

"He did, did he!" Jessamine glared at her father as he stubbornly glared back. To Louis she said, "Remember this, Louis, and don't you ever ask me again. I won't marry you or anybody else in Cavelier!"

His hand found the doorknob, and it gave him the courage to say, "Don't worry about that! I'll never come courting you again. I'm going to go and propose to Dorothée Parlange! That's what I'm going to do!" He squeezed through the door and was pulling it shut as he remembered to call out, "Good night, Mr. and Mrs. Delacroix!"

Delia and Reuben turned on their daughter with fury. "Go to your room!" Reuben demanded in a voice that cut like a whip.

Jessamine lifted her chin defiantly, but she obeyed. As she passed through the dining room, her eyes met Tabitha's.

"Child, child! What have you done?"

"I'll marry Ransome MacKinley or I'll marry no one!" she stated angrily.

Tabitha shook her head and made soft clucking noises, but didn't argue with her.

20

"I NEVER DID SEE WHY IAN WANTED TO MOVE OFF down there," Polly Talbot said as she rocked and knitted. "I told him myself it was a mistake. Now, there he is, laid low with a stroke, and the whole country lying between us."

Ransome poked dispiritedly at the fire and leaned his forearm on the mantel. "Father likes Louisiana."

"Posh! He likes owning a big house and lording it over the neighbors." She peered over the top of her spectacles at her favorite nephew. "You act like a bird in molt. What's ailing you?"

"Nothing, Aunt Polly. I appreciate your giving me a place to stay while I go to law school."

"You always have been like a son to me." She rocked vigorously, the way she always did when she was trying hard not to be obvious about something that was on her mind. "You haven't told me much about your friends in Cavelier. Did you know anybody special?"

"Has Mother written to you?"

"Not lately. Why?"

"I just wondered. Yes, there was someone special. Our neighbor has a daughter my age, named Jessamine Delacroix." Her name felt good in his mouth so he said it again. "Jessamine. She's beautiful. Not only on the outside, but also as a person."

As Aunt Polly's nimble fingers flew over her work, her needles clicked like a castanet. "You never mentioned her before. Is she the one you write to so often?"

"Yes. Aunt Polly, what would you think about a woman saying she loved someone and wanted to marry him, but not ever writing him back?"

"You were in love?"

"I still love her. But I've been here six weeks and she hasn't answered a single letter."

"Does she know the address?"

"I enclose it in every letter, but she hasn't written to me once. We were going to elope, and she was to meet me at the dock. I told her we could be married here. She never showed up, and I assumed her parents prevented her coming, although it does seem that she could have sent her friend Doll to tell me. As soon as I got here, I bought her a boat ticket and sent it to her, along with this address. She never wrote me back, and of course she wasn't on the boat when it docked."

"Do you have her correct address?" Polly asked sensibly.

"Yes, but even if I didn't, everyone in town knows the Delacroixs and where they live. The postmaster would have given her the letter."

"Well, Ransome, sometimes when two young people are together, they think they're in love, but when they are apart for a while, they see that they weren't. Is this Jessamine a popular girl?"

"Very much so. She was the belle of the parish."

"There, now, that must be it. She is probably too busy to write."

"Jessamine isn't like that. No, I'm afraid something may have happened to her. You don't know how angry her parents were when they found out we had been seeing each other."

"Why would that be? Ransome, this isn't the family your mother wrote me about, is it? The one that has given them so much trouble?"

"I'm afraid so. But don't get the wrong opinion of her—she isn't like the rest of her family. Jessamine is a wonderful person."

"I'm sure she is, if you love her. Still, you know that old saw, 'Out of sight, out of mind.' I've heard these Southern girls are quite the coquettes. How old is she?"

"She's twenty. A year younger than I am."

"That's awfully young to be able to decide to leave kith and kin and strike out to Albany on her own."

"You don't know Jessamine. Nothing frightens her."

"Then perhaps she's just enjoying her last days of freedom. She may be a bit reluctant to give up her girlhood for responsibility."

"That doesn't seem likely either."

"If something dreadful had happened to her, Eliza

would have written you. We both know how she loves to gossip."

"That's true." He frowned down at the fire. "I don't like to think she hasn't written because she's having too much fun at parties."

"Dear Ransome, nothing is more difficult than changing from child to adult. I thank God we only have to do it once in a lifetime! When I was your age, I had three fellows courting me, and each one thought he was the only one." She laughed at the memory and shook her head. "How my parents used to worry about me! I was considered the wildest of their children, you know," she said with barely concealed pride. "Thank goodness I had the luck to choose Edward. Otherwise I might have become a Gypsy in a circus or something."

Ransome laughed in spite of himself. His diminutive aunt was the soul of respectability these days. "It might have been an exciting life."

"But it would have been a chancy one. That may be what your Jessamine is feeling. I know sentiments here are still hot toward Southerners, and I assume that down there they feel as bad about the North."

"More so."

"Then her parents wouldn't be against her marrying you only as a MacKinley but also as a Northener. You can't expect a girl to be able to turn her back on her family and even her way of life."

"She said almost the same words to me on more than one occasion."

"Well, there now! That explains it."

"It's not the way I want it."

"Short of kidnapping her and dragging her behind you, there may be nothing to do but learn to accept it. If she hadn't had second thoughts, she would have written to you."

"Maybe you should be the lawyer, Aunt Polly. You argue a convincing case."

"I should. I helped Edward many a time when he was preparing to go to court." She smiled at Ransome. "I wish he had lived long enough to know you were coming back to attend his alma mater."

"So do I."

"So I've done the next-best thing. I've invited his law

partner and his family over after dinner tonight. You'll like them, I'm sure.''

''If they are friends of yours, I know I will.''

''Ransome, about the other matter, I know it's hard to do, but you had better put this Jessamine out of your mind. I just don't think it was meant to be.''

He tightened the muscle in his jaw. They had meant so much to each other! How could Jessamine forget him so easily? ''I don't know if I can ever do that.''

''Then you'll just have to settle for second best the way my younger sister did with her husband—it turned out to be one of the most contented marriages in my family.''

''Perhaps.''

Lila and Robert Sherwin arrived punctually at seven that evening and with them they brought their seventeen-year-old daughter, Vera.

''I do hope Polly's nephew doesn't turn out to be a bore,'' Lila whispered to her husband as they waited on the doorstep. ''You recall what his father is like! Such a dreadful man.''

''Maybe he's like his aunt. At any rate, I expect Polly is going to hint at my giving him a place in the law office as soon as he passes his bar exam. It could be damn uncomfortable if the boy turns out to be a dud. Edward and I were friends, you know.''

''Of course I know, and there's no need to swear. Vera, stand up straight and remember to smile.''

Vera, who was already standing straight, nodded solemnly. She was painfully shy and the prospect of an evening of conversation with a stranger made her feel almost ill. She also wondered if she had been invited. Few people ever thought expressly to include her, because she was so quiet.

The elderly maid opened the door and showed them into the parlor. Vera hung back as introductions were made, scarcely daring to glance at the handsome young man. People who looked like this Ransome MacKinley rarely gave her a second look anyway, for she dared not even try the flirtatious skills her mother had tried so hard to instill in her.

To her embarrassment, Vera found herself seated near Ransome and a bit apart from the others. She clasped her cold hands in her lap to keep them from visibly shaking.

''Is it snowing yet?'' he asked.

"No, not yet."

Ransome had to lean toward her to catch her soft voice. She was pretty in a plain sort of a way, with medium brown hair, pale skin, and large brown eyes that held a startled look, as if she weren't certain of herself.

"It is quite cold out," she added.

"Do you have brothers and sisters?"

"No, I'm an only child. And you?"

"I had a brother, but we lost him in the war." He smiled at her. "I guess that makes us both only children."

She glanced at him and smiled. At once her face became prettier. Ransome couldn't help but think she would be very nice-looking if she were wearing a dress of a brighter color, rather than that snuff-hued kerseymere. He tried again. "Have you lived in Albany long?"

"Yes, all my life."

"I've spent most of my life here too. It's surprising we never met, since my uncle and your father were partners."

"Yes, it is, isn't it?"

Ransome curiously studied her. He was accustomed to Jessamine's vivaciousness and quick laughter. Compared with her, Vera seemed to be cloaked in serenity. Most of the girls he knew were at least a bit flirtatious, but she didn't seem to be at all interested in attracting him. Since he was usually in great demand by the female sex as a whole, Ransome was intrigued by her reservation. "Do you enjoy dancing?" he asked.

"Oh, no!" Her eyes widened, and she looked frightened at the very idea.

"I wasn't suggesting we do so immediately." He looked about Polly's fashionably cluttered parlor. "I was only speaking in general."

Vera glanced at her parents, who were chatting with Polly and ignoring her. "To tell you the truth, I'm always terrified that I'll trip myself or my partner and we'll both land in a heap."

She said this so earnestly that Ransome was caught completely by surprise and laughed out loud. At first she thought he was laughing at her, but then he said, "The same thought has occurred to me more than once too!"

Vera smiled, then laughed just a little, as if she were trying it out, and when he seemed to approve, she laughed in real enjoyment. For the first time in her life, she had found someone who appeared to be genuinely interested in what she had to say.

Polly glanced over at the young people with satisfaction. There was no better cure for the heartache of a lost love than the beginning of a new romance. "I'm so glad you brought Vera," she said to Lila in an undertone. "You must promise to bring her back often." At once she began to plan a dinner party for the following week and a musicale for the week after that. In no time, she was certain, Ransome would forget all about that heartbreaking Southern belle.

21

Susanna Delacroix wrapped her heavy woolen shawl more securely about her and smiled at her father. Even though her visitors were only her parents, she was determined to conceal her pregnant bulk. "Thank you so much for bringing me the jar of fig preserves, Papa. I know it's silly, but I just can't get enough of them."

"I know, *chérie,*" her mother said as she patted Susanna's cheek as if her daughter were still a child. "It's your condition. Before you were born, I couldn't stop eating watermelon. Luckily you were born in the summer!"

"Now, Marie, no woman-talk," Arnaud Leslie cautioned with a wink at Jerome. "There are men present."

Jerome forced a smile and tried to position himself to block his mother-in-law's view of the layer of dust on the side table.

"Mama, I made the most adorable nightie for the Little Stranger. Would you like to see it? I'll send Dulcie to fetch it."

Jerome tried not to grimace. Susanna and her mother's habit of referring to the unborn child as the Little Stranger was galling every time he heard it. "We really ought to be thinking of a name, you know. It's almost Christmas."

"Plenty of time," Arnaud boomed. "Plenty of time. It's not due until May."

Jerome looked at his father-in-law in surprise. He had assumed either Susanna or her mother would have told him the baby was really due in March.

Susanna threw Jerome a warning frown. "We've been over that a dozen times, Jerome. We aren't going to jeopardize our luck by choosing a name ahead of time."

"I should say not!" Marie seconded. "Everyone knows it's bad luck. Very bad luck indeed!"

Mr. Leslie grinned broadly. "Let the women have their way, my boy. Life goes smoother like that."

189

"I'll see the Little Stranger's things another time," Marie said to Susanna. "We have to go. I'm to meet Delia to go shopping. Your papa is driving me to town." She kissed the air to either side of Susanna's face and said, "Come along, Arnaud."

As soon as they were gone, Susanna turned on Jerome. "Have you lost your mind? I thought for a minute there you were going to tell Papa the baby will be born in March!"

"I assumed he knew."

Susanna went to the sideboard in the adjoining dining room and came back with a spoon. Unscrewing the lid on the jar, she began eating the fig preserves.

"Aren't you at least going to wait until supper?" Jerome asked in disgust. "You know Dr. Griggs told you to stop eating so many sweets."

"What does he know? Mama says I have to eat for two now. Besides, I'm hungry."

"You're always hungry these days." He looked at her puffy hands and arms and her broadening face. "If you keep this up, you'll gain too much weight."

"You're just a selfish pig," she snapped. "Mama says a stout woman is healthier than a thin one."

"Could that be because your Mama outweighs your Papa by at least twenty pounds?"

"Don't you dare talk about my mama like that!" Susanna said as she ate faster. "You're just used to seeing your skinny sister and mother."

Jerome glared at her. "You may not like my family, but at least Mama and Jessamine keep a clean house. Look at this!" He swiped the dusty tabletop and held his begrimed fingers under her nose. "I was mortified! And look at the dust balls under the edge of the curtains. When was the last time you had Dulcie clean in here?"

"I don't like having her around when I'm in here. She stirs up the dust and makes me sneeze."

"Then sit on the porch or in your room until she's finished!"

"I won't be fastened in my room for your convenience! And I certainly won't sit on the porch. It's cold out there!" She finished off the jar of preserves and dropped the spoon into it with a clatter. "If you don't like the dust, then you can clean it after I go to bed."

"Like hell I will!" He leaned menacingly over her.

"I work damned hard all day, and I won't come home and do your work as well. Now, I'm going for a ride. When I get back, this room had better be clean!"

Susanna began shouting, but Jerome paid no attention. This day was no different from most days when he was at home, and he knew the room would be just as dirty when he returned. With studied placidity he put on his coat and hat and went out into the frosty air.

He circled the house and saddled his gaited horse. There was one advantage to being married to Susanna. The shipping business let him indulge once again in the fine animals he so dearly loved.

He tried not to think about Susanna and what a shambles his life had become. Every day she became more shrewish. Every day was more difficult than the one before. He had talked to Father Theriot, but the priest had told him that all he could do was to practice forbearance and pray over it. Given Susanna's waspish temper, Jerome doubted the priest discussed it with her at all. If he had, it had made no difference. The years stretched out in front of him like a view of eternity. "Until death do you part" would be a very long time indeed, he dismally reflected.

He rode out of town and by habit took the road that led toward Ten Acres. As he neared the house, he recalled that Marie Leslie was meeting his mother in town that day, and that implied that his father would be with Arnaud. He considered visiting Jessamine, but they hadn't completely reconciled things between them since that embarrassing incident over Ransome MacKinley two months before. Instead, he rode past the turnoff to Ten Acres and down the logging road his father and Sam had opened to the sawmill.

Jerome absently looked at the familiar sight of skeletal woods and fields. Off to one side lay the swamp in its frigid stillness. The hard freeze of the night before had left the air uncomfortably cold. Skirts of thin ice surrounded the water-encircled trunks of the somber trees, and coldness seemed to be trapped in the garlands of silver moss. He dreaded returning to Susanna, though he knew that eventually he must. Was there to be nothing more for him all the rest of his life than her grating complaints and filthy house? He had tried—why hadn't she? He could almost believe she hated him.

From the corner of his eye he noticed a house that he had never seen before, nestled in a grove of huge live oaks, the green leaves of which hovered over the roof like a protecting hand.

Out of curiousity, Jerome rode closer, his horse picking his way daintily over the crisp, dry grasses. As he neared, the door opened and Doll stepped out onto the elevated porch. Jerome reined in his horse. He had seen her only a time or two since his marriage and hadn't exchanged a word with her except in the presence of others.

He dismounted and tied his horse to a low-hanging branch. Slowly he climbed the steps to join Doll on the porch.

"Jessamine told me you had a place of your own," he said at last.

Doll met his gaze and wished her heart wasn't beating so fast in her throat. She couldn't count the number of times she had envisioned him here in this very spot. "You'd better come in and warm up."

He followed her into the house and nodded in appreciation. "Now, this is my idea of a house," he said as he looked about, feeling very comfortable to be there. With a nostalgic twinge in his deep voice, he asked her, "Do you remember that playhouse we had up in the tree at Roseland?"

"I should. I fell out of it."

"I remember. It scared me half to death. I thought you were dead."

Doll awkwardly smiled. "It takes more than that to kill me." She felt surprisingly unsettled around him. "Sit down, sit down."

Jerome took one of the chairs, and she sat on the other. "Do you get lonely out here?"

"You sound like Pa. He can't seem to understand you can be just as lonely around people as you can be when you're by yourself."

"You didn't answer my question."

Doll knew this was one person who always saw through her. "I get lonely sometimes, but never lonely enough to move back in with Ma and Pa."

She looked away from his searching gaze. "I'm making friends with a family of deer. Every evening I feed them down by the swamp. I wanted to train them to come closer to the house, but I was afraid a hunter might shoot them in the meadow." She turned her dark eyes back to Jerome.

Silence hung thick about them. "Would you like to see the deer someday?"

"Yes. Will you let me come here again?" he asked quietly.

Doll knew he was asking about more than a bunch of wild deer. "Susanna might not like that."

"She won't ever know. I suspect she's glad of any excuse to get me out of her house."

Doll didn't miss the reference to the house belonging to Susanna. "Then you really aren't happy? Jessamine said you weren't, but I had hoped she was wrong."

"I never said I wasn't happy," Jerome protested automatically, then stopped and looked miserably at his childhood friend. "I can't lie to you, Doll. I made the worst mistake of my life when I married Susanna. No, that was the second-worst mistake. The biggest one was what got us to the altar in the first place. She'll have the baby in March—born 'prematurely,' of course."

"I'm sorry, Jerome. I really am." She longed to put her arms around him or at least touch his hand in comfort, but she didn't dare.

"All she does, all day, every day, is sit in her chair and paint or sew. That baby has a bigger wardrobe than most adults. She never tells Dulcie to clean the house or gives her orders for dinner. Her father brings her jar after jar of fig preserves, and she actually eats them in one sitting right out of the jar."

"I knew a pregnant woman once that craved clay," Doll said with a smile.

"That would be worse, but clay isn't fattening as far as I know. You wouldn't recognize Susanna anymore. I've never seen a woman gain so much so fast."

"She had better be careful or the baby may be too large. I recall Susanna as having narrow hips."

"Nothing is narrow about her anymore." He sighed and shook his head. "That was unkind of me. It's just that I've made a mistake that will last all my life."

"Maybe once the baby is born you two will be happy again."

"I doubt it. This goes deeper than a pregnant woman's capriciousness. She baited her trap carefully, Doll. Up until the wedding, butter wouldn't melt in her mouth. Now she complains and rails at me constantly. She even had me move into . . .'' He stopped awkwardly. Some things he couldn't admit even to Doll.

"So it's like that, is it?" She drew a deep breath and made herself say, "I could go to old Asiza and get you a love charm to make your marriage right again."

He shook his head. "Even if I believed in that, I wouldn't want one. I no longer want Susanna or her love. Doll, what am I going to do?"

"I don't know," she replied honestly. "But you're welcome to come here anytime, day or night. If I'm working at Ten Acres, I'll leave the key in the crook of that lowest limb. You can come and go as you please."

"Thank you, Doll. You always have been the best friend I ever had." He reached across the table and covered her hand with his own, unprepared for the impact of that innocent gesture. Startled by the excitement that suddenly raced through him, he found himself looking at Doll, not as his childhood friend, but as a sensuous and beautiful woman.

Her oval face was the shade of coffee laced with cream and her lips were as pink as the roses in the garden at Ten Acres. Her large dark eyes were tilted slightly, giving her an exotic look of innocent passion. Incongruously he found himself wondering if her hair would be coarse or flowing if she took it from the bun she always wore.

"I have to go," he said abruptly. "I don't want to wear out my welcome on my first visit."

Doll didn't trust herself to speak, so shaken was she by the look on his face and the expression in his eyes. Silently she held the door for him, and watched him mount and ride away. She laid her face against the cool wood of the doorframe and whispered, "Lord, please send him back to his wife. Because I just can't do it myself." After a while she realized she was letting in the cold air, and she shut the door.

22

"DOLL, I'M WORRIED ABOUT RANSOME," JESSAMINE said as she folded her most recent letter to him and slipped it into an envelope. "He's been gone two months and hasn't written to me a single time."

"I expect he's been busy, if he's started law school. That's bound to take a lot of time."

"How long does it take to write a letter? Maybe he didn't get there safely."

"If he hadn't, you would have heard by now. It would have made the paper if there was bad news."

"Maybe I should go to him."

"All the way to Albany, New York?" Doll put her hand on her hip and gave Jessamine an astounded look. "You'll do no such thing! Why, you don't even know his address or his aunt's last name."

"Maybe general delivery isn't enough of an address to get the letters delivered. Albany must be a lot bigger than Cavelier."

Doll folded away the linens into the lavender-scented drawer. "I'm sure he'll write to you when he has time. It's not like Ransome not to." Her tone was unconvincing, however.

"He loves me. I know he does." Jessamine wrote his name and general-delivery address on the envelope. "Are you positive there was no mail for me when you went into town yesterday?"

"I've told you four times there wasn't. Maybe you should go yourself next time."

Jessamine sighed and touched a drop of perfume to the back of the envelope. "I'm so worried about him."

"Think about something else. Fretting won't help. What about that quilting bee at the Ramseys'? Did you have a good time?"

"Not especially. Do you realize almost all my friends

are married, and most of them are expecting babies? All the single girls there were several years younger than I am.''

''It's not that you haven't been asked, you know.''

''Yes, I know, but I hadn't really thought about it much. I was embarrassed when Susanna made that cutting remark in front of everyone about my becoming a spinster.'' Jessamine pushed the letter away and frowned at herself in the dresser mirror. ''You wouldn't believe how fat she's getting, either.''

''It must be all those fig preserves she eats.''

Jessamine looked over at Doll in surprise. ''What fig preserves?''

Doll's hands faltered as she put away Jessamine's neatly folded blouses. ''Didn't you tell me she's been craving preserves?''

''I don't know what she's craving and couldn't care less.''

''I guess I overheard Miss Delia talking about it, or maybe Mr. Reuben.'' She was surprised at how guilty she felt for having repeated something that she had heard from Jerome during one of his visits. After all, she rationalized to herself, she and Jerome had done nothing but talk, but still, she couldn't look directly at Jessamine.

She smoothed a fold of Jessamine's poplin skirt and placed it in the drawer. She had rarely kept any secret from Jessamine, but this was one she could never reveal. She and Jerome might have exchanged no more than words, but the space between them had felt as charged as the air just before a lightning storm. So far Jessamine had never even suspected that Doll's feelings for Jerome went beyond their childhood friendship, and that was exactly what Doll wanted her to believe. She glanced over at the back of Jessamine's head and reaffirmed to herself that her friend must never know.

''That would explain why Susanna has gained so much. Her hair looks darker too, and not as curly. I always suspected she put lemon juice on it to lighten it.''

''I've heard that sometimes pregnancy will darken light hair,'' Doll said in an effort to be charitable. ''As soon as that baby is born she may be as slim and as blond as ever.''

''Why do you always have something nice to say about people? Don't you ever have the urge to cut someone to shreds?''

Doll smiled but didn't answer.

"It's a shame all my mama's teachings took root in you and not in me. All that about saying something nice or nothing at all, and idle hands being the devil's workshop, and so forth."

"You aren't so bad."

"Yes, I am. I'm in love with someone my parents will never accept, and I mean it when I say I won't marry anyone but Ransome. You want to know how bad I am? I think it's purely a shame that Jerome had to marry that sniveling Susanna Leslie and that Ransome had to go to New York without me. I would have gone with him, marriage or no marriage."

"Jessamine!"

"Well, I would!" She frowned despondently. "If Papa hadn't cut that tree down, I might have made it on the next boat."

Doll picked up Jessamine's sewing basket and plopped it into her lap. "It's a good thing for you that you didn't try. Lord knows where you might have ended up or what might have happened to you, trying to travel alone all that way. Now, you had better work on that embroidered change box for Jerome or his New Year's gift won't be ready in time."

Reluctantly Jessamine picked up the small square of satin she was covering with delicate stitchery. "I wish I were making it for Ransome."

Doll wanted to be making something for Jerome too, but she didn't say it.

"Any mail for me, Leon?" Reuben asked at the bars of the post-office window.

Leon Bierne turned to the racks of pigeonholes and unerringly lifted out the mail for Ten Acres.

"Any others?" Reuben asked in a conspiratorial low voice. He gave the reluctant man a level look.

Leon sighed and reached below the counter to hand Reuben a delicately perfumed envelope. "I can get in bad trouble doing this, *mon ami.*"

"Would you want your daughter to marry a Yankee? Especially one kin to Ian MacKinley?"

Silently Bierne shook his head.

"Neither do I." He gave the postmaster a comradely smile and tipped his hat as he left.

As soon as he was back in the small and cluttered office of the sawmill, Reuben opened the mail addressed to him. Most were orders for cypress chests or coffins or fence-posts. But two were from Albany, New York, and were addressed to Jessamine.

Reuben held the two letters gingerly, as if mere physical contact with them was repugnant. The young man was persistent, Reuben thought. At least he could say that for him. And so was Jessamine. He wished their ardor would cool because he was basically an honest man, and he hated what he was doing. But his love for his daughter was stronger than his scruples.

Reuben went to a tin box he kept high on the crowded shelves and took it down. Almost ceremoniously he laid these letters with the others and closed the box with a click. Someday Jessamine would thank him for this, Reuben thought as he replaced the box. When that day came, he would return the letters to her and his conscience would be clear. Until then, the letters were safe here. No one ever came into this office unless he was here, and Sam, like most of his other workers, couldn't read anyway.

There was a discreet knock at the door and Sam entered. "Mr. Reuben, we having trouble with that new machinery. You asks me, we did better with them mules turning the belt."

"I'm coming, Sam." No one but Reuben seemed to understand the advantage in the new equipment he had recently installed. "As much as it cost, we'll find a way to fix it."

He followed Sam out into the mill, where the familiar shriek of saws and clatter of hammers made conversation difficult.

Doll spooned a generous amount of chocolate into Jerome's coffee and put it on the table in front of him as if it were an offering. "I believe the winter is breaking up early this year. I found some little white violets in the meadow."

Jerome tasted the mocha and sighed his satisfaction. "Nobody makes this the way you do."

She smiled almost shyly and put her own cup on the opposite side of the table. "I know how you like for it to taste." She sipped the steaming liquid. "Did you hear the geese passing over during the night? They're heading back north." Her voice grew dreamy. "Just think what all those birds will see. All that territory you and I never laid eyes on. Think what it must be like to be able to fly like a bird and look down on the tops of trees and houses and rivers. I'll bet that's really something.''

"I guess we'll never know."

They sat for a while in companionable silence. After several minutes Jerome said, "The next time I come out, I'll bring nails and fix that shed roof. I notice the last storm pulled some of the shingles loose. Were you afraid out here alone?''

"No," she laughed. "I've gotten used to it. These oak trees were old before you and I were ever thought of. They'll be here long after we're dead and gone. The way Pa wedged this cabin in the midst of them, it can't go anywhere.'' She touched the whitewashed walls fondly. "I'm safe here.''

"I worried about you all during that storm. Don't ever try to go out when it's that bad. Will you promise me?''

"I promise."

He didn't look convinced, but he nodded.

"Jassamine's birthday is next week. Don't forget to get her a gift.''

Jerome studied Doll's contented face. "It's your birthday too. If you could have anything, what would it be?''

Doll's eyes lit up as she recalled one of the highlights of her childhood. "If I could have anything, I'd want a book.''

"A book? Not diamonds and rubies?''

"No, a real book of my very own. One with gold letters on the front, a thick one that would take a long time to read.''

Jerome looked at her in amazement. "Are you saying you can read? I never knew that.''

She ducked her head in modesty. "Jessamine taught me. It's supposed to be a secret.''

"Why didn't you ask me to teach you?'' He felt curiously jealous that he hadn't been the one.

"I didn't ask Jessamine either. She just did it.''

He laughed with her and shook his head. "When Jessamine puts her mind to something, she always does it. What have you read?''

"Why, all the books from . . .'' She stopped herself in time. Not even Jerome must know about the books Ransome had slipped out of Roseland. She finished lamely, ". . . from her room."

"You amaze me," Jerome said with admiration. "What else do you know that I don't?"

Doll thought of the time she had spent with Asiza learning about her spells and charms. "Nothing."

Jerome looked around the small room. The floors had been scrubbed until they were as clean as the tabletop, and were pale, as if they had been bleached. Colorful rag rugs brightened the room, and snowy curtains hung at the windows. Through the doorway to the bedroom Jerome saw a cheerfully bright quilt on Doll's bed. He looked away quickly.

"How's Susanna?"

"She complains more every day. The baby should come in a few weeks, and I know she must be uncomfortable, but she has become a semi-invalid. She only gets off the settee when she goes up to her room. All her meals and everything are served on a tray. She's driving poor Dulcie to distraction."

"Dulcie is distracted pretty easily." At Jerome's inquisitive look, Doll added, "I know her from church."

"To occupy her time these days, Susanna is cutting silhouettes out of black paper," he said wryly. "They're supposed to be recognizable portraits, but they all look alike to me. The women have a wad of hair and the men don't, but aside from that I can't see much variation."

"Once this baby gets here, she won't have time to cut up paper. She may as well enjoy it while she can."

"That's what I thought, but she already has her father looking for a nursemaid. Knowing Susanna, I doubt she will have any more to do with the baby than is necessary."

"No!" Doll was truly shocked. "She isn't going to take care of her own baby?"

"It doesn't look that way. She still won't even discuss a name. She says it's bad luck."

"I've heard that, but I don't think it's true."

"And she won't talk about it as if it's going to be a person either. She acts as if this is some ailment that will pass in time and have no far-reaching results at all."

"Is her mind strong?"

"Yes, it's nothing like that. She's just so thoroughly self-centered that nothing else matters to her. Not even the baby."

Doll was thoughtful for a minute. "Talk to Emilie Brown. She's the tall old woman that used to belong to the Ramseys. She has that red mule with the lop ear."

"I know her."

"She raised the Ramsey boys and they all turned out to be fine men. She's working for Sheriff Macy now, but she's getting too old to do heavy housework. I think she would be obliged at the chance of taking care of a baby again."

Jerome looked relieved. "That's a good suggestion. I'll talk to her tomorrow." He drained the rest of his mocha and took both their cups to the small sink. "I like coming out here. Sometimes that's all that gets me through the week—knowing I can come see you on Sunday." He kept his back turned so Doll couldn't see the strain on his face.

"Sometimes that's all that gets me through too," she admitted softly. "If you stopped coming, I'd be so sad."

Jerome turned and looked back at her. Their eyes met and unmasked longing passed between them. As if pulled by the same string, they both turned away.

"I guess I had better be going. It's getting close to dusk."

"Yes. I don't like to think you're out on the roads after dark. There's too much meanness about."

Jerome took his hat from the deer-horn rack and looked at her for a long moment, then said, "Good-bye, Doll."

"I'll see you next Sunday." She only wished the week wasn't so tediously long.

While the bayou was swollen from the recent rains and navigable again, Jerome Delacroix worked hard to see that all Cavelier's exports were loaded and shipped on the Leslie shipping company's steamboats and that the imports on their return trip were promptly unloaded. Each day he checked the depth of the bayou. If the level of the capricious water went back down too quickly, a steamboat loaded to full capacity would run aground on the muddy bottom—and it would be forced to stay there until the water rose again. Perishables would be lost and the shipping company would have to bear the economic burden.

Jerome's foreman was an eager young man named Tanner Johnson. He usually supervised the activity on the docks while Jerome checked lists in the warehouse, or vice versa. Jerome walked the lower decks of the steamboat *Calliope,* nothing which goods had been loaded and whether the cargo was being stacked properly. As he headed forward in the hold, he noticed that the fore section had been loaded with mules and horses, which were snorting and nervously rolling their eyes at being penned belowdecks in such unfamiliar surroundings. Jerome looked back to his ledger and frowned. Animals were supposed to be shipped last, because if the bayou dropped before they went out, they could still be driven to the New Orleans market, whereas the cotton couldn't.

He caught sight of Johnson arriving with the last crate of furniture from the Ten Acre mill, and he motioned the man over. "Why has this livestock been boarded? I was saving space for the rest of Roseland's cotton."

"We shipped the last of it on the *Lidy Jane.* See? I made the notation here."

Jerome frowned slightly. "That's all they baled this year?"

"It was a dry summer. Not much cotton made."

Thoughtfully Jerome said, "I see most of this cotton was stamped by the Thayer gin and not by the Leslie."

"I guess Thayer made MacKinley a better offer."

"Pete Thayer is getting on in years. How's his health?"

"You know Pete. He's always got a complaint. They never got that bullet out of his shoulder from the war, and he says it's giving him the very devil. I hear MacKinley sent Gibbons over to ask about buying his gin."

"Do you think he would sell out?"

"He might. Couldn't say for sure."

Jerome closed his ledger and smiled. "You finish the loading and get the boat under way. I need to go talk to a man."

He considered consulting his father-in-law about his idea, but decided against it. Mr. Leslie had recently expanded his shipping lines, and not long before that, he had purchased a second gin, which Louis Broussard had been hired to manage. Jerome knew Leslie's cash was pretty well tied up, but he had saved a bit of money on his own, and he thought he just might have enough.

The Thayer gin looked pretty much like all cotton gins. As Jerome stepped under the covered shed at the rear, he took note of the condition of the scales built into the floor where the wagons of cotton were weighed loaded, then weighed empty, to determine the weight of cotton delivered. Thayer had installed one of the new steam engines and a suction pump that drew the cotton from the wagon up through a large pipe and into the building.

He didn't see anyone about, so he walked inside and up the seven steps to the next level of the gin. Here the cotton was sent through a series of rakes and combs to separate it from the bolls and trash. When the gin was in operation, the noise would be so deafening that the floor beneath his feet would shake. In comparison the silence was eerie. From this point, the cotton would pour in sheets out of the hopper into another set of combs, finer-toothed than the ones before. After several more combings, the cotton was fluffy and clean and finally ready to bale.

Jerome climbed the narrow wooden steps at the far end of the gin to examine the press, which was mounted on heavy boards inside a wooden cage. As the cotton would come pouring in, one of the workers would have to reach in and spread the cotton so that it packed evenly, then yank his arm back before the press slammed down with a loud bang to flatten the cotton that had been added. Jerome knew a man who had once had this job who now had only one arm because he had hesitated too long.

The repetitive packing process would continue until the bale was the right size; then the press would be halted while two sheets of heavy burlap were passed over and under the rectangular mass of cotton, still in the press. Metal strips were then hand-threaded into grooves to encircle the bale, and the press was tightened again until the burlap and the metal straps were as snug as possible. Then the press would be opened and a man would hook the bale and tumble it out onto the open platform in front, where it would be weighed and a cardboard tag would be attached with a wire.

" 'Afternoon, Jerome," the gin owner called to him as he stepped out of his office. "What brings you over here?"

"I hadn't seen you for a while, and I wondered how you're doing."

The man cupped a hand behind his ear because he was hard of hearing from years of working in the gin, and said, "How am I doing? My shoulder troubles me most all the time. You know, they never did get that lead out of me.

Seems like the older I get, the worse it hurts." He relit his pipe and puffed gently on the aromatic tobacco.

"Have you ever thought of selling out?"

Pete Thayer looked at Jerome through the cloud of smoke that surrounded his head and pushed his cap back on his gray head. "Who to? Arnaud Leslie? Never liked him much, just between us and the fencepost."

"No, sir. To me."

"To you? Why, you work down at the docks."

"I know, but the line belongs to Mr. Leslie. I'd like a business of my own."

The old man scratched his crotch as he considered the idea. "What price did you have in mind? Now, I have to tell you Ian MacKinley has been showing some interest too."

Jerome pretended to be thinking about the question as if he hadn't considered having to make an offer. "What would you take?" he said more loudly so that the man could hear him without having to strain.

"I don't know." Thayer shook his head in a pretense that price had never occurred to him either. "You know, I put in a steam engine not long ago." He pointed to a separate building connected to the gin by a metal tube. "I built that new seed house last year when the old one burned. That's something you have to watch for—those seeds catch themselves on fire sometimes. There's a lot more to running a gin than turning on the switch."

Jerome nodded. "I know I would have a lot to learn. I was thinking of hiring a manager to run it."

Pete looked around and pointed to a big black man who had entered the gin at the opposite end. "Claude could do it. He's been keeping an eye on me for years. Knows the machinery better than I do." He looked back at the press as he puffed harder on his pipe. "I might consider five thousand."

"Haven't you heard, Mr. Thayer? There's been a war," Jerome said with a laugh.

"Well, I ain't going to give it away. MacKinley would give me more than that."

"He might, but then, he might not. Everybody knows how tight he is, and I'm making a serious bid. I might offer two thousand."

"For this gin? Why, you see those bales in the field yonder?" He pointed to several long rows of bales wedged together, burlap side up. "Each one is worth two hundred dollars."

"I wasn't buying your cotton, Pete. Just the gin. That cotton will be on its way to market as soon as you can get it down to the docks."

Thayer studied him as he rubbed his grizzled chin. "I might come down a thousand."

"I guess I could come up a thousand."

"I'm not taking a penny less than thirty-five hundred, and that's only if I get to sell whatever cotton is already on the lot."

Jerome grinned broadly. "Sold! You drive a hard deal, Mr. Thayer." He held out his hand to shake the older man's callused palm.

"Now that we shook on it, I've got to tell you I got the best of you," the old man said with a snaggletoothed grin.

"We're both happy with the deal. When can we sign the papers?"

"I can sign them whenever you draw them up. My boys will be hauling those bales to the dock this week. After that, it's all yours."

"Fair enough. I'll talk to Claude now, if that's all right with you."

"It's your gin." Pete grinned again, showing yellowed stumps of teeth. "I'm going to find me a place in the woods where there ain't nothing louder than a mockingbird, and I ain't never coming out."

Soon Jerome was on his way to the lawyer's office to draw up the bill of sale. Now that it was over, he wondered whether he should have mentioned this to Susanna. He was given to impetuous behavior, but buying a cotton gin without any more deliberation than this might seem foolhardy to some. On the other hand, if he had waited to mull it over, MacKinley might have bought the gin before he had a chance to bid on it. This way, between himself and Arnaud Leslie, they owned a monopoly on all the gins within two days' drive. If Ian MacKinley wanted to have his cotton baled, he would have to pay whatever price they set, or haul it loose by the wagonload to Baton Rouge, which was completely impractical. Jerome was almost laughing aloud by the time he got the papers drawn up and signed by Pete Thayer. It took his entire savings, but he counted it well worth it.

23

JESSAMINE WAS WALKING IN THE GARDEN WHEN SHE saw Jerome's buggy swing onto their turnoff. She paused and waited for it to reach the gate, and repressed her emotion when she saw only Susanna and her driver inside. Picking her way through the budding narcissus, Jessamine went to meet Susanna at the gate. She nodded a greeting to the driver, who spoke before driving around to the barn to await Susanna's departure.

Jessamine could tell at a glance that Susanna was in a temper. "What brings you all the way out here? I thought you were to stay close to the house until the baby comes."

"You know I'm not due for another three months," Susanna lied easily. "I can't stay home forever. You have no idea what it's like to be fastened in your own home, whiling away the time as you wait for your first child to be born."

Jessamine ignored the stab at her unmarried status. "All the same, should you have driven out over these bumpy roads?"

"It seems this is the only way I can see my husband on a Sunday," Susanna replied peevishly. "He spends every waking moment at the docks, the gin, or out here."

"Jerome isn't here," Jessamine said in confusion. "What makes you think he is?"

"He hasn't been here at all?" Susanna wrapped the ends of her shawl over her large middle and heaved herself clumsily up the front steps.

"I haven't seen him all day." For that matter, she hadn't seen him in several weeks.

"Well, you might know I'd drive all the way out here on the one Sunday he went somewhere else. I'll bet he's off with one of the Ramsey boys or Vincent Macy. I hope not! Vincent has become a gambling man, in case you haven't heard. You're lucky he never asked you to marry him."

"He did ask me. I turned him down."

"Oh? I had assumed . . . Never mind."

Jessamine barely managed to bite back a retort. She held the door for her sister-in-law and called out to her mother that they had company.

Delia was as poised and serene as ever, but Jessamine knew by the fleeting tightness of her lips that she wasn't pleased to see Susanna. "Hello, Susanna. We weren't expecting you. Where's Jerome? Is he still outside?"

"I came alone, expecting to find him here."

"Why, he hasn't been here all day. Sit down, sit down. I imagine he's over at the Ramseys' and will come by here on his way home." Delia took the chair nearest the window and let Susanna have the more comfortable one. Sunlight touched Delia's blond hair and Jessamine noticed there was more silver there than she had noticed before, and tiny wrinkles were beginning to fan the corners of her eyes.

"I certainly hope so. He's gone all the time lately."

"Isn't that just like a man?" Delia said with a smile. "Reuben is down at that mill more often than he's at the house."

Jessamine listened with only half her attention. She knew Jerome had never been close friends with either of the Ramseys. Since their move to Ten Acres he had been too busy helping Reuben earn their living to sport around with his old friends. As far as she knew, he hadn't renewed the friendship since his marriage. As for him gambling with Vincent Macy, Jerome hadn't had much extra money since he bought the cotton gin. She wondered where else he could be.

"I brought you a surprise," Susanna said to Delia as she reached into her reticule and produced a stiff fold of cardboard. Opening it, she spread out two silhouettes cut from heavy black paper. "These are for you."

"Thank you, Susanna. What are they?" Delia peered at them closely. Her calm gray eyes had become nearsighted, but she was too vain to wear spectacles.

"Can't you tell, Mother Delacroix?" Susanna's demeanor was the one she usually reserved for the elderly and infirm. "They are silhouettes of you and Father Delacroix."

Delia, who particularly disliked the manner in which Susanna addressed her and Reuben, said with deliberate innocence, "Which is which?"

Susanna gave Jessamine a look of exasperated amusement, as if Delia were à bit simple with age. "Did you hear that? She wants to know which is which. Mother Delacroix, you are a sight!"

Jessamine leaned over the cardboard and picked up the one of her father. "Don't tease Susanna, Mama. This one is your likeness." She and Delia exchanged a mischievous glance.

"For goodness' sake, Jessamine. That's Father Delacroix you're holding. Now, all you have to do is glue these silhouettes down on paper and frame them, and they will be ready to hang."

"On the wall, you mean?" Delia asked guilelessly. "How thoughtful of you, Susanna. Jessamine, take these to Tabitha and tell her she's to find just the proper spot for them."

"Yes, Mama." Jessamine managed not to laugh as she left the room. Tabitha would know exactly what to do with them. There was a box in the attic designated as a resting place for all of Susanna's projects.

As Jessamine headed out to the kitchen, she thoughtfully studied the clumsily trimmed silhouettes. Doll had told her that Susanna was making these as gifts. How had she known that?

Across the yard, Sam was sitting in the barn, passing the time of day with Andre, who drove for Jerome and Susanna as well as her parents these days. Sam had a cedar stick that he was whittling as he precariously leaned his chair back against the barn wall. "I guess Mr. Jerome's baby gonna be here soon. I seen Miss Susanna crossing the yard, and she looks about ready."

Andre shook his head loyally. "We gots until May. I reckon it's just gonna be big. Maybe twins."

"Uh-huh," Sam said in an unconvinced tone. "I expect so."

"I seen Tom Smith down at the docks with that load of furniture. He says he walking out with Jane Palmer that used to belong to the Palmers on the west side of town."

"I know her."

"They's a nice-looking couple."

"Anybody walking next to Tom would look nice."

Andre laughed softly. "He is a pretty one, ain't he? I was sort of hoping he would set his eyes on Doll."

"So was I. You knows Doll, though. It has to be her

idea or it's not worth nothing.'' He peeled a pink sliver of cedar off the stick before saying casually. ''So Tom is walking out with Jane, is he? All the time, you mean?''

''I hear tell they's talking about getting married. 'Course, that's just gossip.''

Sam considered all this as he whittled. He had been fairly sure Tom was seeing Doll that very afternoon. Not that she had said so, exactly, but from the way she was smiling in church that morning and rushing to get back home, he had assumed she was seeing someone. Tom Smith was by far the most likely man for her to be spending time with. ''Come to think of it, Tom hasn't mentioned Doll to me lately,'' he mused aloud.

''You know how it is. Jane is a handsome girl. She's not a beauty like Doll, but you can find a lot worse.''

''Well, I'd like to see Tom settled down and married. If him and Doll didn't hit it off, then Jane Palmer is a good choice.'' He kept his dark face impassive, but his thoughts were whirling. He knew Doll and he knew the look of a woman in love. If she wasn't seeing Tom, then who was it?

By the time Susanna gave up waiting for Jerome and sent to the barn for Andre, Sam had whittled the cedar stick down to a sliver. He helped his friend back the horse into the traces and buckle him in, then said, ''See you at church, Andre.''

Andre laughed as he clucked to the horse. ''No, you ain't, neither.''

Sam grinned back, but as soon as Andre pulled out of the barn yard, his smile vanished. He closed up his pocketknife, tossed away the cedar splinter, and strode out toward the swamp and Doll's house. The afternoon sun was hovering just over the treetops and the air was growing chilly by the time he reached the edge of the woods and looked across the meadow at the cabin in the oaks. A horse was tied in the shadow of the trees, but from that distance Sam couldn't make out its markings. He sat down on a fallen log and leaned back against a tupelo gum. He didn't mind waiting.

Inside the house, Doll was smiling as she unwrapped the package Jerome had pulled from his coat pocket. Her dark eyes danced with pleasure as she said, ''You didn't have to bring me a gift, Jerome.''

''I didn't do it because I had to. I did it because I

wanted to.'' He leaned his forearms on the table and watched the delight illuminate her face.

She carefully pulled the paper back as if she were uncovering a priceless treasure. ''Books! Two of them!'' She stroked the cover of the first and read, ''*Vanity Fair*. And *Martin Chuzzlewit!*''

''Jessamine doesn't have either book, so I know you haven't read them. *Vanity Fair* is a few years old, but the lady at the store said it's one all ladies like. *Martin Chuzzlewit* is very popular because Dickens pokes fun at the Yankees in it.''

'' 'Ladies'? Is that how you think of me?'' she asked softly. ''A lady?''

''Of course you are. What else?''

''I'm not sure a lady would have a gentleman visitor, and her all alone in the house.''

''The rules can't apply to us,'' he replied quietly. ''We don't fit in them.''

''We don't, do we?'' Doll ran her hands over the books again as if she were afraid they might vanish. ''Maybe our parents were right and we should have put our friendship aside when we grew up.''

''We didn't want that. I still don't. Do you?''

''You know I don't.'' She looked at him across the table and her eyes were troubled. ''Jerome, what's going on with us? We aren't two children anymore. Where are we going?''

''I don't know. Do we have to be going anywhere?''

''I don't know either. I just don't know. I look forward to Sunday as if it's the only day of the week I'm really alive. I don't have any right to your friendship.''

''Yes, you do.'' He sounded almost fierce, as if the same thoughts had been troubling him. Then, more softly, he said, ''Yes, we do have a right to be friends. What else is there of value but to care for each other?''

Doll's eyes widened. Asiza had said almost exactly the same thing that day in the swamp. Had she known somehow that Jerome would say them someday, and had said them first so Doll would pay attention when he did?

He reached out and took Doll's hands in his. She held her breath and dared not move as his strong fingers stroked the smooth skin on the back of her hand. His touch reached all the way into her soul.

When he finally spoke, his voice was so low she had

to strain to hear it. "Look at our hands, Doll. There's almost no difference in the color at all. When I was tanned from working in the sawmill, I was darker than you are. Why does it have to matter so damned much?"

"It matters," she whispered.

"To you? Does it matter to *you?*"

"No." Her own voice was almost as soft as his. "It's never mattered to me that we're a different color."

Jerome stood abruptly and went to the window and leaned his palms on the sill. "What am I saying?" he demanded harshly. "I'm a married man! I have a wife who's going to have my baby in a matter of weeks!"

Slowly Doll stood and came to him. She stood close, but not quite close enough to touch her body to his. "Don't blame yourself, Jerome. I . . . I went to Asiza the day you got married. She gave me a love chant and a charm to make you come here like this. I only thought about using it, and only once—I swear it! But I guess that was all it took."

He turned to her and saw the anguish on her face. Gently he reached up to cup her cheek in his palm. "Do you really think it took a love charm to bring me here?" His deep voice was husky with suppressed emotion as he gazed deep into her eyes. "There isn't a charm in this world that could have kept me away." Slowly he bent nearer, as if drawn irresistibly to her lips.

"No," she whispered, putting her hand on his chest.

Jerome stopped at once, but didn't pull back. "Why? Are you afraid of me?

"No, never that. But a minute ago you were scolding yourself for being here when you have a pregnant wife at home. I don't like Susanna, and I sure don't like the idea of you being married to her, but I won't take her husband from her. Not because I'm that good a person or because I think it's a sin, but because in the long run, I'd be taking something from you."

Jerome gazed into her eyes and said, "How did you get to be so wise, Doll? How do you know the things that you do?"

"It's like I have a voice inside here," she replied as she touched her forehead. "And I know this is not the time."

"Will there be a time for us?"

"I don't know," she whispered as she ached to feel

his arms around her. "But if there is, then we'll both know it and we'll never feel any regret or guilt."

He drew in a steadying breath and straightened. Reluctantly he stroked the back of his fingers over the velvety texture of her cheek. "In that case, I had better go. I'm not as wise or as strong as you."

As he went to the door, she said, "Will you be back?"

He paused and said, "Of course. Next Sunday I'm going to build a bookshelf for your new library."

As Jerome came down the steps and tightened the saddle cinch before untying his horse and mounting, Sam slowly sat up on the log. His eyes widened and his mouth opened in shock. Jerome Delacroix! And Doll? Sam saw her come out onto the porch and wave to Jerome. He waved back as he galloped across the meadow. Doll and Jerome!

Sam's legs felt like rubber, and he couldn't stand up. All he could do was sit there on the log and stare at Doll's house. This was what she had come to! A fancy woman for a white man! She was no better than the octoroons that lined the balconies in New Orleans!

Incongruously Sam remembered Doll taking her first baby steps, her first lisping words, the rag doll he had made her from one of his old worn-out shirts. Where had that precious baby of his gone? Who was this regally beautiful woman who had somehow taken her place? For to his mind this wasn't Doll. Not anymore.

After a long time Sam stood up and braced himself against the gum tree. Tabitha must never know about this. The way she felt about white men taking up with black women, she might do anything. Anything at all. At the very least her heart would break, and Sam loved Tabitha far too much to cause her pain.

Walking like one of the zombie men he had heard whispered about in the slave quarters, Sam turned back toward Ten Acres. As far as he was concerned, his daughter was dead. Hot tears stung his eyes and slid down his cheeks, but Sam hurt too much inside to notice.

24

REDBUD TREES DRIFTED LIKE FUCHSIA SNOW OVER nodding jonquils and hyacinths, and March blew in with a series of nerve-shattering thunderstorms. Susanna became more and more listless until all she did was lie abed and nibble from endless trays of food. She no longer even attempted to curl her hair, which hung in lank strings from beneath her bed cap. Jerome tried hard not to show his disgust as she became more and more shrewish and slatternly.

Because of the approaching birth, Jerome spent less time at the docks, but instead of his presence having a soothing effect on Susanna, it seemed to upset her more than his absences had. To keep from arguing and upsetting her even more, Jerome developed a knack for concentration that bordered on selective deafness, allowing him to work on the gin's ledgers while Susanna kept up her constant barrage of complaints and accusations.

"Sometimes I think you wish I were dead," she grumbled.

"Don't say that. It's not true."

"I could die, you know. Some women do in giving birth."

He looked up from the columns of numbers. "Are you afraid? Dr. Griggs says you have no reason to be. He says you're perfectly healthy."

"What does he know? How many babies has he had?" she snapped.

Jerome rubbed his eyes, and said in a tired voice, "Susanna, what's happened to us? At one time I thought we would be happy together. I've tried to make you happy."

She glared at him and rubbed the small of her back. "I must say, you haven't tried very hard. Mama says she almost never sees you over there, and half the time you aren't here when they come over."

"I've been staying home more often."

"You used to be so nice to be around. You'd bring me flowers and take an interest in my painting or sewing."

"At the time you didn't snap my head off every five minutes."

"There's no need to be so ugly to me. Mama says you should cater to my whims."

"Lately your only whim has been to lie in bed. How can I cater to that? This is the first evening you've come downstairs in a week."

"I feel so restless. Is there another storm building?"

"I heard thunder when I came home from work."

"I hate storms." Susanna walked in a splay-legged gait to the window and brushed the limp curtain aside as she pressed the flat of her hand against her back. "It's starting to rain." She let the curtain drop back over the darkness. "I want new curtains for this room."

"You know we're trying to spend less money since I bought the gin. Those curtains were new when we bought the house, and are only a few months old."

"Mama has some new velvet ones. They were made especially for her in New Orleans. I told her to order some for me."

"You what? We can't afford velvet curtains now! Especially not like those she bought. We aren't as rich as your parents are."

"No? Well, I think you're just being selfish. You bought yourself a cotton gin, and you won't even buy me some curtains!" Susanna's lower lip protruded in a pout as she restlessly waddled around the room.

"The gin will make us more money, Susanna. I explained that to you."

"You could have at least discussed it with me."

"Ian MacKinley was also trying to buy it. I hear he made an offer the day after Pete Thayer deeded it over to me."

"I would rather have new curtains. You don't care if this house looks shabby, but I do! You don't have to stay in it all day!"

"Neither do you."

"I can't go out like this!" She gestured at her distended abdomen. "The baby isn't supposed to be born for two more months as far as anyone knows. I have to stay inside."

"Soon it will be over," he said pityingly.

"That's easy for you to say. I hate this baby!"

"Susanna!"

"I do! And I'm glad I finally said it! I hate it, and I wish it were dead!"

"Susanna!" Jerome leapt to his feet, his eyes blazing.

Suddenly she grabbed her stomach and gave a choked cry as she bent over. Blindly she groped for the windowsill.

"What's wrong?" he exlaimed as he hurried to her. "Is it the baby?"

She nodded and her face went pasty white. Jerome tried to help her across the room, but when she staggered with another pain, he lifted her and carried her toward the stairs.

"Dulcie!" he shouted.

The maid hurried into the room and stared up at him on the steps. "Yes, Mr. Delacroix?"

"Run and get the doctor. Then go tell Mr. and Mrs. Leslie to come over."

"Mama. I want Mama," Susanna whimpered.

"Dulcie will get her."

He carried her into her bedroom and set her on the bed as he unbuttoned her dress.

Susanna groaned and tried to push him away, but he persistently stripped her to the skin and pulled her nightgown on. She seemed to be torn between pain and embarrassment at his seeing her naked for the first time in months. Jerome noticed with a clinical detachment that her breasts were larger than before and that the skin on her stomach seemed painfully tight. Then the heavy gown obscured her body, and she was buttoning the front up to her neck.

He didn't know what else to do, so he sat beside her on the bed and held her hand until she shoved him away with a look of exasperation. He paced back and forth from her bedside to the window, then finally saw the lantern on the doctor's buggy.

"Lie still. Lucas is here. I'll go let him in."

"I don't want him, I want Mama!"

She screamed as another pain gripped her. When she caught her breath she yelled, "Go away! I don't want you here! I want Mama!"

"You're just upset. Lie back and save your strength."

"Don't tell me what to do! You get out of my sight!"

Jerome clenched his teeth and strode from the room. He met Lucas Griggs coming across the yard from the barn, where he had taken his horse and buggy. "I'm glad you could come so quickly, Lucas."

"How close together are her pains?"

Jerome looked blank. "I never thought to time them."

"No matter. I'm here now." He walked briskly through the house and toward the stairs.

"What should I do? Shouldn't I be doing something to help?"

"Boil water, Jerome. Lots of water." The doctor smiled as he proceeded up the stairs.

Jerome went back to the kitchen, glad to have something to occupy his time. He tossed firewood onto the glowing coals in the black stove and pumped water into the biggest pot he could find. His muscles strained as he set it on the stovetop.

He impatiently stared into the pot, praying for it to boil, while he tried to ignore Susanna's periodic screams. He had rarely felt so guilty and so miserable in his life.

Susanna's parents arrived and hurried in out of the rain, Dulcie on their heels. "Where is she? Where's my baby?" Marie Leslie demanded in a tragic whisper, as if doom were threatening the house.

"She's upstairs. Dr. Griggs is with her."

Arnaud slapped Jerome on the shoulder so hard he almost knocked him off balance. "Come into the parlor, my boy. We may as well have a glass of brandy while we wait."

Hesitantly Jerome said, "Lucas told me to boil water. I don't know if I should leave it."

"I can boil all the water the doctor needs," Dulcie said firmly. "Don't you worry none about that."

"You're wet, Dulcie. You'd better change into dry clothes before you catch a cold." Jerome's face was drawn with worry as Susanna let out a louder shriek than before.

"I'll take care of myself, Mr. Delacroix. You just go on in the parlor."

Arnaud led his son-in-law out of the kitchen as he said, "Do as she says, boy. At a time like this, the women are bosses." From the sideboard in the dining room Arnaud fetched a decanter of brandy and poured a serving for each of them as Jerome stared in concern up the stairs.

"Is it always so painful to have a baby? I was taken out to Tabitha and Sam's cabin when Mama was having Adele."

Arnaud cast a glance toward the top of the stairs. "Just drink this down and quit worrying. Dr. Griggs knows what he's doing. Marie will keep him on the right track, you can depend on that." He settled heavily into a chair and lit up a cheroot.

Jerome shook his head when Arnaud offered him one, and took a stinging swallow of the brandy.

"I'll tell you what I'm going to do," Arnaud said jovially, as if he were completely oblivious of his daughter's bloodcurdling screams. "If it's a boy, I'm going to make you a full partner in the shipping company."

Jerome looked at him in surprise. "You are?"

"I always wanted a son. Maybe now I'll get me a grandson."

"I only hope the baby is healthy."

"Quit fretting. Women have babies all the time. There's nothing to worry about."

By dawn the storm had dwindled to a mizzling rain and Susanna's screams were hoarse but never-ceasing. Even her father was pacing nervously by midmorning, and Dulcie spent all her time running back and forth from Susanna's room to the linen closet and kitchen. Jerome had tried once to see if Susanna was as bad as she sounded, but when she saw him she became so upset that Lucas sent him downstairs with orders to stay there.

"I never knew an early baby to take so long," Arnaud fretted. "I thought it would come pretty fast because it's so small."

Jerome didn't answer. His dark hair was tousled and his eyes were bloodshot from strain and worry. He wondered how a man who was in love with his wife could bear knowing how hard childbirth was on her. He didn't love Susanna, and he was a nervous wreck.

Just when he thought he couldn't stay in the house another minute, Susanna's moans took on a desperate note, and within no time he heard the cry of a newborn baby. Jerome raced up the stairs two at a time and burst into the room as the doctor was pulling the covers around Susanna. Marie, looking more disheveled than Jerome had ever seen her, was washing the baby with a damp cloth.

Lucas grinned at Jerome. "You've got a son! A healthy, strapping baby boy."

"A son?" A foolish grin spread across Jerome's tired face. "How's Susanna?"

"She had a hard time, but she'll be all right."

Marie gave the men a glare as she wrapped the baby in a blanket. "You shouldn't be in here, Jerome."

He crossed the room and gazed at the wrinkled face of his son. "He's so small!"

"Small!" Marie sputtered. "He was nearly the death of Susanna!"

Jerome went to his wife and touched her hand cautiously. She opened her eyes and jerked her hand away as she recognized him.

"Don't you dare touch me, Jerome Delacroix," she gasped hoarsely. "You're never going to lay a hand on me again!"

"We have a son," he said, too overjoyed to pay heed to her characteristic peevishness. "A little boy!"

"I don't care! I told you I hate him! I don't want him anywhere near me!"

Jerome stared up at the doctor in shock. Lucas took his arm and led him away from the bed. "Sometimes new mothers say things they don't mean," he said comfortingly. "Give me some time with her. She'll accept him. You'll see."

Jerome paused as he passed the baby in Marie's arms. Almost reverently he touched the dark fluff of hair that hugged the tiny scalp. "His name is Pierce Spartan Delacroix. After my brother."

Marie pulled the baby away from his reach. "Don't touch his head, you'll hit his soft spot."

Jerome looked at the doctor in concern, but Lucas smiled reassuringly. "All babies are made like that. Otherwise they couldn't be born. You get some rest. I'll see to things in here."

Going to the head of the stairs, Jerome called down to his father-in-law, "Draw up those partnership papers! I have a son!"

25

JEROME LEANED OVER THE BABY'S CRADLE AND SAID over his shoulder to Susanna, "He's sure growing fast. And he's coordinated, too. Look at him catch this rattle." He held the brightly colored gourd in front of his son and the baby grabbed it with his chubby hands and tried to stuff it in his mouth.

Susanna pouted. "You pay more attention to Pierce than you do to me."

He took the gourd and gave the baby a sugar cube tied in a napkin, then drew the soft blanket up. He leaned over and kissed his son good night before blowing out the lamp.

When they were in the hall, Jerome said, "I talked to Lucas Griggs today."

"Oh?" Susanna breezed past him into her bedroom.

After a brief pause at the doorway, Jerome entered the forbidden territory. "He says two months is plenty long to wait."

Susanna whirled on him. "You discussed our private life with this . . . this friend of yours?"

"Lucas isn't just a friend, he's a doctor. He says it's all right if we resume our marriage."

"I don't need his permission for anything! And we aren't going to resume . . . that."

"Yes, we will. What are you talking about?"

"I'm not taking a chance on having another baby. Just look at me!" She gestured contemptuously at the reflection of her plump figure in the cheval glass. "Pierce has ruined me. I may never be slim again."

"Don't blame that on the baby. It was all those sweets you ate. Lucas told you this would happen."

"Everybody knows a mother-to-be has to eat for two. I'm convinced that doctor doesn't know what he's talking about. No, this is all that baby's fault, and I'm not having another one."

Jerome frowned. "Isn't there something you can take so you won't have another?"

"For shame, Jerome! What if Father Teriot heard you say that! Besides, herbs don't work. No, we're going to do exactly what my own parents did after I was born, and that's continue to live separately."

"You mean to tell me they don't—?"

"Don't you dare speak to me in that low way!"

Jerome went to her and put his hands on her arms. As always, Susanna made no effort to return his touch. "Susanna, we're husband and wife. It's natural and right for us to sleep together. You don't seem to understand about my needs. I want our marriage to be happy, but I can't live the life of a monk."

"You have no choice."

With strained patience he tried again. "I've been coming home earlier and talking to you more. Susanna, I don't want us to continue like we have been. I can't live like this. We constantly snap at each other or ignore each other altogether. Marriage is supposed to be better than this."

"I didn't realize you're such an expert. Did Lucas Griggs tell you all this too?" she asked with dripping sarcasm.

"No, I know it from watching my parents."

"Yes, well, we won't go into that." Susanna's lip curled in a sneer.

"There's no reason for you to look down on my family."

"No? Have it your own way." She shrugged off his hands and went to her dresser to remove the cameo brooch she wore at her collar. "If you'll excuse me, I'd like to go to bed now."

"Don't dismiss me as if I were a servant!" He angrily crossed to her and jerked her around to face him. "Don't do this, Susanna!" He stared down into her coldly hostile eyes, then commandingly pulled her to him for his kiss.

Susanna remained frigidly stiff and kept her lips clamped shut. Jerome pulled back and frowned down at her. "What's happened to you? How could anyone change so much in such a short time?"

"Every girl flirts with her beaux. How else could I get married?"

"But you seemed so sweet, so docile! You even let

me make love to you. Now you yell at me and throw things and won't let me near you.''

"Did you ever consider that it might be your fault? That you disgust me so much that I can't stand your touch?'' When Jerome flinched, Susanna knew she had finally touched a nerve, so she fiercely elaborated. "I can't stand having you paw at me, and your kisses repulse me! As for what used to happen in this bed, the very idea makes me nauseous!'' She thrust her chin out to emphasize her contempt.

Jerome stepped back. He had known Susanna wasn't a passionate woman, but he'd had no idea she felt this way. All his pride crumbled as he said, "You really feel this strongly about it? I thought you liked it a little.''

"I hate it! And I hate you!''

"Then why in the hell did you marry me?''

"What else could I do? By then your disgusting rutting had made me pregnant!''

Jerome felt as if he had been hit in the stomach. Even in the early days she must have felt this contempt toward him. "Then why did you let me sleep with you at all?''

"For one thing, it was my duty. For another, I was afraid that you would force me.''

"You were afraid of me?'' He stared at her as if she were a stranger. "I would never have taken you against your will!''

"How could I know that? Look what you did to me before we were even married!''

"You let me!''

"You're so naive, Jerome. You were my only beau. Did you think I would take a chance on being an old maid like your sister? Once you had ruined me, it was only a matter of honor for you to have to marry me. The baby only speeded up the inevitable.''

Jerome's face was pale as he stared at his wife, trying to reconcile this virago with the blushing girl he had courted. "You tricked me into marrying you!''

"Of course.'' She smiled cruelly. "And now that we are married and have a son, there isn't a damned thing you can do about it!''

He knew she was right. Divorce was impossible, not only because of his religion but also because of his standing in the town. Susanna had won. Without another word he turned and strode from the room. He heard the baby start to cry as Susanna slammed her door and locked it, then the soothing sounds of Emilie Brown as she quieted the infant.

He left the house in a daze and saddled his horse in the light of a full moon. Even though it was nighttime, he couldn't bear to stay under the same roof with Susanna. He had to get some distance between them. Within minutes he was heading out of town.

Later he couldn't recall turning his horse in any particular direction. His only thought was to get away from the sharp pain Susanna had caused. By habit the horse took him down the bayou road and along the edge of the swamp.

When he saw the lights in Doll's windows, he almost turned back. He wasn't in the mood to be good company, and he didn't want to inflict his pain on her. But she had evidently heard his horse's hoofbeats, because she came out onto the porch and looked across the meadow in search of him.

He rode closer and called out in order not to frighten her, "It's me, Doll."

"Jerome? What are you doing out so late? The baby's not sick, is he?"

He stopped his horse below her steps and said, "No, Pierce is fine."

For a moment they looked at each other through the silvery night. Then Doll said quietly, "Put your horse in the barn and give him some feed, while I put on a pot of coffee."

She went into the house and pumped water into the fire-blackened pot. Her fingers were shaky, and she was as nervous as if this were his first visit. Kneeling on the hearth, she put another log on the fire and raked some coals under the spider before placing the coffeepot on it. When Jerome came in, she looked up quickly. Again their eyes met, and time seemed to stand still. Slowly Doll got to her feet.

"What happened?" she asked. "You look like you're all torn up inside."

"I feel that way. My marriage is over."

"Not a divorce!"

"No, I can't. But it's ended just the same. I'm going to move out tomorrow."

"What about Pierce?"

"I'll take him with me. I can find a wet nurse somewhere."

"You can't do that! A baby belongs with his mother!"

"She never goes near him except to nurse him."

"Maybe so, but he's still her baby. Besides, if you take him, the law will make you give him back."

Jerome hung his coat on the antler rack. "I never thought about that. I just can't live there anymore."

Doll went to him and touched his arm with her fingertips. "If you want to see your baby, you'll have to. What happened?"

"Susanna told me how she feels about me. Since we got married, she's treated me as though she didn't like me, but now I know she's hated me all along. Really hates me! She says my kisses repulse her and my lovemaking makes her sick to her stomach." He tried to laugh, but the sound was shaky and Doll could see tears in his eyes. "I never knew I was that bad."

"Hasn't it occurred to you that it might be her? There are women that no man could please."

He shook his head. "I don't know that. She's the only one I've ever been with. Maybe any woman would feel that way about me."

"No one that loved you would," Doll replied softly.

"Well, I know for a fact that she doesn't love me. Do you know, she has never once said that word to me? Not once!"

Doll got their two cups out of the cabinet and poured the thick black coffee. "How do you feel about her?"

"I don't love her either. I thought I did, but I guess I'm not the first man to confuse love and lust."

She smiled at him and handed him a cup. "You won't be the last, either."

Their fingers touched as he took the cup, and he closed his hand over hers. "Doll, you have such keen insight. How do you know so much about people and what they think and feel?"

"Didn't you know? I have the 'knowing,' " she said lightly. "Asiza told me so."

"Asiza? The witch woman back in the swamp? I always thought she was a legend."

"She's real enough. Did you think I made it up when I told you she gave me a love charm?"

Jerome stared at Doll in fascination, the tension in the small room building with words not yet spoken.

"If I was truly a good person, I would have figured

out a way to use the charm to make love grow between you and Susanna.''

''You can't do the impossible. And you are good. I've never known anyone who was more kind and giving.'' He watched as she prodded the fire to life as if she needed something to do with her hands. He found himself contrasting her to Susanna's slovenliness. Even though it was late, Doll's dress looked fresh and her hair was neatly combed. ''You know, I've never seen your hair loose,'' he said almost to himself.

Doll looked at him in surprise as she replaced the poker against the chimney. For a long, wondrous moment their eyes held and the world dissolved, leaving only the two of them in the mellow light of the small room. As if she were moving in slow motion, Doll pulled the pins from her hair, letting it unroll like a black skein of heavy silk onto her shoulders and down her back in thick waves to her waist.

Obviously moved by the sight, Jerome stepped closer and ran his fingers through her hair. It was still warm from being pinned close to her head, and it smelled of jonquils, just as Doll did. In texture it was not as fine as Susanna's, but it was richly soft. Jerome wound it around his palm and rubbed it gently on Doll's golden cheek.

Not daring to speak, he lowered his head and claimed her lips, kissing her almost shyly, as if he were afraid she might pull away in disgust. Doll lifted her head to return his kiss and experimentally ran the flat of her hands up his back to pull him closer.

Jerome embraced her with growing confidence and lifted his head to look into the deep brown of her eyes. ''Doll?'' he asked, not knowing how to frame the questions that burned within him.

''Don't you know I've always loved you?'' she whispered.

A muscle tightened in his jaw as his eyes searched her soul. He was almost afraid of the emotion that was spreading through him. ''You shouldn't love me. You should tell me to get back on my horse and get out of here.''

''I won't do that.''

''If I stay, we'll never be the same again.''

Her lips parted and he saw the smooth edges of her white teeth. ''I love you.'' she repeated softly.

''I love you too.'' The words were strange in his

mouth, but they felt perfectly at home in his heart. "Why did I never see that before?"

"Does it matter, as long as you know it now?"

"No." His voice was husky with emotion, and he felt passion building that enriched and magnified his love for her. "Nothing matters but us."

Again he kissed her, and this time she returned his passion full measure. The barriers of race and social propriety vanished as they let their newborn love grow and expand until it enveloped them both in a bond of light. When he lifted his head, he was visibly shaken.

With an inviting smile that bespoke the feeling in her heart, Doll took his hand and stepped toward the bedroom. Jerome hesitated, but only out of deference to her. "You're sure? What if you wake up tomorrow and hate me for this?"

"I could never hate you, Jerome. Love—real love—isn't like that. Do you doubt what you're feeling for me?"

"No. I have no doubts at all." He reached back and shut the bolt on the door, locking out the world. "I'm only amazed it has taken me so long to recognize it."

"You never thought to look for it in this kind of package," she said with a twinkle in her eyes.

He put his fingers to her lips. "Don't ever say that again. Close your eyes." When she obeyed, he put her hand on his smooth-shaven cheek. "Can you feel what color I am?" She shook her head, and he put her hand on her own cheek. "Can you feel color there? Then what difference does it make? You're a woman and I'm a man and we love each other. That's what matters."

She opened her eyes and gazed at him. "Do you really love me? If you don't, please tell me now. It won't change how I feel about you, and it won't stop what we're about to do, but I have to know the truth."

"The truth is that I've loved you all my life and was too stupid to realize it. I don't know how I could have missed it, but it's true. I love you, Doll." He looked at her with wonder etched on his face. "How could I have been so blind?"

"That's just it—you weren't."

Jerome pulled her to him and kissed her again before he lifted her and carried her into the bedroom. Slowly he lowered her feet to the floor, breathing deeply of the heady perfume that she had prepared for herself. He paused as if he wasn't quite sure what to do next. Doll reached up and unbuttoned his shirt collar and waited for him to react.

Carefully he unbuttoned her cotton dress, exposing her smooth skin inch by inch. Moving gently, he pushed the fabric from her slender shoulders and gazed down at the twin treasures of her full breasts, barely concealed beneath the filmy fabric of her simple chemise.

He helped her remove his clothing and let her, too, look upon him. His muscles were hard from years of work in the sawmill and his shoulders were broad. His waist tapered to narrow hips, and he was glad to see his manhood held no horrors for her. She was shy, but not repulsed.

He removed her chemise and they stood close, but not quite touching. "You're so beautiful," he said finally, after admiring her at length.

Pleasure washed over Doll's expressive face, and she said, "So are you."

He reached past her and pulled back the quilt to expose the white sheets. She lay down, and he stretched out beside her. Like twin flames, her nipples grazed the dark hair of his chest, and she looked up at him as if the touch had been electrifying.

Gently he cradled her head on his shoulder and ran his other hand down the pale copper flesh of her chest to cup her breast. Her nipples were dark rosebuds that pouted for his touch, and he stroked them as he kissed her. Doll's lips parted beneath his, and she met his tongue's questing with her own.

"Doll," he murmured into the night of her hair. "I love you."

She answered him with kisses, and caressed him as he did her. He made no move to stop her as she explored the ivory muscles of his arms and chest and the taut firmness of his buttocks. "You're so pale," she said in wonder. "Where the sun hasn't touched you, you're as white as an angel."

"Who says angels are white?" he countered. "Maybe they're golden—like you."

He lowered his head and took her nipple between his lips. Doll gasped at the pleasurable sensation, and when he flicked it with his tongue before drawing it deeper into his mouth, she arched toward him with growing passion.

She loved the things he was doing with her, and how his hand half-spanned her waist before cupping her buttocks and pulling her tightly against him. She enjoyed the hot hardness of his manhood as he moved against her, and she moved with him in an instinctive rhythm.

Letting her desire guide her, she traced the tip of her tongue over his neck and tasted the slight saltiness of his skin. Her hands explored him freely, and she quickly learned what gave him the most pleasure and how to show him what she liked as well.

When he finally entered her, she felt a brief moment of pain and gasped in surprise. At once he stopped and drew back in concern. Doll smiled seductively and pulled him more securely into her embrace. "Love me," she murmured.

He moved slowly until she also began the rocking motion, and she sighed his name as pleasure replaced the mild pain. She moved with him and felt the pleasure mount into ecstasy, then suddenly she reached her peak and cried out as tumultuous waves of pleasure shook her. The pulsing contractions triggered Jerome's own release, and he murmured her name as he let himself go.

Languishing moments later, Doll raised her head from the warm hollow of his shoulder to look into his eyes. She was surprised at the worry she saw there. He stroked her cheek, but said nothing. Understanding dawned on her, and she said gently, "You're wonderful, Jerome. I love you more now than ever."

His eyes were glistening as he drew her close and his voice was choked with emotion as he said, "I love you, Doll."

26

Throughout the hot summer of 1871, Jerome went to Doll's house as often as he could. His life with Susanna had settled into one of cold indifference on his side and shrewish complaints on hers. By the time little Pierce learned to sit alone, Jerome couldn't recall a time he hadn't loved Doll, and by the time his son began to crawl, Jerome could no longer remember ever thinking he had loved Susanna.

Fall crept slowly into the South, but by October the leaves of the sweet gums were vivid reds and yellows, and fat orange persimmons hung on the trees in the woods. One cold spell came and passed, then another came and stayed. The horses grew lusterless coats against the winter to come, and squirrels packed their nests with walnuts and pecans. And Doll became pregnant.

She hummed while she worked, often with a secret smile on her lips. Unlike Susanna, she felt as if she were blooming.

"Why do you smile so much lately? Have you got a beau?" Jessamine asked as they gathered walnuts in the woods.

"No, of course not. Tom Smith married Jane Palmer, and he was the only one that was showing me any attention."

Jessamine didn't look convinced. "I know you as well as I know myself, and something about you is different."

Doll smiled her mysterious smile and put a double handful of green-jacketed walnuts in the tow bag.

"You know what I think? I think you're in love with somebody."

Doll sneaked a glance at her, but didn't answer. At times she ached to share her happiness with her friend, but she knew she couldn't.

228

"You aren't denying it," Jessamine said with increasing curiosity. *"Are* you in love?"

"Of course not." Suddenly it occurred to Doll that her condition couldn't be hidden indefinitely. What would happen then? And how would she explain the baby—a very light-skinned baby. A slight frown puckered her forehead despite her struggle to appear unconcerned with the subject.

Jessamine dropped a walnut into her bag and inquisitively surveyed her friend. "Why do I get the feeling you're keeping secrets from me?"

"The truth is, I am in love," Doll said with a smile, choosing her words carefully so she could share her joy without revealing everything.

"I knew it! Who is he? Are you getting married?"

Doll wasn't prepared for that question, and wished she hadn't admitted she was in love. Gathering her courage, she continued, "He's already married."

The smile faded from Jessamine's face. "Not Tom Smith!"

"No, no. Not him. You . . . you don't know him."

"And he's married? That's terrible! Does he love you?"

A softness came into Doll's eyes, and she nodded. "He loves me very much."

Slowly Jessamine resumed gathering walnuts, obviously moved by what Doll had said. "I guess that's what comes of sharing the same birthday. We're both star-crossed."

"You still haven't heard from Ransome?"

"Not directly. I read in the paper that he's in Albany Law School, and has been offered a position with his uncle's former law partner. Sherwin, I think was the name."

"You could write to him in care of the school or the law firm, then!"

"I could, couldn't I! I hadn't thought of that. At last I have an address other than general delivery. Now we must solve your problem."

Doll shook her head. "Mine has no solution. He's church-married. A Catholic."

"Oh." Jessamine shared her church's views on divorce, but she had thought it might be a common-law marriage or just a civil one.

"Don't look so stricken. We love each other, but there's no talk of him leaving his wife. I couldn't let him, even if it was possible,'' she added, her voice filled with adoration. "I love him too much to expose him to scandal.''

Jessamine reached out and clasped her friend's hand. "If you ever need me for anything at all, just tell me. I want one of us to be happy.''

Doll nodded, but she wondered what Jessamine would say if she knew the man in question was her own brother.

They finished gathering the nuts and hauled them on a sled back to the house. Jessamine went inside to scrub the stain off her hands, and after Doll spread the walnuts on racks in the drying shed, she went into her parents' house.

As Doll poured water out of the chipped ceramic pitcher into the bowl and lathered her hands with her mother's pine-scented soap, she tried to decide how and when to tell her parents about her baby. When the child was born, she would have to come up with some explanation for its pale skin. She thought of her own white father, and wondered if that might be explanation enough. Jerome's baby. The idea made her feel soft with love and maternally protective of the fruit of that love. So far she hadn't been certain enough of her pregnancy to tell him, but she decided she would that evening if he came out.

The door opened, startling her from her rumination. To her parents, who had just come in, she said in a conversational tone, "We got a lot of walnuts.''

"That's good, '' Tabitha said as she took the napkin off the pan of cornbread she had baked for their supper while cooking for the Delacroixs. "You is eating with us, ain't you? I'm frying up some jowls, and we've got crowder peas.''

Doll felt her stomach rebel, and she shook her head. "I'm not hungry, Ma. If I could take a square of that cornbread, I'll eat it with buttermilk later on tonight.'' She looked over at Sam and smiled because she knew this was one of his favorites too. But instead of returning her smile, he turned his back to her.

"Miss Delia sent clear to Paris for a little spring coat for Mr. Pierce's first birthday,'' Tabitha said with a laugh. "Ain't white folks something? They's no telling how big that boy will be by next March, and he's already got him a coat on order. And why on this earth would he need a coat in the springtime?''

Sam gave Doll a long, accusing look, and her eyes widened apprehensively. Why was he staring at her like that?

"I hear he's a pretty baby," Doll replied.

"He is for a fact. 'Course Miss Susanna don't never come out here, but Mr. Jerome has brought him by a time or two. It's a shame you is always gone when he comes to visit. You used to enjoy seeing the babies."

It was true that Doll was always gone when Jerome came to Ten Acres. They were both afraid they would give themselves away, so Jerome would tell her when he planned to visit so Doll could take the opportunity to run chores in town or go home early on some pretext. "I still like babies, Ma." She thought of Jerome's other child, the one she was carrying. "I'm not surprised the baby is pretty. The Delacroixs are a handsome lot."

Again Sam gave her that strange look, and Doll felt a prickle of fear on the back of her neck.

"Sam, Doll was telling me her horse is cribbing. Why don't you go over there tomorrow and nail some sheet iron on the top of the stall?"

"I got work to do tomorrow," Sam said gruffly.

"Now, don't I know that? How long you reckon it takes to nail down a piece of iron?"

"It's all right, Ma. I rubbed aloe on the wood and the horse isn't doing it as much. I think it's his teeth hurting him." She exchanged a look with her father, and he scowled before turning his back on her.

"You best sell that horse," Tabitha was saying. "I never heard tell of one that could be broke from cribbing."

"Do you think I ought to sell him, Pa?"

"You're all growed up, and I can't tell you what to do anymore," Sam ground out.

Doll drew herself up taller, a quick pulse hammering in her temple. He knows, she thought. Pa knows!

Tabitha looked at her husband in surprise. "What's wrong with you, Sam? It ain't like you to snap at Doll like that."

Doll held her breath until Sam finally said, "Quit pestering me, woman." He took up his straw hat and strode out.

"Now what on earth is ailing him?" Tabitha asked, her hand balled on her hip.

"I don't know, Ma." Doll watched her father go into the barn. He knew, but evidently he wasn't sharing his knowledge with her mother, and Doll felt a wash of relief for that. She knew all too well what her mother would think about her and the Delacroixs' son being lovers.

Tabitha put a slab of salt jowl on the countertop and began slicing it for the frying pan. Once more Doll's stomach knotted with mild nausea. "I have to go, Ma. Thank you for the cornbread."

"Take that jar of sweetening too. Sam don't like honey and I don't need it."

Doll took the jar and the cornbread and hurried out before her father could return.

That night Jerome rode out to Doll's house and put his horse away in the barn as if he were coming home to a wife. He was whistling as he came up the steps, and broke into a grin at Doll as he went into the house. "Something sure smells good. Don't you get enough cooking to do at Ten Acres?"

Doll laughed and hugged him as she said, "I baked you some gingerbread. Sit down and eat it while it's hot."

"You're good to me, Doll."

She beamed with pleasure and poured him a glass of milk. "How's that baby doing?"

"I wish you could see him." Jerome took a bite of the gingerbread. "He's starting to pull up and tries to stand now. And do you know what? I could have sworn he said 'Papa' today!"

"He didn't!"

"Yes, he did."

Doll sat opposite him and rested her chin on her hand. She loved to watch him do anything. Since he had started coming to her house, he had the old spring back in his step and laughter in his eyes. "Are you happy, Jerome?"

He reached across the table to feed her a bite of gingerbread as he said. "I've never been happier in my life than when I'm with you. I don't ever want this to change."

"There's going to be one change before long."

"Oh? What's that?"

She paused and hoped he loved her as much as he had said, because suddenly she realized he had never once told her he wanted her to have a child. "I'm going to have a baby."

Jerome stared at her in amazement for a moment; then, as her words sank in, a wide grin spread over his face. He leaned forward. "A baby? We're going to have a baby?"

She nodded.

He jumped to his feet with a whoop and pulled her up to hug her. "You're sure?"

Again she nodded as she smiled up at him. "I figure it will be born late summer."

Suddenly Jerome's smile faded. "You aren't unhappy about this, are you?"

"Of course not," she laughed. "I want very much to have your baby."

"You'll have to take good care of yourself. I'll send Lucas Griggs out to see about you."

"Now, how would you explain that? No, I'll go to Nanine Boudreaux. She's the best midwife in the parish."

"Don't you worry about a thing. We won't make love again until after it's a couple of months old."

"We most certainly will. I love you, and it'll be months before we have to stop making love because of the baby."

"Will you be all right out here? In your condition? Maybe you ought to get a girl to move in here with you until after it's born."

"I'll be just fine. I don't want anyone here that can spread rumors about you." She paused thoughtfully. "I won't be able to hide it for too long, though, and as soon as I start to show, I'll have to quit working at Ten Acres."

"That's good. I don't want you to carry heavy loads or work so hard. I make more than enough to support you."

"No, I won't let you do that. I've thought about it, and I'll bet my needlework will buy all I need. You might spread the word that I'm selling embroidery and lace and tatting. Maybe I could even send some to New Orleans and put it in a store there."

"I think I know just the place. William Macy's wife sells handwork through a Mr. Fred Barnhardt. He has a small shop in the *vieux carré* there that sells women's notions. I'll ask about it for you."

She sighed with relief. "I was almost afraid to tell you about the baby."

"Knowing how much I love you?"

"It's one thing to love your mistress and another thing altogether to want her to have a baby."

He kissed her before he said, "You aren't just my mistress. I feel as married to you as any man could ever feel. If things were different, we'd be married, and you know it."

"They would have to be awfully different indeed." Her mirthful expression became serious as she recalled her father's suspicious behavior. "I think Pa knows about us. He didn't say anything, but it was the way he looked at me. He hasn't been friendly toward me in months."

Jerome cradled her head against his chest and held her in the security of his arms. "We knew somebody would find out eventually. If there's trouble, we'll leave together." He pulled back and looked at her with hope. "Will you leave with me? You might be able to pass for white, if we left here where you're known."

She shook her head. "You can't leave Pierce, and we couldn't take him with us. Besides, I don't think I'm light enough. We would spend all our time wondering if anybody suspected, and moving on if they did. No, we'll stay here."

"I love you," he said as he gathered her back into his arms.

"You just be thinking of a good name for this baby. I have a feeling it's going to be a girl."

Jerome laughed softly and held her as if he would never let her go.

27

RANSOME MACKINLEY STUDIED HARD AND PROVED himself an able law student, and by the summer of 1872 Robert Sherwin was glad he had had the foresight to offer him a position in his law firm early on. After his graduation with honors from Albany Law School, Ransome received numerous offers, but turned them all down in favor of the man who had recognized his potential and had encouraged him to attend law school in the first place. Not only was Sherwin professionally interested in Ransome, but he personally enjoyed the younger man's company and sense of humor and regularly invited him to visit in the Sherwin home.

Ransome doggedly continued to write letter after letter to Jessamine, even though he never received an answer. In an effort to hear something—anything—about her, he took out a subscription to the Cavelier *Tribune*. In it he read that Jerome had bought the Thayer gin, which he already knew from a letter his mother had written in which she expressed her contempt at what she called another example of the Delacroix underhandedness; and that Jerome's wife, Susanna, had had a baby boy, which didn't interest Ransome at all other than to know Jessamine was now an aunt.

He read the paper from front to back, even though all the news was well out-of-date by the time he received it. On the back page of each issue was a local gossip column. This, he soon found, was the best source of news about Jessamine. Parties were reported, as well as the formation of a literary society, and Ransome was certain Jessamine must be attending at least the latter.

Early in May he had received the paper and turned first to the gossip column to read, "Louis Broussard is hinting strongly that wedding bells are in the offing, and not too far in the future. This is hardly news to this reporter, as we all know Mr. Broussard bought the Thomlin house

235

last month. As for his blushing bride-to-be? That can scarcely be a mystery, either, to all who know him and have seen him squiring this beauty about town.''

Ransome wadded the paper in his fist and his face became set with hurt and anger. Who else could this "beauty" be but Jessamine? He strode into the parlor and said, "Aunt Polly, I have to go back to Cavelier at once!"

She was shocked to hear him say such a thing, for they had had long talks about his relationship with his father, and he had made it quite clear that he wanted nothing else to do with the man.

"Read this," he said as he unwadded the newspaper. "There! It must mean Jessamine. I know for a fact Louis was courting her and was serious in his intentions. I'm leaving by the next train."

"Now, now. Wait a minute. Let me think. This doesn't mention her name. Maybe Mr. Broussard has found someone else."

"Cavelier is very small. There aren't many to choose from, and the term 'beauty' must point to Jessamine. She's the prettiest one in town."

"Maybe so, but you can't leave now! Your final exams will be in a couple of weeks. If you don't take them, the entire semester will be wasted."

"But if I don't go, I'll lose Jessamine!"

"Ransome, be calm. I think you've already lost her. If she has agreed to marry this Broussard fellow, she has obviously forgotten you. Why, she never even wrote to you in all the time you've been here!"

"That's not like Jessamine. Maybe she's not able to write for some reason." He frowned as he tried to think what might have prevented her.

"Now you're being silly. Unless she's a prisoner, she could go to the post office and mail a letter, or she could send this Doll Farmer you've mentioned. Once it's in the mail, a letter would come here, and even if she didn't have this address, she could have sent it general delivery. Didn't you say you had been checking with the postmaster?"

"Yes, of course. They all know me by sight now." He sank tiredly into a chair. "You're right, Aunt Polly. I just hate to admit it. You don't know Louis Broussard, but I can't see what she could possibly admire in him. He manages a cotton gin for her brother's father-in-law, and I guess he has a bit of money, but physically he's unattractive, and worse than that, he's a bore.''

Polly comfortingly patted her nephew's arm and said gently, "Sometimes money goes a long way toward making a person attractive.''

"Jessamine isn't like that!''

"Perhaps you didn't know her as well as you thought, or perhaps she has changed. Sometimes people do. I hate to point this out, dear, but you also have money.''

Ransome frowned. What she said was true. "I don't believe she could fool me like that.''

"I'm not saying she didn't care for you, but look at the facts. By marrying you, she would eventually regain Roseland, which is evidently important to her and her family, from what Eliza writes and what you've told me. That must have been a strong incentive for her.''

Ransome stood abruptly and strode to the fireplace. He leaned on the mantel and glared down at the Boston ferns that covered the mouth of the fireplace during the summer months. "I don't want to believe that of her.''

"I don't want to hurt you, but what else could be true? She must know the extent of the trouble between you and your father and she must realize that marriage to her would mean Ian would disown you—thus preventing you from ever inheriting Roseland. Why else would she not have written?''

The painful words made sense, and Ransome felt them all knot in his middle. Nothing else could explain it. "I find it very hard to believe that she played me for a fool,'' he said in a dull voice.

"She may have cared for you a bit,'' his aunt said to soften the realization.

With anger rising to cover the hurt he felt, he said, "She couldn't have cared much, if she's already agreed to marry Louis. And the paper says he bought the house a month ago. A man doesn't buy a house unless he plans to marry. At least not a man as stingy as Louis Broussard.''

Polly sat quietly. "I wish I could stop you from hurting. Being young and in love is so painful at times.''

"I'm not in love any longer,'' he said firmly as he clenched his fist. "I was a fool to let her get to me like this, but I'm not fool enough to waste my life over her!'' His pain was so deep his only defense was to convince himself that she had duped him and he had to let her go. Even though he still loved her, he planned to do everything in his power to put an end to that as well. He went to the hall tree and took his hat from the peg.

"Where are you going?"

"The Sherwins have asked me over this afternoon. I want to walk for a while and get my thoughts together first. Aunt Polly, what do you think about Vera Sherwin?"

Polly shook her head sadly. "Don't do anything rash, dear. Give yourself time."

"There's no better way to get over one love than to find a new one. Do you like Vera?"

"She's a sweet girl. Certainly there's no coquetry or duplicity in her. She's so terribly shy that I hardly know her at all."

"She's the exact opposite of Jessamine." He hesitated at the door. "The exact opposite. Would you say she's trustworthy?"

"Yes, I believe she is."

"I thought so," He smiled, but his eyes remained sad. "I may not be home for dinner, Aunt Polly. Don't wait for me."

She agreed and he strode out.

Ransome walked for miles, until at last he became physically so tired that the aching pain subsided. What his aunt had said was true, but he had tried not to think about it before. Jessamine would have had easy access to Roseland by marrying him, and she had known his parents were not in excellent health. He knew she loved her former home and regretted the move that had deprived her of it and their cotton income, though he had assumed she had long since accepted it. Now he saw why she had avoided the subject. She didn't want him to know how important Roseland still was to her.

Jessamine was an accomplished flirt—she even admitted she was herself, and took pride in it. She had told him once that her mother still managed her father by feminine wiles. Was it so unlikely that she was doing the same to him in their secret meeting place at the bend of the creek? True, she had let him make love to her, but she might consider her virginity a small price to pay for Roseland. Why, she had even *said* she hoped she would get pregnant so their families couldn't prevent their marriage. Had this originally been a scheme hatched by Reuben Delacroix to get his daughter married back into Roseland the same way his son had become married to the richest girl in town? But when Ransome had tried to take her to Albany, Reuben had been outraged. Had he somehow learned that Ian MacKinley had threatened to disinherit Ransome if he had anything more to do with Jessamine? He must have! Ransome felt sick to his stomach. How close he had come to believing her sweet words and honeyed kisses.

Squaring his shoulders and pulling himself up to his full height, he walked to the Sherwins' house and knocked on the door. He was a lucky man to have come to this realization in time. From that day on, Jessamine would be dead to him, he decided with grim resolution. In time he hoped the love would die too, for despite all his intentions to the contrary, he still loved her with every ounce of his being.

He was shown into the parlor that had become as familiar to him as his own. Vera was sitting on the window seat, sewing. When he entered the room, she stood up and shyly smiled.

"Don't let me disturb your sewing."

"You aren't."

He came to her and took the cloth from her hand as they sat down on the padded seat. "What are you making?"

"It's a collar for my blue cambric muslin."

"You do beautiful work." His hand dwarfed the thin cloth with its tiny stitches of flowers and leaves.

He looked at Vera closely. She was no beauty, but he had come to think of her as pretty. Certainly she wasn't one to entice other men with flashy smiles or bubbling laughter. Vera rarely laughed aloud at all, and when she did, the sound was soft and controlled. Her brown hair was always shiny and clean, even if it wasn't a mass of luxuriant black waves, and her calm eyes were simply brown and not sparkling gray like quicksilver. Even now when the pulse in her throat told him she was very aware of his nearness, Vera's movements were calm and her manner demure.

Ransome took her hand and turned it up in his to look at her small pink palm. Vera didn't pull back, but she blushed and glanced away when he raised his eyes to hers.

"Vera, in all the times I've been over here, you have never once given me any encouragement. Is it because you don't care for me?"

Her startled eyes met his and her lips parted in amazement. "Not given you encouragement toward what? You know how we all admire you."

"I'm not talking about your parents. I'm wondering about you."

"I . . . I admire you a great deal." She blushed again and looked away.

Ransome put his thumb and forefinger on her chin to gently draw her back. "Do you admire me only as your father's future law partner, or do you care for me as a man?"

"I don't know how to answer you."

"Just tell me what you feel. I've come to be very fond of you. Perhaps more than merely fond."

Her eyes widened and she moistened her lips with the tip of her tongue in an unconsciously enticing manner.

"Vera, I'm asking you to marry me."

For a moment she seemed tempted to run from the room, and her hand trembled in his. Instead, she lifted her head and met his eyes bravely. "I would love to be your wife, Ransome."

He smiled and leaned over to kiss her, hoping to erase the sudden twinge of sadness that tugged at his heart. Vera's lips were soft and her breath sweet in his mouth, and surprisingly, her lips parted the least bit beneath his own. He didn't feel the earth-shattering love and passion for her that he had felt for Jessamine, but he did feel a different sort of love. One paler and calmer, but a love nonetheless. Not one that would move mountains, but also not one that could rip his heart out.

"I love you," she said shyly. "I have for ever so long."

"I wish you had told me sooner. I didn't know how you felt at all."

She looked deep into his eyes and said, "Do you love me? You haven't said so."

Ransome smiled, and this time it reached his eyes. She needed him, whereas Jessamine had not, and she would make him a wonderful wife. In time her calmness would soothe the wound in his soul. He meant it when he said, "I love you, Vera." He only wished he felt a portion of the fevered abandon he had felt with Jessamine and less guilt over saying the words to someone other than her.

28

"DOLL, I CAN'T TELL YOU HOW DISAPPOINTED I AM in you," Delia said in a grieved voice. "Why won't you tell us who this man is who got you in trouble? Reuben will see to it he marries you."

"No, ma'am. I can't tell you who it is." Behind her she could hear Tabitha banging pots and pans, and she knew her mother was in a rare temper, though she would say nothing in front of Delia. Doll held her head at a proud angle and waited for the woman to finish.

"Were you forced?"

"No, ma'am."

"I surely thought better of you. You must know you can't continue working here."

"Yes, ma'am. I know that."

"What will you do? Once this baby is born, you'll have to take care of it. Surely you don't expect Tabitha and Sam to be responsible for your child."

"No, ma'am." Doll's reply was almost drowned out in the clatter behind her.

Delia frowned at Tabitha, but didn't scold her. She knew from the woman's protruding lower lip and rigid back that Tabitha was even more upset than Delia was. "When is the baby due?"

"Late summer, I think. Toward the end of August."

Delia looked at Doll's waist. She was thicker than before, but showed no obvious signs of pregnancy, probably because of her height, Delia thought. Not every woman got big as fast as Susanna had. "You could have worked several more weeks before I would have noticed. Why didn't you?"

"I didn't want you to have to find out. I thought I owed it to you to tell you. This way you have time to find someone else to do my work."

Delia turned away. "That was admirable, but foolish. Now that I know you're *enceinte* and refuse to marry the

241

father of your child, I have no choice but to let you go at once.''

"Yes, ma'am.'' Doll kept her voice calm and her face impassive, but she was terribly upset. She should have waited until her pregnancy was more obvious, and worked for as long as she could.

Delia went to her reticule and counted out some money. "Here are the wages you're due. I'm sorry, Doll. I wish you had been more reasonable.''

Doll looked at the money for a moment before closing it into her fist. "Yes, ma'am.''

When Delia left the kitchen, Doll turned reluctantly to her mother. "I'm sorry, Ma.''

"Sorry!'' Tabitha whirled to face her daughter and spat the words out in a half-whisper so Delia wouldn't hear. "Who gave you that child!''

"I can't tell you.''

"Can't or won't? Who you been laying with? Don't tell me you is as free as that Dulcie girl!''

Doll drew herself up taller. "You know me better than that, Ma.''

"Well, what am I supposed to think! Here you are telling us you in trouble and you won't name the man. I can't help but think they must be a passel of them if you can't name him!''

"There's only one, Ma, and it wouldn't do any good to name him, because he's already married.''

"Give me his name! Sam will whale the tar out of him!''

"No, Ma. I won't.''

"Then maybe he ought to whale the tar out of you!''

"I'll never tell you his name, Ma, and Pa can't make me.''

Tabitha glared in frustration at her daughter. "I should have known you'd bring me grief, looking and talking the way you do. You look like a New Orleans fancy lady, and now I come to find out you act like one too!''

"I'm sorry,'' Doll repeated.

"Sorry don't fix it. Just get out of my sight.'' She abruptly turned back to the cabinet, but before she did so, Doll saw the tear run down her cheek.

"I'll make do. I can sell my handwork. I won't go hungry.''

Tabitha ignored her, so Doll turned and silently left

the house. The sun was warm on her back and shoulders, but inside she was cold. Sam was splitting kindling under the kitchen window and Doll paused to say, "You heard?"

"Damn right I heard. But I ain't surprised. I've knowed about you and your man for months."

Doll went to him and said, "You won't tell Ma?"

"And see her heart break over the likes of you? No!"

"Can't you understand at all?" Doll whispered so her mother couldn't overhear. "I love him!"

"Pah!" Sam snorted in derision. "You think he really gives a damn for you? I'd have said you was smarter than that!" He slammed the hatchet into a stick of wood and cleaved it in half. "Why did you have to pick a white man? I can't ever forgive you for that."

"I love him and I always have. In spite of what you say, he loves me too."

"And what the hell does that make your bastard! He won't be neither their kind nor ours."

Doll drew back and crossed her arms over her breasts as if she were chilled. "For one thing, it makes my *child* one step away from being legally white. You and Ma are always saying the white folks could bring back slavery at any time. Well, my baby will be born free, and a child takes the freedom of his mother. My grandchildren will be white by law, because this baby will be a mamelouque."

"You plan to raise your young'un to pass? You won't have white grandbabies unless it takes up with whites. Ain't you got no pride? What about our people? How could you turn you back on you own kind?"

"I haven't done that, Pa. I'm proud of who I am and what I am. I didn't fall in love with him because of his color. I did it in spite of it."

Sam looked at her a long time, heavy lines creasing his face. "From now on, I ain't got a daughter. Neither has my wife. I don't want to see you nor hear from you for the rest of my life. If anybody asks after you, I'm gonna tell them you died. Now, get out of here."

"Pa!" Doll's anguish was sharp in her voice, and she took a step toward him as if she would embrace him.

Sam stopped her with a dark scowl, then went back to viciously chopping the kindling.

Doll turned and ran from the yard, skirting behind the chickenhouse to avoid Jessamine, who was working in the flower garden. She couln't bear to tell her friend what had happened. Jessamine would be upset at hearing about her condition from Delia, but Doll knew it was best this way. Jessamine couldn't possibly continue to be her friend now that Doll was about to bear an illegitimate baby—especially since Jessamine's brother was the father. Doll cared too much for Jessamine to put her in that position. It was far better to let Jessamine think she had been as false a friend as Ransome MacKinley had proven to be.

Despite her good intentions, Doll was crying as she walked away from her family, her best friend, and her source of income. She only hoped her sewing would sell quickly before she ran out of money altogether, because she would never ask Jerome to support her.

She walked over the field past the sawmill and into the woods. Despite her brave words to Jerome, she was very much afraid. There was no guarantee that her sewing could bring in enough money for her to live on, much less enough to support a baby as well. And that was another thing. She lived all alone down there by the swamp. What if something went wrong during the baby's birth, and she couldn't get help? She and the baby might both die.

As her rising panic brought a brassy taste to her mouth, Doll thought of Asiza, and the image of the witch woman gave her strength and peace. Asiza wouldn't crumble and let this destroy her. Asiza would rise above it. "It's all a matter of who's gonna be the boss," she would say. "You can lie down and die, or you can take hold of the reins."

Doll lifted her head and shoved the tears from her cheeks. Asiza had taught her a great deal, and it wouldn't be thrown away now. As she neared her secluded house, Doll's strides were firm and her back was straight.

29

WHEN JESSAMINE LOOKED UP FROM THE COOKIES she was making and brushed aside the kitchen curtain, she saw a buggy driving toward their house. "Looks like we have company, Tabitha."

Tabitha put her sad-iron on the hearth and picked up the heated one to finish pressing Reuben's Sunday shirt. "I'll go see who it is when they gets to the door," she said with a sigh as she smoothed the wrinkles beneath her dark hands. Since Doll had shamed her, she scarcely seemed to have enough energy to get through the day.

"It looked like Jerome's horse, but I only saw a woman. You don't suppose Susanna is condescending to visit us?"

"Yes, ma'am, I guess," Tabitha replied in the flat servile tone she used when she didn't want to talk to her white employers.

Jessamine dusted the flour from her hands and untied her apron. "You're busy. I'll go to the door." Delia had not hired anyone to take Doll's place, and they all had more to do than before.

"Yes, ma'am." Tabitha methodically pushed the iron back and forth, the smell of hot starch filling the kitchen.

As Jessamine opened the door to see who it was, Susanna rushed in, and without so much as a greeting, she demanded, "Where's Jerome!"

"I have no idea. Have a seat, Susanna. Can I get you some lemonade?"

"He must be here! He said he was coming to Ten Acres!"

Delia heard their voices and came into the parlor to see who was there. "Why, Susanna! What a surprise. Did you bring the baby out for a visit?"

"No, no. I have to find Jerome. Something terrible has happened." Her plump hands shook and her voice trembled. "It's Papa!"

Delia pulled her down on the settee and sat beside her, holding both of Susanna's hands. "What has happened?"

"I had gone over there to have Mama show me a new crochet stitch. Papa came in early and said he wasn't feeling well. Mama said he should lie down, then all at once he looked really strange, grabbed at his arm, and fell over. Mother Delacroix, he's dead!"

"Dead!" Delia echoed. "Oh, surely not! Not Arnaud!"

"Yes! Yes, he is. Mama sent Andre for the priest and the doctor, but Papa was already gone by the time we got Silas to carry him up to bed. What ever will we do without him!" Susanna buried her face in her handkerchief and brokenly sobbed.

Delia turned to Jessamine. "She must find Jerome. Do you have any idea where he might be?"

"No, I have no . . ." Jessamine's voice trailed off. She suddenly recalled how Doll had known about Susanna craving fig preserves and how it had been Doll who told her about Susanna's new hobby of cutting silhouettes from black paper. A dozen small remarks and turns of phrase returned to Jessamine. Her eyes widened and she whispered, "No!"

"I'm positive he's here," Susanna repeated with a wail. "He said he was coming here."

"Jessamine, look down the bayou and see if he has gone fishing. Or maybe on the sawmill pier where he goes crabbing sometimes."

Jessamine's mind was racing. This time she couldn't deny the evidence. "I think I may know where to find him."

She hurried from the house in the direction of the bayou, but as soon as she was out of sight, she cut back toward the swamp and ran through the forest of sweet gum and persimmon. She had been to Doll's house only once before, but she had no trouble finding it. Her momentum carried her plunging into the meadow out in front of the house, but there she paused. Jerome's saddle horse wasn't in sight, nor was anyone to be seen at all. A well-worn trail crossed the billowy silver-green grass at an angle toward town. Jessamine tried to keep her mind on the trail and not think about the house at the end of the trail. Doll could have beaten that path, she thought hopefully.

Jessamine walked slowly to the house and stepped into the cool green shade of the massive oaks. As if Jerome had been watching her all along, he stepped out onto the porch.

Jessamine stared up at him in silence. The door opened

behind him and Doll also stepped out. She held her head up proudly, but didn't speak. Jerome warily watched his sister as if he were waiting to hear what she would say about his being there.

On numb legs Jessamine climbed the steps, grateful for the railing so she could pull herself forward. When she reached the porch and no one said a word, she said. "Jerome, Susanna is looking for you. Mr. Leslie is dead."

"Dead!"

"It sounds as if he had a heart attack." She looked at Doll and saw fear lurking in her beautiful eyes. Looking back at her brother, she saw a matching concern there. "No one else knows. About you, I mean."

"How did you know?" he demanded.

"I didn't. Until now."

Jerome turned back to Doll and touched her affectionately on the arm. She automatically lifted her hand as if to stroke him in return. "I have to go, Doll."

"I know." Her frightened eyes returned to Jessamine.

Turning to his sister, Jerome said, "I suppose you'll feel obliged to tell Susanna and our parents?"

Jessamine's voice was little more than a whisper. "I'm not obliged to tell anyone." She couldn't stop staring from one to the other. Then she recalled the urgency of her mission, and she added, "You'd better go, Jerome."

"I'll saddle my horse." He exchanged a long look with Doll.

Doll knotted her fists in her full skirt when she was left with Jessamine on the porch. "I don't know what to say to you."

"Why . . . why didn't you tell me?"

"How could I?"

"Jerome is the man you were talking about in the woods that day we were gathering the walnuts? The man you loved, but he was married?"

"Yes." She steeled herself for an outburst of anger and disgust, but none came.

Jessamine was still stunned. "You said that you love him. That he loves you!"

"That's right."

"Then the baby . . ."

Doll spread her hand protectively over the swell of her stomach and nodded.

Jessamine didn't know what else to say. For the first time in her life, she was actually speechless.

Jerome led his horses out of the barn and closed the door before he mounted. Riding to the porch, he said to Jessamine, "Get on behind me."

She looked back at Doll. "I won't tell anyone."

"Do you hate me, Jessamine?" Tears caught in Doll's voice, but she retained her proud carriage.

"No. No, I don't hate you. Neither of you." She paused before adding, "But I can't condone this, either. It's wrong. You know it's wrong!"

"Get on the horse," Jerome snapped.

Jessamine dropped her leg over the horse's rump as she had when she was a girl, and held to the back lip of the saddle. Jerome kicked the horse into a lope, and Jessamine heard Doll call after her, "Don't hate us, Jessamine." She didn't look back.

Jerome didn't speak during the ride back to Ten Acres, and Jessamine was glad to have the opportunity to compose herself. All her life she had been taught that the racial barrier was absolute and insurmountable. She had felt quite daring to have Doll as a friend and confidante and knew none of her other friends were nearly so close to their ex-slaves. She had heard of half-caste babies being born on other plantations, but that was never the case at Roseland. She even knew Doll herself was the result of Tabitha's former master's lust, yet somehow it had been far removed from her—a thing that happened among strangers. Not something that involved her best friend and her beloved brother.

At the house, Jessamine waited for Jerome to take his left foot out of the stirrup and push it within reach of her toes. She reached around him to the saddle horn and swung to the ground. As she brushed horsehairs from her skirt, he dismounted and silently stared at her for a moment. His dark eyes were sad and his face drawn into rigid lines.

"One word from you and it will blow wide open," he said in a low voice. "I just want you to know that it isn't what it must seem. I love Doll. I love her the way a man ought to love his wife. This isn't a tawdry affair in my eyes. If I'm forced to choose between Doll and Susanna, I'll take Doll."

Jessamine gave him a long look before she said calmly, "Jerome, I have no idea what you're talking about. I found you down on the pier, and what you were doing there is none of my business."

A slow smile lifted his lips and he released his pent-up breath. "Thank you, Jessamine. I'll never forget this."

She nodded and went toward the house.

Jerome felt a sharp tug of longing as he rode up the curving drive of Roseland. The tunnel of live oaks was unaltered and the magnolias beyond still held their leathery leaves up to the sun. His mother's rose garden still nodded in the perfumed breeze and the fountain splashed as steadily as ever. There were, however, changes. The old pecan tree toward the back of the house had been cut down, and the flowerbeds that had always held violets were now filled with marigolds. The courting swing was gone from the veranda and in its place were several rattan chairs and a small slate-topped table.

Feeling oddly out of place, Jerome tied his horse to a ring embedded in a post under the shade of the nearest oak and mounted the ever-so-familiar steps to knock on the front door. When he had lived here, Sam was instructed to open the door wide to visitors before they had to knock. Jerome waited several minutes and had knocked again before the door was half-opened by a suspicious white butler.

"I'd like to see Mr. MacKinley." Jerome said.

The butler looked as if opening the door farther was the greatest of impositions, but he grudgingly did so.

Jerome was shown into the foyer, and as he waited he stared about in surprise. The walls were painted a dull shade of blue instead of the soft rose he had remembered, and the elegantly carved hall tree from his youth was gone altogether. In its place hung an enormous gilt-framed mirror adorned with cupids, roses, and fat ribbons. Jerome saw in disgust that its surface reflected poorly, showing a ripple when he moved.

After a brief conference with the master of the house, the butler returned and belatedly took Jerome's hat. At last he was ushered into the formal parlor.

Here Mrs. MacKinley's taste was even more apparent. Heavy burgundy rugs covered the honey-oak floors, and matching draperies made the room gloomy in spite of the sunshine outside. Side tables of various shapes were cluttered with every imaginable form of bric-a-brac and photographs and lamps. The furniture was dark brown horsehair that looked decidedly uninviting, and the walls had been papered with dark blue and gold medallions in stripes of brown ivy. Most of the walls' surfaces were covered with portraits of relatives and poorly executed pictures of chubby

Greek women carrying nonsymmetrical jugs of water beside streams that seemed to belong to the British countryside.

Eliza sat on a lady's chair with her plump feet on a tufted stool. Ian MacKinley held court from a massive wooden chair that looked more like a throne. One side of his face was drawn into a permanent scowl and his right hand lay puffy and helpless in his lap. "What business do you have here?" he demanded, his words slurring out of only one side of his mouth.

Jerome wasn't offered a chair, so he walked to the mantel that was bedecked in an Indian shawl with thick gold fringe. "I've come to make you a proposition."

"How's that? A proposition?" He glared from Jerome to Eliza, who promptly began sewing with swift little stitches.

"I want to buy Roseland."

"It's not for sale," Ian barked.

"Don't be too hasty in your answer. First I should remind you that Mr. Leslie's death left me the sole owner of the shipping company. The cost for you to ship your cotton has just tripled."

"You can't raise the price like that! It isn't legal! It's robbery!"

"No, it's not robbery. It's dirty dealing. However, you have no choice."

"Don't I! I'll haul my cotton to market by wagon! That way you won't see a penny of my money!"

Jerome shook his head. "A large wagon can haul eight, maybe ten bales at a time. That would put the weight at, say, five thousand pounds. Even a good team of oxen can't make more than fifteen miles a day with a load like that. By the time you reach New Orleans you will have spent more than I'm charging and you'll be very late to market."

"I'll just haul it to the Mississippi and put it on a boat there."

"No you won't. Leslie shipping works very closely with all the other shippers that work the Mississippi, and after I tell them that you won't do business with me, they will refuse your cotton."

"Then I'll pick early and haul it to New Orleans myself!"

"I happened to ride through one of your fields, and the bolls are just starting to open, and here it is August. You have a late crop this year."

Ian wet his fleshy lips. "I'll send them by flatboat!

That's faster than oxen and I can load a couple of hundred bales on one."

"You must know something I don't," Jerome said with studied innocence. "Even assuming the water in the bayou stays high enough to float your boat, and assuming you stay clear of brush rafts and jams, why, you're still going to have a job on your hands."

"Why?"

"Loose cotton tends to blow off in the least little breeze."

"Loose . . . Are you saying you won't bale my cotton?"

"Now, don't get so upset," Jerome said with a patronizing motion to calm him. "All I mean to say is that the gin owner decides what to gin first."

"It's always been first come, first served!"

"It was that way at one time, wasn't it? I don't guess I need to remind you that I own all three gins and that the next-closest one is over two days' ride from here. That's a lot of hauling, since a cotton wagon won't hold the equivalent of one bale."

"Get out of my house!"

Jerome strolled across the room and looked about in wry amusement. "If you change your mind, Mr. MacKinley, send me word. I'm willing to give you much more than Roseland's worth, now that you can't bale or ship your cotton."

"I'd burn this house down and salt the ground before I'd let a Delacroix live here again."

"Funny. That's more or less what my father said about you Yankees."

Jerome was smiling as he retrieved his hat from the stony-faced butler, and as he mounted his horse, he laughed softly. Losing Roseland's income at the docks and the gin was a small price to pay for being able to hold the whip over the MacKinleys.

He was feeling so good, he rode to Doll's house rather than to town. "You should have seen old man MacKinley's face when I told him I won't ship his bales or give him preference at the gin over the other planters."

Doll slowly dusted the latest book Jerome had brought her and put it on the nearly full shelf. "I wish you hadn't done that. I don't have a good feeling about it."

"Now, honey, it's just because of your condition."

Jerome placed his hand on her distended stomach and felt the baby roll and kick. "The baby is agreeing with me."

"I still don't feel right about it. No good will come of keeping the feud alive."

"I'm not trying to keep it going. I'm trying to buy back Roseland."

"Who would live in it? You and Susanna? Miss Delia, Mr. Reuben, and Jessamine? All of you at once?"

"I'd give it to my parents, of course. In time, Pierce would inherit it."

"Roseland is just a house. The land it sits on is just dirt. Can't you see that? It's not important enough to bring up hard feelings all over again."

"Not important?" Jerome exclaimed. "It's who I am! It's my heritage! You just don't understand."

"No. I can't understand that." She turned away from him and began dusting with quick, angry strokes.

Jerome sighed and ran his hand over his black hair. "Doll, I'm sorry. This is the closest we've ever come to arguing."

She tossed aside the dust cloth and went to put her arms around him. "I'm sorry, Jerome. It's not my place to tell you what to do."

"It's more your right than anyone's," he said as he kissed her forehead. "I just don't agree with you."

She smiled up at him and said, "Since I don't plan to live there myself, you can suit yourself about it. I just wish you were doing this to please your father rather than to destroy the MacKinleys."

"What difference does it make if the results are the same?"

"It makes a big difference as to what happens to you in here." She touched his chest above his heart.

"You worry too much."

Ransome tied his cravat and smoothed his hand over the rich gray suede of his new coat. His perfectly tailored trousers were a pale buff and his silk brocade vest was deep garnet. An expensive gold watch was in his pocket and the chain looped flat across his lean stomach. He looked like exactly what he was—a young lawyer who had just passed his bar exam and who was about to enter into two very important partnerships. His name was already stenciled on the frosted glass door of the Sherwin law office. "Sherwin and MacKinley," it now read.

He reached in his vest pocket and fished out a flat ring box. Slowly he opened it and looked down at the wide gold band inside. It was so thick it covered almost the entire joint on Vera's small hand, but it was the one she had wanted. One that wouldn't wear out, she had said, in all the years and years that stretched before them.

Years and years. Ransome snapped the box shut and closed his fist around it. If he were marrying Jessamine, would all those years seem so endless as they did to him at this moment? He looked back at the mirror and saw the crease of consternation on his brow. Surely this was no more than last-minute nervous jitters. Nothing else.

Nevertheless, he sat at his desk and rolled the top up to take out a pen and paper. Within the hour he would marry Vera. As a last salute to Jessamine, he wrote to tell her so, letting the bold strokes of the pen pour out for the last time his grief over her treatment of him and the last affirmation of love that he would ever be free to give her.

When he was finished, he sealed the letter with a blob of red wax and addressed it to Jessamine. He held the thick envelope in his hand as if he were considering whether or not to mail it.

A knock sounded on his door and his aunt called out, "Are you ready, Ransome? We mustn't be late."

"Coming, Aunt Polly."

Resolutely he put the letter in his coat pocket to post on the way to the church. For better or for worse, from this day forward he would belong to Vera.

Reuben took the thick envelope from his pocket and leaned his forearms on his scarred desk. Outside he could hear the high-pitched snarl of the saws and occasional snatches of the workers' songs. Whoever would have guessed the MacKinley boy would still continue to write to Jessamine and she to him? All these letters, and not an answer to a single one.

Reuben wasn't an insensitive man, nor was he cruel. He had only wanted to save his daughter from making a terrible mistake. Now he was beginning to doubt the wisdom of that decision. Not once had he ever read one of the letters, but this time he was tempted. If he had misjudged the young man, he wanted to make it right.

He scowled at the envelope. As head of the family, he had to be strong, and he had to be indisputably right. At the moment he felt neither. He loved Jessamine and wanted only what was best for her, and he knew Ransome Mac-Kinley wasn't the man she should have. So why did he feel so damned guilty? He wished he had never heard of that accursed family.

Jessamine adamantly refused to even consider attracting a husband, and now that Louis Broussard had married Dorothée Parlange, Reuben had to admit her chances were slim. Louis had been the last really eligible beau in town. Instead of bemoaning her fate of spinsterhood, Jessamine seemed to accept it with a stoicism Reuben had never suspected. Delia had even hinted they might have been hasty in their refusal of young MacKinley, and Delia, of course, had no idea about the letters in the tin box in the sawmill. Reuben sighed heavily. He wished he had never thought of intercepting their mail. Once begun, it was difficult to stop.

As he had done so often, he pulled the box from the top shelf. It was full to the top with letters in Ransome's large hand and Jessamine's flowing script. One more, he promised himself. If one more letter came from the boy, he would give the box to Jessamine and buy her a ticket to Albany. This salved his conscience once more, and he closed the box on Ransome's letter.

He went back to his desk and unrolled a large sheet of paper. Putting his inkwell on one corner and a plumb bob on the other to hold it open, Reuben studied the layout of his newest enterprise. The lowlands between the mill and the road had been put up for sale, and he had bought them cheap. Everyone else thought they were good for nothing because whenever the bayou flooded on one side or the *coulée,* on the other the fields became a shallow lake. These fields, as well as the land cleared by his sawmill operation, were almost always in a state of semibog. He had thought they were useless too, until he had happened upon a book about growing rice.

Painstakingly Reuben mapped out the water lanes and irrigation ditches for the crop that would support them when the cypress trees had all been cut into lumber.

30

THE RAIN DIDN'T COME, AND THE SKY WAS BRASSY with the heat. Old-timers throughout southern Louisiana said they had never seen so severe a drought. The flowers were first to go; then the grasses withered and the ground cracked open. Even the trees seemed to draw into themselves, their leaves becoming limp and pale and seeming to lack the strength to stir in the faint breeze that blessed the land all too infrequently.

Jerome stepped out on Doll's porch and looked up at the night sky through the moon-silvered leaves on the oaks. "There's a full moon."

"Maybe it will change the weather," she speculated as she came out to join him. "I knew months ago when the new moon had both its horns tilted up that we wouldn't get rain for a while. I never guessed it would be this scarce." She walked down the steps with him and strolled out into the meadow while he saddled his horse.

The grasses were dry and yellow under her feet, and she moved heavily with her advanced pregnancy. The unusually severe heat had bothered her more than she let Jerome know. She lifted her face to catch whatever breeze might cool it, and gazed up at the moon.

"Jerome, look up. Have you ever in your life seen anything like that?"

He followed her gaze. The moon was fat and yellow against a black sky, but was encircled by a pale but distinct orange ring that was enormous. "No, I haven't."

Doll apprehensively shifted her weight, saying, "Neither have I. What do you think it means?" Because of their close ties to the moods of nature, weather signs were important to them both.

"Maybe we're going to have some rain. That ring must be on a mist of clouds. Look, there aren't any stars out."

"I don't smell rain. The wind is blowing from an un-

255

usual direction too. Normally this time of the year it's coming in from the Gulf.''

"Maybe a storm is finally brewing. We could use one.'' He put his hands on her arms. "Are you going to be all right?''

"Of course I am. I'm just tired. You would be too if you had this load to carry.''

"It won't be much longer. Maybe I should have Nanine Boudreaux move in until the baby comes.''

"No, she has to be handy for all the other babies that are due. Besides, she has her own family to look after. From all I hear, I'll have plenty of time to send for her when the pains start.''

"I'll be back in the morning before I go to work.''

"You can't keep coming out twice a day. Susanna will start to wonder.''

"She couldn't care less. I figure if I'm here that often, I'll be around in time to send for Nanine.''

"She passes by here on her way to and from work,'' Doll reminded him with a smile. "If I need her, I'm to hang a cup towel out the window.''

"I'm coming out anyway. My horse has been here so often he thinks this is the way to and from work.''

Doll laughed softly and tiptoed up and leaned forward to kiss him. "You're good to me, Jerome.''

"I love you. I just wish like hell the world was different, and we could always be together.''

"Go home,'' she said gently as she patted his arm.

"I am home.'' He swung up into the saddle and waited for her to get back into the house before he rode away.

All the way to town he wished he were staying in the haven beside the swamp. He worried about Doll almost constantly. Whenever he recalled Pierce's birth and the pain Susanna had endured, it as all he could do not to race back to Doll and see if she needed him. What if she went into labor during the night and was too incapacitated to hang out the cup towel? Susanna had all but collapsed with the first pain and hadn't even been able to walk to her room. Jerome almost turned his horse around and rode back. But Doll was right. Susanna didn't love him, but she wasn't about to let anyone else have him or to tolerate any suspicions over his absences. If trouble arose, he knew Doll was the one who would be vulnerable. The Knights of the White Camellia, the state band of the Klan, were on the lookout for any blacks who stepped out of line. That included mistresses, and he knew Susanna would tell the Klan if she ever learned exactly where he spent his time.

Jerome stabled his horse and went into the house. Even though he had become accustomed to the dusty disarray and the slight odor of mildew that lingered in the curtains and throw rugs, he always noticed it and didn't like it.

"So you've finally come home," Susanna complained. "Don't you think you owe me the courtesy of arriving on time tonight?"

"What's special about tonight?"

"It's our second anniversary!"

"Is it?" he asked in genuine surprise. "That's right!"

She pouted as she said, "You could at least come home early tonight of all nights."

"Why, Susanna? Does this mean you're developing a wifely fondness for me?" He hung his hat on the hall tree and crossed the room to straighten a curtain. "Tell Dulcie to air this room, and for goodness' sake, have her sweep the floor."

"Tell her yourself. No, I'm not becoming fond of you. Far from it. Mama was here for dinner tonight, and she remarked several times on your absence." Susanna petulantly leaned back on the settee and watched him closely as she said, "I'm lonely here in this big house."

"I tried to tell you we didn't need a house this size. Do you want to move?"

"And have everyone think we have lost our money? Never!"

"Then do you want a companion? I've told you before that I'll hire someone to stay with you if you like."

"I do have something like that in mind. I've asked Mama to move in with us."

"What!"

"She was overjoyed and has agreed to do it right away." She found a perverse delight in his appalled expression. "Surprised, *dear?*"

"I don't want her here," he said bluntly. "Tell her tomorrow that your offer is withdrawn."

"No, Jerome. And neither will you. See, I took a carriage ride this afternoon, and you weren't at the gins or the docks. Exactly where were you, Jerome?"

He frowned and said, "I don't have to give you an accounting of where I am every hour of the day."

"No? Then it will be to your advantage for Mama to move into the guest room so I won't have so much time for rides, won't it?" She pushed herself up from the couch and glared at him spitefully. "If I was a more suspicious person, I'd say you have a woman tucked away somewhere."

Jerome gave her a withering look and she said with genuine surprise, "Did I hit a nerve, Jerome? *Is* that what you're doing?"

"Would you care?"

"I would care a great deal if word got around town." She shrugged to show how little he meant to her. "Unlike you Delacroixs, we Leslies have a sterling reputation. I wouldn't stand by idly if it were sullied."

"Don't threaten me, Susanna. If you had been half a wife to me or shown me any respect or kindness, I'd have gone the rest of the way."

"You may have your fancy whore. Mama moves in next week."

The muscle tightened in Jerome's jaw, and he strode from the room.

Reuben and Sam climbed the rise of ground on which they had built the sawmill. Beyond the field on one side was the higher knoll where their houses were, and on the other was the swamp. A warbler sang in the neighboring woods, and from deep in the swamp, blackbirds could be heard calling to one another. Reuben looked up at the long, curving bands of clouds on the southern horizon in the faint dawn light. "Maybe we're finally going to see some rain."

Sam looked up and nodded. "I seen a mighty strange circle round the moon last night. Never seen nothing like it."

"Well, we need rain bad." Reuben pointed toward the cleared field below the mill. "When it cools off this fall, that field is the first one we're going to plow for the rice. I figure we can get a crop in the ground next spring if we work at it."

"Yes, sir."

They opened the door to the mill and the team of mules in the adjoining stable pricked their ears. Reuben went to the nearest one and patted the sleek neck. "These are the best animals I've owned since the war. The Ramseys asked a pretty penny for them, but I've never had a team with so much heart."

"They is workers, for sure." Sam slipped the bridle on the other mule. "They is as close a match as twins."

"That's why I named them Castor and Pollux."

"Yes, sir," Sam said with no comprehension.

Reuben looked up the road that led toward town. "Where do you suppose Tom and the others are? They should be here by now. They know we have to haul this lumber to the docks before high tide."

"I don't rightly know. It ain't like Tom to be late."

They harnessed the mules to the wagon and started loading the lumber. After a while Sam paused to rest for a bit and looked out the open window. A pile of dirty-looking clouds was mounded above the trees to the south and a thick haze covered the sky. The birds were calling loudly and fluttering from tree to tree. "I believe you gonna get your wish for rain, Mr. Reuben. Look here."

Reuben joined Sam at the window. "That's going to be a bad storm by the looks of it." He turned to the load of lumber. "Do you think we can drive this to the boat before it hits?"

"I don't know, it sure is building fast."

"We can't afford for it to get wet. It could warp and ruin the whole lot."

"Yes, sir."

"I wonder where the hell Tom and the crew are. If they had shown up, we would be on our way by now."

"Yes, sir." Sam was studying the clouds more closely. Dull lightning glowed silently in their depths, and they seemed to be growing taller and blacker, even as he watched. A strong breeze was blowing from due north, not a fitful breeze that rose and fell, but one that blew steadily and raked the parched grasses toward the Gulf. "Tom lives closer to the bayou. Maybe he knows something we don't."

Reuben again perused the storm clouds. "You don't think it's a hurricane, do you?"

"Yes, sir, I do. Look at how the wind is blowing one way and those clouds is coming up from the other. I believe we got trouble coming."

"And there was a full moon last night. The tides are already running high." He looked around the mill. "Do you think we're likely to take in water here?"

"I don't know. It's never flooded in all the years we been living here." The first low growl of thunder sounded.

"Damn! Well, the boat can't sail in a hurricane. We'll

have to get the load in tomorrow. Turn the mules back into the stalls and help me nail down everything that's loose.''

The pains had started during the night, and Doll had hung out the dishcloth by the time morning rolled around. The air was heavy with thunder and the clouds overhead looked swollen and thick. The air felt moist and beads of sweat pearled on her brow until she wiped them away.

She stepped out on the porch and listened to the birds. They were calling and fluttering restlessly, as if they were discussing the change in the weather. Doll watched the sullen lightning flashes behind the mounded clouds. In a few seconds thunder rumbled over the swamp. She wondered if Nanine would walk this way with it about to storm, or if she would catch a ride into town by way of the road. Another pain gripped Doll's lower back, reaching down her thighs. She decided not to think about Nanine not coming this way today.

She went back inside and made a pot of coffee. Jerome wasn't likely to ride out with the weather so bad, and she wasn't interested in eating anything. She moved restlessly about the house, straightening it and putting everything in its proper place. She and Jerome had made the storeroom into a nursery for the coming baby, and Doll again sorted through the tiny gowns and caps she had sewn and embroidered. Jerome had made a cradle, and she had stuffed a small feather tick to cushion the infant's sleep. She knelt and spread a clean white cloth over the ticking and tucked it in on the sides. Before much longer, the cradle wouldn't be empty.

Doll had seen women give birth in the quarters at Roseland, and she knew her labor was well under way. She looked out the window in hopes of seeing Nanine's large figure crossing the field, but the only movement she saw was that of the birds.

Struggling not to give rein to her fears, Doll tried to remember what she had seen the midwife do at the other birthings, but she had been only twelve, and she wasn't certain she remembered everything.

She pumped water into a pan and poured it into a pot on the fire-arm, then swung it over the fire. She hated to heat the room even more, but she had no choice, so she knelt and blew life into the banked coals and put a log on to burn. Another pain caught her as she was getting to her feet, and beads of sweat popped out on her forehead. When it passed, she stood and went to her sewing basket to get her scissors and heavy thread to tie off the baby's cord. She placed them by the bed and turned back the covers. Moving carefully, she felt her way along the wall, pausing as another contraction caught her.

She took a fresh sheet from the cupboard, along with a waxed birthing cloth. She spread the waterproof cloth over her mattress, then laid the folded sheet over that.

When the next pain came, she sat on the edge of the bed and held her stomach with both arms. Fear coursed through her as she considered whether she *could* deliver her own baby. She seemed to have no choice.

Doll drew a deep breath and forced herself to think over all she would need so she wouldn't forget anything. Since she never used snuff, she put the pepper shaker by the bed in case she needed sneeze contractions to help birth the baby. She placed her largest butcher knife under the mattress to cut the pain.

Again and again Doll went over all she had ever heard or seen regarding the birthing of a baby. Her thoughts focused on three of the slave women who had been born in Africa and who all spoke with a thick patois. When these women went into labor, they hadn't taken to their beds, but instead had walked and walked for as long as they could, then gone into the woods alone and delivered their babies by squatting over a shallow depression. She had once heard an old, old woman say that Indians gave birth the same way. With that in mind, Doll started pacing.

On her fifth trip down the length of her house, she paused and listened, then clapped her hands to see if she had gone deaf. Outside there was nothing but silence. With a frown, she went out onto the porch. The sky had taken on a yellowish hue, and the swamp was completely quiet. Even the thunder had stopped.

Doll's eyes widened, and she groped behind her for the doorway as a sickening fear closed about her. The swamp was always alive with bird calls, the roar of alligators, chirping frogs, the buzzing of insects. Even the very worst storms had never been enough to make the sounds cease.

She looked on the porch rail, where a fat green-backed fly crawled sluggishly. Only when she brushed it off with her hand did it fly, and then only as far as a nearby tree truck. Doll wet her lips nervously. Not a single breeze was stirring now.

She backed slowly into the house and closed the door. Pressing both her palms against the doorframe, she tried to decide what to do. Nanine wasn't coming. Not in this weather. Nor could she hope to walk all the way to Ten Acres. She couldn't even get on her horse in this condition.

Panic mounted within her, along with the next pain, and Doll pressed her forehead against the door as she clenched her teeth and squeezed her eyes shut. The house was strong, she reminded herself. Her father had built it high and tight to withstand hurricanes. The hated word formed before she could block it. Once in her mind it refused to leave.

Suddenly a squall of rain lashed the side of the house and Doll jumped with fright. Through the windows she could see the trees bend and strain under the sudden onslaught. Moving awkwardly, Doll closed the windows on the south side, where the rain was streaming in, and shut the heavy wooden shutters that usually hinged back flat against the wall. She dropped the board in place to lock them shut in case the windowpanes shattered. The room became dark and gloomy. Rain clattered against the tin roof and wind blew smoke back down the chimney into the room.

Doll heard a noise on the porch and stifled a scream as she backed away, not knowing what dread apparition might be blowing in with the storm. Suddenly the door flew open on a gust of wind and Jerome rushed in, slamming it closed behind him.

"Jerome!" She staggered to him and clutched him as if she were drowning.

"It's all right, *chérie*. I'm here." His deep voice had never sounded so reassuring to her. "I'm here."

"It's a hurricane," she whispered as she pressed close to him."

"I know. I'm going to take you farther inland. Are there friends you can stay with in town?"

"Jerome, I can't leave! The baby—it's on the way."

He paled with the thought, but tried not to show his concern. "Now?"

When she nodded frantically, he held her tighter. "Go to bed. I'll ride after Nanine."

"There's not time." She clutched him as another spasm racked her. "Even if you could get there and back in this storm, you wouldn't have time."

"Surely it's not . . . Doll, are your sure?" He drew back and studied her face.

She managed to laugh weakly. "I'm sure, all right."

He kept his arm around her and helped her walk back to the bedroom. How did one go about birthing a baby? He had no idea.

"It's going to be all right," she said as if she had heard his thoughts. "I've seen it done several times. You've helped mares foal. Don't worry."

"I'm not worried," he lied as he helped her sit on the edge of the bed. She still wore her voluminous nightgown and her hair was braided in a thick plait down her back.

He held her hand as the next contraction racked her, but she made no sound.

"That was a strong one," she gasped when it was over. "Maybe you had better bring me a washcloth to bite on so I don't break a tooth."

She lay back and looked out her window at the dark square of sky. The rain had stopped as quickly as it had started and the dense clouds were brassy and bright with an eerie yellow-green glow. Once more the odd silence hung like a separate element in the room as it did over the swamp. Doll's fearful eyes met Jerome's and neither was able to think of anything encouraging to say. Neither of them had ever ridden out a direct hit from a hurricane. The only sound was the dripping of water from the oaks onto the roof and from there onto the ground.

All at once a noise started back in the swamp and spread quickly to all the surrounding trees. Doll half-sat up in the bed. "It's the birds!" she exclaimed. "They're wailing!"

No other word quite described it. The noise was unlike any they had ever heard. All the birds, from the tiny warblers to the blackbirds to the ibises and herons, were shrieking cries unlike mating calls or songs. These were warning cries the birds were squealing in terror.

"I never heard them do that before," Jerome murmured. "I had heard legends that they did that before a hurricane, but I didn't really believe it."

"I'm afraid," Doll whispered as she caught his hand.

He stroked her icy fingers and managed to smile at her. "There's nothing to be afraid of. I'm here with you and I'll keep you safe."

Doll nodded but she looked back at the square of sky. It was a glaring green now. "That's a tornado sky."

"What are you always telling me? These old oaks have been here for a hundred years, and they'll be here a hundred more. As long as they stand, nothing can happen to this house. If the house is all right, we're perfectly safe." He stood up and took off his coat and ribbon tie. "I'm going to the barn and get some boards to nail over the windows down there to protect the animals. Will you be okay for a few minutes?"

She nodded, her eyes large and frightened. "Be careful, Jerome."

He kissed her lightly and walked out. On the porch he paused and shivered. The birds' screams were louder out here and the oak trees above his head were full of noisy birds scrambling for perches as close to the massive trunks as possible. The air seemed overpowering and too thick to breathe.

In the barn he nailed scraps of lumber over the two windows after being certain the two horses and the cow were securely fastened in out of the weather. The horses rolled their eyes and stamped nervously and the cow lowed mournfully, as if she were pleading for help.

As Jerome nailed the last board, the storm broke again, and sheets of rain fell from the sky. He latched the barn door and ran for the house. Before he had gone two steps he was drenched to the skin.

Peals of thunder and lightning crashed as he rushed back into the house. The wind was increasing steadily, driving the rain almost horizontally. Jerome saw a small herd of deer break cover and dash across the meadow. Moments later a panther, its yellow fur matted darkly onto its muscles, raced across the meadow and passed the deer without paying them the slightest attention. A black bear with twin cubs trotted through the woods, all heading inland and away from the swamp. Hard on their heels were several rabbits and an opossum.

Jerome closed the door and tried to erase the concern from his face. He went into the room that would be the nursery, and picked up the cradle. He took it to the bedroom and placed it by the bed. "We're all ready now," he said with all the confidence he could muster.

"I'm so glad you're here! But won't Susanna worry?"

"She has her mother with her and thinks I went to the docks. She'll assume I was trapped there by the storm. That house has weathered several hurricanes so she's in no danger."

"Are we?"

"No, of course not," he said heartily. "Would you like a cup of coffee?"

She shook her head.

Jerome went in the other room and opened one shutter to look out. He didn't see a tornado, but the trees were dancing and scraping as if one were passing over. He could see a bobcat lying in a heap amid the lashing grass, its back broken from being thrown from one of the swaying trees.

A strange restlessness seized Jerome, and he paced from the window to the hearth and back again. His face felt flushed as adrenaline pumped through him, and he felt a kinship to the fleeing animals. He understood now the illogical urge to rush out into the storm—an urge he had heard of but had never experienced.

The wind continued to rise until it whined around the eaves of the house. In the brief lapses between the downpours of rain, he saw the swamp water. It was swept clear of much of the green carpet of duckweed, and the normally placid water rippled and began to wave and whitecap in the wind. The ragged festoons of moss swept into the wind and were torn loose, to roll on the grass like scalps of gray hair.

Jerome again bolted the shutter and went back to sit beside Doll. Occasionally there was a dull thud as a wind-tossed bird or small animal slammed into the side of the house. Doll's eyes were round with pain and fear, but she uttered no complaints.

She was as restless as he was and her slender hands moved constantly, clutching, releasing, and rumpling the sheet that covered her. When the labor pains came, she pressed into the mattress and bit the washcloth as her knees drew up. Jerome sponged her face and held her hands as he talked to her soothingly.

"What's that sound? I hear something!" she said.

"It's just the wind whistling in the chimney. Don't be afraid."

"It sounds like somebody blowing over the mouth of a bottle. A *big* bottle," she added nervously.

He went to her window and drew back the shutter he had closed to block out the storm. The rain was coming down so hard he could scarcely see, but what he did make out caused him concern. "The swamp is coming out of its banks. You can't see the ground for the water."

"The animals! If it gets too deep, they'll drown in the barn!"

"I'll be back."

"Where are you going?"

"I'm going to turn them loose. They'll find high ground and we can get them back later."

"Be careful!"

Jerome nodded and hurried out of the house. He had to hold tight to the slick railing to get down the steps, and for a while he was afraid he couldn't fight his way to the barn. At last he grabbed the door and it slammed open when he released the latch. The horses were shrieking in terror and even the normally calm cow was weaving and kicking in her stall. Jerome opened the stalls and jumped back as the animals plunged past. They galloped out of the barn and instinctively headed for town and higher ground.

Jerome clawed his way back through the knee-deep water and tried not to think what it might have been that thumped against his legs in the muddy froth. When he reached the steps he kicked a water moccasin aside as he climbed them, then forced his way into the relative calm of the house.

Reuben paced the parlor, testing the windows again and again to be sure the boards were holding. Tabitha was crouched against the inner wall with Delia and Jessamine. He could hear the dark woman's near-hysterical prayers. Sam was as restless as Reuben and unable to sit still for checking on first one thing, then another.

Reuben went to the back window and peeked between the cracks in the boards. The glass had been broken out by a tree limb earlier in the morning. "Look at that water, Sam. It's going to flood all the way to the mill!"

"It sure is. I never seen nothing like this in my life. It looks like the end of the world!"

"All I can think about are those mules. I shouldn't have left them down there. I should have known to bring them up here on higher ground."

"Ain't nothing we can do about it now."

"Yes, there is. I'm going after them."

"No, sir, you ain't! You trying to get yourself killed?"

"It's not that bad out yet. You let me out the door and shut it after me. I'll run down, let them out, and run back. I won't be gone more than fifteen, twenty minutes." Reuben's face was flushed and his eyes glittered with storm-fever.

"No, sir!"

"Don't argue with me!"

Sam automatically stepped back and shut his mouth.

Reuben pulled on his oiled coat and buttoned it to his chin, then jammed his hat down tight on his head. "I'll be right back. Don't tell the women I'm going, they'll just worry."

"Yes, sir." Sam helped him out and barred the door behind him.

The wind was stronger than Reuben had expected and the gusts almost lifted him off his feet. His hat spun away as he bent over and ran down the slope to the dark blur he knew was the mill.

Water rose to his knees and then to mid-thigh as he fought his way toward the building. Above the keening of the storm he could hear the frenzied mules thrashing about in their stalls. A loose corner of the sheet-tin roof had pulled loose and as he opened the mill door, the wind ripped the metal back with a shriek and yanked it whirling up into the air as if it were a cumbersome kite.

Inside, the water was halfway up the stall doors. Even in the darkness, Reuben could see the whites of the mules' eyes. He opened the first stall and Pollux leapt out, splashing across the mill and out the door. Castor reared in his terror of being left alone as Reuben struggled with the stubborn latch.

The water was rising fast, and Reuben was increasingly afraid he wouldn't be able to reach the higher ground. He finally opened the latch, and as the mule plunged out, he grabbed a handful of mane and tried to swing onto the animal's back.

Castor shied and reared. Reuben's hand tangled in the mane but he couldn't throw his sodden leg high enough to mount the animal. As they cleared the mill door, Reuben looked toward the swamp in time to see the tidal wave rolling and building as the hurricane pushed the water before it. His eyes widened and his voice merged with the scream of the mule and the storm as his hand lost its grip and he was caught by the rushing water. Castor lashed out with his iron-shod hooves, and one connected squarely with Reuben's temple.

Reuben Delacroix slipped beneath the muddy water as the mule floundered toward high ground and safety.

31

ALL THE NOISE CEASED ABRUPTLY EXCEPT FOR THE low moans Doll made as she fought to give birth to her baby. Jerome never released his grip on her hands, but he looked up fearfully. "We're in the eye," he said.

Doll made an unintelligible response followed by a groan not unlike that of an animal in primeval pain. "It's coming!" she cried out. "It's coming!"

Moving quickly, Jerome stripped back the sheet and caught the shiny head of the baby as it emerged. "Push!" he shouted in the eerie stillness. "Push hard!"

The storm resumed as suddenly as it had stopped. The wind slammed into the house from the opposite direction and again roared down the chimney. Doll strained and groaned and the baby was born.

"It's a girl!" Jerome cried out as he held up the squalling baby. "It's a girl!"

Doll laughed with relief and cried at the same time. He tied off the cord and cut the baby free. After he wiped the tiny face and body clean, he laid his daughter in Doll's arms, then cleaned up Doll and put fresh sheets beneath her.

Although the storm raged on, Doll's total attention was on Jerome and their child. She looked up at him, her eyes shining with pride at their accomplishment. The baby cried lustily and her hands lifted in tiny fists at the indignity of being taken from the warmth and security of her mother's womb and thrust into this howling world. "Look at her," he said with pride, ignoring the creaks from the house as the sheets of rain and pounding wind threatened to tear it asunder. "She already acts like a Delacroix. Look at her defiant expression."

Doll's smile was tired as she said, "She won't ever be a Delacroix. She's a Farmer."

Reluctantly he nodded. "I know, but I don't like to

think my daughter won't bear my name. It's so unfair, Doll.''

"Life is like that."

He touched the incredibly soft skin on the baby's arm. "Little Annie Laurie. She'll be as beautiful as the song." He smiled at Doll and added, "But she won't ever be as beautiful as her mother."

Doll put her hand over his. "I love you." The three of them huddled together, with Doll and Jerome's heads touching over the baby their love had created.

For almost an entire day following the ravages of the hurricane, all of nature's creatures declared a truce. Whites and blacks helped each other pick up the pieces and put their lives back in order, and even the animals were at peace. A coon and a bobcat were seen riding a log through the swollen swamp as if they weren't natural enemies, and a rabbit was seen hopping by a notoriously vicious yard dog while each ignored the other. Gradually the stunned shock of the storm wore away and the smaller animals dug frantically to rebuild burrows and nests before the predators could catch them. Hunting renewed with vigor as the bears and swamp cats returned to find their prey helpless without their familiar escapes. And on the second day, Reuben's body was found in a raft of broken trees and limbs and debris.

The black veil of mourning settled over Ten Acres and both Jerome and Jessamine remarked with worry at Delia's state of mind. "I think she has become unbalanced," Jessamine confided to her brother in a low voice.

"It's only the grief, surely."

"She didn't sink so far when Spartan, or even Adele, died, and I thought she would go mad then."

Jerome looked into the parlor, where their mother sat in heavy black mourning weeds despite the sweltering heat. Delia was erect, but perfectly still as she stared sightlessly out the window. "Has she spoken or eaten anything?"

"No. She hasn't even cried since we returned from the funeral yesterday, and you can see she hasn't touched a bite of her dinner." Jessamine nodded toward the tray she had prepared from dishes brought by friends and relatives who had come to the funeral.

"Has Cousin Aglaé left yet?"

"She went to visit Cousin Athanaise and Jules before

she goes back to Lake Charles. Since they moved to Breaux Bridge they probably haven't heard about Papa. You know Athanaise is his cousin, just as Jules is." Her voice faltered. "I should say 'was.' Jerome, what are we going to do without Papa?"

"You'll move in with us. The house is big enough. I'll take care of you."

Jessamine laughed shortly. "I can just hear Susanna if you suggest such a thing. Besides, her mother lives there too, and you can't see to all of us."

"Of course I can. Sam can continue living here and running the sawmill. We will have to abandon the idea of the rice farm, but Sam never really grasped Papa's notion about that. I'm a rich man. You won't have to worry."

"No, Jerome. I know you would take care of us, it isn't that, but I don't want to leave Ten Acres. Neither will Mama. Can you imagine Susanna and me under the same roof? Your life would be miserable. So would mine."

Jerome moved awkwardly as he tried to think of a tactful way to say what was on his mind. "Have you thought of marrying? What I mean is, well, you were all set to marry Ransome MacKinley. Do you write to each other?"

"You must really be desperate to mention him," his sister observed wryly. "I have a feeling you've already suggested to Susanna that we may move into her house."

"Well, a woman needs a man, and if you marry him, you'll eventually inherit Roseland. If you really care for him, I suppose . . ."

"You're a bit late. Ransome is gone and I have no idea where he is. What a pity you didn't think of all this when I was begging for your help." Her voice was coolly sarcastic, but she didn't care. Her world had fallen apart and she wasn't mollified by Jerome's sudden support. "He hasn't answered any of my letters, and I don't know if he ever so much as received them."

She moved to the window and looked across the pasture to the hill where a raw new grave had been made beside Adele's weathered stone. Sam was working there, fitting the new section of black wrought-iron railing to surround the enlarged plot. "Do I really need a man to take care of me?" she said almost to herself.

"What? Of course you do."

"Why? You said yourself that Sam can run the sawmill. Maybe he didn't understand what Papa had in mind about the rice farm, but I did.''

"You! You can't plant rice.''

"I can hire someone who can. Papa had it all mapped out. All I would have to do is give orders.''

"You can't even think of such a thing!''

"I can too! The Widow Duplantier earns her living.''

"She owns a boardinghouse!''

"And Doll earns hers.''

Jerome was silent.

Jessamine said quickly, "And I can too. I'm not afraid here, and Sam is close by. Tabitha and I can do the work we've always done. The only difference is that I will also give the orders at the sawmill and to the overseer of the rice farm. Whom could I hire?''

"No. I won't discuss this with you. The idea is insane!''

"Not as insane as us all moving into your house along with Susanna and Mrs. Leslie!'' She saw she had won a point. "I'll start interviewing overseers tomorrow. Papa said there's a lot to do before the rice can be planted.''

"You'll do no such thing!'' Jerome frowned at his sister, but he knew he was defeated. "Okay. I'll find you an overseer and I'll hire the workers. I don't want you way out here with just anyone. I suppose,'' he added grudgingly, "that you can handle it if anyone can.''

"I know I can do it. You recall I've always had a good head for business.''

"You're quick at mathematics. Business is something else entirely.''

"Don't be so stuffy. If you can learn ginning and shipping, I can learn about sawmills and rice farming.''

"Jessamine, can't I dissuade you from this? I can have Sam and the overseer report to me.''

"While I sit by the fire and sew a fine seam? Not on your tintype!''

"See? Already you're talking unladylike! I know Mama and Papa wouldn't approve!''

"Papa is gone.'' She looked back at the still figure in the parlor. "Maybe Mama is too.''

"She'll snap out of it,'' Jerome said, but with a lack of conviction. "They were so close. It's just taking her a while. That's all.''

Jessamine went toward the kitchen, where Tabitha was

sewing black bands on their clothes. Jerome followed her. Taking her bonnet from the peg, Jessamine said, "Jerome, stay with Mama until I get back." She tied the new black ribbons under her chin. "I'm going to the mill to look over Papa's records."

"I'll do that."

"No. I'm determined to do this."

She turned to Tabitha, who had stood up to check the pot of clothes she was dying black over the fire. The woman's protruding lower lip and jerky movements told she had overheard the conversation between Jessamine and Jerome and that she was against Jessamine's idea. Jessamine looked back at her brother and shrugged. "I will do what I must. This is 1872! Times have changed. I'm not a featherhead, nor am I still a belle."

"You is still a woman, ain't you?" Tabitha muttered. "Ain't right, a woman going around doing stuff like that!"

Jessamine sighed, but she went to the door. "I'll be back as soon as I can."

She walked over the familiar rise and down the slope to the knoll that held the sawmill. It was quiet today, and deserted, out of deference to Reuben's death. Jessamine let herself in and looked for a minute at the matched pair of mules Sam had found and returned to their stalls. She couldn't see the mules without recalling that they had led to her father's death. "I'd like to sell you for dog meat," she said to the nearest one, "but Papa paid dearly for you. There's nothing that says I can't trade you back to the Ramseys, though."

The mule flicked its ears and nuzzled hay out of the manger.

Jessamine shouldered open the water-swollen door to the office. Already the dank smell of mildew was heavy in the room. She wondered if the smell reminded everyone of death as it did her. Perhaps it took a hurricane to make that association.

She opened the window to let in fresh air. A dark line circled the walls, indicating how high the water had risen. Silt and leaves and moss from the swamp littered the floor, and the chair had washed into a corner. Jessamine retrieved it and spread her black handkerchief over the grimy seat before she sat down.

Fortunately the water had not toppled the heavy desk,

nor reached the papers on top. The ledgers and books were damp and limp, but she could read them.

Shelves stood against one wall, the lower ones washed clean of their receipts and orders, but the upper shelves were untouched.

Systematically Jessamine went through the ledgers that recorded the mill's progress over the years and found the one of recent accounts. She put it aside to take to the house. She could study it while she kept an eye on Delia and sent letters to the ones who appeared to be regular customers. With luck she could convince them to renew their orders, especially if she signed herself "J. Delacroix." Anyone would assume she was Jerome and not a woman.

On the top shelf and pushed toward the back was a metal box. Thinking it might be payroll or papers of importance, Jessamine took it to the desk and gingerly sat on the handkerchief-covered chair. The box was locked, but she pried the hasp open with the letter opener and swung back the lid.

Inside were envelopes. Many envelopes. Slowly, with numbed movements, Jessamine took out the one on top. In bold writing she read her name, and below it her address. Beneath this letter she saw one with her own handwriting. The musty odor of the room didn't disguise the aroma of the gardenia perfume she always used to scent her letters to Ransome.

She dumped the contents of the box on the desk and hurriedly sorted through them. There was the yellow envelope she had borrowed from her mother last Christmas when she had run out of stationery. Here were the pale pink ones she had owned a year before! Mixed with the delicately scented ones were large white envelopes, all bearing masculine pen strokes.

She was stunned. All this time her Papa had been intercepting her mail to and from Ransome! All this time Ransome had written to her, even though he had obviously received no word from her!

Jessamine felt sick and somehow dead inside. Papa had done this? He had sat with her at the dining table and teased her lovingly by the fireside and given her little gifts as he always had, and all the time he was doing this? Her face felt pale and rigid as she picked up the letter that had been on top of the stack. Her fingers were cold and clumsy as she opened it and took out the sheet of heavy paper.

"Jessamine," it began simply. "Today I am being married. She isn't you, but you have obviously turned your back on me. I had expected so much more from you. I had believed all you said. I was a fool. Unlike you, Vera loves me and—"

Jessamine wadded the letter into a tight ball in her fist. For a long time she sat perfectly still. Then she began opening the other letters, one by one.

Shadows were darkening in the office before she again turned to the most recent letter. Slowly she pressed it flat to make out the words on the crumpled surface. Silent tears were coursing down her cheeks, though she had no idea when she had started to cry. Methodically she replaced the letters in the box, then closed it with a metallic click.

If she had needed anything to steel her, this had done it. As if she were an automaton, she stood and almost stumbled as she returned the box to its place on the shelf. She looked out the window toward the place where her father was buried, and her face was devoid of any grief for him.

He had won in separating her from Ransome, and had effectively destroyed all that might have been. But she was alive, and Reuben lay cold in his grave. He had taken her love and ruined her life, but she was in control of all he had worked for.

As she closed the office and went back through the sawmill, she paused again by the mules' pens. After a long moment she said, "I don't think I'll trade you after all."

With a whisper of her mourning weeds, Jessamine went out into the dusk.

III

Yesterday's Roses:
Spring
1896

More exquisite than any other
is the autumn rose.

—Théodore Agrippa d'Aubigné

32

Ransome MacKinley carefully folded his mother's letter and put it in the portfolio where he kept all his important papers. A ray of sunshine fell on his dark red hair, now touched with silver at the temples. In deference to the fashion of the early nineties he had grown a mustache several years before, and because Vera admired it, he had kept it. Unlike her father's whiskers, which bristled like a small bush, Ransome kept his neatly clipped.

He closed the portfolio and buckled the strap that fastened it. The room looked bare and the house echoed eerily with so much of their furniture packed or sold. He had told Vera there was no need to take anything at all to Roseland, but women became attached to such things as sofas and bedsteads.

Across the hall he could hear her talking to their daughters. She sounded as calmly content as if they were merely planning new Easter bonnets and not a whole new way of life. He envied Vera's tranquillity. In their twenty-four years of marriage he had almost never seen her nervous or upset. While they had never developed the tumultuous passion he had hoped for, they had a deep and abiding love.

When Vera broke off her sentence to cough, Ransome frowned, for although she made light of it, her persistent cough bothered him. Spring was blooming outside the window, and she still had the hacking cough that had troubled her all winter. The move to the South would be good for her.

He heard a clatter of noise in the hall and smiled as ten-year-old Ethan, their youngest, raced into the room. While everyone else moved quietly to keep the house from echoing, Ethan had no such qualms for the simple reason that he couldn't hear the noise he made.

"Hello, son," Ransome said, looking directly at the boy so he could read his lips. "Are you ready to go?"

Ethan nodded eagerly and said in his flat voice, "Can we leave now, Papa? Fritz and I are ready." He knelt to pat the small brown dog.

"Go see if Mama and the girls are ready." Ransome consulted the heavy gold watch he wore in his vest pocket. "It's time to leave."

Ethan ran to obey, his skinny legs skipping as the mongrel dog ran in and out between his feet. He's happy, Ransome thought. At least someone is glad to be going. Since Ethan's bout with scarlet fever five years before, his health had been precarious. The disease which had rendered him almost completely deaf had also left him susceptible to colds and anything else that came along. In Louisiana's sultry air, Ransome hoped the boy would finally grow strong and begin to fill out. He only hoped the children there wouldn't be unkind to Ethan because of his deafness. Children could be so cruel.

Ethan ran to his mother and took her hand so she would face him. In his deafness Ethan sometimes forgot that others didn't need to read his lips as he did theirs. "Papa says it's time! We can go to the station now."

"I don't know why you're so glad to leave our home," Pearl, the younger daughter, said peevishly. "I have to leave simply everyone and I may never see them again as long as I live."

Vera smiled at her daughter. "They can come down and visit, Pearl. Papa says Roseland is big enough to house an army. When we get settled in, you may write and ask several of your friends down for the summer."

"Besides," her older sister teased, "think of all the new boys you'll meet."

"Cadence, how can you be so heartless?" Pearl demanded as she patted her blond hair to be sure her curls were still artfully arranged. "You know I'll love Jimmy Dobson forever."

"Just as you loved Harry Berson forever six months ago, and Ed Thompson before that?"

"Now, Cadence, don't tease your sister. Pearl has plenty of time before she has to pick one boy and settle down. She's only eighteen."

Cadence sighed. "Maybe so, Mama, but I'm twenty, and I've never found the one for me. Why, you and Papa were married when you were my age."

"Your papa is very special. Before I met him I had never had another boyfriend."

"Really, Mama? That's hard to believe. I think you're just saying that to make me feel better."

Vera went to her elder daughter and stroked her auburn hair back from her face. Cadence, in spite of having a red tint to her hair, was by far the prettier of her two daughters. She was so pretty, in fact, that boys seemed too much in awe of her to ask her to walk out with them. And then there was Cadence's awful independence.

"I had hoped to go to the National-American Convention this year," Cadence said wistfully.

"There will be a suffragette movement in Louisiana, I'm sure," Vera said.

"In a place like Cavelier? I can't even find it on the map!"

"It's an old map, dear. I'm sure it's there. Papa says it's not too far from Baton Rouge." She pronounced the name the English way, with a soft T and a hard G.

"It won't be the same."

"You shouldn't be so interested in that stuff, anyway," Pearl said sanctimoniously. "It's not ladylike."

"Don't be unpleasant, Pearl," her mother admonished gently. "Cadence feels as badly about the move as you do." She smiled down at Ethan, who had been dashing from window to window in his eagerness. "Ethan, take Fritz out for a run before we get in the buggy."

"Mama," Cadence said, "don't you mind going at all? You'll never see your friends again either."

"I'll make new ones, and I expect we'll be back for an occasional visit. Now that the trains are in such good order, it's not like it was when your papa was young."

"Then why have we never visited Grandmother?" Pearl asked.

"You know what Grandfather was like," Vera said in a soft voice so Ransome couldn't overhear. "He was so dreadful to your papa. Having them here even for a few visits was such a strain on us all."

"And now we have to live in their house," Pearl complained.

"It's not *their* house any longer, now that Grandfather is dead, and you like Grandmother. I've heard you say so."

"I like her for a *visit,* not to *live* with her!"

Cadence frowned at her sister and took her bonnet

from the bed. "If I can do without my suffragette friends, you can make do as well. At least *I* had intended to make matters better for us all!"

"Cadence, that's enough." Vera's voice was calm, but the tilt of her head warned her daughters not to start an argument. "Now, gather your valises and let's go. The men will be wanting to get in this room to pack."

She ushered her daughters into the hall as Ransome came out of his office. "We're ready, dear." He smiled at her, and Vera felt the warm glow she always experienced in her husband's presence. Ransome was a good man, the very essence of kindness. Vera often thought that his love was nothing short of a miracle and that without him her life would be as meaningless as it had been before she met him.

The girls went down the hall, and though Vera could hear them arguing under their breaths, she ignored them. Dissension was permissible as long as it wasn't disruptive, though she couldn't for the life of her see what Cadence found so appalling in women's lot in life.

"I see our Susan B. Anthony is at it again," Ransome said with a smile toward Cadence. He tried not to show it, but she was his favorite, perhaps because her fiery independence reminded him of someone else he had known so long ago.

"Cadence has always had a cause. It's a shame Pearl can't be interested in something besides boys. However, I must admit that I liked it better when Cadence was trying to save the elms on that side street downtown or when she was taking in stray dogs and cats. I don't understand this suffragette talk."

Ransome laughed softly and put his arm around Vera's shoulder. "They are very different, aren't they? And then there's Ethan, who is different from both of them. He sees this move as a grand adventure. I wasn't much older than he is when I first moved to Roseland, now that I think about it."

"I wish I had known you then. To think we grew up here in the same town and our families were connected by business, and we never met until we were grown."

He bent his head in thought in the same manner he used in the courtroom. "Do you regret leaving your parents? Now that Aunt Polly is dead, I'm not leaving as much behind as you are."

"I regret it a little bit," she said carefully. It wouldn't

do to let Ransome know just how much she dreaded this move away from all she had ever known. He had a responsibility to his mother, and Vera knew that responsibilities were not to be shirked, even if she was afraid to face them.

"You'll like Roseland. I guarantee it. And we'll be back to Albany for visits. Perhaps your parents will visit us, as well."

"Mother on a train?" She laughed in spite of herself. "That's highly unlikely. You know how frightened she is of them."

They went down the narrow, dark steps as Ransome said, "I still can hardly believe Father is dead. It's like hearing that the devil died."

"Ransome!"

"You didn't know him quite as well as I did, and by the time you met him he was more or less a helpless cripple." Ransome unconsciously touched the faint scar on his right cheek. "He wasn't always so feeble."

"Nevertheless, you shouldn't talk about your father that way." She went to the etched-glass front door and turned the ornate knob for the last time. In this light, Ransome could see the fine strands of white in her brown hair. Her face was thinner than it had been in her youth, and was beginning to crinkle about her eyes and the corners of her mouth. She was still painfully shy, though she tried to hide it.

Ransome caught her hand before she could put her hat on, and bent to kiss her. "I know this is hard for you," he said softly.

She pulled away with a blush, though she smiled. "What if the children see us?"

He returned her smile, but allowed her to move away. For Vera, physical affection was proper only in the bedroom. Ransome followed her out into the noisy street.

Jessamine looked up from the ledger she was studying to watch her mother moving among the rose gardens. Louisiana's early spring was ripening into summer and buds were bursting on all the lovely roses. Delia's head, now more silver than gold, was bent over the nodding flowers in perfect contentment. She preferred the flowers of her childhood, the China rose named Agrippina with its carnelian pink, the Général Kléber moss rose, the dusty-peach hues of the Duchesse de Brabant. Over the years Jessamine and

Jerome had given her some of the really old varieties, such as the Apothecary roses that had originated in ancient Damascus and had become the red rose of Lancaster, which looked more like a red daisy with its twelve flat petals. There were also damask and gallica and dog roses, even an alba rose, which was said to have a history all the way back to Rome and which had an unusually strong perfume. But none of the varieties were more recent than the Civil War, which had become the popular name for the War Between the States, for Delia still lived in 1860.

Jessamine laid down her pen and watched her mother move contentedly among the flowers. Since her husband's death in the terrible hurricane, Delia had retreated into a happier time. As far as she was concerned, Reuben was out overseeing the cotton, Adele was playing with her dolls just out of sight, and she constantly confused Pierce with her older son, Spartan.

At times Jessamine almost envied her mother's retreat from reality. Since her father died, Jessamine had taken over the running of both the sawmill, with Sam's help, and the rice farm. With Jerome's recommendation, Jessamine had hired Jules Landry, a Cajun who was very adept at rice production, and business was good. So good, in fact, that Ten Acres bore almost no resemblance to the old dogtrot cabin still embedded within its walls.

An office had been added so Jessamine could work at home and keep an eye on her mother. Tabitha had died several years before, and the woman hired to replace her, Maribelle Jackson, didn't live on the place and wasn't as attentive to Delia as old Tabitha had been.

A back parlor had also been added and the kitchen enlarged. Jessamine had built another bedroom for herself that was larger and more airy than the old one, which was now used ostensibly for guests, but was most often used by Pierce in his frequent overnight visits. He was always glad to escape to Ten Acres, Jessamine thought with a smile. His mother, Susanna, had become an almost intolerable shrew and Pierce looked to his aunt for motherly affection. Jessamine often thought of Pierce more as a son than a nephew, and was teaching him all he would need to know to take over the sawmill and rice farm when she could no longer manage them efficiently. This, along with Jerome's cotton gins and shipping, made Pierce by far the most eligible bachelor in the parish. Someday he would own virtually all of Cavelier.

"We haven't done badly," Jessamine said softly to the mottled black-and-gray collie that lay at her feet. The dog raised his head and thumped his tail on the floor. "Good Donnie. You're always here to talk to, aren't you?" Despite having her family around her, Jessamine was often lonely. She was a woman who needed a man, but she had always wanted but one—the one she couldn't have.

Jessamine stood and went to the window that looked toward Roseland. The house was, of course, hidden by trees and all the acres between, but Jessamine could see it in her heart. Old Ian MacKinley was dead and buried, and the rumor around town was that Eliza MacKinley would soon put the place up for sale and move back to New York. Jessamine was waiting for the sale notice, as was Jerome. No matter what Eliza asked, they were prepared to pay it. Once again Roseland would be back in Delacroix hands, where it belonged.

How strange, she thought, that deaths seemed to go in threes. First Ian MacKinley, then the man who ran the dry-goods store, then Louis Broussard's Wife, Dorothée. She recalled Louis, much thinner in those days, and still sporting a full head of hair, sitting on the porch swing, trying to get up the courage and the privacy to propose to her. Jessamine's lips tilted in a smile at the memory, and the dimple appeared in her cheek. "How young we were," she commented to the merle collie, who wagged his tail in response to her voice. "It seems like forever." She touched her hair, still dark despite her forty-five years. She wondered if she had changed as much on the outside as she had on the inside. The laughing and coquettish belle was gone, as if she had never existed at all.

For a forbidden moment she let herself remember Ransome and the fevered love they had shared by the creek so long ago. Was he happy? Was he well? She knew he was still alive because Eliza MacKinley put all the family news in the Cavelier *Tribune*. She wondered if he would return to help his mother dispose of the property, but she didn't believe he would. Ransome had not come back, even once, in twenty-four years. Jessamine felt the now-familiar hatred well in her—not toward Ransome, but toward the hussy who had lured him away despite himself. She could just picture that woman. She must be as hard and conniving as any woman who ever lived. Jessamine would be willing to bet she led Ransome a miserable life.

"Tante Jessamine? May I come in?"

Jessamine turned with a welcoming smile. "Pierce! How good to see you. Of course you may."

He bent to pat Donnie and looked at his aunt. "You looked sad when I came in. Is Grandmama not well?"

"No, no. She's quite all right. I was only thinking about poor Dorothée Broussard."

"It's really a shame. She was a kind person."

"You know, I believe you look more like your papa every time I see you. Of course, you're taller and your eyes are blue, but other than that, you're the spitting image of Jerome when he was twenty-five."

"I think Mother will never forgive me for that," Pierce said with a laugh. "She constantly lists my resemblance to him as one of my greatest faults—she wanted me to look like a Leslie, whatever that means."

"Be glad you don't. None of the Leslies were very attractive. Are you here to stay for a while?"

"If I may. I wanted to ride over the rice farm with Jules and see how the crop is progressing."

"You're welcome anytime. You know that. I'll have Maribelle put fresh sheets on your bed. How is your father today? He had a cold when I talked to him a few days ago."

"He was in bed for a day, but is up and about now. I think having to spend so much time in the house with Mother makes him get well fast, if you know what I mean."

"Yes, I know exactly."

Pierce paused before he said, "I had thought he might be out here. I rode by the gins and he wasn't there, and Tanner Johnson said he hadn't been at the docks all day."

Jessamine turned away in the pretense of putting away her ledger. "I haven't seen him. Perhaps Tanner was mistaken. Jerome could be over at the new warehouse."

"Maybe. Tante Jessamine, there's talk in town that Papa is . . . well, seeing another woman."

"Oh?" Jessamine glanced at her nephew over her shoulder. "Who says so?"

"I overheard Mr. Bierne talking about it at the post office to the new postal clerk."

"Did they mention a name?"

"No. He said no one knows who it could be. I know I shouldn't be talking to you about this, but I'm concerned, and it's certainly not something I could say to anyone outside the family.''

"Believe me, Pierce, my heart won't stop at the sound of gossip. I'm made of sterner stuff than that. Even an old maid has some idea what goes on in the world.''

Pierce grinned. "I never think of you as an old maid.''

"Good. If you did, I'd box your ears and send you packing. As for this ridiculous rumor, I'd pay it no mind at all.''

"But I think it may be true.''

She looked at him in surprise. She knew for a fact that Jerome was the soul of discretion, and he had kept Doll a secret for so many years that Jessamine couldn't believe he would make a slip now.

"Mother has accused him of it too.''

"Is that all? Your mother also thought the mermaid in Mr. Barnum's circus was real, when anyone could see he had just sewn the front end of a dead monkey to the back end of a fish. She also thinks the world will come to an end in 1900. I wouldn't put much stock in her convictions.''

"All the same, Papa *is* gone a lot when he isn't at the docks or the gins or out here.'' Pierce's dark brows knitted and his blue-gray eyes flashed with offended pride. "I think it's contemptible for a man to have a mistress! No matter who it is!''

"That's very commendable, Pierce,'' Jessamine said dryly. "Also very narrow-minded. Perhaps you resemble the Leslies after all.''

"Tante Jessamine!''

"Don't sound so shocked. I'm not saying for a minute that your papa has a mistress. In a town the size of Cavelier, don't you think everyone would know her name if there was one? How long is this affair supposed to have been going on?''

"According to Mother, he's kept some woman for years.''

"There! You see? Wasn't it all over town when the Macy boy got caught in the woods with William Ramsey's youngest daughter? And doesn't everyone know Dr. Griggs has been secretly courting Betty Ramsey since Robert died?''

"Yes, but—''

"There you have it! If your papa was seeing anyone on the sly, especially for several years, you'd know all about it. Just forget you ever heard such nonsense, is my suggestion.''

"I knew I could talk to you," Pierce said with relief.

"Of course you can. If you hear any rumors like that, you come straight to me and I'll tell you if you should worry about them.''

"For an unmarried lady, you certainly know how life is.''

"I'm going to take that as a compliment.''

"It was meant as one.''

Jessamine unclipped the small brooch watch she wore and consulted it. "If you want to catch Jules Landry, you had better leave now. I'll see you at supper.''

Pierce dropped a kiss on her cheek and hurried out. Jessamine thoughtfully replaced her watch. Jerome must have been careless. She would have to remind him to be more circumspect. The Knights of the White Camellia weren't as open as they had been just after the war, but they still had their ways of terrifying the blacks who stepped out of line. She didn't want Doll to have a cross burned in her yard, or worse. Jerome was strong enough and self-assured enough to ride out any unpleasantness, but Doll and her daughter were often alone in their isolated house.

Jessamine hadn't been to Doll's house since the day she discovered Jerome there, nor did she ever mention Doll to him except obliquely. Jessamine might know what it was like to love a man whom she couldn't have, but she still couldn't condone Doll and Jerome. The fact that she wasn't nearly as shocked by their liaison as Jerome had always assumed didn't matter. There were things a person did and there were things a person didn't, and Jessamine couldn't give her approval to a married white man loving a black woman. But sometimes in the lonely night she wondered if her lack of understanding was really jealousy because Doll had a lover, and Ransome was far, far away.

Jessamine heard her mother come in the house, and she went to meet her in the parlor.

"Hello, darling," Delia said in her elderly but still cultured voice. "Was that Spartan I saw riding away?" She carried an armful of roses to the vase on the sideboard.

"Yes, Mama." She had long since given up explaining it was Pierce and not Spartan.

"He's grown so tall. Just like his papa," she said in reference to Reuben. "But his eyes are light, like my family's. Such a handsome man he's becoming. Before long he'll be courting a belle.''

"Yes, I imagine he will,'' Jessamine said in surprise. Delia almost never mentioned the future.

"I hope we like her, since he will probably move her in here. It's only right, with him being the eldest. Someday Roseland will be his.''

"You mean Ten Acres, Mama.''

Delia gave her daughter the pleasantly blank look she always used when facts regarding reality were mentioned. "Have you seen your papa today?''

"No, Mama.''

"I guess he's off with Mr. John in the back fields. The cotton will be ankle-high by now. The slaves must be chopping it.''

"I'm sure you're right, Mama.''

"Tell Tabitha to cook that catfish *étouffé* she makes so well, and some of her iced lemon soufflé. I suppose there's still ice in the icehouse?''

"Yes, Mama.'' Delia also never grasped the idea of the icebox that sat in the kitchen, and always addressed the iceman as James, who had been the slave who had done the heavier menial chores about Roseland.

Delia poured water into the vase from the crystal pitcher and began arranging the roses. "The joint on my thumb has been itching. That means we'll have an unwelcome visitor. And this morning I dropped a knife—that means it will be a woman. You don't suppose that Susanna is coming out to see us, do you?''

"I doubt it. Susanna hasn't been out in years.''

"Well, if she does, I hope she doesn't bring any more of those paper cutouts,'' Delia said with a laugh.

Jessamine smiled. She never knew what Delia might or might not remember. "I wouldn't worry about a visitor, Mama. Those old superstitions don't come true.''

"Sometimes they do. You just ask your papa. When I was a girl I heard a dove coo, so I sat down to wait. Reuben was the next person to come down the road. He stopped to talk to me, and within the week we were keeping company.''

Jessamine smiled. She had heard the story many times.

"We've always been so happy,'' Delia added softly. "I just can't imagine a life without him.'' A puzzled hurt clouded her gray eyes. "Have you seen him today? I can't seem to find him."

"He's just fine, Mama. I'm sure he'll be in any time now."

Delia smiled again and her worry vanished. "Of course he will, *chérie*. Now, you run along and tell Tabitha to cook that *étouffé*. Spartan has always loved it so."

"Yes, Mama." Jessamine went to give the order to Maribelle. Once again she envied Delia's dream world, where nothing bad ever happened, and where time was frozen at the happiest of moments.

33

"IT'S GOING TO BE A HOT MONTH," DOLL COMmented to her daughter.

"It's hot every summer," Laurie snapped as she finished drying the last plate and put it away in the cupboard.

"What's bothering you, honey? You've been irritable all week."

Laurie sighed and frowned as she hung the damp towel over the rack. "I don't like it here, Mama. There's nobody I'm interested in. I'm twenty-three years old. I ought to be married and settled down."

"You don't give people a chance. As soon as they start liking you, you run them off. Besides, there are worse things than not being married."

Laurie turned on her mother, her dark eyes flashing. "You don't mean to say you want *me* to live like you do!"

Doll had known for a long time this was coming. There had been signs for years. Now that it was here, she found herself surprised only in that Laurie had waited so long to speak her mind. Moving with calm deliberation, Doll put back the box she had been taking off a shelf. "I wondered when you would get around to talking about that. Your papa is a good man. He can't help it if he can't marry me."

"He's *white*, Mama! White *and* married! He's got a wife and son in Cavelier that are both as fish-belly white as anybody I've ever seen."

"When did you see them?" Doll asked in alarm. "You're not supposed to be in Cavelier!"

"I got tired of always riding to Palizada to shop. It's further than Cavelier."

"Maybe so, but nobody from Cavelier goes there unless it's one of our people. The white folks don't shop in a mulatto settlement."

"*Our* people, Mama? Who are *our* people? Look at

me! My skin is as light as Papa's and my hair may be dark, but its got reddish highlights. Do you know who I look like? I look like Jessamine Delacroix!''

Doll studied her daughter as if she hadn't seen her in a long time. ''Your eyes are shaped like mine and your cheekbones are higher than Jessamine's, but there is a resemblance.''

''Is that why you don't want me to go to Cavelier?''

''Yes. There's no reason to call attention to yourself.''

''There!'' Laurie triumphantly crossed the room to push open the door. ''I knew it. I don't belong anywhere!''

''No, baby, that's not right. You belong to both. Or to either,'' Doll added carefully.

Laurie spun about to face her mother. ''What do you mean by that? You mean for me to pass?''

''I never said that.''

''But you meant it, didn't you!'' Laurie's eyes widened. ''Mama, how could you?''

Doll went out on the porch, sat on the top step, and leaned back against the rail. She patted the space beside her and Laurie reluctantly sat down, her back rigid.

''One of the things your grandma worried most about was whether the white folks would bring back slavery. She fretted about it all the time as she got older. I don't think it will happen. Not after all these years, but I was a slave like she was. When something like that has happened to you once, you can't help but think it might happen again. When you were born, I was a free woman. It was the law that a child born to a free woman was free. But at the same time, I'm black and was born a slave—and anybody looking at me can tell I'm black. If slavery comes back, I might be taken in by the paddyrollers and sold.''

''Mama, you know nothing like that is going to happen,'' Laurie said petulantly.

''How do you know? Have you suddenly taken up prophesying? It could happen, girl. It could.'' Doll paused. For a minute there, she had sounded just like her own mother all those years ago at Ten Acres. In a gentler voice she said, ''But it won't ever happen to you. Not only were you born free, your skin is pale as cream. You could pass— if you had a mind to.''

''Well, I don't have any such thing in mind. Slavery is all your generation seems to think about. Even at church we sing songs about being free and the promised land and all that. If you ask me, we aren't free to this day.''

Doll laughed softly, but with no mirth. "Girl, you don't know what you're talking about.''

"Now, don't go telling me how much you suffered and how deprived you were as a slave!''

"I wasn't going to say any such thing. The Delacroixs were good to me and my family. But we were still slaves.'' Doll emphasized each word distinctly, as if Laurie might not quite grasp the import. "We weren't free. Your children, now, they could be not only free but also completely out of reach of the law. They might not have to pass.''

Laurie stared at her mother. "There's only one way my children would be white. That's if their father was white.''

"I know.''

The silence strung uncomfortably tense about them. Doll had never before stated her hopes so plainly, and she was afraid she had said it badly.

"You want me to turn my back on what we are? You want that?''

"I want you to be safe! I want you to be able to get a drink from the fountain on Main Street and to go into Ramsey's Café and order your dinner and to get a job doing something besides needlework or laundry or scrubwork. That's not too unreasonable, Laurie.''

"You want me to deny all we are! Is that why you took up with Papa? Is it? So your child would be light and your grandchildren white?''

"No!'' Doll snapped, glaring at her angry daughter and leaning forward. The cords in her neck were standing out and her strong hands were clenched. "Your papa and I fell in love in spite of our differences, not because of them! As for me, planning all this just so you would be born with light skin is absolutely ridiculous! A child was the last thing I had in mind at the time.''

Laurie paled and stood up. Her mother had rarely raised her voice to her in her entire life. "I'm going to Palizada.''

Doll didn't answer, but merely stared after her daughter, too full of conflicting emotions to speak. Soon she heard the barn door slam and the sound of a horse loping away, and she knew Laurie was gone. She covered her mouth with her shaking hand and doubled over as if she were in physical pain. At last the words had been said. Laurie would have to think it out for herself. No matter what Doll wanted, she knew Laurie would stubbornly live her life the way she wanted to. She was so much like Jerome.

Slowly Doll stood and went into the house to resume her routine chores. She again took down the worn box that contained her special herbs and the charms she had made over the years. Many of the herbs were the same ones she used for cooking, although these had been gathered with great ceremony and at specific times of the moon's phases. The rosemary that was tied together at the top of the sprigs had been gathered from the branches Doll had trained to grow downward so as to symbolize forgetfulness instead of better memory. From a small cotton pouch she counted out seven juniper berries, one for each day of the week. She added thyme for strength, bay for victory, and a large measure of mugwort for safety.

Doll carefully laid the herbs on a square of blue cloth that represented her faith in the charm. Over this she sprinkled dried leaves of nightshade to ensure forgetfulness. Over the herbs she laid a bit of mandrake root to guide the charm to do her will. With great ceremony she tied the four corners of the square as she sang the song taught to her by Asiza so long ago. The words were simple, the tune little more than a chant, but Doll firmly believed that all these things together had prevented anyone from learning of her liaison with Jerome. For twenty-four years now it had worked.

Doll took a silver spoon from the box and carried the packet of herbs outside. She knelt beside her steps as she did once every week and buried the charm. When she had patted the earth firmly in place, she stopped singing and stood up. As she wiped the earth from the spoon she wondered what to do about Laurie. Even Asiza hadn't taught her any spells to use in raising a headstrong daughter.

Doll lifted her head and looked down the path worn across the meadow. He wasn't in sight yet, but Jerome was coming; she could feel him drawing nearer. She went inside to put away her box of charms.

Laurie used the ladies' block to dismount from her horse in front of Palizada's general store. Palizada was a town in its own right, governed by a family of mulattoes who had been freed before the war and populated since then by the new freemen. It had a drugstore and Baptist church, in addition to the general store, a doctor who also served as a barber and a veterinarian, and a blacksmith shop.

Laurie walked down the town's only boardwalk to the drugstore and nodded a greeting to the elderly druggist before taking a seat on one of the stools at the new soda fountain. The boy behind the counter brought her an *eau sucré* and a straw. Laurie took a coin from her reticule and pushed it across the counter.

She was still so upset with her mother that she couldn't think straight. All her life they had lived as outcasts. Even her own grandfather barely acknowledged their existence. As far as Laurie knew, Sam hadn't spoken to her mother since Tabitha died. Laurie had never been taught to call him Grandpa, but she did anyway. Now her mother wanted her to completely sever her ties to her heritage by marrying white. Laurie knew what that would mean—she would have to leave Cavelier, where her resemblance to the Delacroixs was already too noticeable, and she would also have to lie to her future husband about who and what she was. All this so that children she might never have would escape a fate that might never happen. Perhaps she couldn't drink from a public fountain in Cavelier or eat at Ramsey's Café, but she could move about quite freely here in Palizada, and there were a few other mulatto towns nearby, as well as the well-known Isle Brevelle where the mulattoes even owned large plantations and had been slave-owning citizens before the end of the war.

Laurie had been close to the Boudreaux girls all her life, and their mother, Nanine Boudreaux, had told her story after story about their people and even about Africa, where Nanine's mother had been born. She still spoke with a faint Gullah accent, which Laurie had tried to imitate as a small child. Doll, however, had seen to it that Laurie spoke white, just as Doll herself did.

She sipped her sugar water and wished she had been born into a nice, normal black family where all the rules were easy and where she wouldn't be expected to choose one life or another. She heard someone sit down beside her, but she didn't look up. There was far more on her mind than civilities.

'' 'Morning, Miss Laurie. You ain't speaking to friends these days?''

Laurie looked up and smiled at the familiar face.

"Good morning, Tommy. I didn't expect to see you in here."

"I ain't been to work yet. Pa was taking a load of pine to the docks and your grandpa don't need me over to the sawmill till Pa brings the wagon back." He motioned to a young man beside him, who was frankly staring at Laurie. "This here is my cousin Tobias Wilson, from up to Shreveport. Pa talked Mr. Sam into hiring him at the sawmill. Tobias, this here is Miss Laurie Farmer."

"Farmer?" the young man said. "I thought . . ."

Laurie turned away in embarrassment. She knew exactly what he thought.

"No, man. She's one of us. Her mama is Mr. Sam's daughter." Tommy leaned toward Laurie and nudged her to make her smile. "My daddy tried to court her mama before he met Ma. Why, we could have been brother and sister!"

Laurie finally brightened and said, "Tommy Smith, how you do go on." She looked past him to say, "Welcome to Palizada, Mr. Wilson. I hope you like it here."

"I'm liking it better by the minute. Call me Tobias."

She took his measure with interest, for she had met few strangers in her life. Tobias was a deep chocolate in color and looked like the very picture of robust health. She could see some family resemblance in the shape of his face compared with Tommy's, and his hair was the same shiny, close-cropped cap of black curls, but Tobias was much more handsome than Tommy Smith, and his shoulders were as broad as the length of an ax handle. When he smiled, his cheeks were round and shiny, his teeth white and perfectly straight. Laurie felt a stirring of interest. "Do you plan to go into the sawmill business or are you just passing through?"

"I plan on staying."

"You do?" Tommy asked in surprise. "I thought you said you was going back to Shreveport come fall."

Tobias jabbed him with his elbow. "A man can change his mind, I reckon."

"Do you have a family, Mr. Tobias?" Laurie asked as she lowered her long eyelashes.

"Yes, ma'am." When she looked up quickly with disappointment in her eyes, he added, "I got a ma and a pa and a whole passel of brothers and sisters. My oldest brother gone out West and made hisself a cowboy."

"A cowboy? How exciting!" She smiled wider, and

a faint dimple appeared in her chin. "I've never known a cowboy."

"I worked with him last summer. I reckon that makes me a cowboy too."

Tommy looked from his cousin to the girl and back again. "I thought you told me not to tell that, so as Mr. Sam would think you knowed more about sawmilling than you do."

"I'm learning it fast. I can learn anything once I set my mind to it." His black eyes never left Laurie's face as he spoke to his cousin. "You live here in Palizada, Miss Laurie?"

"No. No, I live outside of town. In fact, I think I should be getting back. Mama may need me for something."

"I'd be much obliged if I could see you home. A pretty girl like you shouldn't be riding out alone."

Laurie looked at him with frank interest. No one had ever considered that she wasn't perfectly safe anywhere she might go, including herself. She rather enjoyed the idea of needing protection. However, she replied, "No, thank you, Mr. Tobias. I can find my way home just fine."

"Then let me walk you around town a bit if you're not in a hurry. I'd be proud to have you tell me all about Palizada."

"What you talking about?" Tommy began. "You know this town as good as—"

Tobias jabbed him again and came to Laurie's stool and held out his hand. "Miss Laurie?"

She put her pale hand in his dark one and felt the strength beneath the hard calluses. "I'd be honored to show you around, Mr. Tobias. Good day, Tommy. I'll see you in church."

They walked out into the wisteria-scented air and strolled down the dusty street toward the bayou. Tall oaks and walnuts, intertwined with huge clusters of wild purple wisteria, laced their branches over the couple's heads. Back in the trees were fogs of dogwood blossoms, floating like flurries of snow suspended in time.

"I guess spring is my favorite time of year," Tobias said as he looked sideways at her. "How about yourself?"

"I've always liked spring. It's summer I don't care for. Too hot."

"Yeah, it is for a fact."

They walked along in silence; then he said, "How come they call this place Palizada?"

"That was an old name for the Mississippi River. It goes back to the conquistadors."

Tobias whistled softly. "You sure know a bunch. You a schoolteacher or something?"

"No, but I'd like to be. I guess that's the only thing Mama and I have in common, our love of books. I wanted to apply for the teacher's job here in Palizada, but Mama wouldn't here of it. She has something a bit different in mind," Laurie finished gloomily.

Tobias looked down at his feet, then up at the wisteria, then over at the dogwood. Without meeting her eyes he said, "I don't reckon you could teach me how to read, could you? I mean, with me being so old and all."

"You can't read?"

"Just forget I said it," Tobias said with a scowl as he turned to walk away. "I was just fooling around with you."

"No, wait." She put her hand on his muscled arm and pulled him to a stop. "I can teach you to read. I would enjoy it."

"Sounds like too much trouble to me." His deep voice was surly with embarrassment.

"Tobias, I wasn't born knowing how either. It's something that has to be taught. If you weren't ever taught, it's nothing to be ashamed of. Why didn't you go to school?"

"We was always moving and following the crops. Can't nobody in my family read. Not even my brother, the cowboy. But we're bright! It ain't that!"

"I can tell you are."

He scuffed his worn shoes in the dirt and turned a leaf over with his toe. "I figure if I could read a bit, I might could get to be foreman of a mill or something. I guess that's dumb."

"No," she said softly. "I think it's very admirable. I'll tell you what. The sawmill shuts down about two hours before sunset every day. You meet me at that old shack just off the road between the mill and Palizada. You know the place?"

"Yeah, I knows it."

"I'll be there every day I can get away."

"On the days when it rains, maybe I could come to your house so as you don't get wet."

"No. No, I don't think that would be a good idea. If

you knew my mama and papa, you wouldn't think it was either.''

"They ain't mean to you, is they?'' Tobias asked with concern.

"Oh, no. Nothing like that. They're just . . . private people. We don't have visitors.''

"Not ever?''

"I'll meet you at the shack. I'll bring pen and paper as well as books, and teach you to write at the same time.''

"You reckon I can learn all that?'' His face split into a broad grin.

"I guarantee it. Until tomorrow, then?'' She held out her hand.

His velvety black eyes looked deep into hers as his fingers closed over her hand. "Tomorrow,'' he said softly.

Laurie again felt that quivering excitement deep inside her. She had never met a man who affected her like Tobias Wilson. Nor one whose mere touch caused fire to race up her arm and center deep in her middle. Laurie managed a smile and walked briskly back to the stores and her horse. Tomorrow seemed much too far away.

Long before daylight Jessamine put on her heavy boots and went out to the barn. Dew lay heavy on the grass from the rain the night before and her skirts slapped damply against her legs. She lit the barn lantern and went to the stall nearest the door. Inside it was a guernsey cow, large with calf. Jessamine patted the animal's brown neck as she snapped the lead rope onto the cow's halter.

The animal reluctantly followed her out of the stall, and Jessamine blew out the lantern in passing. Tugging on the slow-moving cow, she headed over the rise beyond the newer barn and down toward the woods that led to the swamp.

The waxing moon wasn't quite full, but it gave enough light for Jessamine to find the way. She had seldom walked this path, but when she did, it was usually at this time of night, and she unerringly avoided the low spots, which were prone to be muddy, and the tangle of stickered vines that ensnarled a part of the oak thicket.

Despite the cow's slow pace, they reached the meadow before the sun was up. The sky was now a leaden hue with a faint pink glow in the east. Jessamine could see no movement in the house nestled in the stand of oaks in the middle of the meadow.

Moving as silently as she could, she led the cow to the porch steps and tied her halter rope to the railing. Again she patted the cow's neck, and left as silently as she had come.

Doll awoke thinking she had heard a noise from outside, but as she listened, there was only silence. Nevertheless, she slipped out of bed and padded barefoot through the main room to look out the window. Jessamine was halfway across the meadow, but Doll had no trouble recognizing her. She leaned out and looked down at the cow tied to her handrail. A smile lifted her lips. Her old cow was ailing and too old to breed, and she didn't have the money at the time to buy a new one. Jerome had offered to get her another, but as always, she had refused his generosity, preferring to handle things in her own way. She had planned to buy a cheap one when she was paid for the last bundle of embroidery she had sent to Barnhardt's store in New Orleans, but even a cheap cow was expensive when money had to be stretched so far. Somehow Jessamine had known of her need—again.

Over the years they had never visited, but often Jessamine had done something like this. In fact, the old cow had also been a predawn gift from her friend. Doll shook her head lovingly. She and Jerome and Jessamine were inextricably connected somehow. Sometimes Doll couldn't help but wonder if Jessamine didn't have the sight, as well.

She went back to her bedroom to put on her shoes so she could put the new cow in the barn. As she did, she planned a dress for Jessamine, using her finest embroidery and best design. Jessamine wasn't the only one who gave predawn gifts.

34

JESSAMINE HADN'T PLANNED TO GO TO TOWN THAT day. Sam had told her of a new man he had hired that showed unusual promise, and Jessamine had intended to meet this Tobias Wilson. It was time to begin training someone to serve as manager after Sam's retirement, and Sam had indicated that Tobias might be just the one. Then there was the problem Jules Landry had mentioned with one of the irrigation pumps. Jessamine knew very little about machinery, but she had told him she would ride over so he could explain the problem to her. No doubt the pump would have to be replaced, and it wasn't that old. She had had enough on her mind without Delia insisting that she needed the bottle of cologne water she had ordered from Vincent Macy's Emporium. But Delia had said that if Jessamine didn't have time to run the errand for her, she would go find Reuben to do it, so Jessamine went.

She knew everyone in town, and her progress to the Emporium was further delayed by the necessity of passing the time of day with the grocer, who was putting out his crates of apples and oranges, all wrapped in crisp green and yellow paper, then with Old Father Theriot, who could no longer always recall her name, and Betty Ramsey, who dashed out of the café to say that she had seen Lucas Griggs the night before and thought he was just wonderful and that he was a fine doctor as well as a fine man.

By the time Jessamine worked her way through the laughing jumble of young Ramseys and Macys and Johnsons who were playing marbles and hopscotch on the boardwalk, she was exhausted. With relief she entered the Emporium, and was pleasantly greeted with the familiar fragrances of lemon verbena, lavender, and rose. At the counter she said to the young female clerk, "I've come to pick up my mother's order."

Instantly recognizing Jessamine Delacroix, the new

salesgirl hurried to the back room and promptly returned with a bottle of Trailing Arbutus. Jessamine nodded her approval and added, ''I'd like a tin of bath powder too, please.'' Since she had made the trip in, she thought she might as well get something extra for her mother.

The young woman carefully wrapped the bottle and the powder in heavy brown paper and tied the package with twine from the metal string holder. Jessamine counted out the money and took the parcel. She lingered for a moment among the displays of perfume oils and sachets, and remembered the days of her girlhood when she had wished for such a modern store in Cavelier. Those days were long past, she thought with a sigh. Just as her youth was fading fast. She touched her hair beneath her stylish leghorn hat and wondered if there was any gray there that she had not noticed. Jerome's hair was still as dark as her own. Perhaps they would both keep their dark hair into old age, as their Grandmama Delacroix had. Jessamine didn't like the idea of getting older, so she decided to make the gardenia perfume again that she had always liked as a girl. Nothing store-bought had ever pleased her as well.

She went back outside and nodded coolly to the aging postmaster, Leon Bierne. Even after all this time she couldn't forgive him for his part in intercepting her letters to and from Ransome MacKinley.

With interest, she looked through the new plate-glass window of Macy's dry-goods store as she walked along. Vincent Macy had recently turned the store over to his eldest son for remodeling, and Jessamine noted that the change was refreshing. As she studied the displays, she noticed that styles were changing again. Bustles were completely out of vogue, as was skirt drapery, except for a few folds or shirred peplums on the hips. She rather liked the simpler bell-shaped skirts with the short trains. The blouses had leg-of-mutton sleeves that puffed to the elbow and fit snugly over the forearm. Jessamine might be the town spinster, but she always took care to be stylish.

As she walked briskly around the corner, her mind was filled with plans to sew a new gored skirt from the bolt of cambric she had bought recently. Perhaps, she considered, if she made one that was cut a bit fuller for her mother, she could get her out of the old-fashioned style she had always worn and into something a bit more modern.

She was so engrossed in her musings that she actually

ran headlong into a man before she saw him. Jessamine gasped in surprise when she found herself staring into a pair of brown eyes she had thought she would never see again. "Ransome!" she whispered.

He had automatically put his arms around her to keep her from falling, but even though she clearly was no longer in danger, he continued to hold her close. She noticed that his auburn hair had silvered at the temples, and he now sported a mustache and had laugh wrinkles that fanned out from the corners of his eyes, but she would have known him anywhere. Even with that stunned look on his face.

"Jessamine," he murmured, as if her name had escaped his lips without his realizing he had spoken.

She knew she should say something. Do something. All she could manage, however, was to stare at him.

There was a movement behind him, and Ransome abruptly dropped his arms and stepped back as a thin woman came out of the doctor's office to stand by him. Jessamine stared at her as well. She was pretty in a gentle sort of way, though her face was drawn as if she had a physical pain that she never spoke of. Her hair was a medium brown, liberally sprinkled with gray, and her eyes were as calm as the waters of the bayou.

"I'd like you to meet my wife, Vera MacKinley," Ransome awkwardly managed to say.

Jessamine looked sharply at him and back at the woman. Of course. She would be his wife.

"Vera, this is Jessamine Broussard."

"I'm glad to meet you," the woman said as she held out her gloved hand to Jessamine.

Jessamine took the woman's hand politely. "My name isn't Broussard. It's Delacroix."

Ransome studied her as if he couldn't have heard her correctly. "What?"

"Louis Broussard married Dorothée Parlange. Unfortunately, she passed away recently." She looked Ransome straight in the eye and said quietly, "I never married."

He looked even more dumbfounded than before, and his mouth opened as if he were about to demand that she elaborate.

Jessamine turned back to Vera. "Welcome to Cavelier, Mrs. MacKinley. I see you've been to see Dr. Griggs." She nodded at the doctor's shingle on the wall. "Are you ill?"

"It's a lingering cough. Nothing, really."

By the look of concealed pain and Vera's thinness, Jessamine wasn't so sure her disease was minor, but she made her stiff lips smile and said, "I hope your indisposition won't mar your visit." Somehow Jessamine had never expected Ransome's wife to be so frail and delicate. All the hatred for her that had built over the years dissipated and Jessamine felt only defeat and a deep sadness.

"Oh, we aren't visiting. We've moved to Roseland," Vera said.

"Moved there! I thought—"

"I've already spoken with your brother," Ransome put in. "Roseland isn't for sale."

"I see." Jessamine could scarcely contain her emotions. Overriding her shock and anger at learning Ransome had moved with his wife back to Cavelier was a terrible longing to throw herself into his arms and kiss away the long empty years that had separated them. "I see," she repeated. "Well, I must be going. Good day." She nodded to them both and hurried away before the tears that were stinging her eyes could spill down her cheeks.

Ransome stared after her until Vera touched his arm and spoke to him. "What?" he asked.

"I said, we should be going. By the way, who is she?"

"Jessamine?" He looked at his wife as if he needed to come up with a good answer and to do it fast. "She's . . . a neighbor. Her family once owned Roseland. Back before the war."

"Oh, yes. Now I recall the name." Vera watched the graceful movements of the woman who looked much younger than herself. Vera's face remained calm but her mind was spinning. Ransome looked as if he had been pole-axed, and when she had come out of the doctor's office he had looked most definitely guilty. Vera put her thin hand on his arm and together they walked back to their tea-cart buggy.

35

SITTING ON THE WINDOW SEAT IN HIS PARLOR AT
Roseland, Ransome MacKinley watched his womenfolk chat
over tall glasses of minted tea. Eliza had grown more child-
like and absentminded in the past years, and he could see
by the way Vera leaned toward his mother that they would
become close. Assertive, loud people frightened his shy
wife, but Eliza MacKinley had never been either of those
things. Vera could pamper and cajole her, and they would
get along famously.

He studied the fine lines of Vera's face. She had the
delicate sort of skin that wrinkled at an early age, and already she had small creases in her cheeks and on her high
forehead. For so many years she had been such a perma-
nence in his life that he had almost forgotten to look at her.
Earlier in the day, seeing her next to Jessamine, he had been
amazed to find that Vera actually appeared older than Jessamine, though he knew she was younger by several years.

Jessamine. She had changed so little! Her hair was
still as dark and as lustrous as ever and her eyes still sparkled with life. She was more self-contained than he remembered. More aristocratic. And she had never married! He
looked back at his mother and wondered if her news clip-
pings about Louis Broussard's love interest and her carefully
worded letters had been sent for the sole purpose of killing
his love for Jessamine. If so, they had worked.

With a slight frown he fingered the gold fringe on the
heavy blue draperies. If his love was so dead, why was he
thinking how beautiful Jessamine still was and how she had
felt in his arms? He shifted uncomfortably and gazed at
Vera. He loved his wife. Not with an unbridled passion that
would have frightened Vera half out of her wits, but with a
deep, calm devotion that had weathered bad as well as good
times, deaths and births and sickness. Surely, he thought,
this was better and more lasting than a passion that boiled

303

in the veins. But was it? After all these years, Jessamine had never married, and he found her as desirable as ever.

Ransome slapped the curtain's fringe and received a reproving look from his mother. Whatever he felt—or thought he felt—for Jessamine, he was married to Vera. Jessamine might or might not still want or love him, but Vera loved him and needed him. Besides, the doctor hadn't actually said so, but Ransome knew from the questions Dr. Griggs had asked and the answers Vera had given that she was much more ill than she had led him to believe.

A sick knot tightened in his middle. He truly loved Vera, and he couldn't bear the idea that she might have consumption—that she might die. No matter how wayward his thoughts were toward Jessamine, he was married to Vera and would remain as faithful to her as he had always been. Somehow, some way, he would put Jessamine out of his mind.

Cadence and Pearl came in and kissed their mother, then hugged their grandmother and kissed her papery cheek. Eliza patted Pearl's plump hand and pulled her down to sit beside her on an overstuffed footstool. Pearl, who had never been anyone's favorite, was lapping up her grandmother's attention.

Cadence sat on an uncomfortable horsehair-covered chair and leaned back.

"Cadence," Eliza said, "a lady never allows her back to touch the chair."

Cadence looked at her mother for confirmation, and Vera gave her the small shrug and smile that meant she should humor the older woman. "Yes, Grandmother," Cadence replied dutifully as she sat up straight. "Grandmother, is there a suffragette group here?"

"A what? Would you girls like some tea? I'll have Jenkins bring in some more."

"No, thank you," Cadence said as Pearl nodded. Eliza motioned for the butler to bring one glass, and Cadence repeated her question. "A suffragette group. You know, women who are advocating equal rights."

"Equal rights with whom, dear?" the old woman asked in puzzlement.

"Why, with men!" She leaned forward eagerly. "I once heard Miss Susan B. Anthony speak!"

"Oh? I don't believe I've met her. Is she new in town?"

"No, Grandmother. She's heading the suffrage movement. She and Mrs. Elizabeth Stanton and Mrs. Matilda
Gage have written three books on women's rights, and I've
read them all."

"Have you? I was never one for reading. You can ask
your father. I wager I've not read a dozen books in my life.
I do enjoy *Harper's Weekly*, though."

"So do I," Vera put in. "Did you see that scathing
article last February against the sending of valentines?"

"Cadence reads *Bicycling World*," Pearl said, making
a face at her older sister.

"It's better than reading *The Wayward Heart* or *The
Garden Path*," Cadence retorted.

"I don't read trashy books like that!" Pearl said with
an offended glance at her mother.

"Then why do you keep them under your pillow?"
Cadence chided.

"Girls, stop it," Ransome said. "If you can't be civil,
go sit somewhere else."

Eliza shook her head and the ribbons on her housecap
bounced. "What's this world coming to? I can't imagine a
child of mine speaking out like that in front of Mr. Mac-
Kinley, God rest his soul."

Ransome gave his mother a long look, but said nothing.

Cadence stood up. "I'm going for a walk. Are you
coming, Pearl?"

"No, I'd rather stay here and drink my tea. It's hot
out there."

Cadence let herself out and strolled down the grassy
lawn. She was glad Pearl wasn't one to enjoy walking, because she preferred being alone with her thoughts to hearing
the complaints of her sister. To hear Pearl, she detested
every aspect of Cavelier and the South. Cadence had expected to dislike it here, but she had found she felt just the
opposite. True, there wasn't the bustle and activity of Albany, and the suffrage movement seemed to be practically
unknown, but she loved the massive oaks, festooned with
clouds of Spanish moss, and the lazy waters of the bayou,
and the countless birds and butterflies that abounded here.

When she was out of sight of the parlor, Cadence
turned and went into the woods. No one had specifically
told her to stay out of them, but she knew her grandmother
would say a lady wouldn't go there and her mother had

already spoken of her concern that some harm might come to her in the "wilds" of Louisiana. Cadence smiled. Her mother couldn't understand that neither of her daughters had a shy bone in her body. To Vera the woods were frightening and the swamp was a place best suited for nightmares. She had admitted as much to the girls, but told them not to tell their father how she felt, for she didn't want him to worry.

She followed an old path down the slope to a shallow ravine where a fair-size creek bubbled and tumbled over mossy rocks and logs. When she came to a picturesque bridge made of cedar that was greenish in cast from the algae and lichen that appeared to have been growing there for many years, Cadence eyed it warily, then cautiously tested it before stepping onto it to gaze down at the water. The flat surface of the water beneath the bridge faithfully mirrored the green lace of the tree leaves and blue sky above her, but a few feet beyond, the creek narrowed and the water bubbled and bounced over tiny rapids toward a series of miniature waterfalls.

Cadence crossed to the other side and wandered on through the woods, keeping the creek within earshot so she wouldn't get lost. She had rarely been in a forest alone, and she loved the exhilarating freedom of knowing she could run or dance or sing and no one would know. Being in the woods gave her an entirely different feeling from being in the tree-filled parks of Albany. Here the wildness of unrestricted underbrush and tangled wild grape vines touched a passionate part of her that neither of her parents had ever suspected existed.

She smiled as she thought of her parents. She was so different from them both. Not in her wildest imagination could she picture either of them giving rein to a great passion. Papa had his stuffy law practice and Mama had her teas and orderly house, and they were both as solid and respectable as the church building. And about as exciting, Cadence thought irreverently. They couldn't possibly know of this yearning she had for something more, something better than a monotonously calm marriage. That was one reason she was such an advocate of women's rights. She dreamed of being a lawyer, too. Not one like her father, who dealt in civil suits, but one to champion the downtrodden—namely, women.

She was so deep into her thoughts that she had come

upon the swimming hole without realizing she was no longer alone.

A young man who appeared to be in his mid-twenties was swimming in the small confines. A few strokes took him across the length of the pool, and then he reversed and swam back. Cadence knew he hadn't heard her, because he was swimming with his head in the water. She knew she should turn and hurry back the way she had come, but instead she sidestepped behind the cover of a nearby bush and unabashedly watched. She couldn't see much of him in the cloudy water, but she could see enough to know he wasn't wearing a bathing costume. His bare back and chest were corded with hard muscles beneath his water-slicked skin. She could only guess at the rest, but she knew this alone would be enough to give her grandmother apoplexy.

She knew what she should do. She knew what she ought to do. Instead, she crept nearer.

His black hair was plastered wetly to his head, and although she couldn't see his eyes, she assumed they, too, would be dark. The tan of his skin suggested that he must swim like this often. She was fascinated by him and couldn't stop staring at his broad shoulders and the way his muscled arms pulled him through the water. Cadence had learned to swim during one of her visits to the seashore with friends—a fact she had kept carefully concealed from her mother—but she swam nothing at all like this!

As the man neared the grassy bank, he stood up, the water pooling about him just below his navel. Rivulets of water streamed down his lean body, leaving behind glistening droplets that clung to the crisp, curling hair on his chest. She was intrigued, for unlike her father, whom she had once glimpsed without a shirt, this man's chest was furred with curls that spread across, then tapered down in a line over his taut stomach and disappeared into the water.

Cadence crouched lower behind the clump of bushes and peered around the large tree as he hoisted himself onto the soft mat of grass that grew along the bank. Her mouth gaped open. She had been right. The man wore no bathing costume at all! A blush brightly colored her cheeks, and she chastised herself for not having left long before now.

He stood, and as he dried himself with a square of linen, the nakedness of his hard body drew her eyes back to him. His movements were lithe and confident, as if he owned these woods and came here often, though Cadence had certainly never seen him at Roseland.

He turned as if to face her, and Cadence pulled back behind the tree, wishing desperately that she had already gone. From the sounds she could hear, she guessed he was pulling on his pants, and she decided that the noise he was making would cover her escape. Cautiously she took one step back, then another. Knowing she had to put the next clump of bushes between them if she was going to get away unseen, she turned to run. Her foot caught in one of the vines that covered the forest floor and she fell, knocking the breath out of her.

Pierce half-crouched at the unexpected noise, and his eyes narrowed. Who could be there? In all the years he had come here, he had never seen anyone. Carefully he crept forward, and to his amazement, he found a woman lying on the ground. He quickly surmised that the noise he had heard was her falling, and because her pale green dress blended so well with the surrounding trees and bushes, it was no wonder that he hadn't noticed her sooner. He strode over to her and knelt beside her. She was conscious, but just opening her eyes. "Who are you? Do you work at Roseland?" he asked.

Cadence lifted her head and found herself staring into arresting blue-gray eyes banded with dark blue, as hypnotic as a mesmerist's. Her lips parted in surprise, and she stammered, "No. I . . . I don't work at—"

"So you're trespassing too!" He smiled, and she felt her heart stop. "Strange, I've never seen you in town. Are you new here?"

She nodded as she pushed herself to a sitting position.

He continued to smile as he studied her face. Never had he seen anyone like this in Cavalier! Her hair was deep red and her eyes were as brown as the pine-tree bark behind her. Her nose was small and straight and her lips were the sort that always seemed to smile. "I'm Pierce Delacroix. Welcome to Cavalier."

Cadence finally found her voice, and realized she needed to set him straight. "My name is Cadence MacKinley and you're trespassing on my land."

"MacKinley? I heard old man MacKinley's son had moved back, but I hadn't heard of a red-headed daughter."

"My hair is auburn, not red! And I'll thank you to put your clothes on!"

Pierce looked down at his bare chest and then back at her. "How long have you been watching me?"

"I wasn't watching you at all! If you want to swim in a creek, it's no business of mine." She realized what she had admitted, and blushed again. To hide her embarrassment, she snapped, "Except when you choose to swim on our land! Do you have permission to be here? I've never seen you among the workers at Roseland."

"I don't work there." He fetched his shirt from a bush and shrugged into it. As he did so he said, "As you said, I'm trespassing. My aunt and grandmother live at Ten Acres."

"Where's that?"

"Don't you bother to learn your neighbors' names? It's through the woods there." He nodded in the opposite direction from Roseland. "Do you mean you've never heard of the Delacroixs?"

"Never. Your fame hasn't reached New York, I'm afraid." She was all too aware of a throbbing pain in her ankle, and she longed to unbutton her shoe to relieve the swelling. "Could you help me up?" she asked as he pulled on his coat.

Pierce came back to her and extended his hand. Cadence hated to take it, but her foot hurt too badly for her to be proud. He drew her effortlessly up, and she balanced on one foot while she tested the toe of the other against the ground.

"We don't often hear a MacKinley ask a Delacroix for anything. It's a shame we don't have a photographer around to record the occasion."

"I have no idea what you're talking about. I'm going home now, and I suggest you do the same." She nodded haughtily and tried to step away from him. Her ankle buckled, and she cried out as pain shot through her.

At once he caught her, and kept his arm around her to prevent her from falling. "Are you okay?"

"No. No, it's my ankle. I twisted it."

"Steady yourself on this tree." Pierce put her hand on the rough bark, and before she could stop him, he knelt and put his gentle hands on her leg. She could feel the imprint of his fingers through her stockings as if his touch branded her, and she tried to pull away. "Be still," he commanded. "I'm trying to unfasten your shoe."

He finally mastered the buttons and carefully pulled it

off. Her ankle was puffy, but the fact that she had let him remove the high-topped shoe told him her ankle wasn't broken. He stood and handed her the shoe. "You can't walk on that foot. You have a bad sprain."

"I must!" Her face was pale, but she said imperiously, "Go to Roseland and have them send a cart for me."

"I have a better idea." Before she could stop him, he bent and picked her up in his arms.

"Put me down! You're going the wrong way!"

"It's closer to Ten Acres, and I think our reception might be warmer. Although I don't think I'd tell Tante Jessamine and Grandmama that you go around watching men swim in the raw." He grinned at her obvious embarrassment.

"I don't! I . . . I saw you by accident. Only the barest glimpse!" She jerked her head away when he laughed softly. "I mean, I hardly saw you at all. Just . . . just your arm and part of a shoulder. I was trying to discreetly leave when I fell."

"Of course you were."

"Well, I was!"

"Stick to that story when you explain all this to your parents. It's the sort of thing a parent might believe."

Cadence gave him her coolest look but it was impossible to be aloof when he was carrying her so intimately. The image of his magnificently naked body came back to her, and she tried to pretend a great interest in the distant trees. Unfortunately, each step rocked her against his broad chest, and she could smell the clean woods scent of his skin and hair. Then there were his eyes—so startlingly bright in his tanned face, and with such thick eyelashes. Eyes that could set a woman aflutter at a hundred paces.

As they left the woods, Cadence saw an impressive white house flanked by two log cabins and the usual barns and outbuildings. "How pretty," she exclaimed before she remembered she was being aloof.

"This is Ten Acres."

He carried her through the gate and up the walk beneath the trellises of roses. Although it wasn't grand like Roseland, Cadence had never seen a place she liked better. On the porch a merle collie wagged his tail and waited for them to approach.

"Don't worry. Donnie doesn't bite," Pierce assured her.

"I'm never afraid of dogs. Or anything else, for that matter."

"Obviously. Otherwise you'd never have stayed in the woods and watched a strange man swim like that. What if I had been the sort to take advantage of a young woman all alone in the forest?"

Cadence's eyes grew round. "I never thought of that!"

"No? What *were* you thinking when you were watching me?"

She glared at him and clamped her mouth shut. He laughed as if this were proof of her wayward thoughts.

"Pierce!" Jessamine said as she came to see who was in the parlor. "What on earth . . ."

"Spartan, you put that girl down at once," Delia said with gentle disapproval. "The very idea."

Pierce put Cadence on the sofa and turned to his aunt. "She hurt her ankle."

"Where did you find her?" Jessamine demanded. "Surely she wasn't just walking along the road!"

"She was over by the swimming hole."

"What were you doing over there? And who is she?"

"I can speak for myself," Cadence said testily. "I was . . . walking . . . in the woods, and fell. Luckily Mr. Delacroix happened by and offered me assistance."

"Surely you can call me Pierce." He chuckled. "After all, I did give assistance."

Cadence glared at him and held out her hand to Jessamine. "My name is Cadence MacKinley from Roseland."

Jessamine's eyes widened, and she dropped the young woman's hand as if she had been burned. "Ransome's daughter. Of course. I see the resemblance."

Cadence was surprised by the reaction, but turned her attention to the elderly woman as Delia spoke. "MacKinley," she said with a charming smile that deepened the wrinkles in her face. "An unusual name in these parts. It seems oddly familiar, though. Spartan, do we know the MacKinleys?"

"Not well, Grandmama."

"Spartan?" Cadence asked in a curious whisper. "I thought your name was Pierce."

"Grandmama calls me by my middle name."

Jessamine knelt and examined the swollen ankle. "It's turning purple. She should be put to bed at once."

"I'll take her home in the buggy, Tante Jessamine."

Jessamine looked up almost fearfully at the lovely young woman. Ransome's daughter! "Yes, she mustn't stay here." When Cadence looked offended, Jessamine added, "It's not that you aren't welcome; it's because of the feud."

"What feud?"

Jessamine's hands faltered as she felt the puffy ankle. "You've never heard of the bad blood between the MacKinleys and the Delacroixs?"

"Never! What's this all about?"

"I'm sure you'll hear all about it when Pierce delivers you to Roseland." She got up and looked thoughtfully at Cadence. "Do you have brothers and sisters?"

"I have a sister and a little brother."

Jessamine nodded as if she wanted to say more but couldn't. "Pierce will see you home safely. You can trust him."

Delia said, "Must you rush off so soon? We have so few people drop by to visit. You haven't even had refreshments."

"I'll come back, if I may." Cadence looked at Jessamine for approval. To her surprise, the woman drew back.

"That might not be a good idea."

"Tante Jessamine, you aren't going to act like Papa does, are you? It's not hospitable."

"That's right, Jessamine," Delia agreed. "I'm quite surprised at you." To Cadence she said, "Don't mind her, Miss MacKinley. You're welcome here anytime."

"Mama!"

"Perhaps I'd better not come back. I don't go where I'm not welcome."

"It's not me, Miss MacKinley. It's all of us. There are things you don't know. Things you wouldn't understand." Jessamine gripped her hands together tightly. She couldn't bear to see this girl that should by all rights have been her own daughter but was born of another woman. She was living proof of Ransome's marriage, and Jessamine couldn't be friends with her. To keep from showing her weakness, Jessamine turned and left the room.

"I don't understand," Cadence said in a hurt voice.

"Neither do I exactly," Pierce told her. "All I know is, my family and your family have always been at odds. I'll go get the buggy."

Cadence talked to Delia while she waited. She soon

realized the older woman wasn't quite right in the head, as her mother would have put it. In fact she seemed to think the year was 1860. Even so, Cadence found herself drawn to Delia's gentleness, and before she left, she promised to come again. Pierce's aunt might want to keep this strange feud alive, but Cadence was much too modern in her thinking to consider such a thing.

Pierce carried her out to the buggy as Delia waved good-bye. Cadence clutched her shoe to her chest as if for security as she said, "Can I really trust you? After all, you're the one who suggested you might be a masher, and I can't run from you."

"Miss Cadence, your virtue is as safe with me as if you were a nun. I'm not interested in ravishing a helpless maiden today."

"You needn't be so testy about it!"

"Do I detect a trace of regret? Perhaps I'll ravish you next time."

Cadence glared straight ahead. "I can't say I care much for Southern gentility if you're an example of it."

"You lack a certain gentleness yourself." Pierce grinned over at her as he turned the horse down the road. "I think that's what interests me so much. I never met a girl who would hide and watch a man swim naked."

"I've never done such a thing before, and I assure you I never will again."

"No? That's a shame."

"Must you keep making such insulting innuendos? You're embarrassing me."

"No, I'm not. I may be making you angry, but you aren't embarrassed at all. Is this one of those suffragette ideas I've heard about?"

"What would a person like you know about woman suffrage?" she asked haughtily. "I'm amazed you know the word!"

"I read one of Miss Anthony's books. I hear it's a burning issue everywhere but in Cavelier."

Cadence stared at him in amazement. "*You* read Miss Anthony's book? I don't believe it!"

"It's true. There's a copy in the library. Of course the library is still small, but so is Cavelier."

"She did send copies around to libraries that would agree to take them," Cadence said doubtfully. "I suppose you might have read one."

"Now that Wyoming has come into the Union, I imagine the issue for women's votes will come to a head. If you can vote in one state, you should be able to vote in any of them."

"What?"

"Doesn't it make sense? Now, you take my Tante Jessamine. She's as well-read as any man in town, and smarter than most. Since there's no man in the house, neither she nor Grandmama is represented. That's not right."

Cadence felt as if she were hearing an angel speak. Not even her father ever said things like this! "I agree completely!" She leaned toward him eagerly. "Is there a suffrage group in Cavelier?"

"No."

"Then I'll start one! If Miss Anthony's book is here, there must be some interest. Perhaps I can get the library to order her other books as well." She sat back with obvious enthusiasm. "Whoever would have guessed I'd meet someone who thinks so much like I do!"

The buggy rolled to a stop in front of Roseland's wide steps. Pierce hesitated, then got down to tie his horse and lifted Cadence out of the buggy. He had heard of Roseland all his life, but since it wasn't visible from the road, he had never seen its impressive columns and wide porches. As he looked up at the tall house, he tried to figure which of the rooms had been his father's and which one his aunt's.

Before he could reach the door it was thrown open wide and a tall man with hair the color of Cadence's strode out.

"What is this!" Ransome demanded.

"Papa, this is a friend of mine," Cadence begin uncertainly. She had rarely seen her father angry.

"She fell and hurt her ankle," Pierce said quickly. "My aunt says it's not serious, but she should be in bed and shouldn't walk on it for a while."

Ransome scooped Cadence out of Pierce's arms as she confirmed it. "Who is this aunt and what were you doing at their house?" he demanded of his daughter.

"She fell in the woods. Luckily I heard her and was able to rescue her," Pierce said in a clipped tone. He didn't like the man's attitude. "As I said, she's hurt. I'd have the doctor out if I were you."

Ransome's eyes narrowed as he stared at the shape of the stranger's face, the color of his hair. Ransome's heart seemed to be hammering almost audibly as he said, "Who the hell are you?" He heard Vera and Eliza gasp at his profanity, but he resolutely continued to glare at the young man.

"I'm Pierce Delacroix. And you?" Creole pride rang in his voice.

"All you need to know is that I'm her father." Ransome knew he should thank the man or ask him in to show his appreciation for rescuing Cadence, but he could feel Eliza's bristling anger and knew she would never let a Delacroix through the door. Besides, he looked so familiar! Surely he wasn't . . . "Who are your parents?"

"My father is Jerome Delacroix."

Ransome felt a wave of relief. For a moment there . . . "Thank you for bringing Cadence home safely, Mr. Delacroix."

"If I might look in on her to be sure she's all right, say, in a day or two—"

"No! It won't be necessary for you to see her again, nor will it be desirable." Ransome strode into the house as Vera and Eliza bustled around Cadence in concern. He kicked the door shut and wished he could shut out his thoughts with such firmness. The boy looked amazingly like Jessamine. For one terrible moment Ransome had thought their loving had had a result that he had never suspected.

"Papa, don't be like that!" Cadence protested. "He was very good to me and I like him."

"I forbid it!" Ransome said as he carried his daughter upstairs. "Do you understand me? You are never to see him again!"

Cadence stared at him in amazement. She had never been forbidden to do anything in her entire life. She didn't like it one bit.

Outside, Pierce frowned at the door. They would take care of her, of that he had no doubt. But he hated to leave her in such a hostile place. No wonder she was so independent, with a father like that one! Pierce wanted to kick open the door and carry her back out again and into the loving security of Ten Acres.

On the other hand, his aunt actually had been rude to Cadence—something Pierce would have sworn wasn't even possible. Shaking his head, he went back to the buggy. Surely one of his parents would be reasonable about him seeing a MacKinley. Pierce had never known them to agree on anything, so he figured if one of them protested, the other would approve. Although as a grown man he didn't need their permission, he would prefer to have their approval, for he had no intention of obeying her father's unreasonable injunction. No woman had ever intrigued him the way Cadence MacKinley did, and he was determined to get to know her better.

36

Jerome Delacroix sat behind his copy of the Cavelier *Tribune* drinking his bourbon-laced coffee. He wasn't reading the paper, for he had done that earlier during his lunch hour at work, but he pretended to be doing so. As a concession to Pierce, who lived in the *garçonnière* out back, and who was very observant of his parents' actions, Jerome had developed the habit of coming home from work and reading the paper over a cup of coffee. As usual, Susanna was complaining and deriding him, which led Jerome to see to it that his coffee was well-fortified, but he was in the house, giving the appearance of normal family life at the end of the day. Under the cover of the society page, he consulted his watch to see if he could make his excuses yet and leave for the tranquillity of Doll's home.

Susanna stuffed a forkful of cake in her mouth and said, "I don't know why you aren't down at the docks tonight. With all the rain we've had, I imagine the bayou must be up."

"Tanner Johnson is seeing to the ship loading."

"Papa used to say anything worth doing is worth doing yourself."

"He did spend an unusual amount of time away from home, didn't he? I wonder why." Jerome gave Susanna a cold look over the top of his paper.

"What's that supposed to mean!"

"Just an observation."

She finished off her cake and drank the last of her hot chocolate. A dusting of crumbs sprinkled over her swelling bosom and down onto her overstuffed lap. "Where do you suppose that boy is? He knows I worry when he doesn't come home on time."

"Pierce is a grown man. You have to let him come and go as he pleases."

317

"No, I don't. Not as long as he's living under my roof!"

"The *garçonnière* wasn't under this roof the last time I checked."

"He's getting to be just like you," she said scathingly. "Always at the gin or the docks and never at home. Where do you two go so often?"

"I'm not sure where Pierce spends the time he's not either here or at Ten Acres. I suppose because he's very popular, he goes to a lot of parties. I don't grill him for information as you do."

"You should find out! He's your son!"

"He's twenty-five years old! Turn him loose!"

"There! I knew you'd raise your voice to me! I suppose next you'll start beating me."

"Susanna, if there was the remotest possibility of that, it would have happened long ago."

"You don't care about me. Mama says you never have. I think you only married me because of . . . well, the unfortunate situation."

Jerome turned the page. He had never in all these years told Susanna he had gone to her house that awful day to call off the wedding. "Where is your dear mother?"

"Lying down. The heat prostrates her and it has gotten hot so early this year. I want to move to a cooler house. There's a lot for sale on the north side of town, where all the better people are moving. We could build a really fine house there." She leaned back with a ponderous sigh and rested her ridiculously small hands on her protruding belly. "Or better yet, we could buy the Monson house on Peach Street. It's one of the nicest houses in town, and goodness knows you can afford it."

"This one is larger than we need."

"But it's so old! I'm ashamed to have anyone in."

Jerome looked around at the unkempt parlor. Dirt was ground into the rugs, and the windows hadn't been cleaned in years. One curtain had a raveling tear at the hem, but Susanna refused to let him buy new ones because her father had given them to her—though they had been charged to Jerome. A day's worth of dirty saucers and cups littered the tabletop, but Susanna refused to let Dulcie clean the room while she was in it, and she left it only to sleep.

"I agree," he said. "You shouldn't have guests in."

"Now, don't start on that! I do the best I can!" She

looked up at the sound of a door closing. "Pierce? Is that you?"

"Yes, Mother. Hello, Papa." He came in and sat down beside Jerome.

"No kiss for your mother?" Susanna scolded.

Pierce leaned forward and automatically placed a kiss on her fat cheek. "You'll never guess what happened to me today. I met an angel."

"A what?" Jerome asked with a smile. "I didn't know there were any around here."

"She just moved here. She turned her ankle and I took her home. Her name is Cadence. Isn't that a pretty name? Cadence MacKinley."

Jerome lowered his paper and stared at his son. Even Susanna looked more surprised than petulant. "Who?" he asked.

"Cadence MacKinley. From Roseland."

"Not Ian MacKinley's granddaughter!"

"Yes, that's right. Wait until you meet her, Papa. She's not like anyone you've ever met before."

"Not a MacKinley!" Susanna exclaimed. "They're Yankees! Why, they aren't our kind at all!"

"You're not to see her again," Jerome commanded. "Do you hear me?"

Pierce drew back, and his smile faded. "I don't need your permission."

"I will not have that white trash in my house!" Susanna snapped. "Imagine!"

"Cadence is not white trash." Pierce's voice was showing his growing anger, though he was trying to control himself. "I won't have you talk about her like that!"

"She's a MacKinley!" Jerome made the name sound worse than Susanna's label.

Pierce looked from one to the other. He had never heard them agree on anything before. "She's not like that. I know old Ian MacKinley was a pain, and her father doesn't seem to be any better, but Cadence is different."

"You met Ransome? You went to Roseland?" Jerome thundered. "How could you do a thing like that!"

"I told you she was hurt. I took her home."

"There must have been someone else around who could have done it. Don't ever go there again!"

"I don't intend to, but I do plan to see Cadence again!"

"Not as long as you're under my roof!" Susanna shrieked. "You're no better than your father!"

Jerome glared at her, then crumpled the paper and stood up. As he put on his hat, he heard Pierce say, "Maybe it's time I moved, then, because I will see her again!"

As Jerome left the house, he heard Susanna scream something about all the Delacroix men being womanizers. He didn't bother to answer. He saddled his horse and mounted, wishing he had the freedom to move away as Pierce did. He knew where he would go. Nothing ever disturbed the peace of Doll's house.

The horse found the well-known destination and nickered softly to the other animals in the barn. Jerome unsaddled him and turned him into the lot. He planned to stay as long as possible. He had to be home only in time to put in an appearance for breakfast.

Doll looked up as he came in and went to give him a hug. "Supper's nearly ready. I was hoping you'd ride out tonight."

"Only two plates?" he asked as she set the table. "Where's Laurie?"

"She's eating with friends in Palizada. They'll see her home."

He looked at her more closely. "What's wrong? Don't walk off, come here." He put his arms around her. "Tell me what's bothering you."

"It's Laurie. She's met a boy, and I think she's seeing him tonight."

"Well, it was just a matter of time, *chérie*. She's growing up."

"You haven't noticed her lately," Doll said with a short laugh. "As Ma would have said, 'She's done there.' " She laid her head on Jerome's chest and closed her eyes. "I just wanted so much more for her."

"Oh? Who is this boy?"

"It's Tobias Wilson from over at the sawmill. He's kin to Tom Smith."

"That doesn't seem so bad. I know Tom, and they're good people. Don't you like this Tobias?"

"She won't let me meet him. That's part of what worries me. I wouldn't know about him at all, except Mr. Edwards told me they meet at his soda fountain so often. He assumed I knew it."

"Why doesn't she bring him home? I want to meet this man."

"Now, why do you think she doesn't?" Doll looked up at him in exasperation. "My cornbread is going to burn."

He let her go and said with a frown, "He must know she doesn't come from an ordinary family. Anybody can tell that by looking at her."

"I'm surprised he hasn't figured out who she's kin to. He must know Jessamine. What if he tells someone?" She took the heavy black iron pan of bread out of the oven. "Wash up."

Jerome worked the pump handle as he said, "If you think about it, it's amazing that everyone doesn't know."

Doll didn't answer. She never told even Jerome about her spells to protect them.

"Is there something I don't know about this man? Does he drink or is he wild?"

"Not that I know of."

"Then what's the problem?"

"He's black!"

Jerome looked at her blankly, then begin to laugh.

"Don't you laugh at me, Jerome Delacroix! Don't you do it!"

"Come here." He pulled her down onto his lap. "Now, don't you think that's a pretty strange reason to object to him?"

She smiled despite herself. "Not when I had something else in mind for her."

"Doll, for Laurie to pass, she would have to move away. We might never see her again. You could never meet her husband or hold your grandchildren. We don't want that."

"You don't know what it's like, being black! What if some crazy man up in Washington decides to bring back slavery!"

"It won't ever happen, honey."

"It might! And even if it doesn't, I want her to have the advantages of *your* people—not the heartaches of mine."

"It's Laurie's life. She has to decide."

"You don't understand." Doll jumped up from his lap and shoved the skillet of cornbread on the table. Her movements were jerky with suppressed emotion as she poured the black-eyed peas into a bowl and took out the jar of pepin. "You can't ever understand because you can't walk around in my skin."

He went to her and put his arms around her to calm her down. "You're right, Doll. I can't. I can't feel the hurt and hear all the insults and snide comments and experience all the frustrations. I know that and it tears me up that you're treated this way. But I love Laurie and I don't want her to leave us forever."

Doll turned to embrace him. "I don't either. I want it both ways, I guess. I always have wanted your kind of life and my own heritage. I guess it won't ever be possible."

He held her tightly, wishing he could absorb her pain and unhappiness and make it right for her. "It's better than it was, *chérie.*"

"It's not good enough." She tiptoed up and kissed him. "Sit down and eat before it gets cold."

37

Ransome sat at the head of the polished cherrywood table and carved slices of roast beef for each of his family members. Eliza preferred to take her dinner from a tray in her room, on the theory that if no one saw her eat, no one would notice she was gaining weight. Ransome wished all their problems could be so easily wished away.

"I rode out with Oliver Gibbons today to look at the new cotton crop, and he's right. The land is worn out. Besides, Father was having to pay exorbitant prices to have it baled and shipped."

Vera touched her napkin to the corners of her lips and said, "You'll soon have a law practice established. We won't need the cotton as well."

"I'm afraid we will. Roseland costs considerably more to run than did our house in Albany. Besides, it may take years to build a clientele here."

"Everybody here is as old as the hills," Pearl complained. "Maybe you could buy out one of the ancient lawyers and have his practice."

"You don't understand the politics here," her father said. "We're newcomers, and people prefer to deal with the old stock."

"But Grandmother and Grandfather have lived here thirty-one years! You grew up here."

"Thirty-one years is a drop in the bucket to Cavelier." He passed the green beans to Ethan. "Eat some vegetables, son. They'll make you grow tall." He interspersed his words with gestures so the boy would understand.

Cadence had insisted on coming downstairs for dinner, but she kept her bandaged foot propped in a chair. "How long have the Delacroixs been here?"

Ransome gave her a warning glance. "Forever."

Vera pushed the beans and carrots around on her plate

323

to disguise the fact she didn't feel like eating. She felt as if she were running a low-grade fever again. "Perhaps we could grow peanuts, Ransome. I hear there are all sorts of uses for peanuts these days. Or maybe sugarcane. I understand many of the plantations have switched to that."

"I'll look into it."

"I think you're being completely unfair," Cadence persisted. "Pierce Delacroix is a perfect gentleman. Just because our grandparents hated each other is no reason for us not to be friends."

"I've explained all that to you. Be glad your grandmother isn't downstairs to hear you!"

Cadence turned to Vera. "Mama, he has actually read Miss Anthony's book!"

"That's very commendable, dear, but so have a lot of people."

"Not in Cavelier!"

"If your father says not to see him, then you mustn't."

"That's not fair!"

"No one ever said life has to be fair," Ransome said. "This is the way it's going to be. We won't have any dealings with that family. None!"

"If Ethan were my age, and he wanted to spark a girl, I'll bet you wouldn't tell him who he could see and who he couldn't!"

"Whom," Vera corrected as she passed the rolls to Ransome.

"You aren't going to turn this into another suffragette debate, Cadence." Ransome took a roll and handed the plate to Pearl. "This has nothing to do with women's rights, and everything to do with my rights as your father!" He grimaced when he noted that he had sounded disturbingly like his own father. In a softer tone he said, "Cadence, try to understand. They aren't socially acceptable to us." His frown deepened as he realized this sounded even worse. "Eat your dinner."

"I'm not hungry," Cadence said with great dignity. "I may never be hungry again."

"Suit yourself." Ransome refused to get further involved in the argument with his daughter. If only she wasn't his favorite, he thought, he would have less difficulty controlling her. If only the young man hadn't looked so much like Jessamine. The food on his plate suddenly seemed unappetizing.

Jessamine again! Since accidentally meeting her in front of the doctor's office, he had been haunted by her memory. Even the room Vera had chosen for them to share had been Jessamine's, and he could imagine her spirit in every corner. Today, when he had met Pierce, he had been certain for a dreadful moment that this was her son—*their* son.

The scent of wisteria drifted through the open windows, and he could almost hear Jessamine's laughter. Earlier he had walked down to the bridge, tormenting himself with the idea that he might find a leaf stuck in the railing that would signify her desire to meet him in secret the next morning. Of course, there was no such indication, and there would be no secret meeting, but nevertheless, he had severely chastised himself for his mental infidelity.

Cadence stood and said, "Excuse me, please. I find I'm not hungry and wish to go to bed."

"She acts like Ada Rehan," Pearl said with sisterly disgust.

"And what do you know about actresses?" her mother asked.

Pearl pretended to be engrossed in finishing her vegetables as Cadence painfully hobbled out of the room. Ethan swung his head from side to side in his effort to see everyone's lips so he could understand this bewildering family confrontation.

Ransome laid down his fork. "I'm not hungry either. Will you excuse me?"

Vera nodded. She knew he was more troubled about Cadence's new beau than about what crop to plant. He had been nervous ever since they arrived at Roseland. She thought about the woman they had met in town, and wondered if she had anything to do with Ransome's odd behavior. After all those years of marriage to Ransome she knew him as well as she knew herself. He had never been unfaithful before—she would wager anything on that—but she also knew he was still very attractive to women. She found that she had lost her appetite, but she forced herself to stay at the table for her children's sake.

Ransome went out onto the porch and sat on the rail. Lightning bugs flickered on the lawn and frogs vied with crickets in the evening's chorus. He had always loved Roseland, but now he wished like hell he had stayed away. Why had he ever thought he could come back here and feel nothing for Jessamine, whether she was married to Louis Broussard or not?

From what Cadence had said, she must have been walking somewhere near the old swimming hole. That had been his rendezvous point with Jessamine. The bower of tall gardenias was only a stone's throw away. He recalled that hot summer when he and Jessamine had hidden in those bushes and loved and planned an impossible future. He had been young enough and foolish enough to believe dreams came true if only a person wished hard enough. And perhaps they would have if his father hadn't found them that terrible day and if the consequences had been different. He absently touched the scar on his cheek. He couldn't look in the mirror without remembering.

"Ransome?"

He looked up to see Vera framed in the doorway. With a smile he held out his hand to her.

"Would you rather be alone with your thoughts?" she asked as she came to him. "I don't want to intrude."

"How could you intrude? Come sit beside me." He couldn't help but notice that she appeared thinner since the move, and he felt even guiltier for his thoughts. "We've had a good marriage," he said without thinking.

"Yes, we have. There have been hard times. Ethan's sickness, those first years before your practice became established, Aunt Polly's death."

"We've had more good days than bad."

"Is that what you're doing out here? Thinking about our marriage?" She put her folded hands on the rail, and he covered her fingers with his.

"I was wondering what to do about Cadence. I hate to refuse her anything. I guess it's because I heard the word 'no' so often myself as a boy."

"Sometimes it's necessary. We have a responsibility to protect our children."

"Even after they're grown? Cadence is old enough to make her own choices. I just don't want her to make this one."

"Are the Delacroixs really so bad, Ransome?"

"No," he said softly. "They aren't bad people at all. Vera, how does life get so damned complicated?"

She had no answer for that, but the way he had asked the question caused a prickle of anxiety to creep from the nape of her neck to the base of her spine. Never in all their years of marriage had she ever thought Ransome might be yearning for another woman. Not until the past few days. "Did we make a mistake in moving here?"

"No," he firmly answered, lifting his head. "No, it was no mistake. I love you, Vera. We'll figure out what to do about Cadence." He pulled her to him and kissed her. As always, Vera was gently responsive, but then she pulled back and smiled at him with a rare twinkle in her eyes. "What if someone steps out and sees us like this?" Then, taking his hand, she said, "Come upstairs with me?"

For Vera this was tantamount to a brazen proposition. Ransome returned her smile, knowing how hard it had always been for her to be the one to suggest they go to bed and make love. "I guess it is getting late."

Together they went into the house.

Jessamine went into the grocery store and handed her shopping list to the man in the white bib apron. "Good morning, Mr. Travis. Is your wife feeling better?"

"Tolerable, Miss Delacroix. Dr. Griggs was by to see her, and he gave her some medicine. I imagine she'll be up and about in a day or two." He consulted the list and began stacking the goods on the worn countertop.

Jessamine stepped between the cracker barrel and the potbellied stove to count out a few sticks of horehound candy for Maribelle's children. She liked buying them surprises now and then. She wished Pierce would find a nice girl and settle down to raise a family. But not, she thought firmly, that MacKinley girl! Fate couldn't possibly be so cruel as to throw her together with Ransome and his clan on every family gathering.

"Miss Jessamine?"

She turned and said, "Louis Broussard. How nice to see you." She noted he still wore somber colors, but had already removed the mourning band from his sleeve. Even mourning seemed to go faster these days, she thought.

"I'm beginning to go out into society again," he said solemnly. Then in a brighter voice he added, "I was talking to your brother the other day, and he said you're expanding the sawmill."

"That's right. We're going to start making more furniture on the premises."

"Well, that's wonderful news. How's your mother doing?"

"She's fine. Of course she never will be her old self again after all this time, but I think she's happier than any of us."

"I imagine she is." He tapped his thinning hair and his round belly jiggled as he chuckled. "I guess all of us at one time or another would like to turn back the clock. Do it all again, as it were."

"I suppose so." But only if we could change the outcome, she added silently.

"I hear the MacKinleys have moved into Roseland. Ransome's family, I mean."

"Yes. So I hear."

"Funny how things go full circle, isn't it? I never would have guessed he would come back to Cavelier or even give it a second thought."

Jessamine pretended to be ignoring what Louis had said as she counted out the money for Mr. Travis.

"Yes, it all comes full circle. Say, I've been meaning to ask if I might drop by for a visit one day before long."

Jessamine looked at him in surprise. "Yes, I suppose that would be all right. We're at home on Sunday afternoons."

"Sunday. Good, good. Well, Miss Jessamine, I'll see you then."

"All right, Louis."

"Good day. Good day, Mr. Travis." Louis bowed with a jerky movement and went out.

"Now, what do you suppose that's all about?" she murmured to herself. With a shrug, she dismissed the matter entirely.

38

"LADIES, WE MUST UNITE TO MAKE OURSELVES heard," Cadence said to the group of women. "Today we meet in the library in Cavelier, Louisiana, but someday I expect us to meet in the Senate in Washington. Great Britain is changing its attitudes about women. So is Australia. Only the United States is stubbornly refusing to allow complete representation of all its citizens. And why? Because all forty-five states have written constitutions which require a majority vote before they can be changed, and all the voters are men!" Cadence's flashing eyes swept over the room. For the third meeting of the Cavelier Suffragettes, this wasn't a bad turnout.

A tall young woman in the front row held up her gloved hand. "Miss MacKinley, what can we do to change things? I'm not married, so I can't talk my husband into voting for woman suffrage."

"I'm married and I can't either," the woman behind her commented, to a twitter of laughter.

"We all have fathers, brothers, uncles, cousins," Cadence said firmly. "We must work through them."

"All I hear when I mention suffrage is that if women have the vote, they'll neglect their homes and families," a woman in the back said. Her neighbors nodded.

Cadence said, "I've heard that too. It's the favorite argument of all the men who would keep us suppressed. But it's not true. Men vote. Do they neglect their families because of it?"

"My husband is scared to death that women would vote against drinking," another said. "He also says Scripture is against it. If he knew I was here, he'd have my hide." The woman beside her patted her hand sympathetically.

Cadence nodded. "There are many reasons they have thought up to prevent us from being heard. But we *will* be heard. And I promise you, we *will* vote!"

Muffled applause from a dozen pairs of gloved hands brought a broad smile to Cadence's face and elation burst within her. In time they would win. She could feel it!

"Miss MacKinley," the tall woman said, raising her hand again, "what will be our next step?"

"Organization. We must formally elect officers and join the National-American Convention. I've taken the liberty to write to Mrs. Caroline E. Merrick in New Orleans and ask her to speak to us. She and Mrs. Elizabeth Saxon have been active since 1879 in trying to alter the state constitution. Since 1884 there has been an active suffragette club in that city. She has nobly agreed to come and show us how to organize. At present she is lobbying against the lottery and will be unable to get here until fall. In the meantime, we will do our best to further her efforts here in Cavelier."

Cadence sorted through her papers and said, "Last December I had the fortune to attend the National-American Convention in Rochester, New York. It was held at the First Universalist Church and was presided over by Mrs. Lillie Blake, who was president for the past eleven years. I heard such notables as Miss Mary Eastmas, the Reverend Anna Howard Shaw, and Miss Susan B. Anthony." She paused while murmurs of awe mumbled through the room. "At that meeting we decided to hold mid-year executive meetings in addition to the yearly convention, and also to educate and send out speakers to form and instruct new groups. With your approval, I'd like to write to our new president, Mrs. Jean Brooks Greenleaf, and ask that someone be sent here."

Again her words were answered with enthusiastic clapping and nods of agreement. Cadence touched her lace-edged handkerchief to her moist brow, for the room was close in the summer heat. They had elections, and as she had expected, she was chosen as president. The tall woman named Daisy Buckner was selected as her secretary, and after the close of the meeting, Daisy lingered to speak to Cadence.

"Miss MacKinley, I can't tell you how excited I am to be a part of this."

"Please, Miss Buckner, call me Cadence. We'll be working together quite closely."

"Then you must call me Daisy." The woman smiled, showing rather prominent teeth in her thin face. "I'm so glad you came to Cavelier. We haven't had so much excitement around here since the Baptist preacher ran off with the organist. Not that this is the same sort, I mean. That was a scandal, and this is progress.''

"Yes, I understand. I imagine the town will be standing on its ear before we're done," Cadence said with a smile.

"I hope so. Yes, I truly do! I guess I shouldn't be so vehement, but I've always felt it was wrong for us not to have a say."

"So do I. Perhaps we could meet at Ramsey's Café tomorrow at noon and discuss our plans for the next few meetings?"

"I would love it! Tomorrow at noon, then." Daisy Buckner said good-bye and strode away.

Cadence consulted her locket watch, then hastily gathered up her papers. She was supposed to meet Pierce at the bend in the creek, and she was late.

She hurried out the door and hopped on her bicycle. In no time she was wheeling through Cavelier's hot streets and down the road by the bayou. Hers was one of the new safety bicycles that had front and rear wheels of the same size. It was faster and easier to ride than an "ordinary," and was similar to the one "Mile a Minute Murphy" had used when he set the incredible record of a mile in one minute. She pushed the bicycle at a pace that was greatly beyond feminine decorum to reach the trysting place before Pierce left.

"I thought you weren't coming," he said as she arrived, panting for breath.

"The meeting lasted longer than I expected. Pierce, there's so much enthusiasm here! Whoever would have guessed I would become a leader in the women's-rights movement? When I left New York, I was afraid it was over for me."

"Is that the only reason you're glad you came to Cavelier?" he asked as he took her hand and folded it into the bend of his arm.

"You know it's not." She smiled up at him and felt the curiously dizzy sensation she always got from gazing into his arresting eyes. "I'm glad because you're here."

They strolled along the banks of the creek, where tiny black water bugs sailed the smooth surface and bottle-green flies hummed in the sun. Not far away was a tangle of overgrown gardenias that bloomed with a heavy perfume.

"Why do you suppose anyone would plant flowers out here in the woods?" Cadence pondered as she plucked a waxy white blossom.

"I don't know. I suppose there was once a house here, but I've never seen the foundation stones. And these are planted in a circle instead of in a row as you'd expect."

Cadence pushed aside the branches that almost closed the entrance and stepped into the circle. "I always feel happy here. As if it's a private world of some sort." She laughed and twirled the flower under his nose. "Maybe fairies planted it and this is a magical place."

"Only a Celtic woman would think of that, Cadence MacKinley. A Frenchman like myself is much too prosaic."

"Is that how you think of yourself? A Frenchman?"

"I'm Creole through and through. I've heard my grandmother refer to non-Creoles as Americans. Whereas you discuss events in Britain, we talk about what's happening in France."

"I never think of myself as being from a British background, though I suppose it's true."

"People need a culture that they can look at and say: This is mine. It's who I am."

"Not for me, thank you. I have enough difficulty figuring myself out." She glanced sideways at him. "I guess you'll settle down someday with a Creole woman and continue the heritage another generation."

"I always assumed so, but now I'm not so sure." He noticed the way the sun seemed to strike fire in her hair and how it silvered the lines of her lovely face. "I've never found a Creole woman that I loved."

"Cajun, then. They're French."

He laughed. "Don't ever let my family hear you suggest such a thing!"

"I don't understand."

"We don't normally mix with each other."

Cadence shook her head and laughed. "It's so confusing. Louisiana is like a different country."

"Yes, it is," he said, as if that were obvious.

"I'm afraid I'll never have the opportunity to say anything at all to your family," she said with a sigh. "Papa won't even consider letting me call upon your aunt and grandmother, let alone your parents."

"My mother is never 'at home,'" he said quickly.

"And they aren't being reasonable either. I've started looking for another place to live."

"Because of me? That's terrible!"

"Not only because of you. It's time I moved from the *garçonnière*. I just never had a reason before." He put his arms around her and enjoyed the feel of her warm body in his embrace.

"Even if you did move out, I couldn't possibly visit you without a chaperon. We suffragettes aren't *that* bold, you know."

"I wasn't thinking of you as a mere visitor. I thought perhaps you'd be my wife."

For a moment Cadence looked at him in stunned amazement. "Your what?"

Pierce bent and passionately kissed her before he answered. "My wife. I'm asking you to marry me, Cadence."

"Marry you?" she whispered. All the love she had tried to ignore swept over her. "Marry you?"

"Is it so unbelievable?"

"Not unbelievable—impossible!"

His arms dropped. "Then you don't love me?"

"Yes! Yes, I do love you. Surely you know that. But how can I marry you when our parents won't even let you court me?"

"We could elope, or better yet, since we're both of age, we could just go to the church, have our banns published, and do it."

"I'm not Catholic."

"You could go for instruction."

Cadence laughed and stared up at him in disbelief. "You're serious, aren't you?"

"I was never more serious in my life. I know this is terribly sudden, but I love you, Cadence. When we're apart I can think of nothing but you, and when we're together I can't bear to leave you. I spend the hours in between thinking of things I want to tell you or show you or discuss with you. Do you realize we actually *talk* to each other?"

"Yes, of course."

"No, not 'of course.' There are people who are married who never talk. They may argue, or they may make sounds as if they are talking, but they don't hear each other. I know because my parents are like that."

"How sad!"

"I never really thought I would marry, for fear of becoming stuck in such a predicament. Because divorce is against my religion, I've been very careful not to fall in love. But then I met you. Cadence, you're nothing like anyone I've ever known before! You care! You're full of life and exuberance, and you want to make a difference in this world. I like that. I love you because of the way you are.''

Her dark eyes brimmed with happy tears. "I never thought I'd hear a man say that! You wouldn't expect me to give up my suffrage cause?''

"Give it up? I'd help you further it! Will you marry me, Cadence?''

"Yes!'' She threw her arms around his neck and held him tightly as tears glistened on her cheeks. "Yes, Pierce. I love you so much!''

"Do you? You've never said so.''

"How could I? Did you think I could propose to you? I may be thoroughly modern, but there are limits.'' She spun away from him and pirouetted in the grass, her arms spread wide. "I'm so happy I could fly!''

He laughed as he caught her and pulled her back into his arms. With a teasing wink he said, "Did you love me the first time you saw me, like it says in novels?''

She blushed and cut her eyes up at him. "No, it was the second time I saw you.'' Then she laughed and added, "The first time I saw you I was struck only by your swimming ability.''

"Oh?'' His sparkling eyes gazed down into hers. "Want another demonstration?''

"No, no! Not now, at least. Do you suppose,'' she asked daringly, "that we might come here and swim after we're properly married? I have a bathing costume.''

"After we're married, you won't need one.'' He nuzzled in the ticklish part of her neck. Suddenly their nearness overcame their exuberance and the smiles faded from their faces.

"Cadence,'' he whispered, "I do love you.''

"I love you, Pierce. I love you with all my heart, and just as important, with all my friendship.'' She stretched up to kiss him, and let her lips part beneath his in the way he had taught her. When he lifted his head, she remained with hers tilted back, her lips parted, and her eyes closed. "You make my world spin,'' she sighed. "I feel dizzy and tingling and excited. Surely no one has ever been so much in love.''

"I can't imagine how a couple could be and not glow from it. You're as radiant as an angel."

She laughed softly. "You're the only one who has ever cast me in that role. Papa loves me more than anyone else, and even he says I'm troublesome and stubborn."

"You are indeed stubborn. So am I. We make a good pair. If you team a stubborn horse and a flighty horse, they're liable to walk in circles. That could get boring."

"I have a feeling we'll never be troubled by boredom." Her smile faded. "Pierce, how can we ever tell our families?"

"I don't know. But one thing is for sure—we won't do it separately. Do you object to taking Catholic instruction?"

"No, not at all."

"I'll arrange with Father Theriot for you to come in. We'll talk to him about it and see what he suggests. He's a bit forgetful these days, but he knows all about the feud and may be able to help us. In the meantime, bring my name up however you can without there being a scene. I'll do the same. Our families may as well get used to the idea that we at least know each other."

"Pierce, I'm afraid. Just all at once I feel afraid!"

"Of your father? He had better not hurt you!"

"No, no. Papa would never do such a thing. I'm afraid for us. There's so much keeping us apart!"

"Together we can overcome anything. If you love me as much as I love you, we'll be able to be together."

"I do love you, Pierce. Hold me. I feel so safe in your arms."

He cradled her securely as the bees hummed in the flowering bower.

Pearl was seldom able to come to town alone. She rode a bicycle that Cadence had abandoned for the swifter one, but Vera seldom let her younger daughter out of her sight. Only because Ethan was running a slight fever had Pearl been able to slip away.

She pedaled to town and was quite out of breath by the time she reached Macy's Emporium. She knew Cadence was holding a suffrage meeting at the library, so she parked her bicycle out of sight in the weed-grown alley and went into the building.

The tall ceiling trapped the heat well above the shoppers' heads and a long soda fountain graced one wall. She sat gingerly on a red padded seat and leaned her forearms on the cool marble counter. "A lemon fizz, please."

Before she could find a coin in her bag, a man's hand pushed one forward. "I'll buy the lady's drink," a deep voice said.

Pearl looked up in surprise to see a man with an impressive black mustache who was wearing, of all things, a plaid suit. "Excuse me, but I don't know you. I don't think it's proper for me to allow—"

"In that case, may I introduce myself. I'm Phineas K. Weatherby, at your service."

"Phineas K. . . . ." She smiled. "I never knew anyone with such an important-sounding name. Are you from around here?"

"Me? Nah. There's a riverboat at the docks. I came up the bayou on it."

The soda clerk frowned disapprovingly at the man's forwardness, but Pearl ignored him to stare at the stranger. "I've never seen a riverboat up close. We always travel by train."

Phineas waved his hand in dismissal. "Not the same at all. Not at all. A riverboat is romantic. Adventurous! A little world that floats on the current of life."

Pearl had certainly never heard such fancy words from a man before. They were like the lovely passages she read in her forbidden romantic novels. "My!" she sighed. "Just imagine! Where are you going, Mr. Weatherby?"

"You must call me Phineas, my dear. After all, I purchased a lemon fizz for you."

"Oh, I couldn't possibly. I mean, you're so much . . ." She realized what she was about to say and caught her lower lip between her teeth.

"More mature? Surely that's not a crime here in your fair city. Besides, I have a feeling we're kindred spirits."

"You do?" Pearl breathed.

"In fact . . . ." He tapped one stubby forefinger against his broad chin. "In fact, you remind me of someone. Yes! I have it! You remind me of my sister!"

"Do I really?"

"Of course her hair isn't quite as blond as yours or her eyes as blue, but yes, the resemblance is quite striking. That's why I felt free to buy your drink."

The soda clerk puffed out his graying mustache at the stranger's gall, but Pearl kept her eyes averted.

"I'll bet," Phineas continued, "that you have a voice as pure and clear as a bird's. Am I right?"

"Well," Pearl admitted with a blush, "I do sing a bit, but only in church or at home."

"I knew it!" Phineas slapped his square hand upon the counter. "So does my sister!" He shook his head dolefully and fingered the black bowler hat in his lap. "Such a pity about dear Millisant."

"Oh? Is she ill?"

"I'm afraid so. I had to leave her to convalesce at our dear aunt's house in New Orleans. Ever been there, Miss Pearl?"

"Never. But I've seen New York City, though!"

"Have you! Well, you're one up on me there. I've never played further north than Richmond."

"Played? Are you an organist?"

He laughed, throwing his head back and showing his big teeth to the ceiling. "No, no, my dear. I'm an actor. Phineas K. Weatherby has thrilled crowds of people all along the Mississippi and points east."

"But we're west of the river."

"I'm here on a sabbatical, my cherub. I needed a rest from my public."

"You actually perform on a stage, Mr. Weatherby?" Her face was rosy with awe.

"Now, see here," the soda clerk spoke up indignantly.

"Please, Mr. Mouton," Pearl said with great dignity. "We're having a private conversation, if you don't mind."

Phineas winked at the older man and helped Pearl from the stool as he said, "Walk with me a bit, my sweet, and show me your lovely city while I elaborate on my adventures on the stage."

"Have you ever met Miss Ada Rehan?" Pearl asked as they went out.

"Ada and I are as close as brother and sister. I've met all the greats—Silvia Starr, who's billed as the American Venus, the Stirk Family, Primrose and West, the Great Kar-Mi Troupe, and Lilly Clay. I know 'em all."

Pearl followed him out in a fog of adulation.

Jessamine put her iced-tea glass onto the tabletop and fanned herself gently. Louis Broussard, who hadn't the advantage of any breeze at all, mopped his face with his handkerchief.

"It's going to be a hot summer," he observed.

"Yes, I imagine that's true. I've never known a cool one." She found herself staring at the angry red line on his neck where his starched collar had irritated the skin. She looked away and hoped for his sake the starch would soon give way to the heat. She wished she could push up her sleeves, but naturally that was unthinkable. "More iced lemonade, Louis?"

"Please. I don't mind if I do."

She poured another glassful and added chipped ice from the silver bucket on the table. "Cookie? I made them myself."

"I couldn't refuse them in that case." He took two. "It's funny, isn't it, how things go full circle?"

She glanced at him as she poured lemonade in her own glass. "You said that in the grocer's when I saw you last."

"I know, but it just struck me again. I mean, here we are sitting on the same porch, drinking iced lemonade and having delicious cookies, just like we used to."

"There are a few differences, Louis," Jessamine said wryly. "You've been married and widowed and I'm forty-five years old."

"You'd never guess it to look at you. Why, you'd pass for a girl of thirty."

Jessamine laughed softly. Louis had always talked foolishness.

"Actually that brings me to the reason for my visit."

"Yes?"

"As you know, my Dorothée has been gone for several months. She was a fine woman, really fine. But she's gone to her reward and, frankly, I'm a lonely man."

Jessamine, whose mind had wandered to the new addition she was building onto the sawmill, merely nodded.

"I was sure you'd understand! Miss Jessamine, will you do me the honor of becoming my wife?"

"What?" she gasped. "Louis Broussard, you ought to be ashamed of yourself! And Dorothée barely in her grave!"

"She was ailing for a long time," he said in his defense. "It's not like it was sudden!"

"Don't you dare sit on my porch and suggest we get married! Don't you dare, Louis!"

"I'm sorry . . . I'm sorry, Miss Jessamine. I just thought with you being alone too, I—"

"Alone? I'm never alone! There's Mama, and Pierce is here most of the time, and there's Sam. Not to mention all the hired help. I'm alone less than any woman I've ever known. In fact, I've rarely been alone in my whole life!"

"Well, I only thought I'd offer," he said huffily.

Jessamine pressed her fingertips to her temples and calmed herself. "Forgive me, Louis. That was deplorable of me. It was just such a surprise."

"Then may I come back to visit? I really am lonely, you know."

"Yes, Louis. You may come to visit—as a friend, that is."

"Thank you, Miss Jessamine. Who knows? In time maybe you'll accept my proposal."

"Who knows, indeed," she said with a straight face. "My life has been a series of surprises."

39

CADENCE IMPATIENTLY FANNED HERSELF, KNOWING that her efforts to cool off would be of little avail, despite the shade of Roseland's veranda and the fact that she was wearing the coolest dress she owned. The air seemed thick and oppressively humid, and the temperature continued to rise.

"You'll adjust," Daisy Buckner said, trying to console her friend. "It takes newcomers a year or so, but you won't always feel so uncomfortable."

"I hope you're right. I keep telling myself it will be worth all this discomfort next winter when I won't have to contend with blizzards and icy sidewalks." She turned back to the papers on the white rattan table. "I heard from Mrs. Merrick. She has agreed to speak to our group in late November."

"How wonderful! I tell you, Cadence, I've never enjoyed anything in my life the way I have these meetings. I feel . . . well, important. I guess it's awfully vain to admit such a thing, though."

"Nonsense. Everyone should feel worthy. Perhaps you would consider being our delegate to the National-American Convention. It will be in Auburn, New York, this year, on November 10 and 11. Miss Anthony herself will be there."

"Me? Represent Cavelier?" Daisy looked as if Cadence had handed her the moon.

"Why not? I'm sure everyone will agree that you're the best choice. Of course, we'll have to raise the money for your train ticket and lodging expenses."

"But as our president, you should be the one to go."

"I've attended the convention before. Besides"—Cadence lowered her voice conspiratorially—"I've met someone and I hope to be married by then."

"You have? Who is he?"

Cadence glanced around to be sure they were alone.

"Pierce Delacroix. Promise not to tell anyone. We have to keep it a secret awhile longer."

"I promise. Pierce Delacroix! What a catch! He's the most eligible bachelor in the whole parish! I didn't realize you even knew each other." Daisy flushed when she recalled the relationship between the MacKinley and Delacroix families that had been the subject of discussion in Cavelier for as long as she could remember. "I had forgotten the . . . problem. I understand why you have to keep it a secret. Does your family know?"

"I keep bringing up his name, but Papa is so unreasonable. He's never been this way about my other fellows."

"I think my parents would welcome any suitor," Daisy said with a mournful sigh. "Especially at my age."

"Why, what a thing to say!"

"Girls marry young around here. I've become reconciled to being a spinster, but my parents haven't."

"And neither should you. A woman of your character should be in demand. I can vouch for your steadfastness and your abilities."

"Unfortunately, those aren't qualities that attract a man. They prefer a prettier package."

"What nonsense. Widow Ramsey is no beauty, and it's plain that Dr. Griggs dotes on her. Mr. Travis' wife is actually homely, and they're perfectly happy."

Daisy shrugged. "I guess those women are luckier than I am."

"I won't hear such talk," Cadence said in the tone of voice she usually reserved for suffragette meetings. "You're a fine, decent woman, and if you want to get married, you should do so. This is just another sign of women's repression. Why should we have to have a pretty face and a curvy figure, and be expected to go around simpering like an idiot so that some man will want us for a wife? It's wrong!"

Daisy raised her head and tilted her chin proudly. "You're right! If I have to be like an addlepated doll to get a man, I don't want one."

"That's right! Any man we choose must revere women as equals, not as pretty toys to do all the work around the house!"

"I hear you! Amen! It's time the women got to pick and choose."

Cadence clasped her friend's hands across the wicker table. "I'm so proud of what we're doing, Daisy!"

"So am I! Who knows? Maybe I'll meet my future husband on the trip to New York in November."

"Stranger things have happened."

The front door opened and Ransome stepped out. "Is something wrong?"

"No, Papa, we're just excited. We've decided it's time women had more choices about their fate. After all, it's our life."

He regarded his daughter as if he weren't too sure he could agree with that. "Within reason, I suppose that's true." He started down the steps. "Do you want anything from town? I'm going to look at the new law office."

"No, thank you, Papa."

"Good afternoon, Miss Buckner."

"Good day, Mr. MacKinley."

"Poor Papa," Cadence whispered as he left. "He and Mama love each other, but I'm sure he's never known a deathless passion." She leaned closer to Daisy. "Let me tell you about Pierce."

Ransome was secretly glad that Cadence and her friend had not suggested riding to town with him. He wanted to be alone with his thoughts. Jessamine seldom left his mind, and he was terribly afraid he might call Vera by the wrong name. Not that he had even so much as spoken to Jessamine since that day in town, but he had seen her several times as she shopped or crossed a street or passed the time of day with someone in front of the Emporium. Each time he had caught sight of her, he had gazed at her as if she were a lodestone to his heart, then realized what he was doing and virtually fled in the opposite direction. Fortunately they went to different churches, and Vera hadn't joined any clubs or women's groups that Jessamine belonged to. Jessamine, he knew, must be completely oblivious of him. After all these years she had made a life for herself, and gossip had it that she and Louis Broussard were seeing each other again now that he was free to remarry. Ransome hated himself for the jealousy he felt.

He pulled his thoughts to Vera, but that was also upsetting. Her health hadn't improved in the warmth, and in fact she was coughing more now than she had in New York. Her coloring was rosier than he ever recalled seeing it, but he was afraid the pink in her cheeks was the flush of consumption. While he was in town he planned to drop by Dr.

Griggs's office and speak to him man to man. If Vera was as sick as he was beginning to fear, he wanted to know. He had done all he knew how to do to make her more comfortable, but maybe something else could be done. Perhaps the doctor would suggest a drier climate, and if so, they would move. He dreaded the thought of hearing he might lose her, but he had to know.

Pearl saw her father ride by, and she ducked back into the alley, pulling Phineas with her. "Do you think he saw us?"

"Was that your father?" the man asked as he straightened his houndstooth-check coat and adjusted his scarlet cravat.

"Yes. I'm afraid he would take a very dim view of my meeting you like this. He thinks I'm still a child."

Phineas carefully appraised her. "Exactly how old are you, if I may be so bold as to ask?"

"I'm eighteen. That's plenty old enough to make my own decisions as to who I will or won't see, don't you think? In pioneer times girls—women, that is—were married by the time they were as old as I am."

"I agree completely. You're as much a woman as any I've met."

Pearl smiled with her head down so she would seem shy. "You must know some very remarkable women. All those great actresses and all." She never tired of hearing the stories her new beau told of the famous people he had met.

"In my line of work, a person becomes accustomed to it. Jaded, even. Then he meets a lovely flower like yourself and sees Woman for the first time."

"Phineas." She laughed with a blush. "You'll turn my head with all these compliments."

"Nonsense. It's impossible to spoil a lady of your caliber." He was hoping to be able to capture more than a few kisses in an alleyway before the week was out.

"Soon you'll be gone and I'll miss you so." Pearl pouted as they strolled along the back street.

A new idea came to Phineas, and he wondered why it hadn't occurred to him sooner. "You needn't be left behind, my pet."

"What? I don't understand."

"You could go with me. Flee this backwater town and see the world."

Pearl's mouth popped open. "Phineas! What are you saying?"

"My darling sister, Millisant, is only a few hours away in New Orleans. We would reach her abode well before dark. I assure you Millisant would make an admirable chaperon. I mean no mischief."

"No, no, I wasn't suggesting that you were!" Pearl's eyes were as round as her mouth.

"By now it would be safe for me . . . I mean, prudent for me to return to my circuit on the Mississippi River. Ah, Pearl, you've never tasted life until you taste it on the Father of Waters."

"But I couldn't possibly ask you to pay my way! It wouldn't be proper at all."

"No, no, my dear. I wasn't suggesting such a crass thing. I had hoped you might do me a small favor in return. As you know, Millisant has been quite ill and may still be unable to sing. Since there is such a resemblance between you two, I thought it would be lovely if you went on for her. Not often, mind you. Only when my sweet sister doesn't feel up to it." He glanced sideways at Pearl and added, "Together we could bring back her rosy health. It was overwork that laid her low. She does so insist on pushing herself to please me."

Pearl's face fell as she said, "Mama and Papa would never let me go."

"And they would be right," Phineas said smoothly. "What am I thinking of? A child of your tender years!"

"I'm not a child, Phineas."

"Of course not, my dumpling."

"I'm old enough to make decisions for myself."

"I suppose so."

"Besides, on your next trip to Cavelier, I'll be older and then no one could object."

"Oh, but I'm afraid you don't understand. I'll pass this way but once."

"What?"

"I'm here this long only because the abominable bayou is too low to float the boat. When I leave, it will be forever."

"Forever!" she gasped.

He patted her hand reassuringly. "It's better this way,

love. You stay in the bosom of your family and meet a nice young man and settle down to raise a houseful of young-sters. That's the proper way to do things.''

Pearl frowned. She didn't like the sound of that at all.

''Tante Jessamine, I have to talk to you,'' Pierce said.

Jessamine looked up from the letter she was writing and replaced her pen in the inkstand. ''Come in and sit down.''

He walked around Donnie, who was sleeping in the sunlight that spilled through the window, and sat in the chair his aunt indicated.

''You look as nervous as a thief, Pierce. What have you been up to?''

''I'm in love,'' he said simply.

Jessamine laughed. ''I guess that's enough to make you edgy. Who's the lady?''

He drew a deep breath. ''Cadence MacKinley.''

Her smile disappeared. ''Are you joking? Tell me you are.''

''No, I'm not. We love each other and want to get married.''

She pressed her fingertips to her temple as if to slow and control her thoughts. ''You and the MacKinley girl want to get married? How can that be? You've only seen her once.''

''No, Tante Jessamine. We've seen each other often. I meet her at the old swimming hole. Do you remember the place?''

Her lips felt dry and her face stiff. As if she could ever forget that place! ''I remember. Pierce, you two aren't . . . ? You don't . . . ?''

''Certainly not!'' he said, taking offense at the sug-gestion. ''Cadence isn't that sort of girl!''

Jessamine's cheeks turned pink as she thought how horrified her nephew would be if he knew that his aunt had been ''that kind.''

''There! I've embarrassed you. I'm sorry, Tante Jes-samine. I forgot you're a maiden lady.''

''Don't worry about it. I've known about the birds and the bees for some time now.'' She came around the desk and leaned back against it, facing him. ''What does your father say about these marriage plans?''

''We haven't told our parents yet.''

"I thought not."

"I decided you should know first."

"So I can pave the way? What if I agree with your father?"

"I know it's hard for you to understand, never having been in this position yourself, but Cadence and I are very much in love. With or without our families' approval, we intend to get married."

A sad smile lifted her lips. "You think I've never been in love, Pierce? Let me tell you something. I was in love. I was about the age Cadence is, maybe a little younger. I fell in love with the most handsome young man I had ever seen." Her face became soft as she spoke, and the years seemed to drop away.

"He loved me too. As much as you love Cadence. We, too, planned to get married."

"Why didn't you?" Pierce asked.

"We tried, but our parents were against it. He came here to the house one day and asked me to go away with him. He said we had to leave then, that very minute. Papa came in and threw him out and locked me in my room." Again she smiled sadly as she recalled the events that had ruined her life. "Papa even cut down the chinaberry tree outside my window so I couldn't climb out and elope. As for my young man, his parents sent him far, far away."

"And you never saw him again?"

She pondered her answer for a moment before she said, "No. I never saw him again." Ransome was no longer the man she had loved. He was solidly married and had clearly forgotten all about their dreams and passion.

"I never knew that. Why didn't you tell me before now? Does Papa know? Who was he?"

"Oh, yes. Your father knows. As for what his name was, I suppose it no longer matters. I'm only telling you now so you'll see that I do understand. In spite of my own experience—no, because of it—I don't want you to marry Cadence MacKinley."

"Tante Jessamine, that makes no sense at all! I'd think you, of all people, would understand and be on our side."

"I think you should tell your father how you feel. Sit down and talk to him, away from your mother, so you can discuss it without hysterics."

Pierce shook his head. "Papa could never understand."

"No? He's been in love." She walked absently to the window and pondered how odd it was that all three of them—Pierce, Jerome, and she herself—had known forbidden love. "In fact, he wasn't as unfortunate as I was."

"You mean with Mother?" Pierce asked in disbelief. "You have to be kidding! Those two hate each other and have all my life!"

Jessamine stepped back from the window. She was talking too much about things that she must never reveal.

Pierce continued, "Papa is so happily married that he stays gone as much as possible. Not that I blame him for that, but I've heard more talk that he even keeps some doxy!"

"No!" Jessamine whirled to glare at him. "That's not true and I won't have you say it."

He looked at her in surprise. "Then he really doesn't have a woman stashed somewhere?"

"I know your father better than you do, obviously. He's never been near a . . . a doxy, as you put it. Never in his life!"

"Maybe it's not something a man can reveal to his unmarried sister."

"You sound as if you have no respect for him at all!"

Pierce looked away. "It's hard to, Tante Jessamine. I know Mother is hard to live with, but dammit, he married her!"

"And he has treated her better than she ever deserved. Susanna has always been a whining brat, whether she's your mother and whether you like it or not. She should thank her lucky stars to have a man like Jerome. He provides for her every wish, he allows your grandmother to live with them even though she causes constant trouble between them, and no matter how much he's gone, he always comes back."

"I think that's one reason I've lost respect for him. Mother makes his life a hell, and he always comes back."

She sighed. "You're still young, Pierce. Sometimes strength looks like weakness when you're shy of thirty."

He went to her and took both her hands. "The point is, I want more out of my life. I want to marry the woman I love and have happiness. Don't you want that for me?"

Jessamine gazed up at the troubled eyes of the young man who had always been like a son to her. How could she stand in his way just so she wouldn't have to face Ransome and Vera at family gatherings? "You're right," she said with reluctance. "I hate to admit it, but you're right. If I could pick and choose, I'd take any girl in the world for you rather than Cadence MacKinley, but it's not my choice. If you two love each other enough to fight your parents, then I guess you deserve to be together."

Pierce laughed with relief and enveloped his aunt in a bear hug.

"Easy, Pierce. You'll break my bones," she chuckled. "Save your strength for the fight ahead. You'll need it."

"You're the core of the family, Tante Jessamine. If you're on my side, Papa will listen."

"I'm what? How odd. I never thought of myself in that way."

"When can you talk to Papa?"

"Oh, no! You have to tell him yourself. Besides, I want to get to know Cadence before I promise you my support against Jerome." She thought of the young woman whose hair was the same shade of auburn as Ransome's. Had fate been kinder, Cadence would have been her own daughter. "I suppose I must get to know her eventually."

"Of course you must! You're going to love her, Tante Jessamine. You won't be able to help it."

"I'll settle for 'abide' her," Jessamine said dryly. "We'll work our way up from there."

Pierce kissed her cheek. "I'll talk to Papa tonight."

"Let's not be too hasty. Ask Cadence to come over here for Sunday dinner tomorrow. Let me talk to her and get to know her before you stir up a hornet's nest at home." A part of Jessamine hoped the girl would prove to be obnoxious, so she could be justified in disliking her.

"I don't think I should do that. I've already put off telling them about her for weeks. To keep being so evasive makes me feel . . . well, unworthy. You know I prefer to meet problems head-on."

"Yes, I know. You've always been remarkably like me. Temper and all."

He grinned. "I could do a lot worse. No, I'm going to take Papa aside as you suggested and tell him how I feel."

Jessamine saw the determination on his face, so she nodded. "Perhaps that is best, but she's still invited for dinner tomorrow. So is your father, if he still feels up to eating."

"You make it sound like the end of the world because I want to marry Cadence."

"No, it's because you want to marry a MacKinley."

He turned to leave, but she stopped him. "Pierce, tell your father that I told you about my young man. Tell him I said to remind him that forbidden love can sometimes be the strongest. It may help." She turned away, hoping Jerome would understand her oblique message, and that she had not said too much.

Pierce saw no reason to wait to confront his father, so he rode straight to the docks. Jerome was in the warehouse that backed up to the water, overseeing the loading of the steamboat. "Hello, Papa."

"Hello, son. I was hoping you'd come down here. Ride over to the other warehouse and tell Tanner I said to send over those crates in the back corner. I have enough room for them in the bow." He studied a sketch of the boat's hull, where he had penciled in his loading plans. He looked back at the boat through the open end of the warehouse. "This damned bayou has never stayed so low for so long at this time of year. I'll bet it's no more than a mud puddle by August."

Pierce smiled at Jerome's familiar grumbling. "Rain clouds are building to the northwest. We'll have rain by tonight."

"It had better be a frog-strangler. Harry," he called to a workman, "don't load those yet. They're too heavy. She never will float free if we weigh her down too much." He glanced back at his son. "There's a town meeting next week and this time I'm going to insist on funds to deepen the bayou. Silt is making it shallower every year." He thought of the overcast skies as he made a notation on the paper. As much as they needed rain, he dreaded the kind of storm that was building because it would prevent him from going to visit Doll after supper. With Susanna in the bad mood she had been in at breakfast, he had hoped to get away that night, especially since he had been too busy to visit Doll and Laurie the night before.

"Papa, could I talk to you?"

"Are you still here? What is it?"

"I plan to get married."

Jerome looked at him blankly for a moment. "Married? Since when?"

"We decided a couple of weeks ago."

"And you're just now telling me?" Jerome slapped his son on the shoulder as he shook his hand. "Harry! Pierce is getting married!" He looked up at his tall son. "Who's the girl?"

"Cadence MacKinley."

Jerome's smile wavered, and he leaned closer as if he couldn't have heard Pierce correctly. "Who?"

"You heard me, Papa. Cadence MacKinley."

A thunderous look knotted Jerome's black eyebrows. "Forget it, Harry!" he yelled. "He was just fooling around."

"No, Papa. I mean it. We love each other, and we want to get married."

"I'll never give my permission for you to marry a goddamned MacKinley!"

"I don't need your permission, Papa."

"Does your mother know about this!"

"No, I wanted to tell you first."

"Come in the office." Jerome stalked away, and when they were alone in the cluttered room, he slammed the door so hard the papers on the wall shuddered. "Now, what's all this about! Is she pregnant!"

"Of course not! Give me credit for some decency! Cadence isn't like that at all!"

Jerome looked away and tried to control his anger. "It's been used as a trap before! You wouldn't be the first to get caught up in a situation like that!"

"We love each other, and we want to get married."

"She isn't even Catholic! Do you plan to leave the church as well? This is going to kill your mother. And your Grandmother Leslie. Not to mention your Tante Jessamine and Grandmama!"

"Tante Jessamine will survive. I've already told her."

"So I'm not the first to know after all?"

"I couldn't tell everyone first," Pierce defended himself.

"I guess Ransome MacKinley and old Mrs. MacKinley are all for it," Jerome ground out.

"No, they don't know. I told Cadence we would tell our parents together, but then I thought it might be best if I prepared you."

A low rumble of thunder sounded from the lowering sky as Jerome glared at his son. "There's no way to prepare me for something I refuse to accept."

"As for her religion, we've talked to Father Theriot and she has begun Catholic instruction. She will join the church before the wedding."

Jerome stared at Pierce. "It's gone that far? It seems to me your mother and I must be the last to know."

"Does it matter?"

"Yes! I would have stopped you!"

"You can't, Papa. I love Cadence, and she's going to be my wife."

"And you expect me to believe Jessamine gave her approval to this harebrained scheme?"

"Not at first. She has told me to invite Cadence for Sunday dinner tomorrow, and she says you're invited if you want to come."

"Never! I won't see the girl or talk to her, much less break bread with her!"

"Not even after we're married?" Pierce demanded hotly. He knew their angry voices must be carrying to the workers in the warehouse, but he didn't care.

"If you marry her, I'll disown you!"

"Tante Jessamine asked me to tell you that she told me about a young man she almost married. That you should remember what happened then."

"Happened? Nothing happened! She never married him." Jerome glared as he ran his fingers over the back of his neck. In a more controlled voice he said, "Did she really tell you about him?"

Pierce nodded. "Everything but his name."

Jerome barked out a laugh. "That figures."

"She also said to tell you that sometimes forbidden love is the strongest."

Silence grew so heavy they could hear the slap of rain against the tin warehouse roof. At last Jerome said, "What else did Jessamine say?"

"That's all."

Jerome closed his eyes with relief and let out his pent-up breath. Slowly he went to his desk chair and sat down to face his son. Not once in all these years had Jessamine ever mentioned his relationship with Doll, but for a minute he was afraid she had chosen the worst possible time to do it.

"Come to dinner at Ten Acres tomorrow," Pierce urged. "Just meet her and get to know her."

"And if I do and I don't like her, will you end it?"

"No." Pierce met his father's eyes steadfastly.

"Then why the hell should I bother?" He pointed his finger at his son and said, "You're about to make the biggest mistake of your life!"

"Like you did, Papa?" Pierce knew he was going too far, but he was too angry to stop. "You married the girl your parents wanted you to marry, didn't you? Is that the kind of marriage that you want for me?"

"Get out," Jerome said, his voice hoarse with rage. "Get out!"

Pierce straightened and gave his father a level look before turning and walking out the door.

After several minutes Jerome leaned back in his chair and swiveled to look at the sheets of rain that were sluicing down the small window. He ached deep inside and he wanted more than anything to talk to Doll. She would know what to say, what to do. A crack of thunder told him the storm would get much worse before it got any better.

Jerome sat in his chair, and wished he could cry as copiously as the sky did.

40

By the time Cadence reached the bend in the river, Pierce was impatiently pacing. She ran to him, and after kissing her, he held her close.

"I was afraid you couldn't get away," he said.

"Mama was asking me about church. She wasn't feeling well this morning, and they didn't go, so she has no idea I went to St. Mary of Lourdes instead of the Presbyterian one."

"You haven't told them you're converting?"

"No. Mama feels about her church like Papa feels about the family. I'm going to put it off as long as possible."

"Are you having second thoughts?" He gazed into her brown eyes and stroked the backs of his fingers over the smooth skin of her cheek.

"Not a single one," she reassured him. "Naturally, when she learns we're going to be married, she will have to accept my change of religion. After all, the wife always takes her husband's religion."

Pierce held her hand as they walked the short distance to Ten Acres. Cadence tried not to be nervous, but she couldn't help it. So much depended on the approval of the Delacroix matriarch. "Do I look all right?" she asked anxiously.

"You look beautiful. Tante Jessamine can't help but love you."

Maribelle let them in the house, and Pierce knew by the maid's furtive glances that she was curious about Cadence, as well. Delia, who was in the parlor, looked up from her sewing with glad recognition when the couple entered. "Miss MacKinley! How good of you to come back." She called over her shoulder, "Jessamine, Spartan is here with his young lady."

"You remember Cadence?" Pierce asked in surprise.

353

His grandmama's memory was especially faulty when it came to recent events.

"Well, of course I do. What a question. Miss Mac-Kinley promised to come back for a visit. I'm glad you could come, my dear. We don't have many young people out to visit these days." She leaned toward Pierce as if she had a secret to share. "Louis Broussard has come courting Jessamine! Reuben and I are so pleased."

"That's good." Pierce couldn't always tell if his grandmother's bits of gossip were from current events or from things that had happened before he was born.

"Mama, you know he hasn't come courting," Jessamine said as she entered the room, having overheard the exchange. With rather stiff politeness she offered her hand to Cadence as her mother winked broadly at Pierce to silently contradict Jessamine's unspoken protests.

"Thank you for having me over, Miss Delacroix," Cadence said as she released Jessamine's hand.

"Pierce tells me we have a need to get to know one another—all things included."

Cadence glanced at Pierce, and he smiled to reassure her. "Tante Jessamine, don't frighten Cadence."

Jessamine looked at him in surprise. Frightening the girl had been the last thought in her mind. She had been thinking how Ransome's hair was the same shade as his daughter's and how the girl had his eyes and nose. Jessamine motioned for her guests to be seated. "Am I so terrifying, then?"

"You can be awesome," Pierce said with a disarming grim. "At least to someone who doesn't know you as well as I do."

Jessamine studied the young lady. She was nervous, but by the angle of her chin, she didn't look as if she needed any protection. "Tell me about yourself, Miss MacKinley."

"Please, call me Cadence."

"I understand you've organized a woman-suffrage group here. Is that so?"

"Yes, it is." Cadence lifted her chin higher. "I feel it's very necessary for us to get the vote and to be allowed to own our own property."

"So do I," Jessamine surprised her by saying. "If it had occurred to me at your age, I'm sure I would have started one too."

"You would? Perhaps you'd be interested in attending our meetings."

"No, I think not. For one thing, I rarely enjoy club meetings of any sort, and for another, I've already liberated myself. As I'm sure you know, I control two of the main industries in Cavelier. Pierce's father owns the other two. For that reason we have to be, shall we say, cautious about whomever Pierce wants to marry. Someday he will be a very wealthy man, and his wife must be able to stand beside him."

"I am quite capable of that," Cadence assured her.

Delia looked at them in confusion. "What's all this talk about marriage?"

"Pierce and Cadence want to be married, Mama. Remember? We discussed it this morning."

"Why, of course! I recall now. Goodness, I had no idea this was the young lady you meant. Reuben will be so pleased!" She reached over to pat Cadence's hand. "My husband will be in soon. He's out inspecting the crop."

Pierce and Jessamine exchanged a glance, but relaxed when Cadence said smoothly, "I'm looking forward to meeting him, Mrs. Delacroix."

Delia tossed her daughter a triumphant look that made her wonder if her mother's memory was as selective it appeared to be. "You must bring your parents by to meet us, child," Delia said.

"No, Mama. That's not a good idea," Jessamine interjected quickly. "Papa knows them and he will arrange everything."

"Good," Delia replied complacently.

"Miss Delacroix, you have to meet them eventually," Cadence said. "Perhaps if we all sat down together, we—"

"No!" Jessamine interrupted as she abruptly stood. "That's asking entirely too much."

Surprised by the vehemence of his aunt's reaction, though not her words, Pierce said, "I think Tante Jessamine is right. Let's take things slowly."

Maribelle came back into the room and announced that dinner was on the table. In a strained silence the Delacroixs and their guest went to the table.

Cadence was quiet throughout the meal. Most of the dishes were foreign to her and were surprisingly spiced.

Although she didn't care for the taste particularly, she asked for the recipes.

"You like to cook?" Jessamine asked.

"Not a great deal," she answered truthfully, "but I can do it. When we're married I want to make dishes that Pierce will enjoy."

Jessamine suppressed her smile. "And you? How do you like Creole food?"

"I've never tasted anything quite like it."

"Crawfish jambalaya is an acquired taste, I hear."

"Crawfish?" Cadence asked, her fork halfway to her mouth.

"From the swamp," Pierce said, not noticing she had put her fork carefully back on her plate.

"Are you full so quickly?" Delia asked. "You scarcely ate enough to feed a bird."

"I had a large breakfast."

Jessamine finished her helping of jambalaya. "I'll write out the recipe for you. This is one of Pierce's favorite dishes." Then, to Jessamine's amazement, Cadence took up her fork and finished the meal. Perhaps, she thought, there was more to the girl than she had expected.

When they retired to the parlor, Delia excused herself and went to lie down in her room as she did every day after the noon meal. Jessamine waited until her mother was out of the room before she said, "Jerome was out here to see me about you two. He's not pleased."

"I know," Pierce replied. "I'm going to tell Mother tonight."

"I didn't want there to be trouble," Cadence said earnestly. "We don't want to hurt anyone. We only want to get married."

"Only," Jessamine repeated. "How simple you make it sound. But here in the South we aren't just individuals. We're our families as well. And our land beyond that." She looked thoughtfully about the room. "That's what started it all, you know. The land. You can't see it, but within the walls of this home is the log dogtrot cabin it was built around. You can see the back of the original house in the kitchen, where Papa intentionally left it uncovered. He wanted us never to forget how it had been. But I can see it even in here. So can Jerome. And every time we see that old dogtrot cabin, we remember Roseland and how your grandfather threw us out of our home."

"But he bought it at auction," Cadence protested. "I've heard the story all my life. Before he came here, he and Grandmother were the poor branch of the family. They came here looking for a new start, and it took all their savings. Papa says Grandfather never had a talent for business, and even less sense for farming. Several times they almost went bankrupt. It was very risky for them."

Jessamine had never known about the MacKinleys' finances before their arrival in Cavelier, and was rather embarrassed to think that she had never even considered that they might have been struggling to succeed as well. "They paid a mere pittance for our plantation. Nothing!"

"It was the sale price. No one would insist on paying more than the going price!"

"He even begrudged us taking two cabins for Sam and to use as a barn!"

"Grandfather was no different from any other man who was having money problems. He was afraid to lose his possessions."

Jessamine thoughtfully considered the sincerity with which the young woman spoke, and found no indication of duplicity. It was difficult for Jessamine to hear of this side of the detestable Ian MacKinley. "He could have been more tactful and far less rude. You have to admit that."

Cadence smiled and said, "To tell you the truth, I never liked Grandfather. He scared me silly. Even Papa never loved him. Grandfather wasn't the sort of man a person could love. I think it's sad. Don't you?"

"I can honestly say I've never once thought of your grandfather as an object of pity. Not even after his stroke."

"That's the only way I ever knew him. He had the stroke before I was born."

"Yes. I know." Jessamine hadn't intended to mention the old man's stroke, for the recollection of that horrifying event was so painful. But now she had to know what had been said within the MacKinley family about that fevered summer. "Did your father ever mention what happened the day Mr. MacKinley had the stroke?"

"No," Cadence said with total innocence. "Why should he?"

"No reason at all. I merely wondered."

"Tante Jessamine, now that you've talked to Cadence, will you help me explain to Papa why I love her? He always listens to you."

"And if I don't, what will happen? Will you two call off your marriage plans and be sensible?"

"No," they said in unison. Cadence added, "I love Pierce and I have no intention of taking him from you. I had hoped you might welcome me into your family, because I might not be as well-received in my own."

Jessamine said, "I'm only one person, and not even Pierce's mother."

"But they all look up to you, Tante Jessamine," he objected.

"What if neither side agrees on this marriage? What then?" Jessamine persisted. "Have you given any thought to what you'll do in that case?"

Pierce gazed lovingly at Cadence as he sat on the arm of her chair so he could hold her hand. "Then we will make a family of our own. Orphans do it every day."

"But you're a Delacroix!"

"Cadence will be too, once we're married. Father Theriot has posted the first banns."

"We looked at a house yesterday," Cadence said. "Pierce is going to buy it. After the wedding we'll live there."

"Oh?" Jessamine saw the hope and determination in their eyes, and she hated having to play devil's advocate. If the girl were anyone else, she would be perfect for Pierce.

"It's the Monson house on Peach Street."

"I know the house," Jessamine answered. "Randolph Monson built it a few years ago for his bride. After she died, he moved away. I wondered if anyone would buy it."

"Isn't it lovely?" Cadence said enthusiastically. "All those bay windows and porches and turrets and gingerbread."

"Yes, it is lovely. Since you're set on doing this, I have some lace curtains you may want for the front parlor. I had them made for my own hope chest, but I never needed them and they aren't right for the windows here."

Cadence clasped Pierce's hand. "Our own lace curtains! Oh, Tante Jessamine, I'd love to have them!" Suddenly she realized the familiar way she had addressed the coolly aloof woman, and she blushed. "I'm sorry, Miss Delacroix."

"Nonsense. If you're going to marry Pierce, you should call me Tante." She didn't let the girl see how touched she had felt at the unconscious term of endearment.

Once again Jessamine reflected that had fate been less convoluted, this could have been her own daughter. She saw the love in Pierce and Cadence's eyes as they looked at each other, and she sighed. Without that quirk of fate these two would be much too close kin to marry. Perhaps fate wasn't so fickle after all.

"I'm going to sign the papers for the house tomorrow morning," Pierce said eagerly. "My own house! I've wanted a place of my own for years, but I didn't want to upset Mother by moving out."

"Pierce, you still have a lot to learn," his aunt observed. "Some things are worth upsetting Susanna over."

He smiled at Cadence. "We'll show this town how happy a marriage can be. You and I won't be like my parents—each with a separate life and no love between them."

"Are they really so unhappy?" she asked.

"Let's just say I'll be more than content to spend my evenings at home with you and not go traipsing off until all hours."

"Your father has his reasons," Jessamine firmly said in her brother's defense. "And he always comes back."

"I don't understand. Do you mean Mr. Delacroix goes on business trips?"

Pierce couldn't resist answering. "You might say it's business of a sort, but not the kind you'd conduct by daylight."

"Pierce," Jessamine said sharply, "that's quite enough! Since you don't know what you're talking about, I suggest you be quiet."

"I'm sorry, Tante Jessamine, Cadence. Sometimes my feelings for him get the better of me."

Cadence stood and said, "I really must be going. My parents think I've gone for a walk and they'll worry if I'm out too long."

Jessamine stood and extended her hand again. "I'm glad you came, Cadence. I see now what Pierce sees in you. I wish I could say my understanding it would make it easier for you, but I know it won't. God go with you both."

"May I come back again?"

Jessamine hesitated only an instant. "Yes. You may come back as often as you please. There must be few places for the two of you to meet in town."

"We never meet there for fear of our families hearing

about it," Cadaence spoke up. "We meet at the bend in the river."

"The swimming hole?" Jessamine said in a low voice. "Near the hedge of gardenias?"

"Yes, that's the place. I didn't think anyone knew of the spot except us."

"That's not a safe place for you to meet. From now on you come here. You may carry out your courting in the front parlor or on the porch. That's much more proper." She knew all too well how hot passions could flare in that gardenia-scented paradise. "You come here," she repeated.

"Very well, Tante Jessamine," Pierce agreed. "If you won't get tired of us under your feet."

"It won't be for long," Cadence added. "Then we'll be married." She smiled radiantly up at Pierce.

"Yes. Well, run along with you before your parents get worried." When she looked at the lovers, she saw Ransome and herself, though with the physical resemblances reversed. Perhaps, Jessamine thought, this combination would be more propitious than her own ill-fated love.

She watched them walk away, and she wondered how it could be that she felt no older than they must inside, yet she was cast in the role of responsible spinster. Looking back on that secret, furtive summer of her love, she marveled that anyone would come to her for advice. But she still didn't regret being Ransome's lover—only that it had ended.

Cadence bid Pierce a lingering good-bye in the still woods and reluctantly released him. The sky overhead had turned a dull pewter and the smell of rain hung expectantly in the air.

"You'd better go before you get wet," he said.

"I know. I just hate to leave you."

"It won't be for long. A few weeks from now, we'll be married."

"I'm going to tell my parents today."

"No, I want to be with you when you do that. I may need to protect you."

"From Papa?" She laughed. "He's never struck me in my life."

"Nevertheless, I want to be there. It's my place to ask for your hand. Maybe he'll give it to me, and we will have worried over nothing."

Cadence knew there was no chance of that, but she

nodded and then kissed him as thunder rolled over the swamp. When the first fat raindrops spattered onto the leaves overhead, she turned and ran for home.

Pierce followed her to the last sloping hill, though she never knew he did this. The woods were relatively safe, but he knew panthers from the swamp and an occasional band of javelinas roamed there. Either would be dangerous if Cadence came upon them alone. He stopped at the base of an enormous sycamore and watched her walk up the incline toward the house.

When he turned to go, he found himself staring down at a solemn-faced boy. For a minute Pierce was nonplussed because he was trespassing as well as following Cadence through the woods.

"Are you a friend of Cadence's?" the boy asked in a curiously flat tone.

"Yes." Pierce squatted down so their eyes would be on the same level. "Are you her brother?"

The boy nodded. "I'm Ethan."

"Cadence has told me about you." By the way Ethan talked and the way he watched Pierce's lips, Pierce recalled that Cadence had said the boy was deaf. "Do you like living here?"

"I like Roseland, but not the school. Some of the boys tease me."

"Have you told your papa?"

"No," Ethan replied with a quick shake of his head. "I don't want to worry him."

Pierce felt sorry for the boy. He thought Ethan was reluctant to go to Ransome because he was afraid of his father. He didn't realize that Ethan knew his father had far more to do right now than there were hours in the day. "Well, I'll tell you what. I know the big brothers and the fathers of every boy in that school, and they all know me. So you tell them that Pierce Delacroix will have a talk with them if they keep picking on you. Can you remember my name?"

"Pierce Delacroix," Ethan said. The pronunciation wasn't correct, but Pierce knew it would be close enough.

"Now, you'd better get in out of the rain before you catch cold. Cadence tells me you get sick easily."

"I'm going." Ethan felt a wave of hero worship for the tall, dark man. "I'm going and I'll tell them what you said." He grinned and added, "Thanks."

Pierce felt a sudden sadness as he watched Ethan making his way up the hill. The boy was thinner and more sickly than Cadence had led him to believe. Malaria was an ever-present threat in southern Louisiana, and Pierce knew the boy would likely not survive even a single bout of it.

When Ethan raced into the house, he almost collided with Cadence, who put her finger to her lips and pointed. Pearl and their parents were in the library, and Ransome was angrily pacing. Cadence mouthed the words, "Let's go upstairs and put on some dry clothes before they see us." They crept away before their parents could see they had been out in the rain.

"Pearl, how could you do this?" Vera said, her gentle voice full of hurt. "A man like that!"

"There's nothing wrong with Phineas. He's a pure gentleman."

"Even you aren't so naive as to believe that!" Ransome bellowed. To Vera he said, "I caught them necking in an alley. An alley!"

"I'll never forgive you for hitting my young man like that!"

"Young? He's almost as old as I am! Where did you meet scum like that?"

"Don't you dare talk about him like that! He's a famous actor."

"Ha! He's a tinhorn shyster, if you ask me. Vera, if you had seen him, you'd never have another calm night's rest. He looks like the villain in *For Her Children's Sake.*"

"Goodness! Surely not!"

"Pearl, how long have you known this blackguard?" Ransome demanded.

Pearl hesitated. If he knew she had slipped out to see Phineas every day that week, he would be even more furious. "I just met him, Papa."

"And you let a stranger take you into an alley and kiss you?"

"I've known him a short while, I mean."

"You couldn't have known him long or you would have told me!"

"You don't suppose she was seen with this man," Vera gasped. "What will people think? Pearl, how could you be so . . . so loose?"

Coming from her mother, these were harsh words indeed, and Pearl dissolved into tears. As always in the presence of a sobbing woman, Ransome felt his anger being replaced by uneasy guilt.

"Don't cry, Pearl," he said as he gathered his younger daughter into his arms. His eyes met Vera's in shared misery over the top of the girl's golden head. "A single kiss never ruined anyone. You did wrong, but now you know never to do it again."

"I'm so sorry, Papa," Pearl cried. "Mama, I wish I had never seen him!"

"I know, dear. It's going to be all right. Surely no one else saw you, and no harm has been done."

Pearl let them pet her and cajole her as she sobbed with racking gulps. All the while, she was congratulating herself on her acting ability. Phineas was right! If you believed in your role, others would too. She was a born actress, just as he had said. She wondered when her straitlaced parents had ever attended a play called *For Her Children's Sake*, however. They had never even hinted at having gone to a melodrama. In her amazement, her sobs tapered off.

Ransome put his finger under Pearl's chin and lifted her head. "Promise me you'll never do anything like this again?"

"Yes, Papa," she said, feigning innocence. As he and her mother hugged her, Pearl wondered when she could slip away to meet Phineas again. Her father had hit him pretty hard, and Phineas had still seemed dazed when Ransome dragged her away. One thing was certain, Pearl decided: they would have to be far more circumspect in the future.

Pierce went to his room in the *garçonnière* and changed into dry clothes as soon as he put his horse away. The building was made of aged red brick and had once been the house of a less-prosperous neighbor. When Pierce had become a young man, his father bought it for him and had several of his dockhands jack up the building, drive a wagon under it, and haul it into the large backyard. After the bricks were remortared, it looked as if it had always sat there in the shade of the black locust tree. Inside, there were two rooms, one of which Pierce used as a parlor whenever he had friends over. For a long time now he had felt cramped in the small house.

He went to his desk and took out the papers to the Monson house. He could still scarcely believe it. Soon he and Cadence would live there as husband and wife. His eyes softened as he thought of having her close by to share all his dreams and plans and hopes.

Carefully he replaced the papers in the desk and rolled the top down. Fortunately the Monson house was vacant, for he suspected he might have to move into it before the wedding. He looked out the window and through the rain to where the main house's lamps were lit as evening approached. He had to tell his mother. There was no way around it.

Pulling on his oiled slicker, Pierce ran up the walk and entered the house through the side door. Dulcie looked up as he came in, and took his dripping coat out to hang on the screened porch. Pierce straightened his collar and cuffs as he went into the parlor.

As usual, his mother was seated on the old settee. This time she was methodically cutting long strips of white paper, curling them into scrolls and flowers, and gluing them onto a sheet of dark red paper. When her son entered, she looked up and absently greeted him.

Pierce sat on the chair at an angle to the settee and watched her unhurried movements as he pondered where to start. The room smelled strongly of mucilage and faintly of mildew and oil paint—smells he always associated with the parlor and his mother. "Has Grandmother already gone upstairs for the night?"

"Yes, she went shopping today and was tired out, poor dear. She's getting too old to walk about town, but no one can tell her so, and certainly she has no one else to do the little errands for her in this house."

Pierce looked over at the empty hall tree. "Papa isn't home?"

Peevish temper lit his mother's eyes as she said, "When is he ever at home? I tell you, he's no good. He has a fancy woman stashed away somewhere. I know it! I'll bet if you rode past Sophie James's establishment you'd see his horse!"

"Mother!" Pierce really was shocked to hear the town whore's name on his mother's lips. Sophie and her girls were known throughout Iberville parish, but they were never discussed in the front parlor.

"I may be a shut-in, but I have my ways of knowing," Susanna said with a sharp nod. "Just because my health is failing doesn't mean my mind is."

"Dr. Griggs says you're in perfect health, or would be if you got about more."

"That charlatan? I don't think he's a real doctor at all." She reached out to pat Pierce's cheek. "Fortunately I have you. You were worth breaking my health for."

Pierce frowned, but endured her brief pat. "Mother, there's something I want to tell you."

"Oh?" She went back to cutting the long strips of paper. "How do you like my newest project?"

"Very pretty. Mother, I've fallen in love and am going to be married."

"What?" Susanna looked at him blankly. "What's that?"

"I'm in love, Mother. She's perfect for me. We like all the same things and have so many interests in common. We're going to be married."

"Love! Marriage!" Susanna roughly shoved the table aside, sending the strips of paper spilling onto the floor. "Marriage!"

"Calm yourself, Mother. You'll wake Grandmother."

"I want to wake her! I want her to know what you're contemplating! Who is this girl?"

"Cadence MacKinley."

"What!" Susanna lurched up from the settee, her double chins trembling in anger. "My son marry Yankee trash?"

"They are hardly that, Mother. The MacKinleys are very respected here in Cavelier."

"Not by our sort, they aren't! Why are you marrying her? She's in the family way, isn't she? That's it!"

"No!" he bellowed to override her shrieks. "I've never laid a hand on her!" He glared at his mother. "Papa asked the same thing when I told him. Why would that even occur to you?"

Susanna snapped her lips shut.

"I'm marrying her for the reason I gave you. We're in love. I wanted to tell you sooner, but I knew there would be a scene."

"Yet you managed to tell your father." She sneered. "Are you saying he took the news calmly?"

"You know he wouldn't."

"Well, you aren't bringing her here. I won't have a Yankee living under my roof and eating at my table."

"I expected you to say that. I'm buying the Monson house over on Peach Street."

"The Monson place!" Susanna had been trying to nag Jerome into buying *her* that house. Her anger doubled. "I guess you'll enjoy lording it over us! I guess you'll have a fine time in that big monstrosity of a house! It's just like a Yankee to demand you buy her the biggest house in town!"

Pierce turned and walked out of the room. At least that was behind him. All in all, his mother hadn't thrown as bad a scene as he had expected. She wasn't in hysterics, and nothing was broken.

"I have one consolation," she shrilled after him. "This will put your father in his grave!"

Pierce took his coat from Dulcie and walked back out into the night.

41

"PAPA. WHY WON'T YOU AT LEAST GET TO KNOW Pierce?" Cadence pleaded in exasperation. "I've never known you to be so muleheaded."

Ransome frowned at her. "Nor have I ever known you to be such a nag. I would never have badgered my parents like this. I asked my father something one time, and if the answer was no, I never brought it up again."

"I can't be like that. I don't think you really want me to be."

"No?" He tried to go back to reading the paper, but she pulled it out of his hands and sat in his lap.

"You're going to listen to me. It's not like he's a scoundrel or a ne'er-do-well. Pierce is the most-sought-after bachelor in town."

"Is that what you see in him?"

"You know me better than that."

Ransome sighed. It was true that Cadence had never cared a whit for other people's opinions. This was the first time in her life she hadn't championed an underdog.

As if she had read his mind, she said, "Admit it. You've always expected me to want a poor crippled orphan no one else would want—now, haven't you?"

"Only if you could find one that was also blind and had a dozen sisters to support," he joked. He slid her to her feet and stood up. No longer smiling, he said, "Dammit, Cadence, he's a Delacroix! I would almost rather have the orphan!"

"At least you can tease me about it. Does that mean you're changing your mind?"

He went to the mantel and leaned his forearm on it, as was his habit, and frowned down at the huge pot of Boston fern on the hearth. "No, I won't change my mind. Not on this."

"But, Papa!"

"Think what you're asking! It's not only my feelings or your mother's, it's your grandmother's. It would kill her to see you marry a Delacroix."

"Then explain to me what's so very bad about them!" Cadence demanded. "I've gotten to know his aunt and his grandmother, and they seem to be very nice people."

"You've what? Since when?"

She faltered. "I . . . I had Sunday dinner with them yesterday. Perhaps Grandfather and Mr. Delacroix had some reason to hate each other, but they're both dead now. Can't we end this feud?"

"You went to Ten Acres?" Ransome asked in disbelief. "You ate there?"

"I was invited."

Ransome felt betrayed by the one child he had loved above all the rest. "You went to Ten Acres," he repeated dully.

"The grandmother is very sweet, but her mind isn't strong. She thinks the year is 1860 and that her family is all still alive. She even calls Pierce by her elder son's name. Isn't that sad?"

When Ransome didn't speak, she continued. "I was afraid of Miss Delacroix at first, but I think she's all bark and no bite. By the time dinner was over she even smiled at me."

Jessamine's smile. How well Ransome remembered it, especially framed by her cloud of black hair spilling over the lush grass in their private gardenia bower. He rubbed his eyes in an effort to erase the memory. Jessamine laughing in the sunlight, or dewy from a summer rain, and bubbling over with plans for a future that had never been.

"You're not to go back there," he said sharply. "Not ever!" Before she could reply, he strode from the room.

Pearl knocked softly on the back window of the boardinghouse as she cautiously looked about to be sure no one was watching her. Silently the window slid up, and she scrambled over the sill.

"Did anyone see you?" Phineas asked as he looked back at the window.

"Of course not. I can put one over on this one-horse town anytime I want to," Pearl said with smug satisfaction. "Did you have trouble explaining to Mrs. Gallier why you wanted to switch to a downstairs room?"

"No, this one is much nicer than my old one." Since he doubted he would be here long enough to have to pay the more expensive rent, he wasn't worried.

"We've had a lot of rain lately," Pearl said. "The bayou is rising. Soon the steamboat will be able to leave."

"And we'll leave this raggedy town behind and head for the city," he said enthusiastically. "You haven't changed your mind, have you?"

"Oh, Phineas, how can I ever go with you? Papa would catch up with us at New Orleans, and you've seen what a temper he has."

"Yes." Phineas rubbed his jaw reminiscently. "However, I have no intention of running crosswise of him again. He expects us to exit stage left, so we will exit stage right."

"What does that mean?" She loved it when he spoke to her in technical theater jargon.

"It means he expects us to leave by boat, so we will leave by train."

"Not by boat?" Disappointment weighed her voice. "I've been on trains before."

"Don't fret, my poppet. We'll take the train up to Natchez and board a real boat on the Mississippi. Not a tub like the one I arrived on."

"But your sister is in New Orleans," Pearl said in confusion. "I thought—"

"Didn't I tell you?" he said quickly. "Darling Millisant wrote me to say she's completely recovered. At least enough to travel. Of course, she is still too frail to perform every night and will need you to go on in her place as we planned." His mustache bristled in brotherly affection as he said, "She is so eager to meet you. She says she has always wanted a younger sister to share her confidences."

"I'm so glad, Phineas. I was afraid at first I would no longer be needed."

He drew her dramatically into his embrace and said, "I will always need you, my heart."

The aroma of cigar smoke that always clung to him epitomized his masculinity. "Oh, Phineas. We'll be so happy, the three of us."

"Yes, indeed." He roughly kissed her, trying to sate his hunger for her. Pearl was so young and vulnerable, he could hardly restrain himself. He silently cursed his stupidity for not remembering about the train days ago. They could have been well on their way, and he wouldn't have a sore jaw.

"Will we be able to reach Natchez and find your sister before nightfall? Otherwise she may think ill of me—you being an unmarried man and all."

"To be sure. Millisant will be waiting for us at the depot, or in the hotel. Don't you worry your pretty little head about that."

Pearl arched back in his embrace to look up at him. "Do you really think I sing well enough to appear on the stage? I have no experience, you know, unless you count the church choir."

"We count that. You'll be the toast of the river. Perhaps we'll even cross the ocean and appear before the crowned heads of Europe!"

"Kings and queens? Imagine!" she sighed as he drew her closer. His full lips covered hers, and she hoped her inexperienced response didn't disgust him. In time she knew she would learn to please him. "Oh, Phineas, I'm going to enjoy being your wife."

"My what?" he gasped.

"Your wife, silly. We're eloping, aren't we?" Doubt clouded her blue eyes, and she said, "I naturally assumed—"

"Yes! Wife! Of course we're going to be married, my sweet. I merely misunderstood you at first. We'll be married on the Father of Rivers, going full steam up the Mississippi."

"But you said we would stay in a hotel when we arrive in Natchez. I couldn't possibly—"

"What a sweet child! No one expects you to do anything inappropriate. You and Millisant will share a room. I will stay on another floor entirely."

Pearl snuggled closer to him and enjoyed the forbidden thrill of his big hand kneading her breast. She knew she shouldn't allow him to do more than kiss her, but surely he could be allowed greater freedom now that they were engaged. Slipping out of the house with a suitcase might be difficult, but she knew she would manage it somehow.

Phineas thought his loins would burst from his desire to throw her on the bed and ravish her tender body, but he contented himself for the moment with feeling her small, rounded breast. In time he would have her far out of reach of her possessive father, and then he could do with her as he pleased. The marriage ceremony might prove to be a difficulty, but not an impossibility. He knew a number of actors in Natchez, one of whom he could surely bribe to play the role of a preacher. The thought that soon he would have this girl in his bed for months to come was the only thing that kept him in check. He assured himself that he wouldn't tire of this one as quickly as he had all the others.

Ransome looked up from the court case he was reviewing when a timid knock sounded on his office door. It was Daisy Buckner. "Come in," he said as he rose. "Have a seat."

"I hope I'm not disturbing you, Mr. MacKinley, but your secretary was out, and I saw you through the doorway."

"Not at all. What can I do for you?" He leaned back in his leather swivel chair and tried to put the young woman at ease. Like many of the people Cadence befriended, Daisy was painfully shy, and as homely a girl as he had seen in Cavelier.

"I came here on my own. Cadence didn't ask me to speak with you."

"Oh?" His dark eyes became wary, and this seemed to make Daisy even more nervous.

"I want to talk to you about her happiness." Daisy pulled at her gloves and clasped and unclasped her trembling fingers. She had always been frightened of this stern-looking man, and was having difficulty staying in the office, let alone speaking her mind.

"Go on, Miss Buckner."

Daisy leaned forward in an imploring gesture, gripping the edge of his desk. "She loves Pierce Delacroix, Mr. MacKinley. I mean, she *really* loves him. Cadence doesn't want to go against your wishes, but she also doesn't want to give up Pierce. I'm not his confidante, of course, but if my observation means anything, I believe he truly loves her too. Oh, Mr. MacKinley, don't stand in their way! Don't destroy their lives!"

Ransome studied her for a moment before he said, "Have you considered a career in law, Miss Buckner? You give a very impassioned speech."

"Impassioned?" Daisy blushed from her tight collar to the roots of her hair. "Me?"

He leaned forward to rest his forearms on his desk.

"I love Cadence, and I, too, want her happiness. However, I'm not at all convinced that her happiness lies solely in this particular young man." Although his voice was calm and he retained his smile, his eyes held the steely glint he usually reserved for the courtroom.

Daisy stood abruptly. "I've said too much. I was afraid I would. Please, don't hold this against Cadence. As I said, she doesn't know I came here." Before he could reply, she turned and ran from the room.

Ransome had automatically stood when she did, and as he sat back down, he rubbed his fingers over his chin, pondering what the young lady had said. Daisy's argument for Pierce's qualities carried no weight with him. He already knew that Pierce's only drawback was the insurmountability of his family name. What concerned Ransome was Daisy's assumption that he would take out his anger on Cadence.

Was he such a tyrant? Ransome frowned as he touched the scar on his cheek. He had promised himself the night Cadence was born that he would never raise his hand to her in anger, and he never had. True, he was stern with her, but how else was he to teach her what she needed to know? He might always have been strict, but when she was a child he had made time almost every evening to read her a story before Vera put her to bed. In later years he had walked with her for miles along Albany's snow- or mud-clogged streets so she could confide some secret or relate to him some dream. He had done this for all his children, though Cadence sought him out far more often than the others did. He had even let her join the suffrage movement, although his father-in-law had said it would be the ruin of her.

So when had he become such a fearsome tyrant? he wondered. He hated any resemblance between himself and his father. The abhorrence was an obsession with him. He even kept the old man's room untouched and under lock and key so he didn't have to see it and be reminded of the cruelties he had endured as a boy. Even Vera didn't know of the beatings and the misery his father had put him through.

Now it seemed Cadence might see him in the same light. Ransome struck the desk with the palm of his hand as he rose and paced to the window.

Outside he was surprised to see Pearl walking briskly along the street. He wondered absently why she was coming from the direction of Mrs. Gallier's boardinghouse, but he had too much on his mind to go out and ask. At least she had stopped seeing that white trash he had found her kissing. If he had reason to worry about any of his children, he knew he should worry most about Pearl.

Although his mother thought the girl was as angelic as she appeared, Ransome knew her looks were deceiving. Pearl wasn't openly rebellious like Cadence or mischievous like Ethan, but she always seemed to be hiding something. He had known her to lie just to see if her parents would believe her. Ransome knew as well as Vera did that Pearl hid romantic novels under her pillow and that she often swiped an extra dessert from the kitchen when she had expressly been told to leave it alone. These were small transgressions, however, and only minor annoyances. The incident in the alley had been something else.

Pearl had been overly fond of boys ever since she learned the difference, so to speak. He had fired two stableboys for flirting with her before she was fourteen, and she hadn't been sorry at all for leading them on and causing them to lose their jobs. Ransome hadn't seen much in the alley before he yanked Pearl away from that despicable man, but he had seen enough to know Pearl was kissing him back. The man hadn't been forcing her.

Ransome sighed as he watched his younger daughter go into the Emporium. How had shy, gentle Vera ever given birth to such daughters as these? Ransome shook his head wearily as he went back to work.

Cadence and Pierce walked hand in hand through the large house, their footsteps on the oak floors echoing faintly off the high ceilings, their voices hushed to soften the reverberation of their words in the empty rooms.

"Pierce, I love it! Our own home! I can just see you in a wing-backed chair in front of the fire this winter."

"And you'll be sitting here knitting or reading a book."

She laughed. "Or working on a speech for the next suffrage meeting."

"We'll work on it together. I can help your cause by speaking to the men around town, people who vote but might not understand your issues."

"Oh, Pierce, we'll be so happy." She put her arms around him and gazed at the cold fireplace as if she could see the imagined flames crackling and dancing.

"That's not the only reason we'll be happy," he said as he bent his head to kiss her. "I love you, Cadence."

"I love you too."

He kissed her long and slow, the way they both liked it. When her lips parted, he ran his tongue over the soft inner flesh and along the sharp edges of her teeth. "You taste so good," he murmured as he rubbed his cheek on her forehead. "I want you so much."

She smiled, her face radiant. "I want you too. I want you the way a woman isn't supposed to feel at all."

"Women feel that way. Ladies lie about it." He chuckled. "Would you like to see the upstairs?"

They went up the gently curving front stairs to the second floor. As he pointed up the straight stairway that led to the third floor, he said, "There is a big nursery and playroom up there, with a small room for a nanny," he said. "The bedrooms are down here." He pushed open the first door. "This is the largest one."

Sunlight streamed into the room from windows which overlooked the side yard and a huge magnolia; the sitting alcove opened onto the upstairs porch. As she stepped out and viewed the street in front of the house, she exclaimed, "How lovely! We can sit here in the cool of the evening and watch people pass by."

"But not *too* late in the evening," he teased.

"We'll be the scandal of the neighborhood. Little old ladies will gather out front and protest how early our lights go out."

"Always forming a rally, aren't you?"

"Do you mind?"

"No, I believe in equality for all. You know that."

"Yes. That's a rare quality in a man, and I love you for it." She hugged him exuberantly. "I can still hardly believe this lovely house will be ours!"

"It already is. I've signed the final papers. I'll start moving in on Saturday."

She whirled about and pointed at the back wall. "Our bed should go there. It's far enough from the front windows for privacy and close enough to the side ones for a breeze. We'll wake up every morning to birds singing in the magnolia tree."

"Did you notice the windows all have screens? No flies or mosquitoes."

"That's wonderful. I don't know if I'll ever get used to those pesky mosquitoes."

"And we'll have a dog," he said

"And a cat. Maybe two of each."

"And children."

She smiled at him affectionately. "Definitely *more* than two of each. We'll fill the house with laughter and noise and excitement."

"I love you so much, Cadence. But maybe after you've had one baby, you won't want another one. That's why I have no brothers or sisters."

"Not me. I want lots of children. I'm not worried about it."

He put his arm around her as they went down the hall and pushed open the other doors to peer into the empty rooms. "I'd like to use this back room as an office. I won't be gone all the time like my father is." His blue-gray eyes clouded. "Not for any reason."

"Nor will I. We can plan our vacations around the National-American conventions and our girls will grow up with rights equal to their brothers'."

"I'm sure of it."

They went down the narrow back stairs that ended in the large kitchen. Cadence opened the lid on the well and looked down at her reflection in the water. Pierce's visage appeared beside hers in the wavery depths. "What if Papa still refuses to let us marry?" she asked, her voice hollow against the stone walls.

"Will you marry me anyway?"

"Yes. Oh, yes, Pierce!" She turned into his arms and held him. "I just wish he would get to know you. He would have to like you—in most ways you two are very much alike."

Pierce recalled the stern-faced father he had seen that day at Roseland. "I don't see the resemblance."

"That's because you don't know him as well as I do. He pretends to be very strict and firm, but underneath it all, he's as loving and kind as anyone you'll ever meet."

"Ummm," Pierce said noncommittally.

"Well, he is. You'll see. Unless he disowns me, of course," she added, as a frown creased her brow. "What about you? Will your father strike your name out of the family Bible?"

"I doubt it. Mother might want to, but Tante Jessamine won't let that happen."

"I think we should go talk to her. If we could convince her to go and see Papa, they might be able to work this out between them."

"Tante Jessamine and your father? I don't think that's such a good idea."

"They evidently know each other from when they were children. Children can't live next to each other and not speak at least once in a while. She seems to be a reasonable woman, and Papa is certainly able to appreciate logic. I'm sure she'll help us in this."

"Me! Talk to Ransome?" Jessamine stared openmouthed at her nephew and Cadence.

"You're the only one who can," Pierce reasoned. "He won't talk to me, and he might shoot Papa."

"How can you be so sure he won't shoot me as well?" she countered to give herself time to think.

"Papa wouldn't do that," Cadence said as she sat on the porch chair beside Jessamine. "He's not so fierce, really."

"No?"

Pierce sat on the porch rail and added, "You might be able to sway him. All we want is for him to meet me. To let me ask him for Cadence's hand."

"And if he refuses?"

"We're going to be married anyway. Our banns have been posted a second week now. Cadence has almost finished her Catholic instruction."

"Then why bother to talk to him at all?" Jessamine asked sharply. "It seems to me you two aren't going to listen to anyone but yourselves anyway."

"It's not like that," Cadence said earnestly. "I love my parents, and they love me. But Papa is so stubborn!"

"He always was," Jessamine mused. "To a point. But not quite as stubborn as I am."

"Tante Jessamine, he's threatening to disown Cadence. I can't stand by and see that happen if I can do anything to prevent it."

"Yes. Ransome would do something that foolish." Jessamine stood and looked at the couple. "All right. I'll go talk to the MacKinleys tomorrow." The words made a tight lump form in her stomach. To talk to Ransome again.

And for such a reason! She felt excited and apprehensive and hot and cold at the same time.

"Thank you, Tante Jessamine!" Cadence said. "I knew we could count on you." She hugged Pierce's aunt and smiled radiantly.

"Hmmm," Jessamine said, seeing the all-too-familiar gold flecks in the girl's eyes. "I don't know how you were so sure of that when I wouldn't have bet a dime on it myself." But she awkwardly hugged Cadence in return.

42

"How's THE NEW ADDITION COMING ALONG ON THE mill?" Louis Broussard asked.

"Quite well, thank you. I expect to start turning out furniture within a few months."

Jessamine and Louis sat in the parlor sipping tall glasses of lemonade as crickets sang outside to the accompaniment of tree frogs. Delia had gone to bed right after supper, and though she had pleaded a headache, Jessamine suspected she was merely leaving her alone with Louis.

"You ought to let me help you on that."

"Why, Louis, you've never worked on furniture. Besides, you're needed in Jerome's cotton gin."

"I have a feeling Jerome will be closing it down soon. With Roseland turning from cotton to peanuts, Cavelier doesn't really need three gins."

"Jerome knows how dependable you are. If your gin closes, I'm sure he'll put you over one of the others." She was careful to speak clearly, because after so many years in the noisy gin, Louis was slightly hard of hearing.

"I suppose he will. Still, it seems I could be of more use to you. I don't know how a woman keeps so much business straight. You need someone to lift the burden from you."

"No, I don't. I enjoy being boss of my mill and rice farm. Jules Landry is a book of knowledge about rice. Sam knows the sawmill inside out. There's a new man there named Tobias Wilson who has a talent for furniture-making. He can even read and write, so I don't have to decipher marks on crates to see where to send them. I'm going to promote him to manager when we start production. So you can see, I really don't need any more help. Not that I don't appreciate the offer," she added politely.

"It's just not right, you working like this. You weren't brought up to toil like a man."

"No, I was trained to ornament a parlor. And that was pretty boring, I can tell you. I prefer using my brain, Louis. I enjoy making a keen deal and haggling over prices and arranging deliveries. It's exciting to me."

"Your father wouldn't approve at all."

"Well, I don't approve of all he did either," she retorted, thinking how Reuben had kept her from Ransome until it was too late. "Now, don't cluck at me like an old hen. I'm too set in my ways to change and too stubborn to even consider it."

Louis looked askance at her, but didn't dispute her words. After a while he said, "You'll never guess what I saw in town today."

"Oh? What was it?"

"I saw a grown man decked out in a yellow plaid suit with a crimson satin vest and a black mustache that looked like the handlebars of a bicycle."

"How odd. Is Mr. Barnum's circus coming to town?"

"No, it seems this man is an actor off that steamboat at the dock. His name is Phineas K. Weatherby, if you can credit that."

"My," she said with a smile. "His parents must have had a keen sense of humor."

"I daresay his real name is Smith or Jones or something quite normal. These actors try to find the most flamboyant names possible. It's a disgrace to let one in our town."

"That hardly seems reasonable, Louis, since he can't leave. Jerome says the boat won't float until the bayou rises another foot."

"That's not all I saw. This actor fellow was walking on the street in broad daylight with that MacKinley girl."

"Cadence?" Jessamine asked in astonishment.

"No, no. The other one. Pearl, her name is. She's barely old enough to appear socially, much less be walking out with a beau old enough to be her father!"

"I wonder if her father knows."

"He certainly does. Mr. Travis over to the grocery store said Ransome caught his daughter and that actor fellow in an alley the other day, and that Ransome nearly knocked the man from here to Sunday. I'm surprised Miss Pearl would even consider stepping out where she shouldn't again so soon."

"I should think not."

Louis looked over at Jessamine and said, "Do you ever see any of the MacKinleys these days?"

"Not often."

"I heard the other MacKinley girl has chosen a mighty interesting beau on her own."

Jessamine gave him a cool look. "If you mean Pierce, I know all about it. Gossip certainly spreads fast in Cavelier, doesn't it?"

Louis ignored her rebuke. "Pierce is getting ready to move into the Monson house this Saturday. He hired several of the hands from my gin to help him."

"So *that's* how you know. Naturally you haven't passed the news on, I assume."

"Only to a few of my most trusted friends," he reassured her. "I'm surprised Jerome will allow Pierce to see a MacKinley. He must be mellowing."

"I wouldn't say that. Have you ever tried to forbid Pierce to do anything at all? The boy is as stubborn as all of us Delacroixs. Besides, I rather like Cadence. She reminds me of myself in some ways—so sure that good will win out in the end, and so wholeheartedly behind anything she believes in."

"The whole town is up in arms about this women's-rights group she has organized. There's even talk of calling in the Knights of the White Camellia."

"The Klan? Surely not!"

"That's the gossip."

Jessamine's eyes flashed, and she said, "Those ridiculous hoods don't fool me, Louis. You tell Mr. Travis and the Macys and William Ramsey that if there's trouble from the Klan, there will be even more trouble from me."

"Now, Jessamine, you can't think our own men are—"

"I know your horse when I see it, too, Louis Broussard, sheet or no sheet. That's why I'm giving you the message."

Louis paled as white as a Klan robe. He had been positive no one knew the identities of the ghostly riders. He looked away to hide the guilt on his face.

"Besides, I may go to some of Cadence's meetings myself. I'm not too old to cram a few new thoughts in my head."

"Jessamine! You wouldn't become a suffragette!"

"Don't sound so shocked, Louis. I didn't say I was proposing to get a job with Sophie James."

His plump cheeks mottled red, and he leapt to his feet. "You know about Sophie! I mean Mrs. James? Jessamine, I'm surprised at you. I'm shocked!"

"I also have my ways of knowing whose horses are tied out back. If I were you, Louis, I wouldn't let anything happen to upset either Pierce or Cadence. You see," she said innocently, "they're in love, and it pleases me for them to be happy." When she leveled her gray eyes on him, he realized she could and would do whatever was necessary to protect her family.

"My goodness, it's gotten late. I must be running." Louis headed for the door.

Jessamine followed him out and whistled for Donnie to come in before she locked the screen door. "Good night, Louis. Come back, now."

She shut the wooden door and locked it before speaking to the dog. "Louis Broussard has always been a pompous jackass."

The dog beat his tail on the floor to show his agreement.

43

JESSAMINE CHANGED HER CLOTHES THREE TIMES before she decided on her new garnet silk dress. The color was daring, especially for a maiden lady, but it was dark enough not to be garish, and it was the prettiest day dress she owned. The gored skirt which was lined in taffeta made a pleasant froufrou sound when she walked. The leg-of-mutton sleeves ballooned fashionably from shoulder to elbow, and fit as close as her skin from elbow to wrist, with tiny jet buttons securing them and the close-fitting bodice. The collar was high and close to her slender neck, and trimmed in frothy white lace that flowed down the front into a jabot. The seams of the dress were trimmed with the same black silk braid which edged the ruffle that barely skimmed above the ground.

Jessamine put on a garnet Rembrandt hat and tilted it toward her face. A dusky-pink ostrich feather rising from a matching satin bow cascaded over the hat, just touching the shiny coil of her hair. She knew she looked elegant, and the knowledge of that gave her confidence.

As her buggy was brought around, she pulled on black kid leather driving gloves and dismissed her driver. She didn't want any of her servants to witness the scene if she were ordered off Roseland's porch. Her confidence wasn't that strong.

After a moment's hesitation, she took a letter from the top of her dresser. It was yellowed with age and smelled faintly of dampness. Once again she scanned the words of love she had written to Ransome so long ago, then resolutely put it into her reticule. She hoped she wouldn't have to use this to sway him, but she wanted to be prepared.

When she ordered Donnie to stay home, she noticed that her mouth was powder dry. She had rarely had to face a more uncomfortable interview. Twice she considered turning the tea cart around and going back home. This, after all, wasn't her affair, since neither of the young people was her child. Then she recalled the depth of her passion for Ransome before they were separated, and how bitter she had become for a while when he was lost to her. It was that memory that gave her the resolve to continue toward Roseland. No one should have to go through such agony as she had.

The front drive was much as she recalled it. The spreading branches of the enormous live-oak trees that lined the drive made a deep green tunnel over the hard-packed road. Three tracks led up the slight rise, one in the middle made by the horses, the two outside it worn by buggy wheels. The trees seemed larger and the lawns beyond had undergone subtle changes over the years—a birdbath here, a new hedge and border of flowerbeds there. Despite her efforts to remain unaffected by this reunion with her childhood home, Jessamine felt a sharp twinge of nostalgia as she reined to a stop at the front steps. She paused for a minute on the pretext of arranging her skirt, but she was really soaking in the remembered splendor of her ancestral home and trying to compose herself.

She tied her horse to the ring on the post and walked slowly up the wide white steps. Tall, perfectly proportioned Greek columns supported the airy upper balcony high overhead. A huge brass lamp suspended from chains hung directly over the porch.

Jessamine lifted her hand to knock, but the door swung open before she could make contact. A butler with a very haughty demeanor greeted her. "Yes, madam?"

"I'm here to see Mr. and Mrs. MacKinley." The words almost stuck in her mouth.

"Are they expecting you, madam?"

"No, but I'm sure they'll see me. Tell them Miss Jessamine Delacroix is here on a matter of great importance."

The butler escorted her into the foyer, then left to announce her. Jessamine looked around with interest, but not approval. Her mother's lovely pink paper that had been hand-painted in Paris had been covered by a dull gray-blue. The wainscoting was painted a similar shade, and a carpet in hues of beige, red, and blue now ran up the wishbone-shaped stairs. In her wildest dreams Jessamine had not expected that Eliza MacKinley would have redecorated to such an extent.

The butler, Jenkins, ushered her into the front parlor,

and when Jessamine saw the changes there, she stopped in her tracks. Even the lovely rose velvet curtains that should have lasted until the turn of the century had been replaced by burgundy ones that ignobly sagged at their hems. The sheer panels of Brussels lace that had covered the windows were gone altogether, and it occurred to Jessamine that without the lace to diffuse the sunlight, the room was probably unbearably warm when the sun sank below the porch roof.

Delia's parlor, like Delia herself, had been pink and calm, and had held only the furniture necessary for comfort, though the walls had been adorned with elegant prints suspended by ropes of gold silk. Jessamine couldn't recognize a single object from her youth. The gentle wallpaper was now a hideous display of blue and gold medallions stalking up the wall like huge regimented spiders between garlands of snuff-colored ivy. Everywhere she looked there were settees, wicker chairs, small tables, poorly executed prints, a collection of fans, another of seashells, and dozens upon dozens of photographs and other bric-a-brac. Jessamine didn't know where to sit, or whether she wanted to.

She strolled through the cluttered room, for it was impossible to walk straight across it, and when she noticed the one familiar object in the room, she headed for it. The old piano on which she and Adele had learned to play songs as children was sitting well into the middle of the room, as was currently fashionable, instead of being backed to a wall. To hide the piano's backboard, which the manufacturer had never intended for anyone to see, someone had tried to disguise it with tasseled draperies and swags of fabric, as if it were a screen or free-standing wall hanging. At the foot of the draperies was a box for the potted plants which served as humidity gauges for the music room. Jessamine felt as if she had been betrayed even by the garishly adorned piano.

Gingerly she eased herself onto the piano stool and let her fingers almost unconsciously trace a soft melody from the keys. Its mellow voice was the same, regardless of how unattractively it had been decorated.

Ransome heard the soft music as he entered the room and closed the parlor doors behind him. For a moment he paused, drinking in the lovely sight of Jessamine seated at the piano, attired in a dress of flame. She looked so comfortable there, so natural and at home, his heart was wrenched. Quickly he cleared his throat to get her attention.

She looked up, her quicksilver eyes startled, her moist lips parted. Hastily she stood and covered the keys. "I didn't hear you come in," she said with some embarrassment.

Ransome felt oddly out of place, as if he were the visitor and not Jessamine. "You play beautifully. I've never heard you before."

She left the piano abruptly and followed his gesture to sit on a lady's chair of blue watered silk. Ransome sat opposite her in a larger armchair and studied her in a way that made her feel most uncomfortable. "There have been a lot of changes in Roseland," she ventured through the cottony taste in her mouth.

"Yes, there have. Did you come to discuss them?"

She wished he didn't look so handsome. The silver wings in his auburn hair were very distinguishing. She didn't care for mustaches in general, but his was perfect, and she soon couldn't imagine him without it. The lines in his cheeks and at the corners of his eyes were somewhat more prominent now that he was in his mid-forties, but they only accented his strong features. He wore a suit of dark tobacco brown over a camel-gold vest. He looked exactly as she had imagined him in her dreams.

"Jessamine?" he repeated. "I asked why you're here."

"I came to speak to you and your . . . wife. Is she at home?"

"Vera is indisposed, I'm afraid. Her health isn't strong, and she's confined to her bed today."

"I'm sorry. Perhaps I should come back another time." Jessamine hid her relief by starting to rise from the chair.

"That won't be necessary. Vera is terribly shy, and I shield her from unpleasantness whenever I can. I assume you did come here to be unpleasant?"

Her conciliatory words dissolved before they could be spoken. Instead she said, "I hadn't planned to be until now. There's no reason to be so rude to me, Ransome. After all, *I* wasn't the one to jilt *you.*"

He frowned at her and glanced back to be sure they were alone. "I'm not so sure of that, but it's neither here nor there. What did you want to talk to me about?" He wished she had aged more or had been plainer to start with, for she looked like a glowing jewel in his mother's overstuffed parlor. Her charm was draped about her like a luminous mantle, and Ransome had to struggle to keep from pulling her into his arms.

"As you must know by now, your daughter and my nephew are seeing each other. While I assure you this was as much against my wishes as it must have been against yours, nevertheless, it has happened. Now they are in love and want to marry."

"So you expect me to agree out of hand and give them a lovely wedding and the Grand Tour."

"Sarcasm doesn't become you, Ransome."

"Nor does manipulation seem to be your forte. Why aren't Cadence and Pierce telling me this, or Jerome? Why you?"

"They thought you were less likely to shoot me than you would be Jerome or Pierce."

"Why would they assume that?"

"Because I'm the weaker sex, I suppose. How should I know?"

Ransome chuckled. "You're a lot of things, Jessamine. But you've never been weak."

"Thank you." She met his gaze and felt pulled into the depths of his enchanting eyes. She knew she should speak or move or do something to break this dangerous spell, but she could only gaze back and imagine the touch of his lips and his arms holding her.

She tore her eyes away. "No matter how much you dislike my family, we must think of the young people. They really love each other and want to marry. Pierce is already a wealthy man and he will inherit riches beyond his expectations. You'll have no cause for concern there."

"Cadence wasn't raised to trap a fortune," he said testily.

"No? I've often wondered what criteria are necessary to marry into the MacKinley family. Tell me, Ransome. What does it take?"

He glared at her. "It takes a heart true enough to withstand a brief separation. A love strong enough to believe in the one she loves. It takes trust and dependability."

Jessamine frowned at him. She knew he wasn't talking about Cadence and Pierce. "In my experience that isn't always true. However, Pierce meets those criteria and I assume that's also true of Cadence. So why aren't you agreeable to their marriage?"

"Don't be a damned fool. You know exactly why. Do

I have to spell it out for you? Tell me, Jessamine, why didn't you ever marry?''

Their eyes met and tension crackled between them. She wanted so badly to blurt out the truth in scathing accusations. Instead she took the faded letter out of her bag and handed it to him. ''Read it!'' she commanded when he was reluctant to take it.

Ransome's face was pale and his eyes grew darker with emotion as he read the letter from Jessamine that he had never received. Slowly he let the paper fall to his lap. She took it and put it away again. ''I had hoped not to have to use that. I wouldn't have if we hadn't been alone. Ransome, as much as we loved, they love. Oh, I know it's in a different way, and they talk more of causes than of moonbeams, but the point is, they love! Such wicked injustice must not ruin two more lives!''

He stood, and she got to her feet. ''Why did I never receive that letter?'' he demanded with growing indignation.

''It was Papa. He kept all our letters in a box down at the sawmill. I never saw yours either. I thought you had forgotten me or never loved me at all. By the time I found the letters, Papa was dead and you were married.''

''Jessamine.'' He breathed her name in a whisper of agony. ''What have we done!''

''It's too late for us, but it's not for Cadence and Pierce. Give her your blessing.''

''I can't. It's not just me, it's Vera and Mother, and Jerome and all the others rising up out of the dust to tell me I can't! Don't you see?''

''I see your father,'' she said coldly. ''You were always a braver man than this. I never thought you'd let your own child's happiness be forefeit to your pride.''

Her words cut him deeply; he towered over her. ''How can you of all people be so sanctimonious? You speak of pride and bravery, and yet you don't know my burdens or my responsibilities!''

''Don't I? I haven't lived in seclusion these past twenty-four years! I, too, have pride and commitments.'' She faced him squarely, her eyes flashing silver fire.

''Why did you never marry?'' he asked her again. ''Tell me the truth.''

Her breath caught in her throat as she said, ''There was only one Ransome MacKinley to be had.''

Ransome didn't plan to kiss her. He certainly never planned to kiss her in a way that made the universe spin away, leaving only the two of them. But it happened, nevertheless. She felt small and firm and rounded in his arms. Her breath mingled sweetly with his and his eager tongue delved into her mouth to taste her, and again he felt as if their hearts beat in unison. Passion made his blood thunder, blocking out everything in the false world. Only Jessamine, with her aura of gardenia scent and soft skin, was reality.

Ransome heard a strangled sound behind them, and instinctively pulled free and thrust his shoulder protectively in front of Jessamine.

Pearl stood in the doorway, her face a study in shocked disbelief. She stared at Jessamine, who raised her fingers to her moist and rosy lips, then at Ransome, who looked as fierce as a protective lover could. With a hoarse cry Pearl ran from the room and up the curving stairs.

"I'm so sorry!" Jessamine gasped, her eyes round with horror. "I never knew . . . Perhaps I could talk to her. Explain somehow."

"Leave, Jessamine. Just go!" The harshness in his voice was not anger, but the result of having to say the opposite of what he meant. Dread was fast sinking into his bones.

Jessamine ran from the house to her buggy and whipped the horse to a quick trot. Ransome glanced after her and walked like a stunned man to the stairs and peered up at the empty hall. He had to find Pearl, to talk to her, to explain. Above all, he had to protect his gentle and blameless Vera.

He clambered on rubbery legs up the stairs to try to mend the rip in his world before it crumbled into ashes over the only indiscretion of his entire married life.

44

ALL RANSOME'S ARGUMENTS AND PLEADINGS AND threats were of no use. Pearl kept the door to her bedroom securely locked and refused either to open it or to speak with her father. By peeping through the keyhole, Ransome could see her sitting slouched down in a chintz-covered chair, nibbling at her fingernails. Since she seemed to be in no physical distress or about to jump from a window, he straightened and said in his most patriarchal tones, "Pearl, there is a perfectly logical explanation for what you think you saw. When you are ready to be reasonable, you may come to me and I will explain. Then you will see how foolishly you are behaving."

He scowled at the solid door. He was sure his words sounded convincing. Now he had to conjure up some plausible reason for Pearl to have seen him kissing Jessamine Delacroix with such unbridled passion. He could only hope that from the angle of the doorway his daughter hadn't been able to discern everything. He decided to go back downstairs and check Pearl's view from the doorway as he tried to come up with some convincing lie.

"Ransome?" Vera called out as he passed their bedroom. "Is there a problem with Pearl?"

He stepped in and went to sit on the edge of her bed. "Are you feeling better? I didn't mean to disturb you."

"What is happening with Pearl? She isn't seeing that dreadful man again?"

Ransome managed a smile. "No, no. Nothing like that. We merely had a misunderstanding. That's all." He reached out and smoothed the fine hair back from Vera's temples. She had always been so good and trusting. He hated himself for what had transpired between Jessamine and himself. Vera deserved so much better than him.

As his fingers stroked her, he said, "You feel feverish. Perhaps I should send for Dr. Griggs."

"There's no reason for concern. I often feel a bit warm. I imagine it's this cold I can't seem to shake."

Ransome nodded, but his face became drawn. Dr. Griggs had confirmed that her "cold" was in fact the disease called consumption, but he had advised against telling Vera for fear the trauma of knowing would add further stress on her. "Honey, I've been thinking. Louisiana isn't the healthiest place for you or Ethan. I think we should move to the mountains."

"Move again? So soon?"

"A cold, dry air would be more invigorating for you both. Can't you just see Ethan running up and down mountains? We could get him some sheep or goats to raise. He'd love it!"

"And leave Roseland?"

"He isn't very happy here. I think some of the boys tease him about his deafness."

"He will be deaf in the mountains too."

"We'll hire a tutor. Besides, a move would take Cadence away from young Delacroix before she makes an irrevocable mistake."

"You don't want to move," Vera said gently. "You love Roseland. Besides, what about your mother? She would never leave."

"I'll hire servants to care for her here. We can come back on frequent visits to see about her. Who knows, she might want to leave." He bent over her and placed a kiss on her papery cheek. "Vera, please agree to move away from Cavelier."

Vera gazed deeply into his troubled eyes. "Do you really want to go?"

He recalled the fire Jessamine had ignited so easily in him—and in his own parlor. "We have to leave here."

She felt the cold knot of dread tighten again inside her middle. There was much more going on here than he was saying. Slowly she nodded. "Whatever you think is best, Ransome."

He smiled with relief. Once he was away from Jessamine, he could again fasten her memory away in the closet of his mind. "Get well quickly," he urged gently. "When you feel up to it, we'll leave."

Vera was restless all that night, and her tossing kept Ransome awake. He longed to comfort her somehow, but she slept so lightly that he was afraid the slightest touch would awaken her completely. Even in health, Vera could rarely go back to sleep if she awoke during the night, so Ransome lay still, trying to think of a place they could relocate that would be both cool and dry and where he could earn a living practicing law.

By dawn he was as exhausted as if he hadn't gone to bed at all. Vera's eyes were still closed, though she fitfully moved her head from one position to another. Ransome carefully eased out of bed and dressed with practiced silence. Perhaps without his body beside her, Vera would rest more comfortably.

Cissy prepared breakfast as usual, but only Ransome and Cadence showed up to eat; the others were presumably sleeping late. The meal was taken in relative silence, with only a few pleasantries exchanged about the weather and Cadence's vague plans for the day. He felt guilty about not telling his daughter about the decision to move, but he couldn't handle a scene with Cadence so early in the morning, and he knew she would be upset. For that matter, he still didn't know what he was going to tell Pearl. A girl of eighteen could certainly recognize a passionate kiss when she saw one, and Ransome had never been adept at lying to anyone.

Ethan wandered in as they were finishing the meal, and dropped dully into his chair.

"Good morning, son. Are you ready for breakfast?" Ransome asked after touching the boy's arm to get his attention.

"No, Papa. I'm not hungry. I feel so tired."

Ransome frowned as he touched Ethan's forehead. "You have a fever. Do you feel ill?"

The boy nodded. "I feel sick at my stomach, and I had a nosebleed off and on all night."

"He looks sick, Papa," Cadence observed as she came around to kneel by her brother. "Look how shiny his eyes are and how the whites are sort of yellowish."

Ransome tilted the boy's head up for a better look. His eyes did seem odd, and his skin had a jaundiced hue as well. "Back to bed with you, young man. I'll have Cissy bring a tray up to you later."

Ethan nodded and fished his handkerchief from his pocket as he felt another nosebleed starting.

Ransome stroked his lip in concern. "How do you feel, Cadence?"

"Perfectly well, Papa."

"How is Pearl? She hasn't been down yet."

"I heard her moving around earlier, and I think she came downstairs about the time it started getting light enough to see. I guess she went to the necessary house and then went back to bed. She does that sometimes." After a pause she drew a deep breath and said. "Papa, there are some things we need to talk about."

"Not now, Cadence. We'll talk later." Ransome strode from the room. He had a sinking feeling that Vera might have come down with whatever Ethan had, and that Pearl might have it as well.

He went to Pearl's room and knocked on the door. When there was no answer on the second knock, he tried the doorknob. To his amazement, the door opened easily. He stepped in and looked about the empty room.

Pearl's room was seldom as neat as Cadence's, but today it was more disheveled than ever, with the drawers gaping open and the door to her armoire unfastened. A quick glance told him her tapestry traveling bag was missing, and it appeared that quite a few of her clothes might be gone too. Ransome hurried to the top of the stairs and called for Cadence.

When she joined him in Pearl's room, he said, "You know her things better than I do. Does it look as if some of her clothes are missing?"

Cadence sorted through the jumble of her sister's belongings. "Her new pink dress is gone, and so are her better cotton ones. And her Sunday dress. Why aren't they here?"

"Could the laundress have them, do you think?"

"No, I asked to borrow her yellow cotton dress yesterday, and Pearl said no. The others were hanging here then. Where's Pearl?"

A deep dread was settling on Ransome. "Do you know if she is still seeing that man named Phineas Weatherby?"

"Who?"

Ransome brushed past his daughter and ran up the wide stairs to the third floor, then up the narrow flight that led to the servants' rooms in the attic. At the end of the short hall he opened the door onto the balcony. From this vantage point he could see the bayou glistening and twisting in the early sunlight. And at a distance he could see the white bulk of the *Lidy Jane* billowing a trail of black smoke as she floated toward New Orleans.

"Damn!" he growled as he gripped the railing. "She wouldn't have!"

As if in answer, the steamboat blew a mournful note that drifted faintly back to him. "Damn!" he repeated.

He ran back downstairs to his bedroom to get his pistol and his traveling coat. He could ride to New Orleans almost as quickly as the boat could get there, and haul his foolish daughter back.

As he pulled on his coat, Vera raised up weakly. She tried to speak, but wavered and fell back onto her pillow. Ransome stopped what he was doing and went to her side. Her skin was a sickly yellow and was moist from perspiration. Her breathing was rapid, and the veins distended at her temples and on her neck and arms and hands. As he watched, a thin trickle of bright blood formed at the corner of her mouth.

Ransome's eyes widened and his heart beat wildly as he backed away. At the door he yelled for Jenkins.

The butler came running as Eliza popped her head out of the door to see what was wrong. Ransome pushed his mother away from his bedroom door as he shouted at Jenkins, "Send Oliver to get the doctor, and move fast! If you can't find Oliver, ride for him yourself!"

"Sir?" Jenkins asked.

Ransome said in a tight voice, "I think it's yellow fever."

Jenkins stared a moment, then turned and ran.

"Mother, try to remember," Ransome said as he bent toward her. "Have you ever had yellow fever?"

"Why, no," she said vacantly. "I've had malaria, of course, as so many people around here have. But I don't believe I've had yellow fever. It seems like Mr. MacKinley did, but I can't recall now. I suppose it doesn't matter now if he did or not, does it?"

"Mother, Vera and Ethan are very sick. I want you to stay as far away from them as you can. Will you do that?"

"Yes, if you say so. Pearl isn't sick too, is she? Where is Pearl?"

"I'm not sure." He frantically looked around. Pearl couldn't have picked a worse time to run away with that scoundrel, for he was sure that's what she had done. He couldn't possibly leave Vera and Ethan to ride after Pearl.

"As soon as Oliver comes back with the doctor, I'll send him to look for her."

Eliza smiled and nodded as if this made perfect sense to her. "You men always know just what to do. I'm so lucky to have you to look after me."

Pearl was nervously shifting from one foot to the other as Phineas bought their train tickets. "We should have taken the boat," she said for the third time. "It sailed nearly an hour ago."

"As I told you, my dumpling, that's the first place your papa would look." He gave the porter their tickets and tossed their bags on board before handing Pearl up the metal steps. "This is a much better plan."

She followed him down the narrow corridor and squeezed into a gray felt seat by the window. Visibility from the window was poor because of the road grime and soot that covered the glass, so Pearl busied herself looking about the coach to see if she recognized any of the other passengers, but no one looked familiar. Even as far back from the engine as they were, she heard the hiss of steam that meant departure was imminent.

"Are you certain Millisant will know where to meet us?" she asked as she nervously squirmed in her seat. "Perhaps we should wait until she writes to us in reply."

"To turn back now is to forfeit our claims to success."

Pearl turned to him in delight. "Is that a line from a play?"

"Quite possibly, my dear. Quite possibly."

The porter called for the stragglers to board, then waved at the engineer. The engine belched black smoke into the air and the train jolted and bucked in its effort to move. As it began to roll forward, the porter swung up onto the platform, hauling the steps in with him. Pearl strained for a last glimpse of Cavelier as the train steadily picked up speed.

"Phineas, look! That's Oliver Gibbons, our overseer! He's going into Dr. Griggs's office."

"No doubt the search has begun," Phineas said as he craned his neck to see who it was she was talking about. "We've made our escape just in time."

Pearl leaned back and smiled. "I hope I never see this backwater town again."

"Never! For you, the lights and gaiety of the stage. Accolades from adoring fans! Command performances before royalty!"

"But first Natchez and a preacher," she reminded him coyly.

"Naturally."

Pearl settled back as the train accelerated, taking her from the banality of her childhood to the uncertain excitement of her future.

Vera and Ethan weren't the only residents of Cavelier, Louisiana, to fall victim to the dread yellow fever. By the end of the second day, one-third of the townspeople were too sick to move. The next day the count was almost half, and it was then that the disease claimed its first victim of the current epidemic.

Jessamine tirelessly mopped her mother's fevered brow for hours on end. Following Dr. Griggs's orders, she fed her mother copious amounts of calomel and gum camphor, alternating that regimen with morphine. Delia had broken out in a hard sweat, as the doctor had said she would, but she seemed unable to rid her body of the poisons of the fever. Delia was sinking fast, and Jessamine knew it.

Sam stood mutely in the doorway, his seamed face drawn with worry. Jessamine sent him on one errand after another to keep him busy, but at last she gave up and let him stand watch like a sentinel against encroaching death.

"You gots to get some rest, Miss Jessamine," he said in a hushed voice. "You ain't slept since night afore last."

"I can't leave her, Sam."

"I can get Maribelle to spell you. Yellow jack don't hit us black'uns like it does you folks."

Jessamine shook her head. "I've seen black and white die from it, and so have you. I'll stay here a bit longer."

"Yes, ma'am." He didn't need to be told that his old mistress couldn't last much longer.

Delia opened her eyes and looked around the room. "Jessamine?" she asked, as if surprised to find herself in these surroundings. "Are we at Ten Acres?"

"Yes, Mama."

Delia looked over at Sam, and he made a half-bow as he clutched his battered hat into a shapeless wad. "Where's Jerome?" Her voice was weak, but for the first time in years it held reason.

"He's in town with Susanna and Pierce."

"They aren't sick too, are they?"

"No, thank God. He'll be out in an hour or so to see about you."

Delia reached up to touch her daughter's cheek, and Jessamine leaned closer, straining to hear her mother's fading voice. "We were wrong," Delia whispered. "All those years ago. We were wrong."

Tears gathered in Jessamine's eyes. "Don't talk, Mama. You need to save your strength."

Delia's gray eyes roamed across the room to the doorway. Slowly the reason evaporated from her, and her voice took on the coquettish tones of a much younger woman. "Reuben!" she sighed happily. "You're here at last."

Sam shifted hastily out of the doorway and looked uneasily over his shoulder as Delia's eyes appeared to be following something no one else could see.

"Reuben," she murmured softly. Her lips curved up in a smile, and at that moment Jessamine realized her mother was no longer with them.

Slowly Jessamine straightened her tired back, and gazed down at her mother. "He came to get her. Somehow I thought he would."

She looked over at Sam, whose eyes were wide and staring. "Tell Maribelle we will see to laying her out now. You bring in the best cypress coffin we have in the mill. Tom Smith is down there to help you. Send Tobias into town to get word to Father Theriot that my mother has passed away. Thank God she was already given Divine Unction."

For quite a while Jessamine sat beside the still figure of her mother, remembering the good times and the bad that they had faced together. And in the end, her mother had apologized for denying Jessamine the happiness of a family of her own. Curiously, Jessamine found she felt no bitterness at her mother's admission of having done wrong. Her life had not turned out the way she had hoped, but she hadn't been unhappy. She had spoken the truth when she told Cadence she was a liberated woman. More so than she probably would have been as a wife.

"I forgive you, Mama," she said softly.

As with so many, Laurie's symptoms of the fever developed rapidly, and in the absence of specific knowledge of the disease and how to treat it, Doll resorted to her intuition. She knew prolonged high fever was damaging, so she fed her daughter large amounts of wild ginger tea and a tea made from pennyroyal leaves. And when she wasn't helping her to drink, she was sponging her off with cool water.

The day before, Tobias Wilson had come knocking on her door, but Doll had sent him away without letting him so much as peek in at Laurie. She gazed down at her daughter and shook her head at the idea of Laurie settling for a mill hand when she could live like the Delacroixs if she just would.

Doll's hands shook as she wrung out the washcloth. For two days she had struggled against admitting that Laurie wasn't the only one with yellow jack, but she could deny it no longer. Her temperature was elevated and she was losing her strength rapidly. The only remaining question was whether Laurie would recover soon enough to care for her when she could no longer get about.

Laying the damp cloth on Laurie's forehead, Doll stood up and tried to clear her muddled thoughts. She knew she had to get help. Laurie was holding her own against the fever, but Doll was not, and she had to fight hard against the compelling desire to lie down and go to sleep. She couldn't go to Jerome. That was unthinkable. He hadn't been out, and Doll was afraid either that he was sick himself or that he was keeping the same vigil she was with Pierce or Susanna, or both. There was only one other person she could turn to.

Doll went through the house and out the door. When she became aware that the summer air felt cool against her skin, she knew she must have a great deal of fever. Not letting herself dwell on her weakness, she followed the path along the edge of the swamp, pausing when she had to in order to catch her breath. The air hung still and close beneath the huge trees, as though the curtains of Spanish moss were holding back the breeze. The stagnant water was hazy in spots where clouds of tiny gnats hovered just over the surface. Doll forced herself past all the familiar scenes and thought only of getting help.

She made her way past the mill, where no one could be seen at work, and struggled up the hillock beyond. At last she saw Ten Acres and her father's small brown cabin. She forced herself to climb the two steps and cross the small porch. With a trembling hand she pushed against the door and it swung open.

Sam was sitting at the rough table drinking coffee from a chipped cup. When he saw that it was Doll who had unexpectedly come in, his look of surprise immediately changed to a scowl. "What are you doing here?" he demanded.

Doll drew herself up. He hadn't spoken to her at all in years, but the harshness in his voice was nonetheless more than she had expected. "Laurie is sick. I need help."

"Not from me, you don't. You ain't never needed nothing from me." He slurped his coffee loudly.

"That's not true, Pa."

His head snapped back as he glared at her. "We all got trouble these days, girl. I can't go off and leave Miss Jessamine."

"Jessamine? She's sick?" Doll stepped closer.

"Nah. She done had the bronze john years back, *Miss* Jessamine did. It's her ma. Miss Delia died yesterday. We just finished burying her up by Mr. Reuben and Miss Adele. I can't leave to go nowhere."

"I'm so sorry," Doll said. "Miss Delia was a good woman."

He snorted derisively and lifted his cup again. "I'm surprised you can tell one when you see one."

Tears stung Doll's eyes. "Pa, don't do this. Laurie's so sick, and I can't manage by myself."

"So your man's left you, has he? Don't surprise me none."

"He hasn't left me!"

"No? Well, I'll tell you what. You promise me you won't ever see him again, and I'll come help you."

Doll drew back, the tears flowing down her face. "I won't do that, Pa."

He looked at her in disgust. "I'm sorry for the way you turned out, girl. You broke your ma's heart, and you broke mine too. And still you hang on to your evil ways."

"I'm not evil, Pa. I love Jerome, and he loves me! It's not like you say!"

Sam deliberately turned his back on her. "I know what the Good Book say. It say, 'Git thee behind me, Satan.' That means you. And don't you go up to the big house and hassle Miss Jessamine, neither."

"Pa?" she lamented in a whisper.

Sam didn't answer so she slowly backed out. "I love you, Pa. In spite of the way things are, I love you."

She left without seeing the tears that were flowing down Sam's seamed dark face.

By the time she returned to her house, Doll's head was swimming, and she felt sick to the bone. She hauled herself up the steps and swayed to a halt when a man's voice called out to her. Looking over her shoulder, she saw Laurie's young man approaching.

"Mrs. Farmer, how's Laurie?" he asked, coming to the foot of the steps.

"Are you back again? I thought I told you to stay away from here."

"I know you did, but I's worried about her."

Doll tried to focus on his face, but everything seemed hazy. "You have no call to worry about her."

He stepped nearer. "Are you ailing, Mrs. Farmer?"

"No! Now, get away from here!"

Tobias looked at her as if he were about to challenge her right to order him away, but Doll stared him down. With a shrug, he sauntered away.

Doll rubbed her eyes tiredly. She needed help, but not that much. The last thing she wanted was to be obliged to Tobias Wilson.

Slowly she dragged herself up the last of the steps and into the house. She poured herself some pennyroyal tea and forced it down her throat. Her eyes fell on the box where she kept her spells. She had been so busy with Laurie and so worried that she had failed to make her weekly forgetfulness spell that had protected her secret all these years. And now she was too sick. She doubted she would have the strength to bury it under the steps even if she did make it. She would just have to hope the sickness kept everyone away until she was well enough to resume the practice.

With leaden feet she went back to sit beside her daughter.

Cadence and Ransome somehow stayed well. And although Vera and Ethan remained very weak, when they seemed no worse after the third day, Cadence felt her prayers for their recovery would be answered. With Ransome busy with his wife and son's needs, and Jenkins occupied caring for Eliza and Oliver Gibbons, who had both contracted the disease, the responsibility for seeing to Roseland's daily affairs fell on Cadence's shoulders.

When the need arose for more supplies for the household, she had Jenkins hitch the horse to the buggy and she drove into town. The changes that had come to Cavelier stunned her.

The usually bustling little town was almost deserted. The few people she saw on the streets were hurrying from place to place as if the epidemic were hard on their heels. Most of the stores were boarded up against vandals, and many had signs posted on their fronts warning away anyone from New Orleans, for the general opinion was that the disease had come from there.

Black-bordered funeral announcements had been posted on fences and lightposts, and although many of the ceremonies had already occurred, the notices remained, for no one wanted to venture out to take them down. On the courthouse green the Civil War cannon was being fired at intervals in the superstitious hope that the booming sound would break up the pestilence that hovered over the town. Barrels of tar burned on street corners to purge the disease from the air. In the distance, Cadence saw a crew of men with bandannas over their faces, shoveling lime on the gutters and streets.

She reined her horse to a stop at the grocer's and hurried into the store. At her entrance the owner looked up suspiciously. "Hello, Mr. Travis," she said.

" 'Afternoon, Miss MacKinley."

She offered him the shopping list, but he asked her to read it off to him. She deduced he thought that she, too, was ill and that the disease might jump from her to him through the list. Quickly he stacked her needed items in a box, his movements nervous and jerky, as if he were in a rush to get her out of the store.

"How's Mrs. Travis?" she asked in an effort to put him at ease.

"Sick, like everybody else," he snapped, then recalled his manners enough to ask, "Your folks all right?"

"Mama and Ethan are sick, as well as my grandmother. But Papa and I are fine."

Mr. Travis nodded. "This is the worst the fever has hit since 1878. It's them mosquitoes that brought it to us, I hear. Come out of New Orleans. Leastways that's what folks say."

"Surely it won't last much longer."

"Can't say for sure. The preacher offered to hold a prayer meeting, but most folks is scared to come."

Cadence paid for the groceries, and the man carried them out to her buggy, but he was careful not to touch the buggy itself. As the grocer came out with the last of her boxes, a small procession coming down the street drew their attention. In the lead was a wagon being driven by a red-necked farmer. In the bed of the wagon were two pitifully small coffins. Mourners walked behind, their eyes glazed with sorrow.

Cadence and Mr. Travis watched in silence until the funeral passed by. He said as if to himself, "Ain't nobody making money these days but gravediggers, and they ain't making much because they're spending most of what they make getting drunk enough so they'll handle the bodies."

"Surely the coffins . . ."

"A lot of folks can't find one to buy these past few days. I hear tell the bodies are stacking up faster than they can be buried. I sure wouldn't drive by the cemetery, if I was you."

With a shiver Cadence said, "No, I won't."

She thanked him and climbed into the buggy. The horse trotted quickly down the street, as though he too would be glad to leave the unnatural silence of the town. On the way out of town, Cadence stopped at Daisy Buckner's house to see if her friend was well.

The door opened a crack, and Daisy's mother peeped out.

"Good afternoon, Mrs. Buckner. I just dropped by to see if Daisy is all right."

The door opened another inch, but the woman didn't ask Cadence in. "She's bad sick. I can't let her have visitors. You ought to be home yourself."

Cadence saw the fear and worry in the woman's eyes. "Will you tell her I said hello and that I hope she'll be well soon?"

"I'll tell her. I'm sorry I can't let you in, Miss MacKinley, but we're under quarantine."

"I understand. I didn't mean to intrude." Cadence backed away and hurried back to the buggy. She wanted to see Pierce, to reassure herself that he was still well, but she was afraid of giving him the disease. With everything turned topsy-turvy, she didn't dare risk his health. Instead, she drove back to Roseland as quickly as possible.

She found Ransome in the library, a letter held in his hand. "Papa? What is it?"

He held the paper out to her, and she read it, then read it again. "It's from Pearl. She's married?"

"No wonder Oliver couldn't find her in New Orleans. That scoundrel took her by train to Natchez."

"It says here that they are married. Perhaps . . ."

"You never saw the man! I did, though, and she couldn't have made a worse mistake!"

Cadence looked at the heading of the letter. "Why do you suppose it's addressed only to Mama?"

Ransome closed his eyes as if in pain and ran his fingers through his hair, but didn't answer her.

"She says they are going to live on a steamboat and perform on the stage! Imagine Pearl as an actress!"

"If I thought it would do any good, I'd go after her and drag her home. But she's a married woman now. Her husband has legal rights over her."

"Papa, don't be so hurt. You know how Pearl is. Maybe she will be happier this way."

He shook his head. "You just don't understand."

Cadence laid her cheek against his shoulder. Her father was a dear, but he didn't give her much credit for understanding affairs of the heart. She guessed it took a woman to comprehend such things. "I love you, Papa."

He covered her hand with his and patted it, but he could only see Pearl's stunned face that day she had found him kissing Jessamine. He could only recall the coarse features of the gaudily dressed man pawing at Pearl in the alleyway—and Pearl allowing it. He blinked hard to conquer his tears, and wished it were permissible for a man to cry.

"How are they?" Cadence asked with a nod toward the stairs.

"Your grandmother is a bit worse. Ethan and your mother are about the same."

"Go lie down for a while, Papa. I'll watch over them."

Ransome shook his head. He knew Vera and Ethan had taken a turn for the worse, but he just couldn't admit it out loud.

"We'll both watch over them." With tired steps he followed his daughter upstairs.

45

DR. LUCAS GRIGGS FOLDED ELIZA MACKINLEY'S hands over her chest and sat back with a sigh. The epidemic of yellow fever was on the wane, and he had thought the old woman would make it. He dreaded calling Ransome and Cadence in. They had had to bear so much in the last few days. The first to go had been young Ethan, then Vera. At least there had been the dubious comfort that Vera died without knowing her son had slipped away only a few hours earlier.

Eliza didn't look peaceful in death, but the victims of yellow fever rarely did. She appeared sullen and unhappy, as if she had personally resented the intrusion of the disease to the very end. Her skin was mottled and her veins were distended in the manner so typical of this type of death. Lucas slowly smoothed the sheet across her chest and straightened her beribboned bedcap. There was nothing more he could do.

As he descended the stairs, Ransome looked up and Lucas saw comprehension in his dark eyes. "I'm sorry," he said as he had so often lately to so many families.

Ransome stood and held out his arms to his daughter. Cadence held him for a munute, then went up the stairs, her mourning dress rustling softly.

"She passed away in her sleep without speaking. I didn't have time to call for you to come up," Lucas said.

"We said our good-byes yesterday. Thank you for coming." He firmly clasped the doctor's hand.

Lucas studied Ransome for a long moment. As did everyone in Cavelier, he knew of the feud between the MacKinleys and the Delacroixs, but unlike most, he knew the men of both families quite well. Lucas couldn't figure out what either of them found in the other that was so disagreeable. In fact, if he hadn't known of the feud, he would have guessed that Ransome and Jerome had enough in common to be good friends. He also knew that Ransome's daughter and Jerome's son saw more of each other than most people realized.

Ransome gave orders to the butler to send for the undertaker and went over to the bar. "Brandy, Lucas?"

"No, thanks. I still have to call on the Johnsons, and you know they're Baptist and frown on drinking. Maybe later on in the week I can take you up on it."

Ransome poured himself a drink and sat on the window seat. "So many of them are gone. Vera, Ethan, now Mother."

"Have you heard from Pearl?"

"I got another letter this morning. She said she's sorry to hear about her mother and Ethan being ill, but she won't be back."

"I just don't understand her," Lucas said. "You'd think she would be home for your sake."

Ransome shrugged and didn't reply.

"I know it's little consolation, but nearly every family has lost someone."

"I understand Delia Delacroix is gone."

"She was one of the first."

Ransome gazed out the window as he asked with studied nonchalance, "What about the rest of the family?"

"Miss Jessamine and Jerome had it as children. Susanna and Pierce didn't catch it." Lucas saw Ransome's shoulders drop to a more relaxed state, and he wondered if Ransome was quite as firm in his hatred of the rival family as everyone thought. "I saw Pierce this morning, in fact. You know, he bought the house next door to me. The Monson house."

"So I hear."

"He's a fine man, Ransome."

Ransome looked across at his friend. "You know how I feel about them."

"I know, but I think it's a damned shame."

Ransome looked back out the window.

"Louis Broussard pulled through. I hear he's been seeing Miss Jessamine. Did you know they courted before he married Dorothée?"

"Yes. You say they're seeing each other again?"

"To hear Louis, he's on the verge of proposing." Lucas smiled. "It would be good to see Miss Jessamine happily married. She's had a hard life in some ways. She's had to carry most of the burden of the family.''

Ransome stood abruptly and tossed down the brandy. His black coat contrasted sharply with his pale skin. ''I have to go upstairs.''

''I know. Again, I'm sorry, Ransome. I wish I could have done more.''

''You did all anyone could do.''

Ransome escorted Lucas to the door and said, ''Get some rest. You look awful.''

Then, as Lucas waved good-bye from his buggy, he looked at the heavy black wreath fastened to Roseland's front door. He missed Vera even more than he had thought possible, especially since his mourning was tinged with guilt. Vera must have already been sick with the fever the day Pearl caught him kissing Jessamine. He wondered if he would ever be able to forgive himself. At least Vera had never had reason to suspect he wasn't completely true to her. Other than that one indiscretion, he had been faithful—except in his heart.

Jerome rode at an easy pace to Doll's house. He hadn't been to see her in several days, first because of his mother's death, then because the rising bayou demanded he get as much shipping done as possible. Several times he had considered riding out after work, even though it was late, but fear of taking the disease to Doll held him back. Because her house was so far from town, he assumed she and Laurie were well and safe.

He put his horse in the barn and fed him before going to the house. He was whistling as he went up the steps, but broke off in mid-note when he opened the door and saw the young black man making coffee over the fire. ''Who the hell are you?'' Jerome demanded. ''Where're Doll and Laurie?''

The man jumped up and stared at Jerome before he finally said, ''They's in the bedrooms.''

Jerome's eyes narrowed suspiciously, and he hurried to the room he shared with Doll. As the man had said, Doll was there, apparently in a restless sleep, a washcloth draped across her forehead. Quickly he pushed open the door to Laurie's room, and when she saw her father, she struggled to sit up but was too weak to do so.

To Jerome's back the black man asked, "Ain't you Mr. Jerome Delacroix?"

Jerome whirled to face him. "Yes. Who are you?"

"I be Tobias Wilson, Tom Smith's cousin, over to the sawmill. Miss Delacroix's training me to be the manager of the furniture building."

Jerome looked at him more closely. He was vaguely familiar. "Did Miss Delacroix send you over here?"

"No, sir. Why would she do that?"

"Then I think you sure as hell better have a good explanation for why you're here." Jerome advanced threateningly.

"Papa! It's all right. He's my friend," Laurie blurted out, drawing her father's attention. "I've been seeing Tobias lately."

" 'Papa'!" Tobias exclaimed as he peered through the doorway at Laurie, then back to Jerome. "*This* is your papa?"

Jerome cast the man a scowl of dismissal, then went back into Doll's room and sat beside her. Her skin was hot and her pulse rapid.

"She been real sick," Tobias said as he approached Doll's doorway. "I didn't know who to send for. I tried to find a doctor, but Dr. Griggs was always out doctoring somebody else, and they ain't one in Palizada. Leastways not a real one." When Jerome didn't answer, he added, "I just did for her what Laurie told me Mrs. Farmer was doing for her. Making her drink tea and water and trying to keep her cool." He continued to stare at Jerome.

"Doll?" Jerome said softly. "Honey, can you hear me?"

Slowly Doll opened her eyes and wet her parched lips. "Jerome?"

He lovingly stroked her cheek before turning back to Tobias. "How long has she been sick?"

"I don't know for sure. She was passed out on the floor when I come here yesterday morning. I put her to bed and been tending to both of them ever since, except when I went out to try to get a doctor."

"Did you leave word for Dr. Griggs to come out here?"

"Yes, sir, I tried, but his nurse say he too busy seeing to white folks for me to bother him."

Jerome's dark eyes flashed with anger. "You stay here. I'll be back as soon as I can."

"Yes, sir." Tobias watched him leave, then hurried back into Laurie's room. His expression was foreboding as he said, "You never told me your papa was Jerome Delacroix!"

Laurie looked away petulantly. "I didn't see any reason to."

"No reason! He's white!"

"Don't you shout at me, Tobias. I know he's white. Didn't you ever wonder why I'm so light-skinned?"

He shoved his hands deep in his pants pockets and frowned. "I never thought much about why that was." As he stared out the window, he could see Jerome riding at a gallop toward town. When he was gone from sight, Tobias turned back to Laurie. "Is that why you told me not to ever come to your house?"

"Yes."

Tobias frowned. "I just assumed your parents were like mine, only lighter, maybe. I thought they would be married. I sure thought they would be black."

"Well, now that you know, you can be on your way. I can see you won't have anything else to do with me." Tears gathered in Laurie's large eyes. She had rarely felt so weak and helpless. The idea of losing Tobias was heartwrenching.

"He told me to stay here."

"And I'm telling you to go." She struggled to get to her feet. "I can look after Mama until Papa gets Dr. Griggs."

"You lay back down there," Tobias said gruffly. "Look at you. Just weak as a kitten. I been seeing to you for two days and I ain't going to quit now." He gently pushed her back into the bed and covered her with a sheet. "I sure do wish you had told me about this sooner."

She caught his hand. "Why, Tobias? Does it make that much difference?"

"It's gonna take some gettin' used to. It is for a fact."

"I knew you'd feel this way."

When her tears brimmed over, he reached out and wiped them away with his work-roughened hands. "But then," he said as if Laurie hadn't spoken, "I love you, and that's more important than who your papa is."

An hour later Jerome and Lucas Griggs rode into the

clearing. As they dismounted, Lucas asked, "Who lives here? I never knew anybody lived beyond Ten Acres."

"Her name is Doll Farmer," Jerome said gruffly.

"Farmer," Lucas mused as he untied his bag from the saddle and followed Jerome up the porch steps. "I don't recall a Farmer family."

Jerome went straight into the house without knocking. Lucas paused when a young black man came out of one of the bedrooms, then nodded in greeting.

"In here," Jerome said. "Doll is running a high fever. Laurie seems to be getting well."

Lucas glanced from the octoroon woman to Jerome, who met his stare unflinchingly. "Take care of her, Lucas."

The doctor sat on the bed and checked Doll's pulse and heart before opening her eyelids and studying her eyes. "She's not as sick as some I've seen," he said at last. "Why wasn't I sent for before now?"

"Tobias here tried to get you, but your nurse sent him away. She said you were too busy with your white patients."

Lucas frowned as he said, "I'll see to it that doesn't happen again. You said there's another patient here?"

Jerome led him into Laurie's room. "This is Laurie. She's my daughter."

Lucas again tried to cover his surprise. Now that Jerome mentioned it, he could see a remarkable resemblance between the young woman and Jessamine Delacroix. "I see."

"It's not like that," Jerome said sharply.

"Don't get on your high horse. I didn't mean anything by it." He looked back at the young woman. "She seems to be pulling out of it. Her mother is the one who needs me most." After another appraising look at Jerome, Lucas went back to the older woman's room.

For the next two hours Lucas worked to bring down Doll's fever. When it finally broke, he straightened his aching back and said, "I think she has passed the worst of it. I was taught in medical school to use purgatives and emetics on yellow fever, but this epidemic has showed me that just the opposite works. Give her as much in the way of liquids as you can get down her. Weak soup, tea, lemonade. I'll come out tomorrow and look in on her."

"I'll still be here."

Lucas had a dozen questions, but he was too good a

friend to ask any of them. "That's a good idea. She shouldn't be alone. Laurie is mending, but she won't get her strength back for several days." He looked over at Tobias as if he couldn't quite decide where he fit in this puzzle.

"Don't say anything about this," Jerome said as he walked Lucas to his horse. "Doll and I have been more or less living together for nearly twenty-five years. As far as I know, you're the only one in Cavelier who knows it."

"How in the hell did you ever manage to keep it a secret?" Lucas asked. "Cavelier gossips more than any town I've ever seen."

"I don't know. To tell you the truth, I wonder that myself. Lucas, I know how this looks, but I love Doll and Laurie. They're as much my family as Pierce is. As for Susanna, well, you know as well as I do what she's like. I'll see to it that she and her mother are always well-provided-for, but my heart is here."

"I can see that. Your secret is safe with me." He glanced back up at the house. "This Tobias Wilson, is he their kin?"

"No, he's evidently a man Laurie has been seeing."

"He seems like a good man. They have been well-cared-for." Lucas swung up into the saddle. "I'll see you tomorrow, Jerome."

Jerome waved and put his horse back in the barn before going into the house. He had a lot of questions to ask Tobias, such as how he felt about Laurie and whether his intentions were honorable.

46

JESSAMINE WRESTLED WITH HER REASONS FOR DAYS before she gave in and rode to Roseland. As before, she tied her horse and buggy out front and was admitted into the house by the butler. Cadence and a friend were in the parlor when she entered, and Cadence greeted her with a glad smile.

"Tante Jessamine," she said in the familiar address that had become a habit from the numerous secret visits to Ten Acres. "I had no idea you'd come here!"

"I came to offer my condolences to you and your father. Is he here?"

"Of course. Jenkins, fetch Papa, will you, please?" She led Jessamine to her friend. "I want you to meet Daisy Buckner. Daisy, this is Miss Delacroix."

"I've seen you about town, Miss Delacroix, but we've never been formally introduced. It's a pleasure to meet you."

"I hope I'm not interrupting anything. I should have sent my condolences by letter, but it seemed silly since we live so close." She held her hands together to keep them from visibly trembling.

"Thank you for coming. We weren't doing anything but passing the time of day and planning Daisy's upcoming trip to the National-American Convention in New York."

"So you're also a suffragette, Miss Buckner?" Jessamine was relieved to have something to say so she wouldn't give in to her fears and run back to the safety and security of Ten Acres. Now that she was here, she was appalled at her nerve. Ransome might think she had more in mind than offering her sympathy and trying to end the feud. Especially after what had happened the last time she was here! She wondered if she could manage a graceful escape.

"Indeed I am," Daisy was saying. "You might say I have found my true reason for living. I was just telling Cadence that I've decided to dedicate my life to gaining equal rights for women.''

"That seems to be a worthy cause.'' Jessamine's ears were tuned to the sound of approaching footsteps. Her muscles seemed to be turning to mush and her mouth was going dry.

"When I was so sick with the fever, I made a solemn promise to God that if He let me get well, I'd do all in my power to get the vote for women.''

"Good, good.'' Jessamine was certain that the footsteps belonged to Ransome. At any moment he would be opening the parlor door. "Cadence, I feel a bit faint . . . would you mind if I step out onto the porch by way of the side door there?'' She could be in the buggy and down the drive before anyone knew she had gone.

"Of course,'' Cadence said with concern.

Before Jessamine had reached the outside door, she heard the one behind her open and she froze. For a painful minute there was a strained silence; then Ransome said, "Jessamine?''

She turned with false confidence and said in carefully measured tones, "I came to offer you my condolences in your bereavement.'' The words sounded fake and stilted.

Ransome visibly stiffened. "Thank you, Miss Delacroix. That was kind of you. I've heard you lost your mother. I wish to express my sympathies.'' His voice sounded hollow and strained.

"Thank you.'' Jessamine paused, but she couldn't think of another thing to say. She was all too aware of how fast her heart was beating, just being in the same room with him. "I really must be going. It's later than I thought, and I have a guest coming over.''

Ransome's mouth tightened and he said, "I hear Louis Broussard isn't a stranger at your house.'' At once he could have bitten his tongue. Both Cadence and Daisy looked as surprised as did Jessamine.

"Who told you that? As a matter of fact, Louis is coming over after supper.''

"Good. He's a fine man.'' Ransome clipped the words of any emotion in his effort not to say more. He hated himself for the way he was feeling, but he couldn't help it. He still loved Jessamine as much as he ever had.

As she swept past him to the outside, he smelled the faint scent of gardenias. With a great effort he gave her a frosty smile, but kept his hands at his sides. "Thank you for your expression of sympathy."

Daisy and Cadence exchanged a perplexed look. Neither had ever seen Ransome so ill-at-ease.

Jessamine managed to refrain from running back to her buggy, but her hands were shaking so badly she could hardly hold the reins. From the corner of her eye she saw Ransome standing in the wide doorway, his feet braced slightly apart as if to steady himself. She slapped the reins on her horse's rump and rolled away at a brisk trot.

Later that evening she sat in the front parlor of Ten Acres, trying hard to keep her mind on Louis' rambling accounting of his day. In the room beyond, she heard Maribelle moving about, providing an unseen but necessary chaperonage for her spinster mistress. Jessamine thought how ridiculous it was. Louis Broussard was as harmless as any man she had ever met.

"So as you can see, the business is picking up again and Jerome won't have to close down a gin after all."

"How nice," Jessamine said. She hadn't heard a word he had said about the gin. Why, she wondered, did everyone have to be so circumspect? "Why can't people say what's on their minds?" she heard herself blurt out.

"I beg your pardon?"

"Haven't you ever noticed how people shilly-shally? Before they state their business, they have to discuss the weather and ask about the health of the kinfolk."

"I didn't—"

"If you ask me, the suffragettes have the right idea. Equal rights for everyone." Jessamine knew she was babbling, but she couldn't bear another minute of polite small talk. "If a person has something on his mind, he should be able to just say it right out." She wanted to ride back to Roseland and demand to know why Ransome had been marginally rude to her—and most of all, why he had kissed her the time before.

"Miss Jessamine, I don't know what to say," Louis stammered.

"Say what's on your mind, for goodness' sake. Why did you want to come out here tonight?" Her gray eyes snapped with impatience at all the unanswered questions in her mind.

To her amazement, Louis slid out of the chair and

dropped onto one pudgy knee. "Miss Jessamine, will you marry me?"

"Oh, for Pete's sake, Louis, get up from there before someone sees you." She gave him a chagrined look that sent him back into his chair. Perhaps, she thought wryly, there was a need for social evasiveness after all.

47

LAURIE LEANED HER ELBOWS ON THE KITCHEN TA-
ble and looked from her father to her mother. "Can't you
understand that I love Tobias?" she asked in exasperation.

"You're young, girl," Doll said angrily. "You don't
know what you want."

"I'm twenty-four years old! I'm not a child any longer.
You've never let me walk out with anybody from Palizada
because you say they aren't good enough for me, and I can't
see anyone from Cavelier because of Papa. What *do* you
want, Mama?"

"Calm down, honey," Jerome said soothingly. "Like
your mama has always said, you'll catch more flies with
honey than you will with vinegar."

"I'm not after flies, I'm after a good man. Like Tobias. Papa, you can ask your sister what sort of person he
is. She's made him manager of her furniture production."

"A carpenter," Doll snorted. "Just a plain old carpenter."

Laurie turned on her mother with her eyes blazing,
but before she could say anything, Jerome covered her hand
with his in a gesture that told her he wanted her to let him
speak first. To Doll he said, "I've already asked Jessamine
about Tobias. She says he's a fine worker. In fact she was
afraid I was trying to hire him away from her to work in the
shipping office."

"You didn't tell her why you were asking, did you?"
Doll demanded.

"No, no. Of course not."

"Well, why not?" Laurie asked. "I'm proud that Tobias wants to marry me."

"You can't just throw away your life like this! You
deserve more than Palizada!"

"But I love Tobias!"

Jerome went to the stove and poured himself another

cup of coffee. Instead of going back to the table, he stepped to the window and looked out at the peaceful swamp. "Laurie, can't you see your mother's point of view at all? She just wants what she thinks is best for you."

"She's wrong, Papa. Tobias is perfect for me. He's a good man and he works hard. He's gentle with me, and won't ever hurt me or do me wrong."

"You can't know that!" Doll argued.

A movement next to one of the tupelo gums at the far side of their yard caught Jerome's eye. Squinting, he recognized the figure in the shadows to be that of Tobias Wilson. Even from a distance, Jerome could see the young man looked miserable. "Laurie, why don't you go for a walk, and let me talk to your mother?"

"It won't do you any good, Jerome," Doll said. "I'm not giving in."

He led Laurie away from the table and pushed her gently toward the door. "Go on, honey. Take a long walk." He surreptitiously winked at her.

Laurie gave him a beseeching look and went out.

Jerome watched her from the window until she saw Tobias and hurried to him. Hand in hand, they strolled out of sight. Jerome's smile faded as his thoughts returned to the problem he had to resolve. Solemnly he turned back to the table. "Doll, we've seldom had a real disagreement in all our lives, and I've never once said this to you, but this time you're wrong."

"Jerome, don't you stand there and tell me how to raise my daughter. You know as well as I do that people are judged by the color of their skin. Slavery was abolished, but not prejudice. You don't know what it's like to be black and know you can't ever rise above a certain point."

"She's not only your daughter, she's mine as well. You've done a good job with her, and I only wish I could have been here all the time to help raise her, but you have to face the facts. You may feel it's in her best interest to pass for white, and she could if she chose to, but that isn't her decision. She has told you over and over she doesn't want to."

"How can she know what's best for her?"

"How can you? What makes you think for one minute that she would be happier away from all she knows and everyone she loves? And she would have to live a lie for the rest of her life, you know. She couldn't pass any other way."

Doll tightened her mouth and folded her arms over her breasts. "I wasn't aware that you had taken sides against me."

"I haven't, but I know Laurie has to be the one to decide. Doll, when I got here last week and saw how sick you two were, I knew Tobias had most likely saved your life. He's a good man, and I think Laurie could go a long way and not find one who loves her more."

"You mean he loves her white skin!" Doll snapped.

"No, he loves her in spite of it. We had a long time to talk. When he learned that I was Laurie's father, he was very upset. But we were both afraid of losing someone we loved, and because of that we spoke honestly and openly about things that would never have been discussed otherwise. After he got over his initial shock, he told me that the most important thing was that he loved Laurie, and neither the color of her skin nor the reason for its fairness mattered. You and I love each other, and the color of our skin doesn't have anything to do with it—now, does it?"

"Of course not."

"Then give them the same right."

Doll sighed and looked away. "That's not the point. I just wanted so much more for her!"

"Are you sure you don't mean you wanted it for yourself?"

She looked at him in surprise. "I never wanted anything other than to be loved by you."

"That's all Laurie wants of Tobias." He took Doll's hand and sandwiched it between his own. "We have to let her go her own way, *chérie*. She's a grown woman, and it's way past time to let her go."

Reluctantly Doll nodded. "All right. But if he makes her unhappy, I'll conjure a spell that will make him regret ever seeing her!"

"If he makes her unhappy, I'll help you," Jerome said with a smile. "But I don't think he will."

Pierce looked across the room at his mother lying atop her high bed with a sheet mounded over her body. She had sent for him earlier in the day, but he had been too busy at the shipping office to come until midafternoon, and he expected her to be in a stew. He wasn't disappointed.

"I tell you he's been gone a week!" she complained in a strident voice. "A whole week!"

"Papa has never been gone like this before," Pierce said with concern. "Have you talked to Sheriff Macy?"

"Yes, yes. I've sent Andre over to talk to him every day. He has no idea where Jerome is."

"Something must have happened to him! You should have told me sooner."

"Hasn't he been at the docks at all?"

"No, but with Tanner in one warehouse and me in the other, I often don't see him for days at a time, unless I come by here. Maybe he's been at the gins."

"Cotton harvest won't start for another week or ten days." She plucked at the sheet and pouted. "Mama says he's run off with some woman. And me so sick!"

"You don't seem very sick. Has Dr. Griggs been by?"

"What does he know? Of course he has. I'm getting the fever, I tell you."

Pierce came to her bedside and felt her cool brow. "I think you must be mistaken."

"Since when are you a doctor? I have pains all the time. I haven't been really well since you were born. Do you think I like living the life of a semi-invalid?" Her harsh voice rose and anger flushed her face.

"If you're sick, you mustn't alarm yourself."

"Don't talk to me like your father does! I won't be ridiculed!"

"Mother, I wasn't doing any such thing. What do you want me to do?"

"Find your father and bring him home! What do you think I want? Nothing has happened to him or someone would have found him by now. No, he's holed up with some fancy woman. Just like Mama says."

Pierce hid his distaste of her viperous tone. "All right. I'll try to find him."

As he went out, Susanna shouted, "And you tell him I won't stand for him treating me like this! Do you hear me?"

Pierce didn't bother to reply. As he passed his grandmother's room, the old woman glared at him and made a derisive comment under her breath about all men being alike. Pierce didn't answer that either. Now that he was away from daily exposure to his mother's verbal attacks, he wondered even more why his father had put up with them for so long. Still, Pierce knew he had to find him, even if only to be sure he was alive and well.

He mounted his horse and cantered out of town. He could hardly go around asking if anyone had seen his father or if anybody knew the name of his father's mistress. Instead, Pierce went to the place Susanna had always intimated was Jerome's second home.

Sophie James lived about a mile west of town—far enough out to help protect her clientele's desire for privacy, yet near enough for their convenience. From the outside, the house looked much like any other farmhouse except for the lack of flowers in the yard. Sophie and her girls were interested in indoor sport, not gardening. Pierce discovered a vegetable garden in back and a pigpen and chickenhouse beside the barn. He dismounted and tied his horse to the hitching rail and went into the barn to look for his father's horse. The bright bay with a white star and one white foot wasn't in any of the stalls, but to be sure that meant his father wasn't there, he went to the house and knocked on the back door. After a long wait a big woman he assumed to be Sophie James answered it.

"You're kind of early, ain't you?" she asked. "Most of my girls ain't ready for business yet."

"That's not why I'm here. I'm looking for Jerome Delacroix."

Sophie laughed mirthlessly. "And you think we got him? Come in and I'll ask." She pushed open the screen door and turned away to waddle down the hall. "Tansy! Bernice! You all got Jerome Delacroix up there?"

Pierce reluctantly followed her inside. At the top of the stairway were two reasonably young women, one blond and one brassily red-haired. They were slouched over the railing, neither wearing more than a short shift, and their hair hung down in disarray.

"Nah. We ain't got nobody up here," the blond said as she looked hungrily at Pierce.

"I could use some company, though." The redhead smirked. With a leer, she hitched up one side of her shift, exposing her thigh almost to her waist.

Pierce turned back to Sophie, ignoring the two prostitutes. "Then he hasn't been here all week?"

"Sweetie, he ain't been here in his whole life, 'less he crawled in a back window. My guess is he thinks he's too good for my girls."

"Thank you," Pierce said with forced politeness, then went out into the fresh air. He was relieved to learn his father wasn't in the habit of frequenting such a place, but that didn't tell him where his father might be. Just because Jerome didn't visit Sophie and her girls didn't mean he had no mistress, or that he wasn't with her. But who could it possibly be? Frustrated and perplexed, he headed for Ten Acres and his aunt.

Jessamine was in the rose garden pruning the dead blooms to encourage a few more buds before autumn. She smiled in greeting and motioned for her nephew to join her as Pierce rode into the yard.

"I haven't seen you in a while," she said as he bent to pat Donnie. "I had hoped you'd bring Cadence by."

"I've come for a different reason today, Tante Jessamine. Have you seen Papa?"

"No, is he looking for me? I guess it's over that load of pine crates I promised him. Sam says they'll be finished by tomorrow."

"No, no. You don't understand. Papa is missing."

"Missing?" she said with a disbelieving laugh. "How can anyone get misplaced in Cavelier?"

"Mother says he hasn't been home all week."

Jessamine's smile faded. "What? Have you talked to the sheriff?"

"Andre says Sheriff Macy hasn't been able to locate him either. Mother didn't tell me until today."

"Why, that's terrible!"

Pierce hesitated before he said in an uncomfortable rush, "Are you absolutely sure that he has never mentioned another woman to you?"

"Are you on that tack again?" Jessamine asked as she turned away and started back toward the house.

Pierce hurried to walk beside her. "I know you don't want me to bring this up again, and I know you've said before that Papa doesn't see fancy women, but he does go somewhere! Sometimes he's gone overnight, and frequently is neither at home nor at work."

Jessamine went to the waist-high porch and laid her pruning clippers down, then slowly pulled off her gardening gloves. She said nothing.

"Mother says he must be seeing someone. In spite of what you told me before, I think so too. Papa isn't one to stay out drinking or gambling, and there just isn't anything else to do in Cavelier!"

"I never said your father wasn't seeing a woman," Jessamine said at last. "I said he wasn't seeing a doxie."

Pierce stared at her. "*Do* you know where he is?"

"I know where he might be."

"Well? Who is she?"

"You go back to town, Pierce. I'll find your father."

"No. Tante Jessamine, you know I won't do that. For one thing, it's my responsibility to bring him back, and for another, I can't let you expose yourself to such a low person as his mistress."

"Pierce, I love you, but sometimes you talk like a character in a penny dreadful. Go home."

"I won't do that. I have a right to know where he is."

"Do you?" she asked with curiosity. "Why do you?"

He frowned down at her with a look of determination that she had seen all too often. She sighed. "Very well. Perhaps you should know." While she went in the house to exchange her old straw hat for a sunbonnet and get her riding gloves, Pierce saddled her horse. To his surprise, she didn't head them toward town, but rather turned her horse in the direction of the sawmill. Pierce silently followed her, expecting the worst. After seeing Sophie James and two of her working girls, he could just imagine the sort of house they would find on the swamp. This whole situation was humiliating, and it was all he could do to curb his tongue.

Jessamine guided him through the woods past the mill and into a small meadow where late wildflowers were sprinkled among the rush grasses. In the middle of the meadow stood a grove of huge oaks. As they got closer, Pierce first saw the tidy outbuildings, then the cypresswood house that was almost hidden in the oaks. "This is it?" he asked doubtfully.

"You expected a den of iniquity, perhaps?"

They dismounted in front of the house, and Jessamine boldly mounted the tall steps up to the porch. Pierce was hanging back, struggling to maintain his composure. He caught up with his aunt as she knocked on the door. When Jerome opened it, Pierce drew in his breath sharply.

"Pierce! Jessamine, what are you doing here?" Jerome gasped.

"I might ask you the same thing," his son heatedly replied, his heart pounding against the lump in his throat. "What do you mean by being gone all week!"

Jerome looked up with a defensive scowl at his tall son. "I don't have to answer to you, Pierce."

"No? What about to your wife? Whose house is this, anyway?" Pierce glared around the spotless room. This was such a far cry from what he had expected, he felt off balance.

Jerome glared reprovingly at his sister. "Why did you bring him here!"

"It's time he knew. I don't know why he didn't find out before now. You can't desert Susanna and expect people not to wonder where you are. What was I to tell him?"

Pierce was about to speak when the door in the back of the room opened, and the most beautiful octoroon woman he had ever seen stepped out. His words stuck in his throat. Her thick black hair was gathered in a heavy bun low on her neck and her blue gingham dress was clean and ironed. Her eyes were wide with fear and the cords in her neck were taut. She didn't say a word, but stared at him as if he were the devil himself.

Jerome cast another censuring glare at his sister, then stepped back and gestured to the woman. "Pierce, this is Doll Farmer."

"Farmer? Sam's cousin?"

"His daughter. This is her house."

Pierce could only stare at her as she moved up next to Jerome and he put his arm around her reassuringly. "It's not what you must think. I love Doll and she loves me. We've been in love for years."

Doll stared from one to the other as if she were ready to break and run at the slightest threat. Pierce could see the quick pulse in her throat, but he was also aware that despite her fear, the woman stood her ground. There was nothing servile about her, nor was she brassy. "How long has this been going on?"

"Since just after you were born."

Pierce stared at his father. "For twenty-five *years?*" he gasped.

"I married your mother for reasons that seemed right at the time. It was a mistake, but even if I hadn't married her, I couldn't have married Doll. Your mother will never lack for anything, and even though we never really loved each other, I would have been faithful to her if she hadn't driven me away. Except for the first few months of marriage, she was never a wife to me. You know how she is as well as I do.''

"I . . . I don't know what to say!''

Doll finally spoke. "It's true, Pierce. I never meant to hurt anyone, and neither did Jerome. I never thought anyone would find out.''

Jerome said, "I haven't been home because Doll has had yellow fever. She's able to get around a bit now, but she was so sick she nearly died, and still doesn't have her strength back. She needed me and your mother didn't.''

Pierce gained control of his thoughts at last. "You're wrong there,'' he finally said. "Mother is sick and she says she needs you.''

His father looked at him in disbelief.

"It's true. She says she has the fever. Whether she does or not, she sent me to get you.''

"And you plan to haul me back as if I were some wayward child?'' Jerome asked. "I wouldn't try it if I were you.''

Doll glanced at Pierce's stubborn jaw and put her hand on Jerome's arm. "Go with him. Please. I'll be all right now.''

Jerome hesitated. He had never been one to knuckle under to pressure, and he was half-ready to take his son down a notch. Before he could reply, the front door opened and Laurie came in.

"Whose horses are . . . ?'' she began, then her voice trailed away.

Jerome smiled wryly. "Pierce, this is your half-sister, Laurie. Jessamine, your niece. Quite a family resemblance, wouldn't you say?'' He was gratified to see Jessamine stare at the girl, her mouth agape. Jessamine deserved it, he angrily thought. "Laurie, I believe you know who your Tante Jessamine is. I doubt you've ever seen Pierce.''

If Pierce was shocked at Doll's existence, he was flabbergasted over Laurie. And from the dumbfounded look on Jessamine's face, he wondered if she had truly never seen her.

Laurie proudly lifted her head and stared back at her half-brother. She had often heard her father speak of him, of course, but had never expected to meet him. Nor her aunt. She could see now why her mother had so adamantly refused to let her go to Cavelier, where Jessamine was well-known.

Jerome turned back to Doll. "You've had too much excitement. Go back to bed and try to get some rest. I'll look in on you tomorrow."

"The spell," Doll whispered in a barely audible voice. "First I was too sick, then I forgot! How could I ever forget something so important!"

Laurie went to her mother's side, and glared back at Pierce and Jessamine as if to dare them to hurt her. "It's all right, Mama."

Jessamine said in a soft voice, "We mean you no harm, Laurie." Giving Jerome a reproachful look, she said, "You might have told me about the resemblance."

"I wouldn't let him," Doll said. "It was bad enough that you knew about us. I couldn't let you know about Laurie. I was afraid you would hold it against her."

"We were friends for so many years, and you don't know me any better than that?" Jessamine asked, her voice tinged with the hurt she was feeling.

Pierce looked at the two women with intense curiosity. Naturally, since Doll was Sam's daughter, she and Jessamine would have grown up together. So would Doll and Jerome. All the pieces were beginning to fall into place. He had known Sam had a daughter, but never having seen her, he had always assumed she was dead.

Jerome stepped forward and said brusquely, "You've seen what you came to see. Let's go."

Pierce gave Doll a long look. "I won't tell anyone. Your secret is still safe." He saw her visibly relax. Her daughter, however, still glared at him defiantly. He put his hand out to Jessamine, and they followed Jerome out of the house.

48

ON THE RIDE BACK TO TOWN, NEITHER PIERCE NOR Jerome spoke. Each was too engrossed in his own thoughts about the situation with Doll and Laurie to talk casually. Jerome glanced at his son as they put their horses in the barn, hoping to find a clue to what he was thinking or feeling. But Pierce's expression was impassive; he was trying to hide his emotions. Jerome knew his son's feelings ran deep and that he must be struggling within himself. Was he feeling hurt? Outrage? Anger? He tried to put himself in his son's place. How would he have felt if he had found his own father with a mistress? Especially one with a daughter almost his same age. Did the longevity of their affair make it better or worse? Jerome wished he could ask Pierce, but they had never shared much in the way of confidences, and he knew it would be fruitless to try.

He was frankly surprised that the doctor's horse was out front. If Susanna was sick, if she had the fever, Jerome knew guilt would consume him. They might detest each other, but she was his wife, and he was responsible for her welfare.

On the porch Jerome paused and touched Pierce's arm, the silence between them unbearable. "Son, don't let this come between us."

Pierce pulled away and squarely faced his father. "How could you be so hypocritical to tell me not to marry Cadence simply because she's a MacKinley, when you've had an octoroon mistress all these years!"

Jerome let his hand drop. Of all the things he had thought might be going through his son's head, this was one he hadn't even considered. He had never thought of Doll as being of another race—she was simply Doll.

"How could you have had an affair for twenty-five years!" Pierce continued. "That's almost as long as you've been married to Mother!"

In a steady voice Jerome said, "I'm not looking for your forgiveness, because I've done nothing I regret. I only hope that you are adult enough to understand." He brushed past his son and went into the house.

As he went up the stairs, he couldn't ignore the musty odor and disheveled appearance of the place. He felt a twinge of shame that Lucas Griggs had seen how they lived, but he shrugged it off. Lucas wasn't one to judge such things, and Susanna's health was the issue now.

As he had expected, he found Susanna in her bed, her stringy hair covered with a smocked bedcap. She was moaning as if her last moments had come. Her mother stood near the window, dabbing at her rheumy eyes as she audibly sniffed. The doctor was bent over the bed checking Susanna's pulse. He looked up as Jerome entered; Pierce stopped at the door.

"How is she?" Jerome asked.

"I'm half-dead, no thanks to you." Susanna groaned from behind her closed eyelids. "Tell him, Dr. Griggs."

"I can't find anything wrong with you. Your pulse and temperature are normal. You have no symptoms of yellow fever or anything else. Perhaps if you lost some weight . . ."

"Nonsense," Mrs. Leslie spoke up. "Everyone knows a stout woman is more healthy than a skinny one."

Susanna opened her eyes and balefully glared at her husband. "I could have been dead for a week for all you would have known. Where have you been?"

Lucas glanced at Jerome, but made no sign of having known his whereabouts.

Jerome went to the bed and said soothingly, "I've been away on business." To Lucas he said, "You're sure there's nothing wrong with her?"

"Positive. She's just short of breath because of her weight."

"That's not true!" Susanna sat bolt upright in bed, a strand of hair escaping her cap. "I'm a sick woman, I tell you! And it's all your fault, Jerome."

Lucas pretended not to hear the accusation as he put his medical apparatus back into his bag. He knew a family argument was about to erupt, and he wanted to be out of the house before it did. He nodded to Jerome and Pierce and left as quickly as possible.

"I demand to know where you have been!" Susanna

shouted at Jerome. "Pierce! Was he at Sophie James's house?"

"No, he wasn't."

Jerome looked at Susanna in disgust. "I've never been there in my whole life."

"Then where is this whore of yours? Don't lie to me! I know you've been with one!"

"Susanna!" her mother gasped. "There are things a lady doesn't mention!"

"Keep quiet, Mama. Papa never disappeared for an entire week. Everybody in town must know! Is it one of my friends? Tell me!"

"I'm very tired, Susanna. I'm going to go to my room for a while before I go to the docks," Jerome said.

"No, you're not! This time I have a witness. Pierce, where was he?"

Pierce and Jerome exchanged a look. "He was taking care of a sick friend."

"That's very unoriginal! Couldn't you two come up with a better lie than that?"

Jerome shrugged. "It's true."

"You bastard!" Susanna shrieked. "How dare you lie to me? I know the kind of man you are! There's only one thing on your mind!" She glared at her husband and son. "I'll bet you two are sharing her. That's it! That's why Pierce is lying for you."

Jerome crossed the room and leaned threateningly toward Susanna. "You're going too far! Let it go, Susanna."

She shrank back in exaggerated fear, as if he might hit her. "Pierce! Protect me!"

With a growl of disgust, Jerome turned and stalked toward the door. "When you've calmed down, I'll look in on you."

"You sorry son of a bitch," she screamed. "I hate you! I've always hated you! I only let you call on me because Papa wanted you for a son-in-law."

Jerome ignored her. He had heard all this many times before.

"You make me sick to my stomach!" she ranted. Thin flecks of saliva gathered at the corner of her mouth, and her skin mottled a dangerous shade of red. "I never would have married you if you hadn't raped me and got me pregnant!"

Jerome stopped abruptly and looked at Pierce. The shock he saw in his son's eyes had to be answered. He turned back to Susanna and said quietly, "I never raped you, and you know it."

The silence was heavy in the room, and for the first time Jerome realized this must have been the story Susanna told her mother to explain her pregnancy. A half-smile tilted his lips. "Is that what you thought all these years, Mrs. Leslie? No wonder you've always hated me."

"He's lying, Mama! He's lying, I tell you. He did rape me, just like I told you. I wouldn't have let him do that willingly."

Jerome turned back to his son. "Do you believe me?"

Pierce slowly nodded. He was staring at his mother as if she were a snake.

"That's all that matters, son."

Susanna grabbed the vase of flowers by her bed and threw it at Jerome. It crashed against the wall by his head and the water made a dark stain on the wallpaper. "I hate you! I never want to see you again! Do you hear me? Pack your things and get out of my house!"

With a maddening smile Jerome said, "Thank you, Susanna. I think I will." Turning on his heel, he walked out.

Even from the far end of the hall he could hear her hysterical babbling and her mother's pleas for her to calm herself, but he no longer cared. He found he was surprisingly steady as he took out the heavy trunk from the storage closet and carried it to his room. It smelled faintly musty inside because it had been used so seldom, but it was large enough to hold all his belongings.

Methodically he took his starched shirts, collars, and cuffs from the drawer and laid them inside the trunk. One by one he emptied the wardrobe's drawers, then folded his suits on top. After packing his shaving mug, razor strop, and brush set, he looked around to see if he had forgotten anything. He knew he would never be back.

A movement at the doorway drew his attention, and he turned to see Pierce. "It's amazing, isn't it," Jerome said, "how few belongings a person accumulates when he doesn't feel at home in his own house."

"You're really leaving?"

"Yes. I hope you aren't going to be fool enough to try to stop me."

"Dammit, Papa, you belong here!"

Jerome's voice was flinty as he replied, "I'll tell you

what, son. You move into this room and you take care of
her for the next quarter-century, and then you tell me if you
want to stick around! She's been railing at me like that since
before you were born.''

Pierce scowled at his father, but he didn't argue. Both
of them could still hear Susanna screaming curses at Jerome.

"Have her bills sent to the office and I'll pay them.
I'll give her a monthly stipend to spend as she pleases. But
I swear on my dear mother's grave that I'll never live here
again, and if you try to cause trouble over it, I'll knock you
from here to Sunday.'' He spoke in an almost conversational tone, but he noticed that Pierce made no move to stop
him as he snapped the trunk shut and maneuvered it onto
the floor.

At the door, Jerome paused, and as he fixed his gaze
directly on Pierce's eyes, he said, "I was telling the truth
when I said I never forced her.''

"I know. You wouldn't do a thing like that. I guess
you're going back to . . . her house.''

"I never meant for you to find out about Doll and
Laurie. Not because I'm ashamed of them, but because I
didn't want you to have the responsibility of that knowledge. You may never accept what I've done, and this may
always be between us, but someday I hope you'll understand.''

"And what about me, Papa? Can't you do the same
for Cadence and me?''

Jerome studied his son thoughtfully. "You know, before you came, Doll and I were discussing Laurie and the
man she wants to marry. I was able to convince Doll that
Laurie should marry whoever will make her happy. I never
realized it before, but I see now that I owe you that same
freedom. I married the girl your grandfather wanted me to
marry, and you can see how it turned out.'' He slapped
Pierce on the shoulder. "Go marry your MacKinley, son.
And I hope to God you two are happy.''

Pierce's smile lit up his face. "Then you give us your
permission?''

"No, but I give you my blessing. If you're the man I
think you are, you'll do what you feel is right anyway.'' He
caught the handle of the trunk and pulled it toward the stairs.

"What about you, Papa? Will you be happy?''

Jerome grinned and nodded. "Don't worry about me.

I'm going home." He maneuvered the trunk to the top of the steps and was preparing to drag it down, but to his surprise, the load shifted as Pierce picked up the other end.

"I'll help you put this in the buggy."

Jerome's smile broadened. Pierce was more of a man than he had thought.

Pierce stayed with his mother until she was herself again, but he was glad to ride away to the quiet of his own house. He let himself in the back door, and as always, he felt a welcome sense of belonging. The deep back porch opened into the bright kitchen. The maid was gone for the day, but she had left his supper on the back of the stove. He sat down at the oilcloth-covered table and ate the fried chicken, creamed potatoes, and biscuits. After the turmoil of the scene earlier, the silent house was a balm to his spirit.

After he was finished, he put the dishes in the sink and went into the parlor to relax. The mantel clock struck the hour in mellow tones as he took up the newspaper. The Cavelier *Tribune* was written in the old "tombstone" style in which a single subject might fill an entire page, and because of this and the small print, the newspaper was hard to read. This issue covered the deaths from the recent epidemic and contained a discussion concerning a local preacher's contention that the disease had been sent to Cavelier in retribution for sins. The editor of the paper, however, took exception to that notion and elaborated at length on his reasons.

Pierce was reading the gossip column when he heard a faint knock at the back door. He folded the paper aside and went to open it. "Cadence! I didn't know you would be here tonight."

"Am I interrupting anything? I know I should have sent word to you at the warehouse, but I didn't know I would be able to come."

He gathered her into his arms and kissed her before he said, "You couldn't have come at a better time. Where are you supposed to be?"

"Papa thinks I'm spending the night with Daisy. I visited her for several hours, so if anyone asks if I was there, she can truthfully say that I was."

"We have the entire night?" Pierce asked in pleasant surprise. "That doesn't happen very often."

"Pierce, sometimes I worry that you may change your

mind and think ill of me because I come here. You won't do that, will you?''

''Of course not. I want to be with you whenever we can be. We would be married by now if it wasn't for your father.'' He tilted her chin up so he could look into her eyes. ''Papa has finally given us his blessing.''

''He has!'' Then her face fell as she said, ''But I don't think mine ever will. That's one of the reasons I came to town. We had a terrible argument this afternoon.''

''Oh?'' He led her into the parlor and sat beside her on the sofa.

''I tried to point out that he had married the only woman he ever loved, and you'd have thought I was stirring a hornet's nest with a stick.'' She curled up against Pierce's side. ''He isn't taking Mama's death very well at all. I miss her too, but he acts as if it was somehow his fault. I miss Ethan,'' she added. ''I never knew how dear he was until he was gone. I always took it for granted he would be there.''

''Maybe your father misses Pearl too. Has there been any word from her?''

''We got a letter yesterday. She hadn't heard yet about the deaths. She asked Papa to send her some money. It seems this scoundrel husband of hers is a drinker and a gambler, and some days she doesn't have enough money to buy food.''

''That's too bad! Is she going to stay with him?''

''I guess she will. She says she hopes to reform him any day now, but I think she was just saying that for our benefit. Papa says if he knew how to find her, he would go after her whether she's married or not. That may give you some idea how he feels about us.''

''Surely he doesn't think being a Delacroix is worse than being a drunken gambler!''

''He certainly acts as if he does. If Pearl hadn't been so foolhardy, we would have had a better chance of swaying him. He says it's bad enough that one daughter made a wrong choice.'' She leaned her head back on his shoulder and closed her eyes.

Pierce put his arm around her and stroked the soft hair at her temple. ''What about you? Has your opinion of me changed?''

She smiled. ''No, I still think you're better than a drunken gambler.''

He chuckled as he bent his head and kissed the velvety skin below her ear. She sighed and put her arms around him. "Why did your father give us his blessing?"

"I'll tell you later." He ran the tip of his tongue over the shell of her ear.

"Oh, Pierce, I do love you so."

He took her hand as he stood, and pulled her up. She put her arm around his waist, and as they had done on several occasions during the past weeks, they walked up the stairs to the bedroom.

Pierce had placed the tester bed he had bought for them against the far wall, just as Cadence had suggested. Although she could not be with him when he picked it out, he had chosen exactly what she had envisioned. A white satin canopy, which Pierce insisted on calling a *ciel,* hovered over the bed and was gathered into a rosette in the center, with a gold ornament in the shape of a bow. The thick corner posts were carved in a pineapple design, and between them hung draperies of mosquito netting. The bed's spread was a colorful quilt of the double-wedding-ring design. A *lit de repos* stood at the foot of the heavily carved four-poster, and a bright braided rug covered the gleaming oak floor. Two comfortable chairs sat in front of the screened fireplace, and an armoire of polished golden oak was against the opposite wall. A chest full of extra quilts for the winter's use stood between the windows, and the boudoir altar in the corner held fragrant candles. This room was lighter and more cheerful than most rooms, as was the entire house. Cadence and Pierce agreed they wouldn't conform to anyone else's style unless it suited them for their own reasons.

"I love this room," she said happily as she went back into his embrace.

"It needs you in it on a permanent basis. Marry me now, Cadence. We may have to wait forever for your father to agree to let us be together."

She kissed him longingly but said, "A little longer, darling. Just a little longer. Your father has come around; maybe mine will too. I don't think I should argue with him when he's still in deep mourning. He just digs in his heels and won't be reasonable at all."

He kissed her with an impatient hunger that she returned with mounting passion. His hands caressed her breasts beneath her tailored white shirtwaist blouse. He unfastened the button at the band of her black serge skirt and let it drop to the floor. She knelt and removed her shoes and stockings.

Cadence unfastened the frilled front of his shirt and ran her tongue over his collarbone as her fingers stroked the dark hair on his chest. Only when he moaned with desire did she remove his coat and shirt together. As she stroked his firm chest, she breathed deeply of his clove-and-leather-scented cologne. Because he used no hair tonic or pomade, his hair was soft and felt clean to the touch.

Pierce lovingly gazed at her as he unhurriedly removed the mourning brooch she still wore, then unbuttoned her blouse and pushed it off her shoulders. After untying her petticoat and sliding it over her lace-trimmed bloomers, he unfastened her camisole. As he eased the lacy garment aside, he traced his fingers lightly over her pale skin as it became exposed. Cadence's breasts were small and firm, with rosy pink nipples that beaded with his slightest touch.

"Remember the first time we made love, and you were afraid I would think your breasts were too small?" he said as he covered them with his hands.

"Are they?" She sighed with the pleasure of already knowing how he would answer.

"They're perfect." He rubbed his palms over the twin peaks and molded her pliant flesh to his hands.

Gently he drew her to him, and she rubbed her nipples teasingly across his chest. When Pierce caught his breath at the sensation, she smiled. With him she wasn't at all afraid to discover new delights. She loved to please him, and he pleased her in return.

"I still don't see why Mama said this was shameful," she whispered as she tiptoed up to catch his earlobe with her teeth. "I think it's wonderful."

"If she had told you that you would enjoy it, you might have gone to bed with a man before you were married," he teased.

"Heaven forbid!"

"In my mind, we *are* married, Cadence. Otherwise we wouldn't be here now."

"I know. I feel the same way. That's why I come to you."

He held her close, and she knew he was aching to possess her as much as she wanted him. She felt him loosen her bloomers and wipe his hands over the curve of her hips as he brushed them to the floor. Stepping free of her clothes, she let him lead her to the bed.

He drew back the covers and scooped her into his arms, where he nuzzled the curve of her neck for a minute before laying her onto the billowy softness of the feather mattress. She stretched seductively, knowing he was watching her as he removed the last of his clothing. When he joined her, their bodies matched as if they were made for each other. She ran her hands over the firm swell of his biceps and shoulders, then down his back. She enjoyed the hard roundness of his buttocks and the long, strong muscles of his thighs.

Pierce gently took one of her nipples into his mouth and rolled his tongue over the turgid bud. She murmured his name and gave herself to him as he moved his head to lick her other breast. Her damp nipples grazed his cheek as he kissed the tender skin below them. He put his hand behind her back and lifted her again to his mouth and tugged gently at the pouting nipples.

"I love you," she whispered. "I want you."

"So soon?" He ran his hand over her stomach and lower to stroke the dark red nest of curls. Dipping his finger into her moist recesses, he smiled. "I see you really do."

She laughed as she looped one of her legs over his body and pulled him to her. "Love me, Pierce. Love me now."

He needed no further urging as he smoothly joined with her. Cadence moaned with pleasure as he filled her, and she held him tightly as he stroked deep into her. When they made love she felt transported, as if she were more than she was and as if they were truly one.

Again his hot mouth found her breast, and he teased her nipple to aching tautness as she moved with him. A primeval hunger grew in her as she matched his rhythm with her own. A fire seemed to be spreading throughout her, turning her desire into a keen need. She moved faster, enjoying the feel of his loving her. He claimed her lips and his tongue copied the mating of their bodies as their passion reached a fevered heat.

All at once she found the peak of ecstasy, and gripped him tightly as completion roared through every nerve cell of her body. The contractions of her release brought Pierce to fulfillment, and together they rode the crest of satisfaction.

Afterward they lay in a tangle of intertwined arms and legs and bedcovers. She rubbed her cheek dreamily against his shoulder and wondered if any other woman had ever been as happy. "I love you so much, Pierce," she sighed contentedly.

"I love you."

She looked up to find him gazing at her as if he had something else on his mind.

"What's wrong?" she asked with a smile. "You look so serious."

"*Ma petite*, something happened today that I have to talk to you about."

"Oh?" She moved away slightly to see his face more clearly. "What happened?"

"My father and mother have separated."

"What? They're getting divorced? But you're Catholic."

"No, not divorce. There's no talk of that." He paused.

"Well, where has he gone to live?"

"That's what I have to talk to you about. It seems he was gone all week, and Mother sent me to look for him. I found him, all right. He has a mistress living down by the swamp. He was nursing her through the fever."

"Do they love each other?"

"Cadence, what kind of question is that? I just told you my father has a mistress!"

"Technically, Pierce, so do you."

"It's not at all the same thing. We're going to be married." He drew a deep breath. "She's an octoroon."

"Oh."

"That's not all. They have a daughter that's almost as old as I am!"

"Then they must love each other if they've been together that long."

"Cadence, don't you see what this means? My father has gone to live with his black mistress."

Cadence sat and plumped her pillow as she said, "I can see how that would upset you. What's her name?"

"Doll Farmer. She's Sam's daughter."

"Sam? The one who works for your aunt?"

"Yes." He turned his head on the pillow to look at her. "Does that make a difference to you?"

"No. Your parents were never happy, and now maybe they both will be."

"Not my mother," he said with a short laugh. "She prides herself on her misery."

"Maybe your father will be, at least. You said he gave us his blessing. I think that's a good sign."

"You're very good for me," he said as he put his arms around her again. "I was afraid you'd have second thoughts about me."

"At times you can be a very foolish man, Pierce Delacroix," she said with a twinkle in her eye. "Nothing will ever change my love for you."

They cuddled closer to talk softly about their plans for the future and how they would manage to change the world to suit their pleasure.

49

THE SWELTERING HUMIDITY OF SUMMERTIME IN Southern Louisiana finally gave way to the cooler weather of autumn, and because of an early cool snap that held for almost a week, the trees took on an unusually brilliant display of reds, golds, and russets. Many of the animals were already beginning to grow their shaggy winter coats when the first of the blue geese arrived from the Arctic.

At Cadence's urging, Ransome put away his heavy mourning clothes in favor of the lighter shades of gray and brown, but he was still having trouble reconciling himself with the fact that he no longer missed Vera as much as he had at first, and certainly not as much as he thought he still should. After her father had done so, Cadence, too, traded her dark garments for less somber ones. She was looking forward to the time when she would again be able to wear more youthful colors. She hoped it would be by Christmas. The ritual of mourning clothes made little sense to her, because she felt that what she wore had nothing to do with the reverence in which she held her mother. But out of deference to her father she followed convention and kept her opinion to herself.

Over the months while Ransome was absorbed in his grief over the deaths of Vera, Ethan, and Eliza, he had become accustomed to Cadence's frequent visits to town. He knew he was being too lenient about some things and that his mother wouldn't have approved of the freedom he allowed his daughter, but with Pearl gone, Cadence was all he had left. She was the only bright light in his world, and he hated to darken things by unreasonably denying her requests for permission to run errands to town or visit her friends. However, on one issue he remained steadfast, despite the conflict that invariably arose when the subject was discussed.

"Papa, why won't you at least meet with Pierce? I could have him out for fifteen minutes—no longer."

"Cadence, if you bring the matter up again, I won't allow you to go visit Daisy today."

She frowned at him, but said, "Then I'll drop the subject."

He kissed her forehead. "That's a good girl."

Turning away, she said, "Daisy has asked me to spend the night. Do you mind?"

"Again? You've stayed overnight three times in the past week. You mustn't wear out your welcome."

"There is no danger of that, Papa. I get along very well with her family."

"All right, go ahead. But you must have Miss Buckner stay here with us more often to reciprocate."

"Yes, Papa."

As she left the room, Ransome wondered why Cadence seemed to be acting oddly of late. Perhaps her suffragette activity wasn't going as well as she had hoped. Certainly he had no reason to worry that she would be found kissing some rounder in an alley as her sister had done. Cadence had Vera's sense of propriety, despite her fiery and headstrong nature.

After seeing her off on her bicycle, Ransome went into the parlor and sat down with the paper. The tall clock ticked with pedantic regularity, and from outside he could hear the occasional shrieks of the peacocks that roamed loose on Roseland's lawns. After reading the Cavelier *Tribune*, he read the week-old newspaper he still received from Albany. As dated as it was, it was a refreshing change from Cavelier's biased reporting of national events. Of course it too reflected the editor's feelings, but because it generally presented an opposite viewpoint, Ransome felt he was better informed and better able to form his own opinion.

Cissy made an early supper, since he was the only one to eat the meal. Ransome pensively stared at all the empty chairs at the polished cherrywood table, and poured himself an extra glass of wine.

Someday, he reflected, Cadence would find the right man and marry. As most young people were eager to do these days, she would likely leave Roseland for a place of her own, and he would be left here alone. He looked around at the tasseled velvet curtains, blue-medallioned paper, ornate pictures, and sparkling crystal and silver. As much as he loved Roseland, he had not even considered bringing his bride here. Of course, he amended hastily, his father would have frightened Vera witless, whereas Cadence wasn't easily intimidated.

Ransome got up from the table and strolled into the library. The huge place felt empty around him. Roseland had been built to house a large family. Now there weren't even servants living there, for Cissy and her husband had chosen to live in one of the old cabins in the quarters.

He stood in front of the larger-than-life portrait of his father, staring at the visage of Ian MacKinley, just past his prime, with bushy eyebrows and bristling side whiskers and the threatening glare Ransome knew so well. This was the only portrait of either of his parents, because his father had never allowed his mother to sit for one. After a moment's deliberation Ransome lifted the heavy portrait from the wall and turned its face away from the room. In the morning he would have Jenkins take it to the attic. "I should have done that months ago," he said with satisfaction.

The small mantel clock dinged the half-hour, and he checked his pocket watch against it to have something to do. He wished Cadence hadn't gone to visit Daisy tonight, for he had no legal work to do and no book he was especially interested in reading. He was not only bored, he was terribly lonely.

Going to the shelf, he spotted one of the books Cadence had recently read, *The Mayor of Casterbridge*. Ransome pulled it from the shelf and thumbed through it. Many women, he thought, didn't appreciate the writings of Thomas Hardy, especially since his books dealt with subjects most ladies disdained. But he knew of someone other than Cadence who might appreciate it. A few minutes later he was riding toward Ten Acres with the book in his pocket.

He tied his horse at the gate and went swiftly up the walk. At his rap on the door, Jessamine swung it open.

"Ransome?" she said after a breathless pause.

"I hope I'm not intruding. I brought you something."

As another horse and rider arrived in the gathering dusk, they both turned to see who it was. Louis Broussard quickly dismounted with a box of candy in hand. He faltered when he noticed Ransome at the door, but continued on up the walk at a rapid pace. By the time he reached the porch, he was breathing audibly. " 'Evening, Miss Jessamine. Ransome.''

"Hello, Louis," she said as she stepped back. "Come in, both of you."

Ransome looked over his rival and wondered how serious Jessamine was about him. Louis looked older than he was due to his balding head and paunchy belly. Tiny red veins stood out in his bulbous nose, and when he smiled at Jessamine, Ransome noticed he had lost a tooth. Louis wasn't a handsome man, but looks weren't everything. He was financially well-off, and Jessamine had once been quite fond of him. So much so that Ransome had thought she had married him.

Louis handed the candy to Jessamine and gave Ransome a suspicious look. "I didn't know you were expecting company, Miss Jessamine."

"You're both a bit of a surprise," she said as she tried not to stare at Ransome. Of all the nights for Louis to drop by! "Sit down, sit down. I'll have Maribelle bring in some coffee." She all but ran from the room, and caught Maribelle just as she was tying on her head scarf in preparation to leave.

Jessamine saw the black woman's lower lip begin to protrude, and she said, "Go ahead, Maribelle. I can see to my visitors by myself." The maid nodded her thanks and slipped out the back door and into the night.

Hastily Jessamine poured three cups of strong coffee and cut wedges of the pound cake Maribelle had baked that afternoon. She grabbed three forks and napkins and hurried back to the parlor with the tray.

Both men sat staring at each other in awkward silence. When she entered, both leapt to their feet, but Ransome beat Louis across the room to take the tray from her. Jessamine took one of the coffee cups and a saucer of cake. Both men returned warily to their chairs.

"What brings you out tonight?" Louis finally asked Ransome. "Business?"

"No, I just thought I would drop by to see Jessamine." As he watched Louis frown at his familiar use of her name, he reached in his pocket and brought out the book. "I thought you might like this," he said to Jessamine as their eyes met.

As she took the book, memories of that sunlit summer he had come back to Roseland from New York flashed through her mind. *"The Mayor of Casterbridge,"* she read.

"Do you still enjoy reading?" he asked in a gentle voice.

"Very much indeed."

Louis shifted in his seat, obviously disturbed by the thread of intimacy beneath their words. "Thomas Hardy scarcely seems appropriate as a gift to an unmarried lady. Perhaps Browning or . . ."

"I've already read Browning," she said in Ransome's defense.

"It's not a gift. It's a loan."

To Louis' surprise Jessamine's face glowed as if that made her happier than an outright gift would have. "Ransome, that seems rather—" he began.

"When I finish it, may I borrow another?" she asked, paying little heed to Louis' protests.

"The library at Roseland is at your disposal." His dark brown eyes held a velvety caress and his voice was unconsciously seductive.

Jessamine smiled, and wondered if she were blushing as much as she felt. At her age she thought it was ridiculous, but she couldn't help it.

"Looks like a good crop of cotton this year," Louis said in a hearty voice.

"I wouldn't know since I'm growing peanuts these days." Ransome didn't take his eyes off Jessamine.

"I hear there are all sorts of new ways to use them," Louis continued. "We always used them for hog feed when I was a boy. Now they're making oil from them and all sorts of things."

"Yes, I know." Ransome let his eyes linger on Jessamine's lips before sweeping his gaze down to her hands, then back up slowly. He didn't so much as glance at Louis.

"Jessamine and I were saying just the other night what a charming daughter you have. Even though she does have a bee in her bonnet about these equal rights."

"Louis, I don't recall discussing . . ." Jessamine began.

"I'm afraid it's more than a passing fancy with Cadence. She's very serious about it," Ransome said.

"Yes, well, it gives her something to do. When we were young, we had the cotillions and Starvation Balls and week-long visits to our families' friends. Young people these days don't have enough to keep them busy." Louis smiled at Jessamine. "Isn't that right, *mon cher?*"

Jessamine was appalled by his implication that they were as close as his use of the endearment implied. Ransome drew back, almost as if he were recoiling. His eyes narrowed and darted from one to the other.

Before Jessamine could form an answer, Louis continued. "Jessamine and I plan to attend the social next Saturday. Are you still in mourning or will you go? It seems awfully soon after your wife's death, but I see you've gone to wearing grays already."

"You're going to the social together?" Ransome asked Jessamine, ignoring Louis.

Louis answered for her. "Naturally. We always attend the social functions together."

"I asked Jessamine!" He gave Louis a cold stare to put him in his place. "Jessamine?"

"Well, we *do* usually go together these days . . ."

"There, you have it," Louis said with a triumphant grin. "That's why I wondered at your presumption in dropping by."

"Louis! Don't you dare sit there and—" she tried to say.

"—and not protect you? Don't worry, my dear. I'll stand up for you. Ransome, I must insist that you leave, as you're upsetting Miss Jessamine."

"This is her house, and I won't be ordered out of it by you, Louis Broussard!" Ransome glared at his rival, straining to remain in his chair and not cause a worse scene.

"As Miss Jessamine's protector, I must insist." Louis heaved himself up as if he might be provoked to fight if Ransome weren't careful.

"Would you like to step outside so we can discuss it more effectively?" Ransome growled, taking the bait.

"Both of you, stop it!" Jessamine leapt to her feet and frowned at the two men. "I want both of you to go."

"I'll leave as soon as I see him on his way," Louis bargained.

"No! You'll leave now. I mean it, Louis!" Jessamine was furious.

Reluctantly Louis went to the door, but he waited stubbornly for Ransome to step out onto the porch first.

Jessamine knew she couldn't possibly call Ransome back without causing a scandal since both men knew that if she hadn't been alone, Maribelle would have been the one to bring in the tray of refreshments. She still wasn't sure how the situation had gotten so far out of control.

Together the two men squeezed through the doorway and stiffly headed down the walk. They mounted their respective horses in unison, neither looking away from the other. When Jessamine closed the door, Louis said to Ransome, "You made a mistake tonight, MacKinley, though it was probably an honest one."

"Oh? In what way?"

Louis was glad they were on horseback because Ransome still looked as if he would like to punch him in the nose. "Miss Jessamine and I are keeping regular company. In fact, though it's not yet public knowledge, I've asked her to marry me."

"When is she to give you her reply?" Ransome asked in a tight voice.

"She has already given it," Louis bluffed.

Ransome stared at him in disbelief. Jessamine had chosen to marry this pompous bore? How could she bear an evening of his dull conversation, let alone consider going to bed with him? The thought of Louis' fat hands on Jessamine's naked body made Ransome seethe with jealous anger. "I don't believe it!"

"Nevertheless, it's true. You know we almost married years ago. I swear to you by anything you like that I did propose and she has already answered me."

If what he said was true, then Jessamine must have said yes, or Louis wouldn't have come here in the evening, bringing her candy. Ransome nodded curtly. "Then I suppose I must offer you my congratulations. You got a better woman then you deserve." He reined his horse around and rode off into the night.

Louis heaved a sigh of relief. He had never expected to convince Ransome so easily. He kicked his horse into a trot toward town before Ransome could have second thoughts and come back to question him further.

When Ransome reached Roseland, the house seemed larger and he felt more alone than ever. He stalked through the empty foyer into the dining room to get the decanter of Irish whiskey and a glass. On leaden feet he went up the gracefully curving steps and along the passage toward his room. At the door to the room that had been his father's, he paused.

Opening the long-unused door, he stepped in and set

his candle on the dresser. The room was just as the old man had left it. With a little imagination Ransome pictured his father's shape in the shadows on the bed. He poured a double shot of whiskey and tossed half of it down as he glared about the room.

"You must be gloating tonight, Father," he said in a strained voice. "She's to marry Louis Broussard. I've lost her a second time." He looked down at his father's things on the dresser. His hairbrushes and tobacco humidor, along with other odds and ends, dusty now from months of neglect, were there where they had been left after the old man's death. His mother had kept up the room as if it were a shrine. But since her death, Ransome had told the servants not to bother cleaning it anymore.

"You cheated me out of her, Father. You kept me from her in the only way you could, but it worked. As a child you trained me to feel guilt and fear, until it was stronger than my reason. I should have stayed to fight against you and to marry Jessamine."

He straightened and again drank a liberal portion of whiskey. "But I didn't. I ran like the boy that I was instead of staying like a man, and I lost her. Tonight I lost her again." With an angry sweep of his arm, Ransome pushed all his father's possessions onto the floor. "But this time you're losing too. Tomorrow I'm going to have Oliver Gibbons load a wagon with everything in this damned room and sell it, give it away, or throw it into the swamp. Jessamine can't be in my life, and you won't be either!"

He knew he sounded foolish, talking to an empty room, but for him that room had never felt empty. He had been haunted by his father all his life. Carrying the crystal decanter in one hand, and the glass and candle in the other, Ransome went down the hall to his room. For the first time in his life, he planned to get roaring drunk.

50

CADENCE CAME HOME EARLY THE NEXT MORNING, not because she wanted to, but because she couldn't afford to be seen leaving Pierce's house when all the neighbors were up and about. She hummed softly as she went to the bathroom and filled the tub. Ransome had installed the luxury when they moved to Roseland, and it was one of the few bathrooms in town with indoor plumbing.

After she finished bathing, she put on a kerseymere day dress of pale lilac. She brushed her shining hair into a silken skein and braided it before coiling it low on the nape of her neck. She fastened the mourning brooch that contained locks of her mother's and Ethan's hair, and rebelliously wished she could wear the jonquil dress with the flounces of frothy white lace instead of the one of half-mourning. For a moment she considered adding just one piece of jewelry, but decided against it. This was no time to challenge her father with such an insignificant issue when she had decided it was time to try again to convince him again that he should let her marry Pierce. She was fast losing patience with this seemingly endless wait.

As she reached the bottom of the stairs, the front door unexpectedly opened. A woman stood there with her back to the bright light, and for a moment Cadence didn't recognize her. "Pearl!" she exclaimed as she ran to meet her. "Pearl, is it really you?"

Pearl threw her arms around Cadence and tightly gripped her. "I just heard," she sobbed. "We had left Natchez, and only recently came back to find Papa's letter. Poor Ethan and Grandmother. Not to mention Mama! How are you, Cadence? How can you bear their loss?"

"Is that why we didn't hear from you? We didn't know what to think." Cadence pulled away and looked around. "Isn't your husband with you?"

"Oh, Cadence, you won't believe the trouble I've had!"

444

Pearl gripped her sister's hand as they went into the less formal back parlor. "He never married me! Not really."

"What!"

"He got an actor to pose as a preacher and read the service. I was fool enough to believe him! It wasn't until a few weeks ago, when I saw our 'preacher' acting in a play, that I realized what had happened." She and Cadence sat together on the sofa, and Pearl nervously looked around to be sure they were alone before she added, "I'm ruined, Cadence. He threw me out."

"He didn't!"

"Yes, he did. He said he had a sister named Millisant who was supposed to meet us in Natchez and chaperon us until we were married. When his sister didn't meet us, I became suspicious, but by then it was too late. There we were in Natchez and it was after dark. It wasn't until much later that I found out he doesn't have a sister at all. I had no way of getting back home, even if I had dared to make the trip alone."

"You should have wired Papa. He would have come for you."

Pearl's expression shifted from contrition to contempt. "I'll bet he would have."

"What do you mean by that?"

Instead of answering the question, Pearl changed the subject. "The next day Phineas found this 'preacher' and pretended to marry me. Right after that, he started changing. At first it was in little ways, like being less patient and drinking too much hard liquor."

"He really is a drunkard?" Cadence gasped. Liquor was one of the evils the suffragettes planned to stamp out as soon as they got the vote. "I thought perhaps you had exaggerated in your letter."

"He was worse than I said. He gambled away every cent we earned. Some days I didn't eat at all. You can see how thin I am."

Cadence looked at her sister appraisingly. "You are thinner."

"You still haven't heard the worst."

"How can it be any worse than this?"

"He was already married! One of the other women in the show knew his wife, and once she realized I was being duped, she took me aside and told me all about him. I'm not the first girl he's led astray. There's a whole string of us 'wives' up and down the Mississippi!''

"Perhaps she was mistaken or lying!"

"That's what I thought too, until I saw the 'preacher' playing the part of the villain in *Fallen Among Thieves*. I called the man over and asked him point-blank, and he laughed at me. He said he hadn't been in a church in years!"

Cadence's lips parted in shocked amazement, but before she could say anything, Ransome came in.

He felt terrible. His mouth seemed to be lined with dirty cotton, and it hurt to blink. If he hadn't fallen asleep with the curtains open so that the glaring sunlight awoke him, he would have still been asleep. He stared at the unexpected person sitting beside Cadence and wondered if he could really be seeing right. "Pearl?" he asked uncertainly.

She stood as he stepped nearer, and went behind the sofa. "Hello, Papa," she said unemotionally. "I see you've started drinking in addition to everything else."

"Papa?" Cadence said in surprise. Even when the three deaths had happened, he hadn't turned to alcohol. She had never seen him unshaven before, either.

"When did you come back?"

"She just got here," Cadence said in a rush of explanation. "You won't believe what that scoundrel has done!"

"He's tired of you and has kicked you out." Ransome spoke as though the consequences and been evident to him. "At least you had the sense to come home."

"I had no other choice. I couldn't stay with the play under the circumstances." She tossed Ransome a look full of disgust.

"Does that mean you would have preferred to stay gone?" her father asked. "Did you come back only out of necessity?"

"Yes."

Cadence slowly stood up and looked from one to the other. "What's gong on here? Pearl, why are you talking to Papa like this?"

"Then she doesn't know?" Pearl demanded of Ransome.

"There is nothing to tell."

"Nothing! Do you call it nothing?" Pearl exclaimed. "Men are all alike!"

"Pearl! I won't have you talk to Papa like this! What's come over you?"

Pearl snapped her head around at her sister. "I caught

him kissing Jessamine Delacroix in our front parlor while Mama was sick in bed.''

No one spoke. Staring at Pearl in shock, Cadence stammered, "You must be mistaken."

"How naive you are," Pearl said with a bitter laugh. "There's no way to mistake a kiss like that!"

"Papa?" Cadence entreated. "Tell me this isn't true!"

Ransome stared at Pearl a long time before he turned to Cadence. "It is true, but not the way Pearl thinks."

His younger daughter leaned forward, her hands gripping the back of the sofa so tightly that her knuckles ridged white. "It *is* true! You were kissing her on the mouth as if you were lovers! And with Mama sick in her bed! In our own parlor!"

"Papa, tell me she's lying!"

"Be quiet, both of you!" Ransome rubbed the throbbing pain in his temple, and hoped he could stifle the nausea before it got the better of him. "Jessamine and I have known each other most of our lives. We used to meet at the bend in the creek where the gardenias bloom." He ignored Cadence's gasp. "We were very much in love. I loved her long before I ever met your mother."

"Love!" Pearl snorted. "I know now what it means when a man says 'love.' He means something else entirely!"

"Pearl, I'm going to remind you only once that you're my daughter and I'm your father. I will not put up with open disrespect." He spoke calmly, but in a manner that demanded obedience.

"Yes, Papa," Pearl said with thinly concealed sarcasm.

"I don't believe it," Cadence whispered.

"It's true. My father learned about it, and sent me away. That was what caused his crippling stroke." Ransome touched the scar on his cheek as he recalled all the details of that fateful time. "I was very young and afraid of my father, so I went. I wrote to her but she never answered my letters. After that, I met and married your mother. We were happy and we loved each other. I don't want you to be mistaken about that."

"And when you moved us back here, you picked up where you left off?" Pearl didn't bother to keep the scorn from her voice.

"No. I tried to keep away from her. She tried to avoid me. But I still love her. God help me, I guess I always will. That day in the parlor was an accident. It didn't happen again."

Cadence stared at him. "How could you deny my love

for Pierce when you say you loved his aunt? How can you justify that, Papa?''

Ransome glared at his daughter. ''I don't have to justify it! Not to you. The only person who would deserve an explanation is your mother, and God rest her soul, she's dead!''

''Are you going to marry her?'' Cadence demanded.

''No! She's going to marry Louis Broussard.'' The words left a vile taste in his mouth.

''You see, Cadence? This is how men are. You're lucky to find out like this instead of the way I did.'' Pearl scowled her contempt at her father.

Ransome dug in his pocket and pulled out a wad of bills, then went to the small marble statue on the mantel and put them under it. ''You're welcome to stay here, Pearl, but only if you change your attitude. If you would rather return to your grandparents in Albany, this is more than enough to cover your train ticket and travel expenses. The decision is yours.''

''Papa,'' Cadence persisted, ''how can you stand between Pierce and me when you've loved a Delacroix too?''

Ransome wheeled to face her. In a low voice he said, ''I didn't marry her, did I? You will do as I say!'' The hypocrisy of his words nearly choked him. He abruptly turned and left the room.

''You see?'' Pearl said derisively. ''They're all alike.''

''I don't believe any of this! Papa and Pierce's aunt? It's impossible!''

''You heard it from his very own mouth,'' Pearl said with a shrug as she went to the mantel to count the money.

''Are you leaving?''

''I haven't decided yet. I'll tell you this, though. If I leave, it won't be to go to Albany. No, I'll go to New York City.''

''But why? We don't know anyone there.''

''I found out a lot from Phineas. I know men for the cads that they are, but I love acting. You can't imagine it, Cadence. All those people hanging on your every word. If I leave here, it will be to make a name for myself on the stage. Why, I might even become more famous than Ada Rehan herself!'' She nodded decisively and flounced out of the room.

Cadence stared after her, wondering how her world had turned upside down.

51

Laurie was half-frightened by her own daring, but she didn't let Tobias know. At the edge of the woods they stopped and looked at the white house with its two small log cabins.

"Ain't nobody here," Tobias said. "Let's leave."

"They must be. There's smoke coming out of the chimneys."

"What if Miss Delacroix sees us?"

"What if she does? We aren't up to any meanness. Come on." She squared her shoulders and walked bravely across the lawn to the first log house. Tobias wasn't about to let her go alone, so he hurried to catch up.

Laurie knocked at the door and it was opened by a black man who wore a blue chambray shirt and tan work pants. His attitude was one of deference when he saw the very light-skinned woman on his porch. "You got the wrong house, ma'am. Miss Jessamine lives over to the big house."

"I came to see you."

Sam then saw Tobias and he straightened. His eyes searched the young man's face, then the woman's. On second look, she wasn't white, as he had thought. "Who are you?" he demanded, though he already suspected the answer.

"I'm your granddaughter, Laurie. This is Tobias Wilson."

"I know Tobias. I work with him every day."

When Sam continued to block the door, Laurie said, "May we come in?"

Reluctantly the old man stood aside. Laurie looked around in interest at the unpainted walls and crude furniture. Everything was old, but it was clean.

"So this is where Mama grew up," she said softly.

"I don't know why she sent you here, but you can just go back again," Sam said.

"She has no idea that I came here. I came because I wanted to meet you."

Sam pulled his head to one side and eyed her suspiciously. "Why?"

"Because you're my grandfather." Laurie took Tobias' hand and said, "We're getting married tomorrow at the church in Palizada. I want you to come."

"I goes to church in Cavelier."

"But, Grandpa, we're going to be married!"

"What's that you called me?"

"Grandpa. What else should I call you?"

Sam blinked. He hadn't expected to feel so drawn to this girl. She was living evidence of his daughter's sin, and he had expected her to be brash and uppity. Laurie was neither, though she did look as if she could be stubborn, and she was obviously independent. "What's your mama have to say about you marrying Tobias here?"

Laurie glanced up at her young man and smiled tremulously. "She was against it at first, but Papa talked her into it."

"He did, huh?" Sam stared at Tobias as if he had never seen him before.

"What do you think about it?" Laurie asked.

"Me? Ain't none of my business."

"Yes, it is, Grandpa." Laurie went to him and took his work-callused hand in hers in a gesture of affection. "You're my family too, even if you won't have anything to do with me."

"She's a good person, Mr. Sam," Tobias spoke up. "I had some trouble with her mama having a white man, but after I got to know him, I felt different."

"I knows Mr. Jerome. I knowed him since he was born. You can't tell me nothing about him that I don't already know. But how you gonna feel knowing her papa is white? What your family gonna think?"

"We already told them. They got used to the idea."

"Grandpa, Tobias and I will be happy together. He's built us a little house in Palizada down by the bayou."

"Not too close, I hope. Come a flood, you'll lose everything," Sam warned.

"It's on a knoll and sits on pilings."

"I never felt right about your mama wanting to live by the swamp," Sam continued. "I cursed myself for building her that house. It led to her undoing."

"No, Grandpa. You're wrong about Mama. She just happened to fall in love with the wrong man. Papa lives there with her now, you know."

"I heard he moved out of his house in town. I ain't heard where to until now. He's taking good care of her, is he?"

"Yes, Grandpa."

"I can't have anything to do with her. She's living in sin and I swore when I buried her ma that I wouldn't have no more to do with her until she straightened out." He spoke firmly and turned away so he wouldn't weaken.

"What about me, Grandpa? I've never done anything wrong. You're all alone here, and it's not right when you have family so close. What have I ever done to hurt you?"

Sam glanced at her. The girl couldn't help how she looked. "You ain't done nothing."

"You hold it against Mama because Papa is white, but Tobias is one of our people. Doesn't that make it right?"

"I don't know! You're bound to know I'm not your blood kin. Your ma was heavy with you when Mr. Reuben bought her."

"You're the closest thing to a grandfather I'll ever have, and I'm not leaving until you accept me."

"It's plain whose daughter you are. I never saw a girl more stubborn than Doll was." He turned to Tobias. "If this girl is anything like her, she'll lead you a race."

"I don't mind." Tobias grinned at Laurie. "I reckon I can manage."

Sam sighed. "I guess I don't have a whole lot to do tomorrow. I might could get over to the Palizada church."

Laurie threw her arms around him and hugged the surprised man until he awkwardly hugged her back. "Thank you, Grandpa. And you're to come see us in our new house too."

"One thing at a time, child. One thing at a time."

"Laurie, stand still. I can't fasten all these little buttons with you dancing around the room."

"I can't help it, Mama. I'm so excited I think I'll burst!"

"Brides are supposed to be shy on their wedding day." Doll smoothed her hand over Laurie's neatly arranged hair. "Where's your veil?"

"On the washstand in the tissue paper." Laurie looked at herself in the mirror and tilted it to see her skirt. The dress Doll had made for her was a white lace froth of satin and velvet with cascades of pleats and bows. "My dress is beautiful," she said as she twisted to see the short train.

Doll checked the veil to be sure it was folded so it wouldn't wrinkle. Over her shoulder she said, "So are you."

Laurie went to her mother and pulled her around so their eyes met. "Thank you for everything, Mama. Tobias and I are going to be very happy."

"You had better be," Doll replied sternly, but softened her words with a bit of a smile. "To tell you the truth, I do kind of like him."

Jerome was waiting for them in the front room, looking very proper and dignified in his best black suit and vest. Doll smiled at him as she stepped aside to let Laurie enter the room. "*Ma petite*, you're as pretty as a picture," he said in admiration as Laurie pivoted in front of him. He pulled his gold watch from his pocket. "It's time to go."

Suddenly Laurie was nervous. Her hands went cold and her feet became numb. She felt as if she were rooted to the floor.

"You're not backing out now, are you?" Doll asked.

"No. No, of course not." Laurie walked quickly to the table and picked up the tussie-mussie bouquet Doll had made for her. In the white lace were nestled many different herbs and flowers whose symbolic meaning would lend strength and security to the marriage. Along with roses for love were peppermint for warmth of feeling, marjoram for joy, spearmint for mirth, and potentilla for maternal affection of the babies to come. After the wedding the bouquet would be dried and kept to remember all that it symbolized.

Jerome drove them in the buggy through the rustling fall leaves to the small black settlement.

Doll was taken to her seat up front by one of Tobias' younger cousins who was serving as an usher, and Jerome offered his daughter his arm as music began to play.

"You're shaking," he said in a low voice. "Are you afraid?"

"No, Papa. Just excited. Why are you shaking?"

He laughed softly. "I didn't think of losing you until now."

Laurie smiled up at him through a mist of tears. "I love you, Papa. I won't be so very far away."

"Don't worry about your mother. She really does like Tobias. You know how she is when she gets her mind set on something. She'll come around."

Laurie wanted to tell him how she was feeling, but there were neither words nor time to describe the bewildering array of emotions she was experiencing. She wanted to go back to their safe little house, and to go with Tobias as well. She trembled on the brink between daughter and wife as the music grew louder.

Jerome opened the door and led her slowly down the aisle. The church was packed, not only with friends but also with Palizada's curious. This wedding had been the main subject of conversation for weeks, and no one wanted to miss it.

Jerome was surprised to see Sam, and even more amazed to see Jessamine sitting beside Doll. Everyone in the church craned his head around to see the bride, and hushed whispers spread through the crowd. Jerome smiled down at Laurie and covered her hand with his where it nestled in the crook of his arm, and they began the slow march to the altar.

Tobias waited at the altar rail, looking as nervous as Jerome had ever seen an honest man look. When his eyes met Laurie's, Jerome saw him become more confident. Jerome gave Tobias her hand, and he slipped into the pew beside Doll, more than ready to si: down. "Thank God we only had one daughter," he whispered. Jerome looked at Doll and shook his head in amazement. Now that the wedding was taking place, she was as calm and composed as if she had been in favor of this union all along.

After it was all over and the newlyweds had left for the house Tobias had built, Jerome and Doll asked Jessamine to ride back with them. She tied her horse to the back of the buggy, and Jerome handed her up into the rear seat. As he helped Doll in, he said softly, "I only have one regret. I wish it had been us getting married."

Doll nodded quietly. "I know."

At their house, Doll made coffee laced with cocoa, then cut the pecan pie she had made the day before. Jessamine sat in Laurie's chair at the table. She said, "This is like old times, the three of us together."

"There's a big difference," Doll said as she sat down. "If anyone in Cavelier knew you were here, you'd be ruined socially. That won't happen, though," she said with assurance. She had resumed making her forgetfulness charm and burying it under the steps.

"Everybody in town knows I moved out, but it doesn't

seem to have occurred to anyone where I went. I guess they all assume I moved in with Pierce.''

Doll gave him her secretive smile and sipped her coffee.

''How are you and Pierce getting along these days?'' Jessamine asked.

''We've never been close. He's pleasant enough at the docks, but he doesn't encourage me to drop by his house.''

Jessamine took another bite of pie. ''He hasn't encouraged me to either.'' And I wonder why, she added silently.

''I guess he just can't abide the idea of Doll and me together. Not to mention Laurie. At first I was mad that you gave it away after all these years. Now I'm almost glad you did. You know, I never realized how hard it was to live like that. Now no one screams at me or throws things at me, and I don't spend half my time wishing I was here and the other half dreading when I have to leave.''

''What if there is trouble over you living here?'' Jessamine asked. ''Would you go back to Susanna?''

''No. If we couldn't live together here, we would leave. Out West and up North folks aren't so picky about color, I hear.''

''Nobody will cause trouble,'' Doll said confidently.

Jessamine looked out the window at the silver-draped swamp. ''Remember when we were little how we believed an old witch woman lived back in there?''

''Asiza? She was there, all right. I went to her myself,'' Doll admitted.

''You did? There really was such a person?''

Doll nodded, her eyes dreamy with the recollection. ''I still can't explain how I ever found her or how she knew I was coming, but she was waiting for me. We talked all night.''

''You never told me what you found to talk about,'' Jerome said.

''You'd be surprised,'' Doll answered with a mysterious smile.

''Did you ever go back?'' Jessamine asked.

''A few times. She taught me the things I needed to know. Later, in a dream she told me not to come back again—that she wouldn't be there.''

Jessamine stared questioningly at Doll. ''Is all this the truth?''

''Why did you think no one ever knew about Jerome

and me? That's why I'm not worried about trouble. I cast a spell to keep us safe. The only reason anyone knows about us at all is that when I was sick I couldn't conjure it up. That's how Tobias and Pierce came here."

Jerome looked at his sister and shrugged. "It sounds farfetched, but you have to admit this secret has been kept for a very long time."

"I guess old Asiza is dead now," Doll continued. "That makes me the witch woman," she added with a wry smile.

"At least you're not a hermit," Jerome teased. "I'd miss you."

"Maybe she wasn't either. She said something about not being as much alone as I might imagine. Maybe she had a man who came to her when there were no other pirogues in sight."

Jessamine looked from one to the other. "Are you two really happy? I mean, in spite of what everyone would think?"

"Yes," Jerome assured her. "I should have moved out here years ago and said to hell with Susanna."

"So you would recommend going with what you know is right, as long as no one is getting hurt?"

"You bet." Jerome patted Doll's hand affectionately.

"Why are you asking all these questions?" Doll asked.

"No reason," Jessamine said with feigned innocence. "No reason at all. Well, I've got to be going now." She stood up and carried her plate to the sink.

"Wait a minute," Doll said. She went to the box where she kept her herbs and took out a sachet bag. Quickly she filled it with bay for victory, rose leaves for love, and thyme for courage. With her back shielding her movements, she made several passes over it with her palms. Then she tied it with a red ribbon for fast action and turned with a smile to give it to Jessamine.

"A sachet? Thank you."

"It's a love charm," Doll whispered as she hugged Jessamine. "I know why you asked the questions."

Jessamine blushed and laughed. "Thank you again. I may need all the help I can get."

52

LUCAS SIPPED BRANDY FROM THE GLASS RANSOME had given him and looked around the library. "It's good to have Pearl back, isn't it? Don't worry about her. She's fit as a fiddle, as they say. No ill effects of her adventure."

Ransome frowned at his friend. "I'd say there are a few. You aren't her father."

"I meant she isn't pregnant," Lucas said bluntly. "After the talk dies down, people will forget it ever happened."

"Forget? In Cavelier? You're still considered a newcomer, and you've been here twenty-five years. No one ever forgets a thing here."

"Life goes on," he said with a shrug. "The important thing is that she's back."

With the knuckle of his forefinger, Ransome rubbed his lower lip. "Have you ever seen anyone change so much in such a short time? She's not like the same girl."

Lucas, who had never been fond of Pearl to start with, said, "She's been through a lot. You'd have changed too. She's bitter against men, and I can't blame her for that. She may have had a rougher time than she let anyone know."

"It seems to me she would be more amiable now that she's back where she's safe." Ransome avoided the doctor's eyes. "Did she . . . , well, say anything about why she left?"

After clearing his throat and turning his glass a time or two, Lucas said, "Yes. She did mention something about the parlor."

"Damn!"

"I asked her point-blank. At least she didn't lie."

"I would rather she lie than tell that to anyone who asks! Can't you see, this could ruin Jessamine's reputation?"

"Jessamine? I thought you were worried about your own."

"With Vera dead, what do I care if people talk about me?"

Lucas observed his friend's pacing. After two turns up and down, he said, "There's more I should have told you about Vera's condition before her last illness. She was much farther gone with consumption than I let you know."

"What?"

"She had the kind we call galloping consumption. It moves fast and is almost always fatal. I didn't tell either of you, because I've seen patients lose their will to live when they're told that the odds are against them. I wanted Vera to have every possible chance to survive. Since there was nothing else I could do for her, I took a chance."

"I had planned to move her to a drier, cooler climate."

Lucas shook his head. "It wouldn't have helped. You might have given her a week or so. No more than that."

"Why are you telling me this?"

"From the way you're acting and what Pearl told me, I gather you have somehow decided her death was a punishment on you. Ransome, if everyone who ever kissed the wrong woman had his wife die because of it, there wouldn't be many people left."

"That doesn't alter my guilt."

"I know of the problems between your family and the Delacroixs from the past, but I assume all that must be over by now. You know, Jessamine Delacroix is a fine woman, and you've gone out of mourning. Are you seeing her?"

"No, she's promised to Louis Broussard."

"I see. Well, he's not the worst man in town." When Ransome glared at him, Lucas added, "Women have been known to change their minds, you know."

"Not this one. I know for a fact that if she says she will have no other man, that's what she means."

Lucas sipped the fiery liquid in the brandy snifter as he deliberated whether to mention what was on his mind. Deciding that he should, he said, "I saw Cadence in town the other day."

"She goes there all the time lately. She and Daisy Buckner are always together."

"She wasn't with Miss Daisy." Lucas' house overlooked the back garden of Pierce's, and he knew quite well where Cadence was spending most of her time. "I was talking to Pierce Delacroix yesterday. He's a good man, Ransome. I know you don't like his father, but the boy is in love with Cadence."

"He told you that?"

"He didn't have to." Lucas sipped his brandy complacently. "You ought to give them your blessing, Ransome."

"Keep out of it. First you say Pearl is none the worse for living with a drunken wastrel for several months. Now you say Cadence ought to marry Pierce Delacroix. I can't see much good judgment in either case."

"Suit yourself. But while I'm minding your business for you, if I were you, I would see if I couldn't talk Miss Jessamine out of marrying that stuffed shirt."

"And I think you ought to marry the Widow Ramsey."

Lucas finished his drink and grinned. "Good advice. I think I may just do that. There! See how easy it is?"

Ransome laughed despite himself. "I haven't had an easy day since I moved back to Cavelier."

He showed Lucas out and waved good-bye before shutting the front door against the cold. The first blast of true winter had blown through the night before, and the swampland was settling down into its shortest season.

His daughters were in the back parlor by the fire. Cadence was reading a book and Pearl was staring restlessly out the window. When her father came in, Pearl said, "Well? Did Dr. Griggs tell you there's no blessed event on the way?"

"I had to be sure. If you had been in the family way, we would have had to make arrangements in order to spare you further embarrassment."

"Me? Yourself, you mean!"

Ransome looked at her as if she were a stranger. "No, I was thinking of you. I also wanted to be sure you're healthy, since you've lost so much weight."

"I was too plump before. This is a better size for someone on the stage."

"What? What stage?"

"She's just talking, Papa," Cadence said, trying to cover for Pearl.

"Sure. That's all."

"You were taught not to use slang," he said automatically.

"I was taught not to do a lot of things that I do these days," Pearl taunted.

"*Did*," her father corrected coldly.

"Papa, Thanksgiving will be here soon. May I invite a guest?" Cadence asked.

"Do you mean Miss Buckner?"

"No."

Ransome passed his fingers through his hair. "Are you two trying to drive me to distraction?"

Pearl smiled, but Cadence jumped up and came to him. "I'm sorry, Papa. It's just that I've waited so long for your blessing."

"Don't you know by now you have to take what you want?" Pearl snapped at her sister. "He will never give you permission to marry!"

"That's not true! Is it, Papa?"

"Stay out of this, Pearl. You aren't exactly the best one to offer advice on matters of the heart."

"See?" Pearl came back at him. "I think you're jealous because Cadence is still young enough to be happy with a man. Go ahead and tell him, Cadence."

"What?" Cadence gasped as she turned pale.

"You aren't the only one who goes to town, dear sister. I happened to be riding down Peach Street about dusk." To her father she said, "You think I'm so bad, do you? I'm no worse than your favorite here! I've done nothing she hasn't—and she does it practically under your very nose!"

Ransome whipped his head around to stare at Cadence. "You were with Daisy Buckner! You stayed at her house!"

Cadence lifted her trembling chin and made no answer.

"See?" Pearl crowed. "She doesn't even deny it! She was with Pierce Delacroix all night!"

Ransome felt as if his world of glass had suddenly shattered. "Cadence? Tell me she's lying," he said at last.

"I love him, Papa. We want to get married."

All at once rage burst over him. "No!" he shouted. "You wouldn't!"

Pearl leaned toward him, her fists clenched at her sides. "All this time she has been your favorite, and she's no better than a common slut!"

Ransome's hand reflexively slapped Pearl's taunting face, and she leapt back more in shock than pain. He had never struck either of them before, and both his daughters looked completely stunned. The rage he had always associated with his father boiled through him, and he trembled with the effort it took to control it. "Get out of here, both of you!" he managed to rasp out. "Get out of my sight!" He was terribly afraid of what he might do if they stayed.

When he was finally able to turn around, he saw the room was empty. The money he had put on the mantel was gone as well.

Cadence didn't know what to do. She didn't trust herself to speak to Pearl or to try to reason with her father. She could think only of Pierce. Grabbing her coat from the hall tree, she ran to the door.

"Don't worry about me," Pearl called after her as she waved the money. "I'll be long gone. New York City, here I come!"

Cadence glared back at her sister, and slammed the door as hard as she could. She was afraid to take the time to saddle her horse, so she ran for the woods and crossed the creek to Ten Acres. With great relief she saw Pierce's horse out front.

As she knocked on the door, she was shaking from head to foot. All she could think of was what her father might do to them. Pierce opened the door, and she almost fell into his arms. "Papa knows," she gasped.

Pierce held her as Jessamine said, "Knows? Knows what?"

Pierce looked down into Cadence's frightened eyes and demanded, "Did he hurt you?"

"No, no. But I'm afraid for you."

"Tell me what's going on here," Jessamine commanded. "What have you two been up to?" Sudden realization caused her mouth to drop open.

"We wanted to get married months ago," Pierce said defensively.

The years seemed to dissolve, and Jessamine saw Pierce standing in the same spot where Ransome had stood the day he tried to get her to go away to Albany with him with that same look of frightened defiance. All at once she knew she couldn't let disaster happen again. "Go to Father Theriot," she said. "He's posted the banns long since. He'll marry you."

"Now?" Pierce asked. "Today?"

"Certainly now. And be quick about it. If I know Ransome MacKinley, he'll look at your house first, but he won't think of the church." When they just stood there staring at her, Jessamine said, "Quickly. Go! Cadence, you take my horse. I'll get it later."

Cadence ran to Jessamine and put a tearful kiss on her cheek. "Thank you," she whispered.

"I should have done this long ago. Now, get out of here!"

Jessamine put on her coat and bonnet as they left, and carefully pulled the door shut to keep her dog inside. She stepped down the walk and went into the woods the way Cadence had come. After all the intervening years the woods looked very different to her, but she had to stop only once to get her bearings, and after crossing the mossy bridge she walked with more confidence. The trees were taller and the underbrush thicker, but she knew the way.

When she topped the small rise and Roseland came into view, she stopped for a moment. A flood of memories of her childhood came rushing in: the deep back porch where there was always a breeze, even on the hottest days, the barn where she and Jerome and Spartan had carved the names of their horses, the old tree where Adele's swing had hung.

She didn't let herself think of the possible consequences as she circled under the magnolias and let herself in the front door without knocking. She didn't want to call out for fear of bringing the butler on the scene, so she peeped in one room after another, looking for Ransome.

Just when she was concluding that he must have left to look for Cadence, she remembered the back parlor. He was there, leaning against the mantel, obviously immersed in despondency. He was not aware of her presence, and for a moment she merely watched him. Then she said softly, "Ransome?"

He lifted his head as if he didn't believe his ears. Slowly he turned to face her. Their eyes met, and she saw that his were suspiciously damp, as if he had been crying. In a gentle voice she said, "Cadence and Pierce have gone to get married."

"What!" He strode across the room, intent on going after them.

"No! Ransome, can't you see it? They're like we were. Will you do to them what our parents did to us?"

He stopped short and stared at her. "Do you know what they've been up to?"

"I didn't until a few minutes ago." She unbuttoned her coat as if this were a social call. "Goodness, but it's chilly out there."

"Don't talk to me about weather! That nephew of yours has had his way with my daughter!"

"Well, for goodness' sake, Ransome. It's not the first time something like that has happened, now, is it?" She shrugged out of her coat and laid it over the back of a chair. "I like the wallpaper in here. It's not as dark and heavy as that in the parlor."

"How can you stand there and talk about weather and wallpaper at a time like this?" he shouted.

"There's no need to yell, Ransome. I'm right here. We may as well have a polite conversation, because you aren't going anywhere. It's high time they got married, and that's the end of it." Taking a deep breath, she played her final card. "Incidentally, I'm not going anywhere either."

He frowned at her in bewilderment. "What's that supposed to mean?"

"Just what I said. Cadence and Pierce aren't the only ones who deserve to be together."

He couldn't take his eyes from her, as he seemed to be struggling to understand what she had said. "What do you mean?"

"Ransome, have you gone deaf? I mean you can marry me or not, but I'm staying right here." She smiled and added, "Of course, if you choose not to marry me, there will be an awful scandal."

Hope flickered in his face, but he had to be certain he understood. "What about you and Louis Broussard?"

"Louis?"

"He said you were marrying him! Which one of us do you want?"

"Well, not Louis Broussard," she said with a laugh. "You don't really mean you would believe him! Louis is the biggest liar in Iberville parish." She reached up to remove her bonnet.

"Are you serious about staying here?"

All at once, unexpected doubt assailed her. She studied his face for a moment, then said, "Unless you tell me to leave."

Ransome caught her to him in a grip that left her breathless. "Just you try to leave! You wouldn't get one step out the door!"

She held him tightly as he swung her around. "I love you, Ransome. I always have."

"I love you, Jessamine. I've loved you since the first day I saw you." He hesitated. "I loved Vera too. I want you to understand that. It was entirely different from the way I love you, but I had to tell you."

She nodded. "I know. I wanted to hate her, but I couldn't."

"And now it's our time."

"At last," she whispered as she leaned forward for his kiss.

About the Authors

Lynda Trent is actually the award-winning husband-and-wife writing team of Dan and Lynda Trent. Not only is it unusual for a husband and wife to become coauthors, but Dan and Lynda are living the kind of romance they write about. After dating for only a short time, they were married in 1977, and then began together a new career for them both.

Formerly a professional artist, Lynda actually began writing a few months before she met Dan, when she put down her brush and picked up a pen to describe a scene she couldn't get onto the canvas. The paints dried and the picture was never completed, but Lynda continued to write.

Dan, also a native Texan from Grand Prairie, worked for seventeen years for NASA in Houston before turning to writing full-time. The Trents have written a total of twenty-novels, and when asked how they manage to write together, Lynda says, ''We only use one pencil.''